PRAISE FOR SANDRA BYRD

LADY OF A THOUSAND TREASURES

"A thousand treasures for a reader indeed! Sandra Byrd's new, highly-anticipated novel presents a determined, realistic heroine to care for and to root for. An amazing cast of characters and Victorian settings pull the reader right into the story. And an appealing hero is ripe for redemption. I became happily lost in this compelling, lovely book."

KAREN HARPER, *New York Times* bestselling author of *The Royal Nanny*

"Eleanor Sheffield is desperate to save the family business. Skilled in valuing antiques and separating the authentic from the fraudulent, she must search for clues—and her heart—to decide whom to trust. Is her old love telling the truth or currying her favor for his own selfish ends? *Lady of a Thousand Treasures* delivers mystery, romance, and suspense in a well-researched Victorian setting."

JULIE KLASSEN, bestselling author

"*Lady of a Thousand Treasures* by Sandra Byrd is another adventure into history and the human spirit. Sandra gives us a rich, page-turning plot, golden threads of mystery, a sparkle of romance and a treasure trove of detail about nineteenth-century collections of porcelains and paintings and the role a lady appraiser played in the collections of the English wealthy. You'll be drawn into many vivid images and precious insights about life and faith applicable to this present moment. What a grand book! I'm always swept away by a Sandra Byrd novel, and *Lady of a Thousand Treasures* will be long remembered as one of Sandra's best."

JANE KIRKPATRICK, *New York Times* bestselling author of *All She Left Behind*

"*Lady of a Thousand Treasures* is truly a treasure of a Gothic romance, aptly named! Sandra Byrd is the rare writer whose evocative, atmospheric prose grabs hold and doesn't let go, delivering a complex, intelligent novel infused with romance and faith, an enigmatic hero who will steal your heart along with a clever, antiquity-dealing heroine who will keep you on the edge of your Victorian parlor chair. The Victorian Ladies series is off to a stunning start!"

LAURA FRANTZ, author of *The Lacemaker*

"Like the antiquities prized in this novel, *Lady of a Thousand Treasures* is a rare treasure of its own. I was swept away from the first page, back to Victorian England and into the haunting mysteries of Watchfield House. With stunning characters and impeccable research, Sandra Byrd has woven together an exquisite treasure hunt with an ending that will leave you breathless."

MELANIE DOBSON, award-winning author of *Hidden Among the Stars*

"It's a rare book that I put on my keeper shelf. *Lady of a Thousand Treasures* earns one of those coveted spots. Sandra Byrd's writing is an absolute piece of art! The plot kept me guessing until the very end. The story, the characters, the intrigue all blend into a delicious read, making this tale one that lives on long after you close the cover. If I had to sum up this story all in one word, it would be *satisfying*."

MICHELLE GRIEP, award-winning author of the Once Upon a Dickens Christmas series

MIST OF MIDNIGHT

"Infusing her story with mystery, tension, and emotion, Byrd strikes a fine balance between the darkness of a Gothic mystery and the sweetness of a captivating love story."

PUBLISHERS WEEKLY

"Just the right mix of mystery and romance to keep the reader guessing until the end. Shady characters along with a strong heroine transport the reader to a different time and place. The rich prose will remind readers of *Jane Eyre* or *Wuthering Heights*."

ROMANTIC TIMES

"*Mist of Midnight* is a subtly haunting, beautifully atmospheric, and decadently romantic story that will find a comfortable home among the best Gothic romances of days gone by."

USA TODAY

"Reminiscent of Victoria Holt, [*Mist of Midnight*] includes an intriguing mystery that is so ingeniously planned that, upon finishing, readers will spend time flipping back to see how the clues were laid."

HISTORICAL NOVEL SOCIETY, Editor's Choice

BRIDE OF A DISTANT ISLE

"The stunning second novel in Byrd's Daughters of Hampshire series is captivating and compelling. . . .The intriguing Victorian England settings will appeal to Anglophiles everywhere."

RT BOOK REVIEWS, Top Pick

"Fans of Victoria Holt and Charlotte Brontë will be enthralled by Byrd's atmospheric storytelling, while those new to the Gothic style will find themselves transported to Hampshire, navigating a murky landscape of greed, desperation, madness, and romance."

USA TODAY

"An absorbing, transportive Victorian romance infused with intriguing details and delicious imagery. Sandra is a master of the historical novel. Engaging to the last page."

SUSAN MEISSNER, author of *Secrets of a Charmed Life*

A LADY IN DISGUISE

"This Victorian inspirational romance features everything fans of the genre expect: a plucky, relatable heroine with a visible Christian faith, a dashing but kind love interest, and a mystery element to foster tension until the dénouement and 'happy ever after' epilogue."

BOOKLIST

"Fans of historical Victorian and Gothic romance will feel right at home in these tightly spun, suspenseful pages. Highly recommended!"

SERENA CHASE, *USA Today*'s Happy Ever After, author of *The Ryn*

LADY OF A THOUSAND TREASURES

Lady of a Thousand Treasures

THE VICTORIAN LADIES SERIES

SANDRA BYRD

Tyndale House Publishers, Inc.
Carol Stream, Illinois

Visit Tyndale online at www.tyndale.com.

Visit Sandra Byrd's website at www.sandrabyrd.com.

TYNDALE and Tyndale's quill logo are registered trademarks of Tyndale House Publishers, Inc.

Lady of a Thousand Treasures

Designed by Dean H. Renninger

Edited by Sarah Mason Rische

Published in association with the literary agency of Browne & Miller Literary Associates, LLC, 52 Village Place, Hinsdale, IL 60521.

Scripture quotations are taken from the *Holy Bible*, King James Version.

Lady of a Thousand Treasures is a work of fiction. Where real people, events, establishments, organizations, or locales appear, they are used fictitiously. All other elements of the novel are drawn from the author's imagination.

For information about special discounts for bulk purchases, please contact Tyndale House Publishers at csresponse@tyndale.com, or call 1-800-323-9400.

Library of Congress Cataloging-in-Publication Data
Names: Byrd, Sandra, author.
Title: Lady of a thousand treasures / Sandra Byrd.
Description: Carol Stream, Illinois : Tyndale House Publishers, Inc., [2018] | Series: The Victorian ladies series
Identifiers: LCCN 2018015280| ISBN 9781496426826 (hc) | ISBN 9781496426833 (sc)
Subjects: | GSAFD: Love stories.
Classification: LCC PS3552.Y678 L36 2018 | DDC 813/.54—dc23 LC record available at https://lccn.loc.gov/2018015280

Printed in the United States of America

24 23 22 21 20 19 18
7 6 5 4 3 2 1

For Dr. Alex Naylor

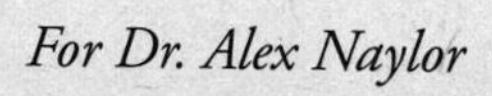

CHAPTER *One*

SEPTEMBER 1866
WATCHFIELD HOUSE, OXFORDSHIRE, ENGLAND

A threading of voices spooled throughout the expansive chamber wherein we waited, voices so decently quiet as to be murmurs. All present quickened as lightning pierced the ground just outside the wide panel of windows, like a finger pointing deep within the earth. Perhaps it was the good Lord's way of informing us exactly where the soul of the recently departed had found its final resting place.

I did not believe Lord Lydney had ascended.

And yet Lydney had been my father's friend, patron, and benefactor. Many spoke admiringly of him. Truth be told, he had on occasion been charitable to me. I had once believed he would be my father-in-law.

That notion had passed.

I was at Watchfield House, English country estate of Baron Lydney, once more to pay my respects and then leave as quickly as possible, putting the past firmly behind me.

My gaze shifted to Harry and, against my better judgment, rested upon him. His fair skin and unruly toss of auburn hair were admirably set off by the black he—we all—wore. I averted my gaze before he could catch me staring.

"A murder of crows." Marguerite nodded toward a clump of unfriendly men who bobbed their heads at one another as if pecking, stiff in their age and black coats.

My dearest friend, Marguerite. Although we were nearly of an age, as a widow, she made a suitable chaperone for me whenever one was required, which was not often for a person of my social status. She knew my habit since childhood had been to sort into collectives, especially as a means of regaining control in any situation which forced my anxieties to the surface. It was a custom particularly suited to the daughter of and assistant to a conservator for collectors. I was now a conservator and valuer in my own right. Almost, anyway.

"A singular of boars." I feigned a yawn.

She looked in Harry's direction. "A rake of mules?" she teased.

I smiled at the jest but knew she could not truly believe that; she had always been fond of Harry, at least until he'd disappeared. Like each of us, Harry had his faults but was certainly not a rake. He'd ever only shown interest in one woman.

Me.

My heart wavered. *Till that interest suddenly waned.* I allowed myself to look at him once more.

He stood tall and sturdy among recognizable peers; he carried himself as a man who was confident, as indeed I'd always known him to be—except in the presence of his father. Near the center of their gathering was a woman I did not know. Her hair was as black as our mourning garments; she was beautiful and young. Her jet jewelry flirted with the lamplight. I held my breath as I watched Harry look at her, his gaze and attention steady.

"An ostentation of peacocks," I whispered to Marguerite. At that, the group of them turned and looked at me. A flush reached up my neck and I was glad for my high collar. I repented of my whisper. It was one thing to reassure oneself, quite another to be unkind, even if born out of sorrow. "Could they have heard me?"

Marguerite tucked a loose strand of her blonde hair back into its upswept style and squeezed my elbow in solidarity before shaking her head. "I think they know something that you do not . . . not yet."

Now that she mentioned it, I had noticed eyes upon me disconcertingly and unusually all morning. I turned and faced her. "And that you know too?"

She nodded. "I only overheard a bit of uncertain gossip whilst in the hallway, but I believe you shall find out soon . . .

if it's true." Marguerite inclined her head toward the dark-haired beauty at the heart of their circle and whispered to me, "She returned with him from Venice." Then my friend slipped away.

I caught my breath and turned away lest my countenance betray my dismay and surprise. To steady myself, I walked toward an over-upholstered chair in which an elderly acquaintance appeared to be drowning, to see if he needed a gentle tug back to the surface. As I made my way forward, a man stepped into my path, blocking my progress. He stood confidently, the stance of a man unused to being told no. His jawline was chiseled and the waves of his platinum hair held in place seemingly without pomade. He seemed vaguely familiar, but I could not place him.

"The Viscount Audley." He bowed. "At your service."

I did not think it was particularly serviceable to prevent me from walking. "Miss Eleanor Sheffield. I'm certain I do not need your assistance, though I'm grateful for the offer."

"Oh, I know your name; we've met." He lowered his voice. "I believe you do need my assistance. You are a woman alone, or soon shall be. That makes you vulnerable, does it not?"

I shivered at the naked honesty and implied threat of his statement but said nothing. He did not need a further prompt.

"My help comes as advice: he'll exploit your goodwill, you know. As he always has, as his father condescended to your father. Their benevolence has never been selfless, has it been, Miss Sheffield? Nor has either proved faithful, at the end."

"I'm sorry, Lord Audley. I'm sure you mean well. But I don't know of whom you are speaking." *A pack of lies.*

"I believe that you do." He looked at Harry, then back at me, and then bowed and returned to the others.

I did not know what to make of Lord Audley's comments except to assume that he, too, knew the secret that was apparently not a secret from anyone but me.

Out of habit, I glanced up at the magnificent mantel clock. Made of French walnut, it was adorned with the three Greek Graces. To my utter surprise, it seemed to indicate the correct time. I looked at my own timepiece; yes, yes, the times were exact. But was the clock's wood brighter than it had been? I thought so. I stepped closer to it. I could not see the works but could faintly hear them; they purred along. The glass face shone. Our firm's associate, Mr. Clarkson, had perhaps polished it when he was here some months earlier to care for the collection in my absence.

I should ask him if he had repaired the works. If so, he was quite a bit more accomplished than would be expected. For that, I was glad.

I looked around the room, now filled with several dozen men and women, titled and not, the rich collectors who had been the baron's friends and, some of them, my father's commissioners. And, of course, Harry.

He caught me that time. He held my gaze as he had hundreds of times over the course of more than a decade, first as a gangly younger man, then as one who had thickened with muscle and maturity. I held my breath. I would not lie:

I had loved both the boy and the man. He smiled. I ducked a slight head bow in his direction before looking away as the tributes began.

Several in the room spoke well of the late Lord Lydney—their kind accolades seemed genuine, and even the vicar seemed at least neutral where the man had been concerned. However, several others looked at the table when the tributes were offered and did not nod or hum an agreement, and the praise soon tapered off.

I prepared to return to my room, but a man touched my arm gently. "Miss Sheffield?"

I nodded, and he introduced himself. "Sir Matthew Landon. I am the late Lord Lydney's solicitor. A word, if I may?" His face looked to have once been angular, but it had been gently larded with years of fine living. His hair, the proverbial snow-white, was pulled back in a short queue.

I followed him to the library. Marguerite trailed discreetly behind, chaperoning. Once we three were in the room, she pretended to browse the many titles on the shelves whilst Sir Matthew led me to the late Lord Lydney's great desk.

Harry's great desk now. All that had been the late Lord Lydney's was now rightfully Harry's.

We sat, Sir Matthew on one side, myself on the other, and then he leaned across the desk. His breath smelled of crushed fennel seed. "I'll come directly to the point. Lord Lydney has requested that you act as temporary trustee of his collection and then dispose of it at your discretion—according to his stated options, of course. You'll be well acquainted, better than most, with the vast treasure that is represented by the pieces in his collection. Hundreds of pieces of art and armor. Glass and porcelain. Jewelry. Silver. Furniture. Portraits. Sculpture."

A collection, as it was commonly known, consisted of all the treasures a person, or a family over many hundreds of years, had accumulated and assembled. The treasures of the highborn and well-to-do represented riches indeed. More than that, they represented family history, affection, personal interests, and the heart of the house.

"There are perhaps as many as a thousand pieces overall," I replied. "We have the inventory."

Sir Matthew nodded. "Perhaps a thousand, then. The late Lord Lydney feels certain that you are the best person to ascertain if the collection should remain *in situ* or be donated."

"Doesn't all this come to his son? As Lord Lydney's only child? Living child," I hastily corrected myself.

"His son has inherited the title, the London house, and the country estate, both of which need considerable repair." Sir Matthew shrugged. "There was nothing to be done about those bequests, one suspects. The horses are his, via his late mother."

"But not the collection?" It was worth an untold sum. Without it, Harry's homes would be stripped bare of everything but the carpets and the drapes.

For as long as I'd been alive, the baron had depended on our family firm, Sheffield Brothers, to acquire, value, caretake, and curate the art. That's what our firm and others like it did for our wealthy patrons. Now, with my papa dead and Uncle Lewis flickering unreliably as he approached seventy years of age, there were no Sheffield brothers. There was only me.

And dear Mr. Clarkson, of course. But he was not family and therefore not a principal in the firm.

"Not the collection," Sir Matthew affirmed. "The late Lord Lydney indicated to me in a letter and legal documents, latterly, when he became certain that his demise was imminent, that he wanted to leave the disposal of his art at your discretion. He does not trust himself to make the right decision because of his persistent grief over the death of his first son, Arthur, and disappointment in his second son. I'm sure you must understand that disappointment better than most."

I remained resolutely silent in word and impassive in expression.

"The late Lord Lydney knows you, as your father's daughter, will understand the care and importance of each piece—as well as have the judgment and experience to determine where it should finally be housed."

I do not want this responsibility. "What would the late Lord Lydney have me do?"

Sir Matthew smiled. "He told me you'd agree, and he is right, as always. His son does not seem to have an interest in art, unless the pieces may be sold to fund the purchase of horses for sport and amusement, that is."

At that, I looked up. "Pieces have been sold?" Mr.

Clarkson had said nothing to me of this after the last inventory, so it would have to have been more recent. "The new Lord Lydney is buying additional horses with the proceeds?"

"I cannot say. I cannot say upon what he draws an income, even. Likely he has none, as his father did not provide one for him."

I nodded. I did not know what to make of that. A year earlier I would have defended Harry's trustworthiness and honor. Now? I was not certain. And it was true—Harry had no love of antiquities.

Sir Matthew continued, "As your final duty toward the Lydney Collection, and as Sheffield Brothers' final task as longtime curators and co-stewards, Lord Lydney would like you to carefully consider the options and then choose to donate the entire collection, in his name, to the South Kensington Museum."

I shivered, suddenly realizing, *He speaks in present tense, as if the man were still alive!*

"Or, upon reflection, you may decide that his son meets the qualifications his father does not currently see, though he once did, and allow the collection to remain at Watchfield House. The late Lord Lydney prefers that it be left in the hands of someone who will not sell any part of it. He wants it to be seen, enjoyed, and appreciated as the pieces relate to one another."

Marguerite slid a book sharply back into the case.

My stomach lurched. "I am to decide if Harry is disinherited or not?"

Sir Matthew grimaced as I mistakenly used that familiar name. "Harry? There is no engagement, is there? His father was given to believe . . ."

I shook my head. "There is no arrangement." That had become clear when he'd promised to return by early last spring but did not return for six months more, and then, I'd since learned, with a Venetian beauty in tow.

"You have no professional contracts with the South Kensington, either?" Sir Matthew asked. "It would be best if, during the period of trusteeship, you have no personal or professional understanding with either party which could call your objectivity into question."

I shook my head again. I could but wish that Sheffield Brothers had a professional arrangement with the budding museum or its supporters.

"Good. I shall make that clear to the potential recipients, as well." The solicitor handed a packet to me. "You are to determine where the treasures will go. Your firm has been paid to carry out its responsibilities until the conclusion of the year, is that not so?"

"Yes," I replied. A commission long since spent.

"Please do not speak of this matter with anyone who might profit from your decision until said decision is final," Sir Matthew continued. "You'll find papers within that may supplement your own inventories and perhaps inform your assessments."

I stood and took the packet from his hands. "How long do I have?"

He appeared to calculate. "It's a little more than three months till the year's end. It will take me that long to conclude probate and further details with the estate. Is that sufficient?"

"Yes."

"Very good, Miss Sheffield. I shall forward any further pertinent documents should I come across them."

As soon as he left the library, Marguerite drew near. "What shall you do?"

I sighed. "I could simply decide, here and now, to have done with it and give it all to the museum. I already know Harry's not trustworthy."

"Do you?" she asked. She must have seen the anger I felt cross my face because she put her hand up as if to quiet me. "I agree, dearest, that his disappearing for six months—especially in light of your, er, unspoken understanding—does not speak well for him. And yet, for the many years that preceded those six months, you trusted him implicitly."

"I was an untested girl. I held foolish dreams. I misinterpreted his actions."

She laughed quietly. "You are far too wise for that. Though none of us is immune to being misled by our hearts."

"You think he should have it, then?" I asked, bewildered.

"I think you should investigate and find the truth, as you always do with your treasures."

I opened my mouth to tell her that Harry was not one of my treasures. Was he? I closed it without speaking.

He left me and did not return when he said he would. Not once, but twice.

Marguerite waited for me to speak, and finally I did, after a realization. "This collection was my father's as much as the late Lord Lydney's. I must see this honestly through—where would it be best placed?—though it's most likely that in the end, I will come to the same conclusion his father did."

"Delivering those valuable *objets d'art* to the South Kensington Museum would be a fine means by which to serve justice to the new Lord Lydney," she said. "Is that what you intend?"

"Does Harry know you are his champion?"

"I am *your* champion, dearest. But I have witnessed several occasions when you were happy together and I want to see you happy again—under whatever circumstances make that possible. I don't want you to rush toward a justice which may not be just."

"Why shouldn't justice be served? I have been led along and then abandoned. Giving the collection to the South Kensington may be just after all."

"That's very possible; perhaps it's even probable. His father has asked you to confirm that. And if you determine that justice will be served, it should be served cold, and I shall be gladdened when you find happiness elsewhere."

Would I find happiness at all? Marguerite had not, not really. Perhaps happiness was not something to wish for.

We left the library, and as we entered the main reception area, all eyes turned to me. Now I knew why. Perhaps

Sir Matthew had told them—perhaps the late Lord Lydney himself had signaled his intentions to his friends. The young woman I had seen with Harry earlier appeared to circulate through the crowd, more hostess, it seemed, than guest.

They all watched as Harry looked at me and I back at him. He began to make his way toward me. I did not move.

Friends and associates of the old man likely believed the late Lord Lydney had placed this decision in my hands because he trusted me but did not trust himself to see or act with impartiality after the untimely death of Harry's older brother, Arthur. Perhaps they were right. But Lord Audley was not amiss in pointing out that the late Lord Lydney had not been a pleasant man, nor one who was reluctant to use other people to reach his own goals regardless of the cost. It had been no gift to force me to decide whether to plunder the house of the man I'd once loved. To do so would be to publicly confirm his father's claim that Harry was neither trustworthy nor honorable.

But did Harry deserve the collection, should it be freely given? That raised the next question: Had he ever deserved me? My heart, so freely given?

Harry finally arrived at my side and drew close to me, the bergamot and spice of his cologne enveloping me. The color of his eyes, which changed from hazel olive to hazel brown with his mood, reflected affection—hazel olive. I took a deep breath to steady the swelling emotions his nearness provoked. Instead, the scent of him made me waver even more.

He glanced at my ring finger and found it bare. "Seven tonight?"

He did not need to say where. I knew.

Duty-bound and prepaid, I could not avoid determining the fate of the riches. I could, however, have declined to meet Harry at seven.

But I did not.

CHAPTER *Two*

The summerhouse was midway between the big house and the stable blocks, deep in the property. It was a private place where none visited or tarried after the gardener had quit of his duties for the day and returned to his home for stew and a pint. Now the garden was being dismantled ahead of winter, and there was but little in the room of the beautiful, butter-colored stone temple with high, long windows and Roman columns circling round it, holding up the roof.

I opened the door, and as I did, leaves blew in a path ahead of me. Some were hands of ruby and amber, supple and newly released from the trees. A few were brown and parchment dry, curled like a lady's locks around a hot iron, the first to succumb to an early autumn. I headed toward the rows of stone benches which faced one another in the center of the room, surrounded by forlorn garden statues with cracked foreheads or a crawl of moss upon them.

In my younger days, when my father had come to stay at Watchfield and care for the late Lord Lydney's collection or strategize a purchase, he brought me along too. After my mother left us, Papa feared that she would visit whilst he was gone and snatch me away. I liked to let him indulge this fear because it made me feel wanted, but I had no reason to believe she'd even recalled my existence.

When Harry was not at school or university, he and I would ride, or I'd first help Papa, and then the two of us would meet in the summerhouse, away from prying eyes and thirsty ears, and talk and play cards and pretend we had no interest in one another except as friends.

Until, of course, we admitted that we did.

The room was dark and cool, and I shivered and repented of having come. I blew out the lamp so as not to draw attention. I soon heard the crunching of footsteps and the creak of the iron hinges as the door opened. Someone stood in the shadows.

He appeared in front of me. Harry. He glanced at the space beside me on the bench, just enough for him to fit near me, closely. I moved to the center and spread my dress out so he could not fit, and he took a seat on a bench across from me.

"I'm on time." He flashed that half-pirate, half–lord of the manor smile at me, and I hoped I did not appear as unsteady on the outside as I felt on the inside. The air between us crackled.

"I'm heartened to know that reform is possible for everyone." I kept my voice tidy.

He laughed aloud, his eyes crinkling with faint lines which appeared to be new. Although he was as delightful to look at as ever, his face appeared more rugged and perhaps somber. I'd heard war could age a man quickly—even a man who was merely midway between twenty-five and thirty. He seemed more mature. Solid. "Ellie. I've missed you so," he said as he leaned toward me.

I looked down and blinked back tears. "I could not have known."

"Please, please look at me." He spoke softly. I looked up and he continued. "I'm only just back with my father's remains, so I could not have reached you sooner. And whilst away, I wrote."

"You wrote that you would be delayed because you needed to help your Venetian friends. Again. Then your father needed you—has he ever needed you? Then but once more to say you'd be home soon and hoped you could call on me. Could call? How very detached."

He nodded. "I'm sorry. I did not realize how careless that may have seemed, and in the rush of circumstances around the war and my father's illness, I'd figured you would see the situation as I did. It was thoughtless of me. I thought of you constantly."

"What happened?" I asked. "Why did you not explain in your letters?"

"I could not," he said with quiet confidence. "A war was under way. While Father was the ambassador to Austria, I was secretly helping free Venice from Austria to return it to its own people. To indicate in any way either by letter, telegram, or even a messenger that I was helping the other side would have compromised my father."

"I suppose that's understandable," I admitted. "But this is not the first time you had to leave to help others. Last year you were needed to ride to deliver documents between Austria and Venice. And you spent an inordinate amount of time in both places."

With his father? With the Venetian signorina?

"I felt I was needed," he said. "I hurried as I could. You'd agreed to it, that time."

That was true; I had. Reluctantly. But each year's situation seemed to delay things, to push us further apart. "The year before, when my father was still alive, you had to help Garibaldi in London—and then back to Venice again, taking months longer than expected. My father died before . . ." I left it unsaid. My father had hoped that Harry and I would be married, that he would see me safely into the hands of a man who could care for me.

Harry held out a hand to me; I did not take it. "I'm beyond sorry, Ellie. If I could undo that, I would, and I'm filled with remorse that I cannot. I have always admired your strength and self-sufficiency, and I hoped both our fathers would consider my purpose and actions in the past years to be noble. I was trying to show them I am a respectable man, though I may not be just like them. I was also trying to do some good in this world with what I had to offer—my ability to ride and to be a go-between. But no matter what good I may have done over the past years, along the way I seem to have, understandably, lost the respect and affections of the one who matters most."

I did not correct him. Perhaps he had. I wiped my tear away with a handkerchief and put on my brusque efficiency again, a cloak which suited me very well indeed. I'd begun to learn to care for myself.

"I hope I have not lost them permanently."

Harry waited for reassurance, which I could not presently give.

He ran his hand through his hair. "May I explain why I was a little late this time?"

"Six months is not a little late, but yes, you may explain." I could hardly hold the man to account, even for the time he'd been gone. We were not engaged. We had not made a verbal promise. Perhaps our love had been, as Juliet spoke in Shakespeare's play, too like the lightning which ceases to be before one could say, "It lightens." But he had given me that ring and that kiss, and we had both known what was implied but unsaid and now undone.

"I'd intended to stay but a month, as I'd told you I would. Then Father became ill, and so I remained in Austria at his request; he repeatedly pleaded that I stay near. He indicated that it would be a comfort to him—yes, I was surprised as well that he wanted me near him. I thought maybe he wanted the two of us to be at peace before he died. But no." He looked down for a moment before looking up again, his countenance lifting a little. "You remember Stefano Viero?"

Oh yes, I remembered Stefano. He had been Harry's closest friend and sworn brother at Oxford. "Of course."

"In addition to my work transporting war documents, Viero asked me to come and secretly collect his family treasures—the blown-glass objects his family has been famous for, in Venice, for nearly five hundred years. Priceless treasures. National treasures, and he didn't want them thieved."

I nodded. "During the last war, Italy was looted." Even British collectors had set off for the Continent to see what ancient artifacts they could carry away in the uproar.

Harry nodded enthusiastically at my agreement. "You'll recall that Napoleon once stole the bronze horses from St Mark's in Venice and brought them to Paris."

I tried not to roll my eyes. Always the horses with Harry. "So you collected the treasures. Glass treasures? Is that all?"

"Yes. I spirited them out of Venice to Austria, and then to England, for safekeeping and protection. Stefano will come to collect them when all is settled again there."

"Is that young lady one of the treasures you brought out of Venice?"

He grew wary. "Francesca?"

My head snapped up at the use of her Christian name. Harry, no fool, noted it immediately.

"Yes, Signorina Viero is Stefano's sister. His mother, widowed, came as well. I could hardly leave them unprotected in a time of unrest. Their son and brother was fighting for his country. I came to know them very well during visits at their family home. They'll remain with me until Viero comes to collect them, too, as soon as the final negotiations are complete. We haven't yet heard from him," he admitted. "We're hoping he is well."

"I hope so too." I liked Barone Viero.

He did not bring up the trusteeship, nor should he have. And yet, I had a question.

"Harry," I began, "did you have the mantel clock replaced? The one in the green drawing room?" I hated to bring up a painful subject, but I needed to know because it worked now, and it hadn't for years. I couldn't imagine Harry had had time to have it fixed. But he was not supposed to have removed anything from his family's collection, either.

"No, but I should replace it." He shifted his gaze, but I caught the look of pain first. His father had had the clock stopped, permanently, at the exact moment that Arthur died. It was, the late Lord Lydney had said, a way to remind any and all that Harry failed to bring the doctor to the house in time—and Arthur suffered fatally for it.

"It certainly would be understandable had you replaced it." No one wanted to be reminded, day in and day after, of their failures, especially if their failure had caused someone to die.

He did not acknowledge that comment. "Why do you ask?"

"The works have been fixed. The clock is keeping accurate time. The past is past."

"Is it?" His voice turned slightly hard. "I'd thought helping in the war would make my father see me as a man. And then, of my own accord, I rode out with Viero's treasures—the antiquities my father prized. All for naught. No reconciliation was ever at hand, despite his misleading. He'd like to continue to mete out vengeance from the grave."

I noticed that he, too, spoke of his father as if he were still alive, and I shivered again. "I'm sorry," I said. And I was—for both of us.

"Ellie . . ." He reached into the pocket of his coat and withdrew a box. "I brought a gift for you from Venice. May I give it to you?"

I took a deep breath but did not answer.

"There is nothing I expect from you in return," he said. "I just thought of you when I saw it. I knew it must be yours."

I nodded. "For times past if nothing else."

He flinched, and I quelled my temptation to soothe him. Things were not now as they once had been. He handed the box to me. "Open it?"

I could hardly accept the gift and not open it in his presence. I lifted the velvet lid and drew out an oval pendant of antique brass with filigreed loops all around it, hung on a brass chain. And then, in the center of the pendant, green velvet upon which rested . . . "A mustard seed!" I exclaimed.

He nodded and smiled. "Under glass, of course. Both brought you to mind—the seed of faith and the glass."

I stared at it, not because I needed to further examine it, but because I needed to collect my thoughts and emotions.

"Thank you, Harry. I appreciate your thoughtfulness." But I did not put it on.

Harry waited a moment, then stood and held out his hand to help me rise from the stone bench; I was glad of it. The cold had bled through my garments to my bones.

He tucked my arm through his. I allowed his arm to remain—it was a gentlemanly offer, and I did not wish to offer an ill-mannered refusal in return. Still . . . the rich promise of the past and the emptiness of the future entwined our arms as the skeletal wisteria entwined around the summerhouse.

"May I call on you in London?" he teased, echoing his letter from Austria.

"I cannot say," I said. Should I let him call? If I did not see him, how could I best judge if he was now deserving of the collection? But if I did, would I be swayed by my former affections for the man?

I would not allow myself to be.

He took my hand in his own and softly kissed the back of it. "My Ellie. If you cannot say, who could?"

CHAPTER
Three

BLOOMSBURY, LONDON

Next afternoon, Marguerite and I took the train back to Paddington Station, London. We parted with a warm embrace at the station, and I took an omnibus, a long, horse-drawn carriage with perhaps six benches on either side upon which travelers might sit, the rest of the way. Home, a place that was—at last—perfectly safe, secure, and dependable.

When I arrived, our housekeeper, Mrs. Orchard, better known as Orchie to all whom she'd endeared, opened the door. She'd been crying.

"Mrs. Orchard!" I rarely called her that, but I was so surprised to see her undone that it threw me off some. "Whatever is the matter?"

"It's your uncle," she said.

My face must have reflected my utter and abject horror because she quickly reassured me with a whisper. "Oh no, he's not . . . gone . . . but he's had a bad upset, he has."

I quickly unwrapped my cloak and hung it on the stand. "Whatever has happened?"

"It's best he tell you," she said, nodding toward Mr. Clarkson, who had suddenly appeared in the hallway which led from our workshop, next door, to our home.

"Let's speak in the parlor," Clarkson said, and I followed him. Orchie followed me.

Once in the parlor we sat down and Mr. Clarkson explained.

"Your uncle said he was going to meet a client, which I thought was unusual, as he has mostly limited himself to valuing in the workshop of late."

I nodded my agreement. Uncle had become more and more housebound, by necessity, of course.

"I did not feel it was my place to interfere. However, I was concerned for his safety and followed him from a distance."

"Thank you, Mr. Clarkson," I said. It was certainly not a part of his professional responsibility to do so but showed his character to be of the best sort that he undertook that responsibility anyway.

"Certainly, Miss Sheffield," he said. "In any case, when he was about a block ahead of me, he took a turn down an alley. I hurried as quickly as possible, but by the time I reached him, two young ruffians were on him, one holding him back whilst another filched whatever was in his pockets. Upon seeing me, they fled, but not before hitting your dear uncle in the face."

"Oh no!" I stood. "I've been gone for but one day and he's been harmed. I must see him."

"He sleeps now," Orchie comforted me. "You'll see 'im at supper."

I nodded and sat down. "I cannot thank you enough, Mr. Clarkson. For thinking to follow him, for reaching him in time, for bringing him back safely."

Clarkson grimaced. "I'm afraid it wasn't entirely in time. He mentioned having an envelope of money and was quite distressed over the loss of his pocket watch."

"Oh . . . oh, dear." My father and Uncle Lewis had been twins and had purchased very valuable twin pocket watches when they first took over their father's business.

Mr. Clarkson nodded, his face reflecting the same distress I felt. "I know how he loved it and how costly it was. A bigger loss than his envelope of money, I'd guess."

"Yes." Tired from my journey, from my commission to determine if Harry would receive his father's fortune or not, and from this terrible news about Uncle Lewis, I decided a rest was in order. I stood once more. "Thank you again, Mr. Clarkson." I took a few steps from the room, and then an icy thought, a worrisome thought, occurred to me.

"Could those ruffians have followed you back to our house? If they knew Uncle had one valuable on him, could they be watching for a time to break in and ascertain if there are others?" Our workshop was constantly filled with the costly rare art of our clients.

Mr. Clarkson looked at me with a little smile, all that could properly be allowed in such a serious circumstance. "I have thought of that. I have taken a piece or two to my residence for the moment and have hidden everything else deep in the cabinets. I will keep a sharp eye out. But I believe it was a crime of chance."

"Dear Mr. Clarkson, thank you very kindly. Words cannot express how valuable you have become to the firm—to all of us, really."

Clarkson smiled more widely then. "At your service, Miss Sheffield. I shall see you at dinner?"

For a moment, I was caught off guard. Orchie came to the rescue. "It is Saturday, Miss Eleanor."

That was right. I'd forgotten. Mr. Clarkson often stayed to dinner on Saturday so he could work late at the workshop. None of us would work on the Sabbath.

"Yes, of course." I nodded to each of them and then made my way to my room. Once inside, I found I was too anxious to sleep, and so I settled in the chair by the window. I opened the folder Sir Matthew had given me and steeled myself. I would glance over the papers for a moment before resting, to see if there were any immediately recognizable irregularities.

Like the newly changed mantel clock.

To my surprise, in addition to the neatly ledgered list of treasures, there was a letter, sealed with the late Lord Lydney's signet and addressed to me.

Merely looking on his handwriting somehow filled me with dread. I'd not thought he liked me; rather he put up with me for my father's sake. I'd felt his lip-curling disdain more than once. But my father had also told me, once, that the baron had been overgenerous with some of the commissions he'd awarded my father, so my school fees might be paid.

I sliced through the black wax.

My dear Miss Sheffield, it began.

My dear?

If you are reading this, then you have accepted my commission, as I knew you would. You are a dutiful girl—well brought up despite some unfortunate circumstances.

In any case, it appears that perhaps family curses stalk all of us. This brings me to the point of this letter. I had always expected, despite your uneven positions in life, that my son Henry would propose marriage to you and you would be the caretaker of the vast collection I've not only inherited but assembled with the help of your dear father. Of late, it became clear that a proposal was not forthcoming, as Henry was keeping close and constant company with the young Venetian woman. He repeatedly refused to return to England despite my pleadings that he do so.

I set the letter down for a moment. Harry told me that his father had pleaded with him to remain until his death. His father, however, claimed the opposite. I could not imagine Harry lying to me. Could I? But I could also not imagine Baron Lydney pleading with his unloved son to remain with him, as Harry maintained. I turned back to the letter.

> *I concluded that my assessment of him after Arthur's death was accurate—untrustworthy and selfish. However, in case anger, disappointment, or illness has clouded my vision, I have decided to leave this decision in your capable hands.*
>
> *In my eyes, Miss Sheffield, he deserves neither my title, my estates, nor my treasures. I cannot deprive him of the first two. Should he be deprived of the third? That is now for you to decide. Would it be true to say that you believe you know him as well as anyone?*
>
> *I am enthusiastic about the new age of museums, Miss Sheffield, as I know you must be, where all can see the many treasures afforded by the few. Perhaps you will determine that this, then, would be the highest and best use of my fortune. The final decision will rest with you.*
>
> *Sincerely yours,*
> *John Arthur Douglas, the Baron Lydney*

I felt as though I'd been chosen to be the blind man in a game of blindman's bluff. Blindfolded and spun around and around till I could not tell which was right and which was wrong. Who spoke the truth? Who lied? Perhaps chess was a better analogy. Whose pawn was I, and to what purpose?

I steadied myself to focus on the weighty decision that lay ahead for me, the stewardship of a great fortune. But from time to time, my thoughts snagged on two sentences and would not be released. *"He was keeping close and constant company with the young Venetian woman. He repeatedly refused to return to England despite my pleadings that he do so."*

Hours later I met with the men at dinner. The lamps were low—too low, I thought, abnormally low. Why? It did help hide the age of the pale-gray wallpaper which, in turn, was designed to conceal the soot powder from coal and lamp splatter. A collusion of small portraits had been carefully hung to hide the worst stains. The table, though it would comfortably seat eight or more, had been neatly set for three. The linens, I noticed, had begun to fray a bit. The men wore ties—though Uncle Lewis's was quite old and startlingly dotted with bits which called to mind meals recently past. Mr. Clarkson was neatly dressed, his thick brown hair parted in the middle without a stray out of place, and newly shaved—a face not altogether unpleasant to gaze upon. His clothing was fashionable though perhaps trailed by a season or two, which I certainly understood. I knew it was important to him to dress as though he were capable of mingling with our wealthy clients but without any pretensions to equality. He did so very well indeed.

I greeted my uncle with a kiss, which he waved away. "I'm so sorry," I said.

"Nothing worse for a man than to be the object of feminine pity," he replied. I retreated to leave him his dignity but was shocked and saddened by the purpling bruise on his cheekbone and the sudden shake in his voice.

"How went the funeral?" Uncle asked after Orchie delivered the first, meager course. It seemed to me that the portions grew smaller as the year grew longer.

"As to be expected," I answered. "Somber."

"I didn't know him well," Mr. Clarkson said. "The deceased, that is."

"I knew Lydney," Uncle Lewis blustered, then raised his hand to Orchie, who smiled and nodded. She returned to the kitchen, as I knew she would, for a platter of Cornish pasties. Again. It was an unusual dinner course, but we indulged Uncle Lewis nonetheless.

"Can't say as I'll miss him a bit—nor will any honest man, a cohort among which he could not count himself—though I'll miss his commissions, that's for certain."

"Dear Uncle, that is most unkind," I responded.

"I'm too old to feign affections. I'm keen on the commissions that will now come to us from those attached to the South Kensington. They are much needed, though I hate to see his son done a bad turn."

"On the few occasions we met, I thought the baron seemed a decent sort of man," Clarkson said. "He certainly assembled an admirable set of possessions and put his riches behind his passion."

Uncle continued, most indiscreetly, "Those museum commissions will come, and I suppose we'll have the late Lord Lydney to thank for that . . . and you, too, m'dear."

I stared intently at my pasty, as though it were about to come to life.

"Isn't that correct?" Mr. Clarkson asked after a moment or two. "With the considerable donation to the South Kensington, right here in London, Sheffield Brothers shall be looked upon in a rather amiable professional light."

"How do you already know—?" I began sharply.

"Everyone knows." Mr. Clarkson cut me off, then looked down. "I'm sorry for that interruption; please forgive me. It's enthusiasm for the future of the firm, of course."

"Please continue," I responded in a more subdued voice. He was right to be invested in our outcome.

He spoke more gently then. "It seems Lord Lydney had shared his plans with a few friends, his solicitor, and perhaps his son. Word traveled in the past few weeks. Swiftly. I learned of it just before the funeral, from Mr. Denholm, when I delivered a piece of jewelry to his wife. Only it seemed proper to let Sir Matthew himself explain the terms to you."

"What shall you do?" Uncle asked me.

I sipped my water before continuing. "I'm sorry, Mr. Clarkson, Uncle Lewis. But Sir Matthew has requested that I not discuss the matter with anyone who may profit by it until a decision is made."

"Then make the decision, dear, and off we go!" A flake of pasty stuck on my uncle's beard, which wagged as he chewed.

"I shan't be hasty with the final duty we've been charged with by the Lydney estate," I replied. "But I shall be deliberate."

After the pudding, Mr. Clarkson excused himself to the workshop. I told him we would meet him there soon and then stayed to speak with my uncle.

"The old man did you a favor," Uncle said.

"Lord Lydney? I think not. He left me to do the task he did not have the courage to do. He did not want to look like the villain, depriving his only living son of his family treasure. Should I decide against Harry, I'll look like a vengeful villainess."

"'Heaven has no rage, like love to hatred turned, nor hell a fury, like a woman scorned.'" He cackled, and my eyes widened at his quote. Then he seemed to rein himself in. "I'm sorry, my dear. I beg your pardon. What I meant was that, rather than give the collection to the South Kensington directly, which would have benefited you not at all, he left it for you to bestow upon them so that you might curry favor with those in charge. It was, perhaps, a gift to make up for what his son did not, in the end, do for you. And for the many years your father worked on his behalf," he reminded me. "It's your papa's collection as much as anyone's."

I heard his sorrow resting atop what must have been a frightening assault. He did not speak of the lost watch. I did not think he ever would—to save me, and perhaps himself, from revisiting the grief. He blinked back a tear. "I shall see you tomorrow," he said. Orchie came up behind us and wiped his mouth with a linen; he had begun to drool just a little but did not seem to be aware of it.

I walked into the hallway that connected our home to our shop and workroom. Our firm had always been run by two brothers. Twins ran in the family, and one brother had always lived in one house and the second in the other. Uncle Lewis had never married, and after my mother had me, she'd said, "Although you're a pretty bauble, I have no desire for any more children." It was clear there were to be no twin sons.

After my mother disappeared, my father had invited Uncle Lewis to move in with us, and they'd converted the second house into our workshop, where we cleaned, repaired, and gave valuations for pieces of fine and decorative art, manuscripts, silver, and the like. In the front was a small storefront—a newish concept in London, for antiquities—mostly to draw the eye and conversation of passersby.

Mr. Clarkson was at work repairing a chip on a fine porcelain cup from China. The workroom was too tidy and bare; we did not have enough commissions.

"Uncle Lewis was unwell and has retired for the evening," I said.

Clarkson nodded at me, then paused in his work. "Miss Sheffield . . . may I call you Eleanor?"

I looked down for a moment and then back up.

"No, no, of course not. Decorum is altogether important for ladies of reputation," he said.

"I'm wondering where I might find the inventory list for the last visit you made to Watchfield House?" I had asked Mr. Clarkson to go in my stead earlier in the year because I had not wanted to be mourning at Watchfield after it was clear Harry was not returning for me.

"It's in here somewhere," he said. "I shall locate it. But may I ask why?"

"I'll have to return to the house for a final accounting."

"Yes," he agreed. "You'll want to let the museum know what they'll be receiving, and the value."

I looked at him intently. The pinched smell of the glaze made me a bit dizzy. "I haven't decided to give it to the museum."

Now he stared. "But certainly, after the way the new baron treated you during his long and unexplained absence . . . When you had me go in your stead, I felt you'd led me to believe . . ."

I had not led him to believe anything. "I'd like to compare what you found then to what is there now. The solicitor indicated . . ." I let my voice trail off. Suddenly I did not want to be forthright with Mr. Clarkson.

"Yes. Yes. If anything has been liquidated. I quite understand. Let me come with you. We can work side by side. There are so many things to account for."

It was a good idea, and I nodded my assent. "Perhaps next month. Soon."

He set down his piece of china and came nearer to me and smiled. "I've been told that the Burlington Fine Arts Club is now accepting discreet enquiries about women members. I've been angling for an invitation myself, and now there is hope that we both may join."

"Truly?" The Burlington, made up mostly of gentlemen collectors, was well-known not only nearby but throughout London. Their members had the largest, richest collections and shared information and conservators. It would be a great boon for the future of Sheffield Brothers if we were to be invited. "I'm delighted!" I allowed a thought which had teased at the back of my mind to present itself fully. *Perhaps I could run the firm even without Uncle's assistance if the time comes.*

"I'm delighted that you are delighted. Mr. Herberts is to visit next week and bring by a piece he'd like me to clean, then offer us a commission to source medieval silver. I thought you might like to meet him."

"Thank you, Mr. Clarkson. I would indeed."

He dug around in the cabinets for a while and finally located the last inventory done at Watchfield House. I was about to ask him about the newly repaired mantel clock, but he spoke first.

"One favor." He handed over the file. "As this is my work, if you have any questions, will you ask me directly?"

I smiled. "Mr. Clarkson, I appreciate your talents and concern more than I can express. But I am capable of reviewing the notes for my own firm's commission and am unwilling to relinquish that responsibility to anyone not family."

He smiled and seemed to understand. I bid him good night and kept my counsel about the clock.

I returned to my room and looked at Lord Lydney's letter once more. To ascertain if Harry was worthy, I must learn if his father's assumptions were wrong or right. Perhaps Harry was the man I hoped—wished, desired—him to be. Perhaps he was the man his father claimed he was. Which of us was the better valuer?

To make a determination, there were three questions I must resolve.

Had Harry tarried in Austria for his own pleasure and desires, as his father asserted, or was he there to serve his father at the end of his life, as Harry insisted?

Had Harry been selling his father's valuables? He did not own them, after all, so they'd not been his to sell.

Was Harry selfish—only tending to his own interests?

I opened the small drawer and lifted out the Adore ring Harry had given me at a time when I'd thought our love was secure.

I closed my eyes, recalling.

The summerhouse was warm enough to make us heave out our breath, and it was but minutes before I would return to London with Papa.

"I must go quickly! It won't do us any good to have Papa find me in here with you . . . alone."

"He won't care about that soon," Harry said.

I tilted my head. That could mean only one thing.

He opened a small velvet pouch and slipped his finger inside. When he withdrew it, something glistened in the summer sun, balanced on his fingertip. He plucked it off. "Amethyst. Diamond.

Opal. Ruby. Emerald. The first letter of each gem spells adore. *I adore you, Ellie. I shall be back home very soon. Within weeks."*

As he bent to kiss me, we heard my father's voice calling, "Eleanor!"

I caught my breath and he his, and though we both wanted to lean in toward one another, we did not.

He slipped the ring on my finger. "Wear it if you dare."

I opened my eyes, in my room once more. After Harry had given the ring to me, he left for the Italian Peninsula, and it took so long for him to return that I pulled it off and hid it away. Before he left for Italy again, he'd asked me to wear it once more, though nothing was formally arranged. I'd looked at him quizzically, and he must have known I was wondering, *Will you propose?*

"Not yet," he'd said. "There are a few more things I must do." I had put the ring back on, then.

Now there were but four stones, and where the amethyst should be there was a gaping hole, like the one in my heart. There would be a fourth question I must answer before determining whether Harry was honorable and trustworthy.

Why hadn't he proposed marriage to me?

CHAPTER *Four*

On the Tuesday of Mr. Herberts's visit, I dressed carefully in one of my better dresses, something I had not taken care to do for many months. I'd sorted through my bootlaces looking for a matching pair, and Orchie finally handed me a dozen of them, in various states of threadbare.

"Thank you, Orchie."

"Important visitor? Mr. Clarkson said it might be better to keep your uncle, erm, occupied and such."

There was no telling what Uncle Lewis might come out with. I nodded my agreement. "Yes. Mr. Clarkson and I hope this visitor will be so pleased that he will extend an invitation to us both to visit the Burlington Fine Arts Club."

She nodded and left me to finish dressing.

Mr. Herberts arrived punctually at half past nine.

"Mr. Herberts." Mr. Clarkson's voice was a practiced instrument. "We are delighted to welcome you to our little shop."

I prickled a bit at Clarkson's use of the possessive *our*, but he did work for the firm, after all.

"May I introduce you to Miss Sheffield?"

Mr. Herberts smiled tightly, took my hand, and after a stiff bow, kissed the back of my glove. "Heiress presumptive of the firm. How do you do?"

It was not the best manners to speak of my uncle as though he were nearly dead. "How do you do?" I responded. "May I offer you some refreshment?"

"No, my dear," he said. "I'm a busy man with a full day ahead, although I appreciate that it's always a woman's inclination to serve. I'm here about silver."

I held on to the retort which first presented itself. "Mr. Clarkson said you were interested in medieval silver? Is there a certain piece or style or any other specific you are interested in?"

His mouth pursed. "Anything authentic, Miss Sheffield."

"You're right to be concerned about authenticity." Autumn rain beaded the windows, trailing down the glass. A sister strand of perspiration trailed down my spine, blessedly hidden by my dress. I somehow knew this was a test.

Mr. Clarkson wiped his brow.

"May I suggest coins?" I asked.

At that, Mr. Herberts looked up. "I'd expected a woman

to suggest a pitcher or jewelry or something pretty and perhaps frivolous."

That was just what I'd needed to starch my resolve. "I can certainly look for a pitcher, if you prefer," I said sweetly.

"No, no." His ears pinked and that gave me strength.

"Fraudulent coins of that era are difficult to pass by an experienced evaluator," I began. "They were standardized, and the details of the mint, and sometimes the moneyer, are well-known." I picked up a small silk pouch I had brought with me that morning, plucked from deep within my father's curiosity cabinet.

I opened it, then sifted through the contents. *A tithe of coins.*

I plucked out one. "This is a later era, of course, but still interesting. I was delighted when I learned that monarchs, on coins, always face in the opposite direction from their predecessor. It started, my father taught me, when Charles the Second wanted to turn his back on Cromwell—and so he did, on a coin, for all to see."

Mr. Herberts took the coin in his hand and smiled. "Happily, our queen looks good with a left-facing profile."

I smiled. "Indeed she does."

I peered back into the pouch, fished out another coin, and handed it to Mr. Herberts. "I've learned that the story behind the item is as important as the item itself. Everyone loves a good story; isn't that true?"

He held the silver coin in his hand, gazing acquisitively at the faint impression. "King . . ."

"Edward the Third," I supplied helpfully. "His visage barely able to be discerned, because you can imagine the hands this coin has passed through over five hundred years. First owned by a rich man, perhaps, paying the wages of his servants, barely missing this one low-value coin. The servant, however, cherished it and took it in hand to pay for the wool his wife must use to make winter garments. The wool seller gambled it away, though he could scarce risk losing it. And finally—" I pointed out the bend at the edge of the coin—"the hand of a pilgrim. Perhaps someone who felt badly for winning the gamble."

He turned the coin over in his hand, seemingly enchanted by my tale. "A pilgrim?"

I nodded. "When our medieval forebears undertook a pilgrimage, they would hold themselves to honest account and intentions by bending the coin to be offered. Everyone knew that bend made the coin unusable in the secular realm. The coin, intended for the abbey or shrine, must now be given to them, where it could be used for holy purposes."

He looked at me, and I saw a bit of unwilling admiration come into his face. "Yes, Miss Sheffield, you are certainly correct. The story enriches the item immeasurably. Do, please, source some medieval coins for me. Holy ones, if possible."

"Gladly." I let my breath out slowly and not in the telling sigh in which it wished to escape.

"I want a dozen. I'd like you, personally, to source these coins."

Mr. Clarkson's face spotted red. He, after all, had cultivated the relationship with Mr. Herberts.

Nothing had been said about the Fine Arts Club. I tried a new tactic. "Perhaps you'd settle for eleven? You may keep the one in your hand. A gift from Sheffield Brothers."

"Truly?"

"Truly," I replied. "With our compliments." I nodded toward Mr. Clarkson to include him in the gift, and he smiled.

By Friday, an invitation had arrived for me to visit the next meeting of the Burlington Fine Arts Club, to be held at Lord Audley's London house.

Lord Audley, issuer of the cryptic warning at Watchfield House.

There was no invitation for Mr. Clarkson.

The carriage wheels threw muck and pebbles, slipping now and again on the rain-slicked roads as we careened through nighttime London. I wondered, briefly, what illness had plagued my uncle that day, as he'd kept to his room, and what I should do if he could no longer work.

If our commissions continued to dwindle, I could not take on work as a governess or a companion, for who would then care for the uncle who had cared so well for me after my father's death?

I arrived at Lord Audley's spacious town house in Mayfair; his butler opened the door. I stood there in the cold, bag in hand, smiling politely, whilst he looked around for a husband.

"I am alone," I offered. "Miss Eleanor Sheffield." I passed

my reticule from one moist hand to the other and back again, awaiting his response.

"Of course." *A censure of grimaces.*

He showed me into an expansive reception room lined with what seemed like acres of well-polished oak cabinetry, all lit with lamps and filled with treasures. Lord Audley caught my eye, and though his earlier manner had been aloof, he was a perfect host and came to greet me.

"Miss Sheffield, I'm delighted you could attend."

"Thank you, Lord Audley. I must admit to some surprise at having been invited, though I am pleased, of course."

Audley nodded toward Mr. Herberts, standing some feet away. "Herberts insisted, and I wouldn't have said no even if he had not. I thought it good you might meet some of the men—and a few women—who make purchases and offer donations for the South Kensington and other museums as well as purchase for their own extensive collections."

Was that an implicit offer? I looked at him, and he smiled. I believed that it was.

The South Kensington, I knew, had grown out of the Great Exhibition our queen's beloved Prince Albert had sponsored some fifteen years earlier. Over the years, the museum had determined to show a complete history of art, including both fine and decorative arts, and that mission required the acquisitions of thousands of items. Perhaps the queen felt that this would be one of her many lasting monuments to her departed husband? Whatever the case, it had her blessing and had fueled further interest in collecting, both for the museum and for individuals among the newly wealthy.

This had been a benefit to Sheffield Brothers for as long as my father had been alive.

"That's very kind of you. May I ask a question?"

His smile dropped. "Of course," he said guardedly.

"You'd mentioned, at the funeral for Lord Lydney, that we had met. I'm so sorry to say I do not recall having made your acquaintance."

"Before my father came into his new title, allowing me to take the Audley title, I was known simply as James Remington."

I knew my eyes opened a bit wider. "Remington." Yes. He and Harry had been friends at school but had a falling-out over something. I had met him at Watchfield House. He'd ridden one of Harry's horses particularly hard, and they'd had a row about horses.

"I've reformed," he said as if reading my mind. He was, perhaps, reading my face. "I mean to do well by you, Miss Sheffield, which is why you are here tonight. Come." He smiled in a friendly, but not overly personal, manner. "I would like to make some introductions."

I followed Lord Audley around the corner into another room, upon whose walls hung beautiful and costly paintings and in whose corners stood breathtaking marble statuary seemingly made of stone quarried from the moon but that was, rather, luminescent Italian marble.

He introduced me to a tipsy shipbuilder, a pleasant tobacco

merchant, a wealthy hackney man—one of whose carriages I might have traveled in just an hour earlier—and a sperm whale oil seller who seemed to me to be as slick as his product. All men. All collectors who might offer commissions. All craving the respectability which had, previously, only been available to the titled but might now be purchased by the pound.

Each greeted me politely but perhaps disinterestedly. I was beginning to despair of ever finding a place among them when I turned and heard pretty laughter coming from a far corner of the room.

Audley himself smiled. "Lady Charlotte Schreiber," he said. "Someone of whom I—all of us—think highly. She's a collector in her own right and quite wise. I have commissioned her several times. I suspect she will be happy to meet you."

He had commissioned a woman to make purchases on his behalf!

He led me to her and made the introductions, then said, "If you'll excuse me, I must tend to my other guests. I look forward to your thoughts and comments after my presentation."

As he left, Lady Charlotte turned toward me. "I knew your late father."

"I miss him greatly."

"I understand that your uncle is not entirely well. Troubling news." Her voice had both a tremor of concern and the note of gravitas which recognized the difficulties my firm would be in should Uncle Lewis pass away or, more likely, be incapacitated, needing continued care.

"My uncle is still working." *When work is to be had.*

"Come." She took my arm. "Let's view some of the cases together. There has been another woman or two at the meetings from time to time, but it seems it is just we two this night."

My fingers tingled. "I'm delighted to learn that other women have been admitted," I said.

"The Burlington was formed to both admire and educate, and its members consider themselves quite progressive."

Would that I be among them. I'd seen other conservators and members of firms often commissioned to make purchases for the well-to-do among the crowd this evening—some who had worked with my father, but who'd left when he died. It was, as has always been, as much whom you knew as what you knew. Perhaps I could make a convincing case for the latter if I was often enough among the former.

As we walked, I knew I was supposed to be looking at the items so beautifully displayed in the cases, but I could not help staring at the striking pendant hanging from Lady Charlotte's waist but nestled in her dress. The front depicted a scene of summer, green glass or jewels along with multicolored flowered ones.

"It's lovely, isn't it?" she asked.

"Yes. I suppose winter is on the hidden side?"

She laughed. "Yes, Miss Sheffield, you are correct—and perhaps the only person who has ever commented on it who would know that there must be a second, equally decorative side to a pendant."

I beamed. "They are made to swing freely, though our current fashions keep them from so doing."

"They are." She led me to a duet of chairs in a far corner where we could sit and talk more comfortably. She fanned herself, and as she did, it lifted her hair slightly from her forehead. Odd gray hair roots hid among the black. She dyed her hair! Was there no end to her daring behavior? I felt, instantly, that we should become friends.

If only she felt the same.

She seemed to notice my glance but took it to be toward her fan. "It was my mother's. Like most collectors, I started with one piece. One small item which came to me laden with emotion and meaning and beauty. I know you're given to collections, Miss Sheffield. Did you come by that as a matter of family practice or as a matter of the heart?"

The drone and heat in the room and Lady Charlotte's pointed question drew forth an unwelcome memory.

After dancing class, Marguerite's mother returned me home. I pushed the door open. "Papa? Mama? Orchie?" The house was strangely quiet. Abandoned.

Orchie appeared in the hallway, her face stricken.

"What has happened?"

She shook her head and said nothing, but the tears flowed. Instinctively, I knew. I had sensed this was to come since I'd overheard Mama and Papa speaking. Since I'd seen Mama clinging to that wealthy man after I followed her, once, when she'd left the house after an argument.

I ran to her room, crying, "Mama! Are you here?" I opened her wardrobe. It was empty. I ran to the kitchen, to the dining room, to the parlor, where she'd loved to sit and read. I sobbed, "Mama! I'm here. I need you. Are you here?"

My heart beat in my throat. Orchie reached for me, and I shook her off.

The door to my father's library was closed, and behind it, he wailed like a struck animal.

Orchie placed her considerable body between me and the door. "No."

I slunk away, back to Mama's room. She had left but one thing that I could see: her beautiful ruby-and-silver perfume bottle. I lifted the cap, closed my eyes, and inhaled. It smelled of Otto of Roses, the hundred-leaved rose, the lingering fragrance of which signaled my mother had been here once. She'd left the bottle behind . . . along with Papa and me.

"Mama," I cried through choking tears. "Why have you left me?"

"Miss Sheffield?" A hand rested on my arm. I shook myself back to the present.

"I'm sorry," I said. "The heat of the room."

"Your collection?" Lady Charlotte prompted.

"Coincidentally, my own collection started with something of my mother's. A silver-and-ruby perfume bottle."

"How lovely."

I nodded and as a matter of will dismissed the past from my mind.

A man who was at least a decade younger than Lady Charlotte smiled at her in a most personal way. She blushed. "My husband, the Right Honorable Mr. Charles Schreiber."

I apparently had not been discreet enough to keep my surprise from my face, but that did not seem to put her off. Indeed, she seemed amused. "I was married to another good man for many years, but he, unfortunately, passed away. Mr. Schreiber was hired to tutor my sons, and after a respectable period, he proposed marriage to me. I said yes."

"And now you collect—together," I said.

"Oh yes." She placed her fan back in her small, tasteful handbag. "We are a partnership in every way, Miss Sheffield. It's most accommodating. You may enjoy something similar," she teased coyly. Did she speak of the pleasant Mr. Clarkson, who was now well-known to be attached to our firm?

We were called to listen to Lord Audley and his father discuss the art, nearly all of which was magnificent, and afterward, the group began to disperse. I had hoped for an invitation to the next meeting, but none was forthcoming. Perhaps Lady Charlotte understood my despair, for she came alongside me before taking her leave.

"It's but your first visit, dear. We can hope for more."

I nodded, trying to remain optimistic.

She continued, "I'm hosting a dinner party and an evening of games next week. Would you care to join us?"

I smiled. "Oh yes, I would be delighted to."

She held up a hand. "Before you so readily agree, I must disclose a detail to you. My husband, Charles, made an acquaintance during some of his collecting in Italy. Lord Lydney . . . the present Lord Lydney."

Harry.

"He will be there, as my husband is keen to learn about the antique glassware he returned with from Venice, though he's been told none of it is for sale. I know about your trusteeship and the decision which must follow it. If you feel comfortable attending, still, I would most enjoy your company; please bring a chaperone if that makes you more comfortable. Give it some thought, and send me a reply." She handed me a calling card, and we said our good-byes.

Later that week, I sent my reply.

Dear Lady Charlotte,

I would be delighted to attend your dinner party. The invitation was so very kind and very much appreciated. I especially appreciate the extended invitation to my friend, Mrs. Marguerite Newsome. We look forward to the event, with pleasure.

Sincerely yours,
Miss Eleanor Sheffield

One night, not long after the note was sent, my bedroom was dark as a closed coffin and as still as the air within it when I awoke to the sound of shattering glass. I heard it once and then twice, the second time more subdued. I sat up in bed, my breath heaving. I could not remain in bed, though. What if my uncle had fallen?

I pulled a dressing gown around my sleeping gown and

slid my feet into my carpet slippers. I lit the lamp on my table and held it out before me as I made my way down the hall. The house, without the coal stove going, was bitingly cold and my teeth chattered, whether from fear or chill I could not discern. I clamped my jaw to stop them.

I went first to my uncle's room. I could hear him, even through the closed door, snoring in jerks and jags. He was safely abed.

Downstairs, next to the kitchen, was the small room which had been made into a bedroom for Orchie. I heard her breaths, in pillowing wisps and bubbles. She, too, was abed. I had to rouse her, though. I could not go out into the rest of the house on my own to see what had happened.

I opened her door and shook her. Her sleeping cap was askew, and when she saw me with the light, she came instantly awake. "Someone is about the house," I said. I could see the fear writ on her face, but she too put on a dressing gown and followed me down the hall. We checked each room, one by one, hearts pounding. What would I do if someone should be there?

"The workshop," I said. "I must check it, too."

"Them men what roughed up your uncle . . ." She whispered my fear and I nodded my agreement. On the way I spoke a silent prayer, asking the Lord to have protected the few pieces of art yet entrusted to us for restoration, most of which were irreplaceable.

Once at the door to the workshop, I quietly turned the knob. I heard Orchie, behind me, inhale and then hold her breath. I was as frightened as she was. But I had to move forward.

I pushed the door open and immediately felt the snake of cold air. A breeze. Orchie and her lamp followed me in. "Hello?" I called into the shadows. "Is anyone here?" I peered into every corner but saw no one. I peeked into the cabinets, but the art seemed blessedly undisturbed.

Thank you, God. And thank you, too, Mr. Clarkson, for having thought to bring the important works out of the front room at night.

"You stay here and run down the street for help if you hear me scream," I told Orchie. Her eyes widened but she nodded and lagged back.

I made my way to the front room.

"Miss Eleanor—look!" Orchie called from behind me, pointing to the front windows. Two panes were broken, only large enough for someone to have reached in and grabbed a relatively inexpensive framed print.

"Not big enough for anyone to have entered." Orchie sighed with relief.

"Follow me back to the house," I said. "And return to bed. I shall get dressed and then sit in the workshop all night until Mr. Clarkson arrives and can call the police. I can't risk anyone coming back to steal anything more. If I scream, run next door for help."

Orchie appeared about to protest but I held up my hand. "I insist."

She grumbled and mentioned 'twas not likely she'd sleep

whilst awaiting a scream, but she did leave the room. I quickly dressed myself and returned to the workshop, where I sat in my chair until I felt a hand on my shoulder.

"No!" I shouted as I came awake.

"Miss Sheffield," came a soothing voice. "Do not be alarmed. It is I, Mr. Clarkson."

I nearly wept with relief. "Oh, dear. I must have fallen asleep whilst waiting for dawn."

He smiled gently and helped me to my feet. "Please don't worry. You've done well. I shall report this to the police and see to having the glass replaced. You've handled this admirably, but it is not a task for a lady. I'm here to care for it now."

I was about to protest but was so overcome with fatigue and relief that I did not have to tend to the situation on my own that I gladly accepted his assistance.

"What should you have done if a burglar had remained on the premises? You could not have protected yourself," he scolded lightly. He was right.

"Do you think it was the people who stole my uncle's watch?" I asked.

He nodded. "Very possibly. You've not had this kind of situation before?"

I shook my head. "Never. Will they do more damage yet? Is my household at risk?"

He looked contemplative. "I hope not. I certainly hope not. But it is entirely possible."

CHAPTER *Five*

Mr. Clarkson had spoken to the police, and they reassured us that they would be walking by our home and workshop each evening for some time, so I was relieved and well rested when it was time to attend Lady Charlotte's game night. Marguerite was to be ready at seven, and when I arrived with the hired carriage, she stepped lightly out of her front door, and someone closed it behind her.

"You seem more enthusiastic than I feel," I said.

"I certainly present myself as more enthusiastic than you do," she said, slightly tart.

"What is that to mean?" I smoothed my dress in front of

me. It did appear a little careworn. I rearranged the folds so the thin areas of fabric would remain hidden.

"Eleanor. You would never allow one of the pieces you manage or place on offer to go as untended or as uncared for as you allow yourself." I felt struck. She reached out a gloved hand and took my own gently. "I'm sorry, dearest. That was thoughtless of me—but still true. You are a most beautiful woman. If only we could be allowed to see that."

"I'm not meant to be beautiful. I'm meant to be capable."

"Cannot a person be both?" Marguerite fluttered her fan at me, knowing I was trapped. If I were to disagree, I would be calling her out as either unlovely or incapable.

"Checkmate," I said, and she laughed.

"Thank you for inviting me to come along. What is a poor old widow to do for an evening's entertainment otherwise?"

"You are neither poor nor old." I quietened my voice. "Though *widow* is still true."

I caught a shadow of sadness before she hid it again. "Yes." Her husband had died two years earlier. She squeezed my hand once more. "*Poor* is nearly true too."

I hadn't realized. I squeezed her hand in return, and we rode on in silence.

We arrived at the Schreibers' home, Langham House in Portland Place, just as the evening lamps were being lit. Lady Charlotte greeted us.

"I'm delighted you could attend. I shall introduce you to some others whose company I am assured you will enjoy and hope that you'll feel quite comfortable. Dinner will be served shortly, and then we will divide up into groups to play games. In addition to collecting fans, I collect board games. Did you know?"

"I did not—but what a delightful idea!"

I conversed comfortably and casually with some of those Lady Charlotte introduced to me, as did Marguerite. I had quickly scanned the room and did it once more. Harry was not yet present.

But then well ahead of the seating for dinner, he arrived.

He still took my breath away. His black tailcoat was magnificently tailored, and under it was a deep-burgundy vest; tucked beneath that was one of the high-collared white shirts he always wore. When he saw me, his face lit up with both surprise and pleasure. His surprise told me that while Lady Charlotte had warned me he would be in attendance, she had not warned him that I would be here. His pleasure seemed authentic. It warmed me, though I remained wary.

He reached into his pocket and lifted a gold chain with a pocket watch, then winked at me. I knew what he was telling me. *"See? I'm not late."*

I smiled and nodded my acknowledgment. Marguerite looked at him, then at me, and smiled too before turning away.

My dinner companion to the right was a man who owned a match factory, and I found him to be most agreeable company. He enjoyed pretty things and made no disguise of that; he had made his fortune providing fire to all and jobs to women who could do no work but assemble matchboxes at home and was proud of both. I made a point to mention Sheffield Brothers and indicated that Mr. Clarkson and I would be glad to value or acquire for him at any time. He said he would think on that and appeared pleasant. I was heartened.

To my left was the wife of one of the other members of the Burlington. She made abrupt conversation when she had to but made it clear she felt that as a woman involved in a profession, I belonged below stairs, if there at all, and not as her dining companion.

After dinner, we retired to the salon, where Lady Charlotte had several tables set with her board games. The room was warm with both the fire and the many lamps which had been placed to best show off their own prizes. It was papered in a pattern which reminded me of the Garden of Eden, thick with vines and flowers and birds, their heads turned so one eye of each spied on the room. We gathered round in merriment—there were sixteen of us in attendance, neatly divided into groups of four.

"I have here—" Mr. Schreiber held out a closed fist—"sixteen straws, each dipped in color. We shall draw straws, and the four that match in each color set will begin as a table group. The winners from each game shall gather for the next round, as will those who came in second place, and so on."

Mr. Schreiber passed the straws. The one I'd selected was tipped in blue, and I went to the blue table, which held an antique version of Game of the Goose. It was a fine place for someone like myself, so deeply immersed in history, to begin. It was the first board game, begun in Italy, perhaps by a member of the infamous Medici family.

In the center of the board was a beautiful illustration of an aristocratic Italian lady sitting at a games table with a band of merry musicians surrounding her. The match maker, my dinner companion, handed a playing piece to each of us. Delightfully, they were not the standard pieces which had come with the game but were little collectibles from, I imagined, the Schreibers' collection. Mine was a thimble which looked to have been about two hundred years old. When I looked up, I saw Lady Charlotte smiling at me as I inspected it. I smiled back.

The game goal was to make it all the way round the board, advancing as we threw dice and landed on spaces which would move us forward, backward, or across. The first person to reach the sixty-third square won. The game was rousing fun, and I quite enjoyed the company of all at the table.

Unfortunately, one of my throws landed me on the skull.

"That means death," the match maker's wife said to me quietly. "You must return to the beginning and start all over again."

There was no way I could win. They all looked at me—none wanting the setback to spoil the cheerful mood. I would not allow it to do so. "Sometimes starting anew is the best way to move forward. Even if it seems like you've lost."

At that, the match maker's wife clapped her hands in approval. The game concluded, and we switched tables.

Just ahead of the third and final round, Lady Charlotte

waved to me. "Miss Sheffield!" She patted the spot beside her. Then Harry effortlessly slid into a chair at that table ahead of another man who'd been hovering nearby.

The man toddled off to a different table, and Harry smiled at me. Had he slid in just in time, just so he could be near me? If so, I rather admired his daring.

Our round was the Game of Virtue Rewarded and Vice Punished. "Lord Lydney will explain the rules," Mr. Schreiber announced to our foursome. He grinned. "Lord Lydney, are you quite familiar with virtue being rewarded and vice being punished?"

Harry looked at me, softly, but without turning away before answering, "Oh, indeed so. And from the prettiest of hands."

A frisson of familiarity passed between us, a wave of intimacy. I imagined the others must have felt it too. I did not wish for the tide of that intimacy to recede.

"Your father enjoyed parlor games, did he not?" Lady Charlotte asked Harry. "I believe I saw him at an evening of games last Christmastime."

Harry nodded. "He certainly enjoyed games. His favorite was Questions and Commands."

His voice held no rancor—I could not recall a time when it ever had, despite the bitterness his father had directed at him—but all present glanced away anyway. Questions and Commands had fallen out of favor in gentler circles.

"Let the game begin!" I spun the totem first and landed on the square marked for the House of Correction, which meant I lost three turns. I think all were aware that I had been significantly set back in the first game, but I was expected to remain a good sport, and I did. "Perhaps this is so I can minister to the ladies therein more effectively."

"Are you part of the ladies' committees which visit the prisons?" Lady Charlotte asked.

"I am," I affirmed.

"Well done." She took her turn and landed on Charity, which meant she could take two more spins. "I think I've robbed you of the charitable position, Miss Sheffield."

"I have known you but a little while, but I have found you to be most charitable. Earned and deserved," I replied.

Harry landed first on Folly, laughed aloud once more and caught my eye, and I could not help but laugh with him. He was such pleasant company. He did not take himself too seriously and yet he could be serious-minded when the situation required it. His conversation was witty and others-directed. Not selfish.

Oh, how I'd missed him. I still missed him. I missed his touch—when he held my arm, my flesh yielded, just slightly, like a newly ripened pear. I missed knowing that . . . I was his and he was mine.

I sat on the bench outside the summerhouse, waiting for Harry. He was just a bit late, which made me slightly cross. I did not want to lose any of our few moments together before my father called me back to assist him.

Harry rounded the corner and walked up the garden, toward the bench. His left arm overflowed with flowers. He waved with his right. When he stood in front of me, he spoke, quoting Song of Solomon. "'Whither is thy beloved gone, O thou fairest among women? whither is thy beloved turned aside? that we may seek him with thee.'"

I blushed. For a gentleman to quote that passage to a lady could only mean . . . well, it was bold. I should reprimand him. But I did not. "'My beloved is gone down into his garden, to the beds of spices, to feed in the gardens, and to gather lilies,'" I quoted the next verse. Marguerite and I had memorized sections of the book as young ladies, role-playing the pieces and wondering if anyone might speak them to us someday. In a rush of indiscretion, once, I had told Harry—and he had remembered.

He sat down next to me and nestled the bouquet of fragrant lilies in my arms before holding my gaze and softly speaking the next verse. "'I am my beloved's, and my beloved is mine.'"

"Miss Sheffield?" Mr. Schreiber said, calling me back to the moment.

"Oh yes," I said, taking a deep, steadying breath.

Harry looked at me quizzically. "Are you well?"

I blushed again, as I had that day near the summerhouse. "Yes. I was . . . thinking of lilies."

The others appeared confused, but Harry's smile, both warm and wistful, told me that he remembered too.

Mr. Schreiber took the next turn and landed in The Stocks. "It appears I shall join you in prison, Miss Sheffield, and can thereby offer some companionship," he jested.

In the end, Lady Charlotte won the game by landing directly on Virtue. It was a perfect ending to a lovely evening.

She pulled me aside as the others were getting their wraps and calling their carriages. "I've heard that you're to be welcomed back to the Burlington. That an invitation to join may well be forthcoming."

"Oh, thank you, Lady Charlotte."

"Please, dear, simply call me Charlotte."

Friends!

"And I must be Eleanor to you, of course," I replied. We walked toward her husband, a handsome man who glanced at her with delight and who was speaking with Harry. I overheard some talk about Venetian glass as we drew near to them. Then she and her husband left to bid farewell to their other guests, and I watched as Marguerite headed in my direction.

"I was delighted beyond measure to see you here tonight," Harry said.

"Thank you, Lord Lydney." The title tripped on my tongue and summoned a picture of his somber father.

"Harry," he said. "Always. At least among ourselves."

My heart pleaded his case. "Harry, then," I agreed. "I'll need to return to Watchfield soon—I, as well as my uncle and Mr. Clarkson, who did the most recent inventory of the collection."

He nodded. "Anytime. Please, telegraph and let me know when. I would like to be present. I'm not always at Watchfield, but when I am, the telegrams are delivered to me promptly."

"Perhaps the second week of October," I said. "I have

some obligations to tend to first—including my work with the aforementioned prison brigade."

"I'm delighted to know you still visit the women prisoners."

"Oh yes. I visit regularly and have earned many faithful friends there."

"A friend to the friendless. They are fortunate for your friendship. As am I."

"They would do what they could for me as well," I said. "At any time."

He took my cloak from the butler and wrapped it around my shoulders himself. It was a familiar gesture. One he'd often used to gather me in his arms in a socially acceptable manner. One I relished. His voice was low, and he spoke in a tone so quiet only I could hear it. "As would I."

I melted into the crook of his arm, my body yielding where my heart and mind fought. I would not reply in like manner because to do so could imply a promise I might not keep.

CHAPTER *Six*

In the workshop Friday afternoon, I wrote letters to sources I thought might have rare medieval coins for Mr. Herberts. I would do what I must to make a success of it for the firm, for my family, and for myself. I would succeed. I turned the lamps high against the encroaching autumn chill, the dull swirl of coal-tainted mist outside the door, and the dread I felt at the decisions I must make. One of the officers Mr. Clarkson had arranged for passed by and waved at me, giving me comfort.

I then took a moment to have a cup of tea and to pray, blessedly easier when I was alone. I asked the Lord for wisdom and guidance as I sought to shore up our finances, two requests of which I knew he approved. I asked for assurance of his presence. *Are you here?* my heart cried out to him.

Silence.

Disheartened, I set about reviewing a teacup and saucer set for a client, Mrs. Priestly—four of each decorated with intricate red landscapes. She wanted to know if they were in fact crafted by Jacques Boselly, the famous Italian artisan. If so, they would be very valuable indeed. I turned one cup over, and then the second, looking for the maker's mark, which more than style identified the creator and a piece's authenticity. The maker's mark was scribbled on both. It looked genuine. I began to grow excited for my client—these were, perhaps, truly rare and valuable eighteenth-century teaware. A shadow of regret clouded my enthusiasm as I realized that if they were a recent acquisition with little or no provenance, then they, too, might have been looted from Italy in the recent war.

I began to see Harry's decision to smuggle the Venetian glass for safekeeping in an ever more sympathetic light.

When I turned over the third cup, although the maker's mark was the same, I could read, beneath it but nearly entirely covered, the faintest impression: *Wedgwood.* It could not, then, be Boselly.

I took the lamp closer to the piece and raked the light across the surface as Papa had taught me time and again to do. Yes. The maker's mark had been painted on above the glaze after the piece had been finished. It was fraudulent. I checked all of them more closely, and indeed, they were all imitations.

I set the items into the box and completed my note with unwelcome news, never easy to deliver, but required by both my integrity and my affection for my clients.

I posted the letter to my client and a deck of antique cards for the game Lend Me Five Shillings, taken from our family's small collection and sent with my thanks for a lovely evening, to Charlotte. Then I returned to the workshop. Shortly after, the afternoon post was delivered, and in it was a large envelope from Sir Matthew Landon, the late Lord Lydney's solicitor. Alone in the workshop, I opened it and began to read.

Miss Sheffield,

As I am concluding the remainder of the late Lord Lydney's estate, several packets of his personal and private correspondence have been forwarded to me from Austria. Among them were some additional information regarding the art pieces and a letter, written and sealed apparently just before his death. It is addressed to you.

Please allow me to be at your service if you have concerns or questions whilst you consider the options before you. I shall look forward to hearing from you when you've reached a decision.

Yours truly,
Matthew Landon, Esq.

I then opened the second letter, sealed in black with Lord Lydney's signet stamped into it, as the first letter had been. It was clearly his handwriting, but much weaker and with blots of ink I would not have expected from a man so scrupulous—some of them still had a few grains of setting sand attached. His hand was spidery and the image of such a creature, and of the man, made my hand recoil in near fear. By the letter's date, I could see that he'd been very near death.

My dear Miss Sheffield,

The bells will soon toll, and I feel that I must share some unwelcome and recently acquired information in case you agree to take on the responsibility I have instructed my solicitor to propose to you.

I've come to understand that my son Henry has, from here in Austria, sold the portion of the Lydney Collection that had been painstakingly assembled by my elder son, Arthur, in his final years on this earth. That was in direct opposition to my instructions. I am heartbroken. It was all I had left of my son. If this is indeed true, then Henry was dealing in stolen goods, as that collection, until my death, belongs to me.

I do not know what else may have been sold, Miss Sheffield, nor why. Perhaps you may arrive at a conclusion.

Yours truly,
John Arthur Douglas, the Baron Lydney

As I read it, I could hear his voice, and it made me quiver as it had when he had spoken to me while he was alive. I knew he was dead—Harry had been with him when he died, and he was well and truly buried, and yet somehow, he felt alive in his ability to reach out, still. I slumped back in my chair. Lord Lydney had always preferred Arthur to Harry; none who had ever observed them could doubt that. Arthur was golden; he was named not only after his father but after the famed King Arthur, a legend beloved of every Englishman. Arthur had traveled with his father—and mine—to collect treasures.

Despite their father's clear preference, Harry and Arthur had loved one another, and their mother had tried to smooth over the widening chasm that their father's disdain for Harry had caused. Unfortunately, overcompensation led her to prefer Harry until her death. The situation had often put me in mind of Jacob and Esau, brothers who might have been affectionate with one another but for the divisive choices of their parents.

In the end, Lord Lydney blamed Harry for Arthur's death—he'd been sent for the doctor and hadn't returned with him in time, though he'd ridden with all speed. His father had never forgiven him. Arthur's collection, like the clock, would certainly have been a thorn in Harry's side. I could not fault him for wanting to rid himself of the unwelcome freight of guilt and disfavor such pieces repeatedly delivered, but it would not have been proper to do so before they passed down to him.

There would now be a fifth concern, a fifth question to

resolve before I could, in honesty, allow Harry to keep the collection: Had he sold Arthur's treasures?

As I was about to pull Mr. Clarkson's inventory from a cabinet to verify the contents of Arthur's collection, our lights flickered, then went out.

Orchie soon burst through the door. "We've got no gas," she said. "No lights at all."

Mr. Clarkson had left early; he had some personal affairs to tend to, he'd said. I missed his help but could address this matter on my own.

Once I'd ascertained that all our gas lamps were out, I walked out the front door and peered up and down. Perhaps there had been a service disruption on our street? But no. The other houses were well and warmly lit. "I shall visit the gas company quickly," I said, pulling on my cloak. "Perhaps there is a line break. If so, it must be looked at immediately." I did not mention the potential for a fire, but by the stricken look on Orchie's face, I knew she recognized the danger.

"Do not fret," I said. "I shall soon return."

I often passed the gas office on my way to the omnibus, so I knew where it was located and made my way there directly. I spoke with the man behind the front desk, explaining my situation. He asked for my street address, and when I told him, he looked it up.

"I'm sorry, miss, but there are considerable monies due. It's the final business day of September, and we cannot wait any longer. We have sent invoices and pleadings to no avail. The gas must remain shut until the invoices are paid."

I reeled. "This can't be. . . ."

"I'm sorry," he repeated, his eyes remaining on the accounts to help me avoid further humiliation. "But it is."

"I have an infirm uncle and an old housekeeper," I said.

"Perhaps your husband . . . ," he began.

I certainly did not want to tell him I had no husband to protect us and risk being robbed once more.

"I shall return on Monday with the amount due. My word is my bond. But in the meantime, would you please restore our gas?" I couldn't image how distressed and disoriented Uncle Lewis would become living in the dark for three long days.

He took pity on me but could not restore the gas until an installment on the amount due was paid. It was too late for me to return with such a payment that night.

I hurried home. Perhaps the envelope stolen from Uncle Lewis had been meant to pay the bill?

Orchie greeted me at the door again in a fluster of upset, which was becoming distressingly common.

"Don't worry," I said. "The gas will be on by Monday."

We spent the evening hours in the dark, with cold meals from the larder and my uncle confused and carrying on to himself about the men from the alley who had hit him and stolen his watch. It was enough to make me cry. After comforting him as best I could, next to the light of the coal stove and with a candle lamp nearby, I walked to the telegraph office and had a note sent to Mr. Clarkson—could he please not come to the workshop, or for dinner, the following night.

Monday morning, I had to explain the misunderstanding to Mr. Clarkson. "One bill was paid, and another let go in error," I said with forced cheerfulness. "It's all been taken care of now."

He nodded but gave me a rather dubious look. He was a smart valuer too. I was certain that he was able to discern the truth of our situation.

Later that afternoon, after the gas had been restored, Orchie came bursting through the door of the corridor connecting the house and the workshop. "There's men here to see you."

"Me?" I asked.

"Well, not you, but Mr. Lewis. He's not well. I thought I'd come get you, I did." She buried her head in her apron.

I straightened my dress and pulled my shoulders back. Perhaps they were here to enquire about a commission?

When I arrived in the parlor, I saw two men, expensively and severely dressed, and a member of the Metropolitan Police Force. They did not smile. My gait grew weak, and I steadied myself on a chair back for a moment.

"Gentlemen? May I help you?"

"We're here for Mr. Lewis Sheffield."

"Miss Eleanor Sheffield. And you are . . . ?" I asked.

The tallest man took off his hat. "Mr. Jacob Adams, ma'am. Solicitor. We're here representing our client, Lord Darlington."

Our longtime landlord.

He continued. "I'm confident our continuing correspondence has been delivered, as promised, by the Royal Mail. Therefore, I must come to the regrettable conclusion that Mr. Sheffield is either unable or unwilling to settle your accounts with us. He is months behind on rent. It is only because of the longstanding relationship with our client—many, many decades—that we have tarried in pursuing this matter. It is now the first of October, and current and past rents are due. Unless we have remittance in full today, we must take the unfortunate action of appearing before the magistrate to request relief, either by complete remission of the debts or by a sentencing to debtor's prison until said remission has occurred. The household will, of course, be evicted as well."

I steadied myself once more on the chair back. "Debtor's prison?"

"Do you, or does your uncle, have the complete payment?"

I was shocked at his direct, impolite approach. He must have read that into my silence. He showed the invoice to me. It was a large sum, indeed. "Perhaps it has been paid already and not credited?"

He shook his head. "It has not. Do you have receipts?"

"I can look. Can you wait but a while longer?"

"I'm sorry, Miss Sheffield. I've little patience at this point. The receipts do not exist as they have not been paid. I have been trying for a few months, on behalf of our client, to collect the debts your uncle signed for."

"I have just now become aware of this matter," I said. "My uncle has been unwell. I wonder if I might ask for some grace. I will have many new commissions, certain to bring the necessary funds. Should my uncle go to debtor's prison, it is unlikely your client will ever see the funds he desires. Perhaps two months? I will continue to remit small payments on the debts due each month in the interim and keep the rents current, of course. I can submit this month's rent by the end of the week." I did not know, even as I said it, how I could possibly pay back rent and our long-overdue gas bill—in addition to the current household expenses—in two months. I'd have to review the accounts.

Mr. Adams stared at me for some time, and I did not flinch, though I wanted to. "Will you personally sign for these debts?" he asked.

I did not answer.

"If you will not, I'm afraid we shall have to press forward."

I thought about my uncle's distress and disorientation the previous long, dark weekend. He would die if sent to debtor's prison. Additionally, if it became known that we were not paying our accounts and were turned out of our home, we'd be unable to purchase additional supplies or have a workshop, and worst, we'd take on a tarnish that our clients would not want to be associated with. In a profession such as ours, reputation was everything. We must inspire trust, or all was lost. It seemed to only have been the better of two or three months since things had gone wrong. Surely I could right them.

"Yes," I finally agreed. "I will sign—if you will give us until the end of the year to clear the account." I'd added on an additional month and hoped he would let that slide by.

He smiled. "Done."

He said he would have papers drawn up and I said I would sign them.

Orchie showed them out, and I sank into a chair and into despair. We'd had fewer commissions, it was true, and Uncle Lewis had been unable to attract as many new clients as my father had; it was the very reason we had hired someone to come into the firm the year before. I'd begun to understand, of late, that Mr. Clarkson desired to be a partner.

I heard a door open into the room. "Miss Sheffield?"

That was Mr. Clarkson now! I was certain he did not know, in full, our dire circumstances, and I could not afford to lose him.

"Yes, Mr. Clarkson?"

"May I be of some assistance?" He looked out the window at the backs of the solicitors and constable.

"No thank you. Those were our landlord's representatives; that's all," I said.

He nodded uncomfortably. He knew there would be no reason for the landlord's solicitors to show up at our home—with a constable, who would only be required when significant debts were owed. "Well, then. Do you know what day we'll be leaving for Watchfield? I'll need to visit Bristol soon. My sisters will be home, and my father is unwell."

I'd learned little about Mr. Clarkson in the previous year.

His father owned a large shop in Bristol—he'd let it slip once that it was a curiosity shop, though he represented it to others as more akin to the higher status of something like Sheffield Brothers—and he was fond of his younger sisters, each of whom depended upon his income to keep them from the poorhouse.

"I had thought, perhaps, the twelfth of October," I responded, gathering what calm and confidence remained.

He stared at my face, which must have blanched during my interactions with the solicitor and police. "Do you need help?"

I shook my head. "No thank you." I softened my voice. "I've sent out enquiries over Mr. Herberts's pieces of silver. I would very much appreciate your opinion when they arrive. I appreciate the many commissions you bring to Sheffield Brothers."

"Consider it done . . . and you're welcome. You will find, Miss Sheffield, that I am most loyal to the firm. And—" he smiled at me—"all within it."

As soon as he returned to the workshop, I went to the kitchen, where Orchie was crying, her head buried in her apron once more.

"What is it, dear Orchie?" I put my arm around her.

"The water. I was so hoping and praying you wouldn't be offering tea to anyone, and you didn't, thanks be."

"The water?"

"The water's been shut too," she said.

CHAPTER
Seven

Uncle Lewis had not, apparently, paid the water, either.

"How can I cook and clean with no water?" Orchie asked. "'Tis difficult enough keeping up on the laundry when there *is* water, and now?" She hiccuped a small sob before getting ahold of herself. She looked so very tired. And it was true: my laundry had become dull and wrinkled, sometimes spotted. Her hands were too old and arthritic to keep up. Dull clothing would not allow me to make my best presentations before our well-to-do clientele.

"Do you know where Uncle Lewis keeps his correspondence?"

She nodded and did not seem surprised by either the

visit or my question. Was this another matter about which everyone but I knew?

"In his study." She wiped her hands as if she was going to show me there.

I put my hand up to stop her. "I should hate to take you from your duties. I shall find them." I was no longer the girl who must obey her; I must take charge of my own household now.

I made my way up two flights of stairs to the level where Uncle Lewis's rooms were—his bedroom, a small study, and a dressing room. I opened the door to the study, which was unlocked. The room was in mostly good order; he had become a little less tidy of late. All the woodwork from floorboards to ceiling was painted dark green, as was his preference. I scanned the shelves first; it appeared something was missing or amiss, though in my distress, I could not put my finger on it.

I opened drawer after drawer until I found many unopened envelopes. The landlord, a few suppliers, the gas company. Quite overcome by it all, I swallowed the sourness rising in my throat. I opened the ledger book; notations as to receivables and payables stopped about a year earlier, though clearly payments had not. I could not know how much was taken in or paid out. Which had truly been paid or not, I did not know. If things were as they appeared after some quick sorting, our current situation would allow me, but just, to catch up by the end of the year. I would visit the bank first thing to ascertain what actually remained.

I took the ledger book with me and knocked on my uncle's bedroom door. "Uncle Lewis? May I come in?"

"Yes, m'dear."

I opened the door; he sat, in his dressing gown, in a chair by the window, looking out. "How are you?" I asked.

"Better," he answered. He glanced at the papers in my hand. "What is that?"

"Invoices," I replied. "All of them unpaid. Many of them unopened."

He waved his hand through the air as if swatting an insect. "Bah. All are paid. You may be certain of that. I paid them myself in crisp notes. These must be duplicates."

I did not argue with him. But I'd seen the dates on each and read the shrill tones in those I'd opened. They had not been paid.

"Perhaps it's your eyesight," I suggested, offering him a way out and thinking how to put the next question delicately. "Can you still see to appraise?"

He grinned. "Oh yes. I just squint a little like this." He half closed his eyes. "Or I blink. On better days, I don't need to do either. It all comes back. Don't worry. I shan't let you down."

"Perhaps I should take care of the ledgers," I said softly. "Till your sight is restored. Things are bound to get better soon." I patted his shoulder, and just like that, our roles as protector and protected had switched completely around. *I don't like feeling there is no one to protect me,* I thought as I left the room.

Next, I visited the water company, which took my cheque

and agreed to allow me till the end of the year to catch up the account but said it would be a day or two before the water would flow once more.

I returned home and asked Orchie for two large, stoppered jugs. "I have to visit the fountain," I said. "Just for a day or two."

"I'll come with you," she said.

"No," I said. "You need not."

"We'll need at least four jugs," she said. I could not carry four jugs on my own, so I reluctantly agreed.

We made our way, heads down, to the public fountain. Perhaps five or six years earlier, a kindhearted banker and barrister of good faith had established the Metropolitan Free Drinking Fountain Association so the poor might not thirst; each year, more fountains were established throughout London. I had never expected to have to avail myself of one and I felt shamed.

It was quite a walk, and I tried to pleasantly pass the time with light chatter. "I've visited the water company, and it shall all be sorted within a few days. The gas company and the landlord have also agreed to my plan, and so we shall be as cozy as we always have been," I said. "I've taken over the accounts from Uncle Lewis, though I didn't quite put it that way."

"I'm happy to hear of it." Orchie laughed sharply. "I was worried it would be off to the workhouse for me, though they'd like as not sell me for glue!" Her eyes looked so shadowed I knew she'd thought it was a real possibility.

"Never," I promised her.

We arrived at the fountain and waited our turns among the long lines of the toothless and those whose clothes smelled of the latrines or the public house. And then there were some who looked very much like me. I did not feel the others in line were my inferiors, but I also did not want to find myself or Orchie in such a place again.

"Look!" Orchie said, pointing to someone about half a block away. "It's Lord Lydney." She elbowed me. "He'll come carry these home for us."

I looked up, horrified to find that she was right! I'd forgotten that Harry's gentlemen's club was nearby. I used my hand to gently push her arm down and then turned so my back was to Harry.

"We don't need his help," I said.

"You mightn't, but I'd just as soon have a man help carry these jugs back," she said. "And he's such a nice man, after all. Or I thought he was until . . . Is that why you don't want his help, then? 'Cause he did not come back for so long?"

"I would prefer he not know we are here," I softly pleaded. She nodded and we both turned our backs and pulled tight our bonnets.

"I have always admired your strength and self-sufficiency," Harry had said to me. I had gone hat in hand to so many in the past few days. I did not want to humble myself before Harry, too. I wanted him to continue admiring my strength and self-sufficiency—it was perhaps all I had left. I wanted him to see me as an equal, not a pauper. I straightened up.

I had three months to clear our debts, and I would.

Normally I took a hired carriage for my monthly visit to the prison, which was both a house of detention—where the accused waited until sentencing—and a house of correction—where punishment and reform were administered afterward. This day, I walked. The mist drenched my face, and I hoped the damp would not be heavy enough to weigh down my cloak before I reached my destination. Dark clouds fell in behind me, chasing me from home and toward the prison. I clutched my reticule and hoped that the small package I'd had Orchie assemble with the portion of bread and bacon I had refused during mealtime would remain dry and somewhat warm. Eventually I approached the prison neighborhood and saw the street children huddling in the corners where boulevards spilled into alleys. In other months, I saw them from carriage height. Now we were nearly face-to-face.

I looked for the younger ones, both for my own safety and for their well-being. As I approached a pair of children huddling together, shivering, I reached into my bag and pulled out the package of food. "Are you hungry?" I asked.

The girl nodded. She looked up at me and smiled, and my heart clenched. Her sweet face was marred by the gloom of rubbed-away coal soot, the deep shadows of black sleeplessness which cupped her eyes, and mourning. I handed the bag to her, and she thanked me quickly before turning her back to me so she and what was likely her brother could share the food before others fell in to steal it from them.

Rounding the corner to the prison, I saw the rows of fine carriages waiting for other, more wealthy members of the committee. *Perhaps someday they will be coming here to visit me, jailed as a debtor. Perhaps Charlotte would lend me five shillings.*

I laughed the sharp, stuttered, slightly feverish laugh found where truth met absurdity and then took hold of myself.

Hysteria would not help.

The ladies' Visiting Committees, first started by Mrs. Elizabeth Fry some fifty years earlier, afforded ladies the occasion to bring comfort, cheer, some minor physical assistance, and the hope of the gospel to those incarcerated. I did not volunteer my hours and charitable gifts only to help them improve their moral standards and outlook on life. As a woman who had been lonely for many years, I understood the crushing sorrow that loneliness brought. Self-sufficiency eased that for me; they had no ability to be similarly eased. I simply wanted to be a friend to them as they had grown to be to me. After my mother left, all my friends did too. Even Marguerite's parents had forbidden her from seeing me; they'd said it might lead to my encouraging her into harmful amusements. After she was married, we could be friends once more.

I entered the prison and showed my credentials to the warden. He then showed me into the open area next to the chapel where the prisoners could congregate, meet those ministering to them, and speak for just a few minutes each week. Prisons were often known as the cold hell—slate floors to better clear the refuse; cheerless, cold stone walls; and peeling, black, cold iron bars on whatever windows were present. The iron released the scent of blood into the air whenever it sweated, which was near constantly. The bars burned like branding irons in the summer. The windows were never cleaned; it was impossible to judge the time of day or celebrate sunshine, even on a pleasant day. The dusk of despair smothered the cells.

"Don't put me in there!" a woman wailed as I made my way down the corridor. Her screams and pleading were met with pitiless silence. She caught my eye. "Help me, miss, please!"

What could I do? Smile? Hardly appropriate. Help? There was no way I could assist her. I nodded and hoped my eyes reflected my concern for her. She was young—perhaps just eighteen—and her hair had been chopped with blunt scissors. It still reached her chin, though unevenly. She was beautiful, fragile as an iris and just as likely to be trampled underfoot. The warden, grown deaf to such pleading, shoved her into her cell and slammed the door shut behind her. It muffled but did not silence her cries.

I kept my head down and continued walking through the fetid, stagnant prison air. I had befriended a prisoner named Jeanette, and her eyes lit as she saw me enter the room. I smiled too, trying to banish the younger woman's misery from my mind, and hurried toward her.

"Miss Sheffield," she said. "I'm so glad ta see ya. I thought perhaps you'd be too busy to visit us." She was, at thirty, five years older than me. In some manner, she seemed much older, perhaps due to the difficulty of the life she'd been forced to live. Perhaps it was her missing teeth.

"Never too busy." Three or four of the other ladies who had been given into my care by the committee came near, and we talked together of the chapel message they had heard very recently, which had brought both tears and hope.

Jeanette held out her hands to me, red and raw. Her fingers were pricked and sliced, torn by the oakum. As part of their work duties, they must pick apart the tight, old, tarred rope used on ships, like the miller's daughter in the tale of Rumpelstiltskin, thereby turning it into something valuable: a mound of loose fiber. The fiber would be collected and sent back to the ships for use in caulking or patching holes. Each woman was assigned a certain weight she must produce each day; if she did not, severe punishment would follow.

I knew Jeanette and other younger women often worked as quickly as possible to help meet the quotas of older women whose hands were crippled by cold and age.

"I am gladdened to see you," I said. I made a note to myself: if in any way possible, buy soothing gloves for the ladies at Christmas, when I would be allowed to bring a small gift to them.

I spoke of news of the world outside and the foods they craved and the books I'd been reading and recited a psalm or two, for comfort. I discussed articles of interest in the ladies' magazines, which they seemed most enthusiastic about, and listened to them tell of their days.

They told me of their hopes and dreams upon release and news of their children, who were allowed an occasional visit, and promised to pray for me.

No one else, not even Marguerite, promised me that.

As I left the House of Correction, I did not want to walk past the row of carriages the other visitors would use to leave. I turned down a nearby street, instead, and then another, and then a third, trying to make my way back to the thoroughfare.

I soon found myself in the center of an unfamiliar tangle of thin streets and alleys. The soot and rain bore down on the day, making it impossible to see clearly. I pulled my bonnet low; still, I could hear two deep male voices just behind me.

I quickened my step as they closed in. My hem dragged through the mud, and the smell of both horse and human muck filled the air. I gagged.

"Hey! Heya, Madge. I'm over here." I looked up to find a woman of about nineteen or twenty years old waving at me. "Come on now. Da is expecting us and he's probably on his way to find us right now." She looked at the men presumably behind me. "I don't think he'll be very happy with those what kept ya?"

I shook my head, not wanting to speak and give away my station in life. My dress, now muddied, had hidden that well.

The young men melted away as the woman pushed a large wheelbarrow across the street toward me; it was filled with towering sacks of what appeared to be laundry.

"Thank you very kindly." I held my hand out to her. "Miss Eleanor Sheffield."

She took my hand in her own, ungloved one. "Alice."

"Miss . . . Alice. I'm indebted to you."

"You don't belong here," she said.

"No," I admitted. "I'd been visiting the women in prison."

She nodded.

"Then I got lost on my way home."

"You'll never find your way out on your own. If you don't mind my saying so. I'm a person who never minds asking for help, meself. Come along. I'll show you the way."

We began to walk. "This is my father's wheelbarrow. That's probably how the lie about our father came so quickly to my lips, God forgive me."

"It's kind of your father to lend his wheelbarrow to you." I wasn't sure what else to say.

She shook her head. "Oh, he's dead, Miss Sheffield. He used to wheel plants back and forth at Covent Garden. When he passed on, he left my mother with six children and a wheelbarrow."

"I'm sorry about your father."

"He drank himself to death with gin." Her tone was matter-of-fact, honest, and unflinching.

I stopped in my tracks and reached out to the brick wall to steady myself. "Gin!"

"I'm sorry to shock you with that, miss," she said. "No way around the truth. We do laundry now. I collect it and deliver it in the wheelbarrow, round here, anyway. My sisters work too, sewing or mending or cutting up bits of wool for shoddy cloth. We could take in more laundry, but the whole street has to share the laundry stew pot." She looked at my collar and my dress. "No disrespect, miss, but your collar is a bit dull and wrinkled." She appraised me anew. "I have one here, for sale." She fished in one of her bags and came up with a lovely, fresh white collar. "Four pence."

I looked at her dress and collar, peeking from beneath an old cloak. Although she was poor, and the fabric was thin, it was clean.

I wondered if she had been a part of the setup with the young men who had been ready to attack me. If I did not take her up on her offer, would they reappear?

"No thank you," I said and waited. The young woman began pushing her wheelbarrow, and I followed her to the thoroughfare. She'd proven true. I knew two things: our laundry needs went far beyond my collar, and I had no extra money. But my water flowed once more.

I thought for a moment before making an offer. I had two reasons for doing so—but I would only tell her one of them. "I have a proposition for you, Miss . . ." I waited for her to give me her last name. If she would not, I would not trust her further with my household.

She blushed. "Cheater."

I tried to keep my face impassive.

"That's the unfortunate truth of it all. Which is why I go by Alice. People tend not to trust you if they know your name is Cheater."

I smiled. "I trust you. If you'd wanted to take advantage of me, you could have earlier. My household does need some laundry assistance, as you can plainly see. Perhaps you could come and do our laundry one day per week. In exchange, I will allow you to use our water, boiler, wringer, and iron on an additional day for your other commissions. Could we try this for perhaps a month? If the arrangement is suitable for us both, we can continue."

I pulled a card out of my reticule but hesitated before handing it over to her.

"I can read," she said, reading my mind at that very moment. "I learned in Sunday school." She looked at the address on my card.

"My housekeeper, Mrs. Orchard, will keep a sharp eye out," I warned her.

"Don't worry. Only my name is Cheater."

"I believe you." She promised to come by the very next day. I wanted to look my best at Watchfield House, and we were to leave soon.

CHAPTER

Eight

WATCHFIELD HOUSE, OXFORDSHIRE

We arrived at Watchfield House on the twelfth of October. Uncle Lewis had insisted on coming, along with his large valise which held his viewing glasses, cleaning cloths and solutions, and notebooks. Mr. Clarkson and I indulged him. I thought perhaps he would do better away from London for a day or two. Mr. Clarkson thought that we could use his help in cataloging. In order that Mr. Clarkson retain confidence in our firm, I did not divulge how difficult Uncle was finding his work, but today, at least, he did not seem to be squinting.

As we approached the house, I recalled why I'd always

loved it. The facade was of blonde stone, the cornerstones matching, nearly. Perhaps browned butter biscuits would be a suitable way to describe them; the deepened sandy color and texture was just right. The four corners of the house each had a tall chimney, and there were several other chimneys on the roof. The windows were high and arched like aristocratic brows. The grounds slept except for the fallen chestnuts and acorns which rolled restlessly in the wind. Ever since Harry's mother had died, the house seemed like a beautiful woman who knew she was no longer loved; kept in style, but no longer cherished, alone and lonely much of the time.

When I'd been at Watchfield for the funeral, the house seemed as though it had been holding its breath during the time it had been uninhabited. Now that people circulated through her once more, she could exhale and be revived. Unless I removed the art from her walls, the armor from her corners, the manuscripts from her shelves, the porcelain from the cases, the tables and chairs, the artifacts from the cabinets—in short, stripped her naked of all that made her what she was by removing the collection.

A new butler, one I did not recognize, took us into the green drawing room. I noticed, immediately, that the mantel clock was missing.

Within minutes, Harry came down the stairs to greet us. He was kind and solicitous to my uncle. "I take it you've met Anderson, my new butler. I've had Mrs. Baker prepare a room for you on the ground floor. Not so much walking."

Harry and Mr. Clarkson nodded to one another.

Then Harry drew near to me under the watchful gaze of both men who had traveled with me. "Here, at last, Eleanor, are your keys." There was a personal tone in his voice, and a smile tugged at the corners of his lips.

Mr. Clarkson flinched—at Harry's use of my Christian name, when I had denied Clarkson permission to use it?

"The chatelaine." Harry held out the large gold ring of keys to me.

I tried not to react outwardly to what seemed, but might not be, a symbolic gesture. The chatelaine held keys to every room in the house, every desk, every pantry and storeroom and jewelry box. In many households, it held the key to the safe. The wife, not the husband, controlled that. The keeper of the chatelaine was understood to be the lady of the manor.

"Ellie, here." Harry held the chatelaine toward me. "Go quickly now, before Mother returns, and take what we need for the picnic."

"She'll see me!" I protested, but not vigorously. "Or Mrs. Baker will!"

"I'll keep them occupied," he said.

I tiptoed downstairs and unlocked the pantry, removed a hamper, then some cheese and a loaf of bread and meat and a pear. Harry loved pears. I walked up the stairs outside the tradesman's entrance and set the basket there so we could retrieve it for our secret picnic in the woods at the edge of the property later, and then went back into the house.

I held out the keys to Harry. He hesitated a moment before taking them back—I knew what he thought. Perhaps one day the chatelaine would be mine. We were eye to eye, nose to nose. Our lips had never touched . . . yet.

Perhaps at the picnic.

I blinked and returned to the present. I looked at Harry and he smiled. He knew of what I'd been thinking.

"Thank you, Lord Lydney. I'll let you know if we require anything further, but for now, we have quite a bit of work to do."

Mr. Clarkson relaxed when he heard my cooler tone, and we set to work.

First, we divided up the areas of the house. We'd account for each item in a given room, noting it on the inventory, and then later, in London, we could compare what was in the house presently to the notes both Mr. Clarkson and Harry's father had made on their last lists.

I took the great reception room and at first was tempted not to note the missing clock. But why? Because I suspected Harry, that's why. *This will never do. I must be scrupulous in my accounting because I will award this collection with honesty and objectivity.* I wrote down the clock's absence. After inspecting and marking down each item, I progressed to the dining room. The sideboard was bookended by delightful beauties. I hefted a hammered silver saltcellar and its cover and admired it anew. Salt was kept in the little niche below the cover; it likely dated from the Elizabethan era, when salt was precious. Because of that, the saltcellar was placed in front of the highest-ranking person at the table, who would use it first before it was passed along.

I set it down and proceeded to the smoking room, where the gentlemen would withdraw after a meal. Although there were many fine treasures along the oak-paneled wall, I stopped at a majolica wine chiller, likely from the last half of the sixteenth century. It was a partner to the majolica pilgrim's flask my father had treasured. I closed my eyes. *Papa.* He had acquired for Lord Lydney the better piece, of course. Lord Lydney had then gifted him with the flask. A rare, expensive piece of art—and history—which Papa had treasured.

A few hours later, Mr. Clarkson and I met in the library. "Could you please open the door to the small room at the end of the third-story landing?" he asked.

I looked at him. I'd opened the upstairs doors, I'd thought. I followed him up—but by the back stairs, which grew narrower each time we turned a bend. I wasn't sure I'd ever been in this corner of the house. It was, if I'd calculated correctly, just above Harry's father's bedroom suite but only accessible by the servants' staircase.

I tried every key on the chatelaine, and none of them fit.

"I cannot imagine why I don't have this key. But I shall find it. Well done for thinking to check here."

"It was open last year," he said. "And empty."

Together, we walked on. "I'd be obliged if you would join me in the study after I finish the work in the statuary. There are some irregularities with the Roman coins."

I agreed, and we met my uncle in the foyer and told him what I was after.

"I know the gatehouse keeper," he said. "I shall seek the key from him, as he's likely to have a complete set."

"I'll help him." Mr. Clarkson was instantly at his side. *"Unsteady gait,"* he mouthed to me as he picked up his bag. I reluctantly agreed.

Clarkson took my uncle's arm and my uncle shook it away, shouting, "I'm not a child!" Mr. Clarkson followed watchfully from a short distance, as he must have done the day my uncle had been robbed.

I went to the study, glad for a moment alone with the coins before Mr. Clarkson arrived. I wanted to be prepared for our conversation. After some time, I became aware that Mr. Clarkson had not yet joined me, and plenty of time had passed. I sought him out—he was just leaving the porcelain room.

"The keys?" I asked. "It's been more than an hour."

"We did not reach the gatehouse. We sat for a moment to allow your uncle to catch his breath, and he fell asleep. I stayed with him for a while so he would not wander off, and then escorted him to his rooms before completing my work in the statuary. I was just about to return to you."

"I shall demand the key myself, then, at the gatehouse. I have been awarded trusteeship. As to the Roman coins," I said, "I have reviewed them and share your concerns."

He nodded. "Last time I was here, I noted that there seemed to be a few coins that were fake. You remember the story of those two men who had been manufacturing forged Roman coins."

I stared at him. "You didn't say anything to me months ago."

He stared back. "Your father had approved the purchase. . . ."

My face heated and he smiled sympathetically.

"I didn't want to shame him," he said quietly, "if he'd been duped while . . . ill."

"Thank you. We should note them now, though."

We returned to the room where the coins were held and jotted down notes together. "More seem to be missing as well," Mr. Clarkson said. "Coins that were, I believe, legitimate. And here several months ago."

My heart sank. Could Harry have been selling things after all, as his father had accused to Sir Matthew?

We worked side by side, noting items and asking one another's opinions. It was pleasant; I could not deny it. Clarkson shared my interests, knowledge, and enthusiasm. What's more, he'd been discreet about Papa. I thought about how happy Lady Charlotte and her husband were, traipsing across the Continent in search of treasure. But hers had been a love match. Must they all be?

After we completed the coins, I returned to the pink room, which had been a favorite of Harry's mother.

There had been three people to whom Harry's father had shown affection: his wife, Edith, Lady Lydney; his oldest son, Arthur; and my father, William Sheffield, whom he had met at Oxford. They'd been sworn brothers much as Stefano and Harry were.

I paused at the pelican pendant which had been Lady Lydney's particular favorite, savoring its story. The pelican looked as though it had a tiny crack, and I wrapped it in fabric and slipped it into my reticule to repair in London if I could.

The rest of the figurines and objects appeared to be intact. Except . . . I couldn't be sure, but as I counted the rare porcelain statues, there seemed to be one or two missing. With a thousand pieces or more in the collection, it was impossible to be certain with a glance, even for someone with my familiarity with the items. After making a few notes, I walked to the gatehouse and looked for the keeper. This gatehouse—one of four, situated at the north, south, east, and west entrances to the estate—was the only one still in operation. We had driven by it hours earlier.

"How can I be of help?" the keeper asked. His voice was cold and defensive; he looked like he'd been drinking or napping, or both.

"I'm looking for the keys to the room at the end of the third-floor landing," I said. "Lord Lydney has requested I do a complete inventory, and I require the key for that."

He crossed his arms over his chest and his eyes shifted. "I don't have that key."

I did not believe him.

"Are you certain?"

He nodded insolently. "Only Lord Lydney has that key. And his valet."

"Which Lord Lydney?" I asked. "The recently deceased or the present one?"

He said nothing.

"Then I shall complete my account of the gatehouse, directly."

He raised his hand in protest. "Again? Your man did it not so long ago."

"Inventories are taken regularly. Mr. Clarkson is inventorying the house at this time, and I will note, afresh, what is in the gatehouse receiving areas."

I did not look around his living quarters, but I did go into the large room where packages were delivered and stored until his lordship or his man called for them.

There were newly arrived boxes from Austria, of course, many of them. I lifted some of the lids, already pried open, and found that they were Harry's father's personal items. Nothing from the collection as far as I could tell. To the side of the room sat two crates stamped in Venetian. I lifted the unsealed crate tops, one after another, and sorted through the hay and cotton protection before gazing at the most beautiful blown glass I had been privileged to see.

The Venetian treasures.

Goblets, in waves of sea blues and greens, fitting for Venice, delicately etched with remarkable skill and openmouthed, ready to receive the riches of Italian water and wine.

A chandelier which glistened and twinkled, even in the relative dark of the room.

Twisted cornucopias, purest glass with threads of gold woven throughout, as intricate as any embroidery I'd seen.

A blown-glass water jug that looked too delicate to be a drinking vessel.

A yellow perfume bottle, swirled like sunrise gauze. My heart clenched. *Mama.*

Venetian wedding cake beads, rolled black but with hearts and flowers shot throughout, to celebrate a woman's best day. Which bride's neck had they graced?

I wrote down piece after piece because, after all, it was on the property even though I knew it belonged to the Vieros. I hadn't told Lady Charlotte, but my personal interest centered upon glass. It was both fragile and strong, liquid and solid, opaque and clear, vibrant and still. Complex as the best of us are. I cherished it.

I put my hand to my still-bare neck. That was why Harry had chosen the mustard seed necklace for me. He knew how I loved glass.

I came to the final, smallish crate, marked with a stripe of blue paint but no wording at all, and found it empty but for the packing straw. Perhaps it had held items used for the baron's burial? As I left the gatehouse, I walked the lawn to collect my thoughts and noticed the door to the summerhouse was slightly ajar.

I pushed open the door and saw the shadow of a figure on one of the stone benches move. "Harry?" I called quietly.

I walked in a little further and could see, of a sudden, that it was not Harry. It was the young Venetian woman, reading a book in the dim late-afternoon light.

She slowly turned to look at me, her dark eyes matching

her dark hair. She stood, smiling, and although I was loath to admit it, she was beautiful.

"Signorina Francesca Viero. And you must be Miss Eleanor Sheffield."

"I am. I'm sorry to disturb you."

"It is not a disturbance. Sit down, *per piasser*."

"I wish I could. But I have much cataloging to do this day."

She smiled and looked around the empty room, as if to ask, *"Then what are you doing here? There is nothing to catalog."* "I see. Harry—Lord Lydney, *me scuxa*—said you were coming to Watchfield today. I enjoy escaping to this very private summerhouse—often. Have you cataloged the Venetian glass? Those which belong to me?" There was now an edge to her lilting voice.

"Indeed, I have," I responded. "They are beautiful. Your family has a treasure and craftsmanship beyond compare. They are on the property, so I must mark them down."

She shifted and, for a moment, looked profoundly uncomfortable. "Do they all seem . . . Venetian to you?"

Was she concerned that her family's treasures would prove false somehow?

"Yes. All Venetian. Of course. You have a concern?"

Relief swept across her face. "No, no. I'm very proud of my family and what we do, what we have always done, and hope always to do."

I nodded. *I'm working as steadfastly for my family tradition as you are for yours.* "I hope you find your visit here in

England to be a lovely time, something to remember when you return home. How long will you be with us?"

She fanned herself. "We've just had a telegram today telling that the Austrian emperor has ceded Venice—we can now join Italia."

Good. Not too long then.

Envy does not suit you, Eleanor. I softened my heart and my tone. She'd just fled a war. "I've met your brother. I found him most agreeable. If there is anything I can do to make your time here more comfortable, please let me know."

She softened too. "I sincerely hope my brother is well. We have not heard. I am most comfortable; Lord Lydney has seen to that. You do realize—" she fanned herself once more—"he is a hero. You've seen the treasures. You know their value. They are five hundred years old, some of them. Without his lordship's help, they would have been looted or demolished—we'd had threats. My mother and I would have been left unprotected, or my brother could not have fought. Harry risked himself for us, Miss Sheffield."

Her thoughts and insights—indeed, her proclamation—further bolstered my growing conclusion that Harry was the honorable man he presented himself to be, that he was to me, and not the duplicitous man his father claimed him to be. According to her, Harry had carried the treasures from Venice out of loyalty and affection for her brother, who deeply valued the antiquities. Despite my happiness at hearing her recount his valor, I twinged with an unwelcome stitch of returning envy.

She had referred to him as Harry.

I said in honesty, "I'm happy to hear of this. But now I must complete my task. Would you please excuse me?"

We said our gracious good-byes, and then I left the summerhouse, determined to put my feelings aside and finish my task. I would retrieve the third-floor keys from Harry. I knew where I'd find him, and it wasn't at the house.

The stable blocks were but a further five-minute walk, and I found him there. The arena had a floor of freshly raked sand, the better to protect the horses' hooves. The windows were high so the horses could not be distracted. Much care went into tending Harry's treasures, for certain.

The horses had been his mother's treasures too, and I knew he cared for them for her sake as well as for his own. *Not selfish,* I thought to myself.

I saw him before he saw me, astride his great white stallion, Abalone, whom he loved.

"Ellie!" He walked the horse near me. "I was just about to ride out. How comes the inventory?"

"It comes," I said, pleasant but reserved. "I have a question for you."

Abalone stamped impatiently, and Harry brought him under control—but only just. "Come ride with me, and you can ask whatever you like. I daren't tarry any longer."

"I really mustn't. The work. Mr. Clarkson."

"Mr. Clarkson seems very capable. And he did do the last inventory on his own." There was an unusual and slightly cool tone in his voice. Jealousy? Had he seen Mr. Clarkson and me working well together? Or was it concern over the last inventory done?

Harry's long legs were sheathed in brown leather boots, his trousers neatly tucked inside, one of his high-collared white shirts on.

I weakened a little at the sight of him and with my desire for his companionship. Mr. Clarkson would do well on his own for just a short while. "I don't have a riding habit with me."

Harry grinned. "Wrap your skirts a bit so they don't scare the horses in the wind."

I spied the mare I once favored being walked by a stable hand. She whinnied at me. I'd missed her, too, and we both deserved a ride.

"All right," I agreed. I did need my answer, after all—that was a part of my work. We rode down the field and into the woods, each of us urging the horses on faster and farther. My father had seen to it that I learned to ride, as would befit a woman of better station; Harry had ensured I'd know enough to keep up with him, and I suppose, if I were truthful, I'd say that I had a way with the horses. Like me, they were skittish, always nose and ears to the wind to avoid trouble. We understood each other.

Harry was well ahead of me, so I purposefully slowed, and he circled back to see if I was well. The moment he reached me, I put my heels into the flank of my horse and urged her toward the stable. Harry caught up with me in time, but barely.

"Victory!" I shouted. A portion of my hair escaped the severe knot into which I'd pulled it.

"That was a clear misdirection, Miss Sheffield," he said as we dismounted. "Cheating to win?"

I smirked. "All's fair in love and war."

He removed a glove, then reached up and took hold of a strand of my hair, running it through his hand before tucking it back into the loosened knot. I felt his touch through my hair and onto my scalp, which tingled and prickled with pleasure. I drew my breath in sharply at the intimacy, which was at once welcome and unwelcome. Was he feigning affection to earn my trust and his treasures? Or would he prove true?

"Is this love or war?" he asked. His face, normally strong and in command of his situation and surroundings, now betrayed real confusion, a sense of bewildered vulnerability fused with hope. I'd seen that vulnerable look before, but only directed at me. He trusted me.

I did not answer.

We walked back to the house slowly. "I'd originally come to ask, do you have the key to the room on the third floor, above your father's rooms and by way of the servants' stairs?"

Harry stopped walking and looked at me long before answering. "I've given you the complete set of keys."

There was something unsettling about his reaction. Was it an evasion?

"I seem to be missing one."

He smiled and took my hand. "I shall make enquiries about the key and deliver it forthwith."

Would he? My mind flitted back to Signorina Viero's flattering account. "Tell me about your time in Venice." I was rewarded with a smile which lit his face.

"Are you certain?" he asked. "I'd thought perhaps you didn't want to know . . ."

"I do," I said softly.

He recounted how he'd ridden back and forth, using his father's diplomatic immunity and his ability to ride for long hours, to deliver documents which eventually led to Austria agreeing to give Venice to Napoleon, who then would cede it to Italy.

"I had, of course, agreed to take Viero's treasures with me, back to England. We just stayed in Austria longer than expected. My father insisted," he said once more.

I recalled his father's letter, which had said quite the opposite. *"He repeatedly refused to return to England despite my pleadings that he do so."*

"Did you know there are crates of your father's clothing and other personal belongings, not yet unpacked, in the gatehouse?" I asked.

He nodded. "I shall have to instruct someone to go through his things and dispose of anything not of personal value. Although Father's valet made trips home to England with new pieces from his collection over the years, he did not return after Father's death. Of course, Father had expected his valet to take care of all his effects and belongings, as he always has, once back in England."

My mouth opened and closed again. Harry's father's valet had been indisputably devoted to him.

"Father left him nothing in his will—and told him so just before he died. His man remained in Austria, with his Austrian wife."

"Your father—so ungrateful, after many years of dedicated service," I said.

Harry nodded. "Yes. Just as well. I plan to replace the few remaining staff after the New Year when I've had time to sort where to go from here. The butler has already been discharged and replaced with a man loyal to me. Until then, I keep the rest at arm's length."

"Wise," I agreed, then turned toward a more pleasant matter. "I'm going to repair your mother's porcelain pelican," I said. "I know it was a favorite of hers. Shall I tell you the story?" We rounded the lawn on the final approach to the house.

"I remember her cherishing it. I await the tale and the sound of your voice telling it."

I smiled and began. "The pelican in its piety is the fable of that noble bird. It has a pouch under its bill, from which it withdraws fish to feed its offspring. Should the parent not have fish, however, it will peck its own breast in difficult times to draw blood with which it might feed its young."

"Piety, of course, is the Roman ideal of filial love. Father would certainly not have credited that to me. But Mama . . ."

"She was a good mother," I agreed. "And she believed you to be an excellent son." In the end, after she'd lost Arthur and was about to die herself, she'd made the baron promise not to sell her horses but to give them to Harry.

"Thank you for repairing her pelican." He looked away, as he often did when trying to regain control of his emotions.

"I take good care of what I've been charged with," I answered.

When we reached the house, I found Uncle Lewis, Mr. Clarkson, and the butler sitting near the foyer. Uncle Lewis clung to his valise like a child being put on a train to school.

"Whatever is the matter?" I asked.

"He's unwell," Mr. Clarkson said quietly. "Says he won't stay for dinner as there are no Cornish pasties remaining—the staff stole them from him and so he must return to London with due haste."

I did not want a scene. I turned toward Harry. "May I come back another time and complete this?"

"Certainly. I hope all is well."

"As do I," I replied.

"Do not worry." He looked into my eyes, those new crinkles creasing as he smiled and paraphrased what I'd just told him. "I also take good care of what is mine."

Did he mean the collection? The horses? Me? I had no time to ask, as the carriage was ready to take us to the train station. As we pulled down the drive, I noticed Harry walking away from the house, in the direction of the stables.

Or the summerhouse, wherein Francesca awaited.

As we made our way back to London, I clasped the keys

I'd forgotten to return. And then, suddenly, I remembered a portion of that earlier memory.

"Did you get it all?" he asked. "Everything we need for our picnic?"

I nodded and smiled. "All but the sweets."

Harry grinned. "Only my father's valet has all the keys, including the one to the confectionery, and I dare not risk stealing it! He is my father's man, and his man alone, through and through. There would be the devil to pay if we were caught."

CHAPTER

Nine

BLOOMSBURY, LONDON

We returned home, and I settled Uncle before speaking to Orchie about the incident. "He seemed disoriented. I think it best if we keep him as close to routine as possible."

She agreed to make some Cornish pasties and serve them to him on a tray in his room. Then she asked, "Are you sure then about that young laundress?"

"Are you not happy with her work? Did she bother you today?" Alice hadn't been working at our home but for a few days, but we'd all been looking a bit spiffier.

"It's not that," she said. "It's just, well, having people we don't know in the house, moving about freely. Maybe this business with the solicitors and robberies and police visiting 'as made me wary, that's all."

Orchie returned to the kitchen, and I walked next door to the workshop and found Mr. Clarkson deep in concentration. He nodded to me but turned his back so that he was between me and the project on which he was working.

Maybe I did trust people too readily—I tended to go with my instincts, and perhaps they were not always right. An unwelcome thought had occurred to me on the train from Watchfield. Perhaps Mr. Clarkson had taken the Roman coins and ascribed the initial mistake to my father, then implicated Harry for the potential theft. I would never know. I could test his integrity, though. He had come to us with the best of references from two of our wealthiest clients and had done well for us since. Still, I must test him. I must test Harry. Along the way, I was testing myself. Was I a discerning evaluator, worthy to carry on my family's firm?

Was I a clearheaded judge of the heart and intentions of the man I once loved?

Still loved?

As I had almost weekly, I wished my father were alive to advise. I recalled what Alice had said to me just days before. *"You'll never find your way out on your own."*

And yet, I must.

One day the week following, I left the workshop for a few moments to allow the fixative to set on Lady Lydney's pelican.

I thought I'd return to my rooms for a light wrap, as the day had grown cool. When I arrived at my bedroom, I found that it was not empty.

"Alice! May I be of assistance?"

Not only was she in my room, but she was also standing near my curiosity cabinet. Though some cabinets were as large as a room, mine was perhaps the size of a small writing desk. Papa's was larger, squatter, and had many compartments. Uncle Lewis felt no need for a cabinet—his few treasures were openly displayed in his study.

Alice jumped at my voice. A rope of faux pearls hung from her hand. "I'm sorry, Miss Sheffield. Mrs. Orchard said that you had not brought your laundry down to the room today, that it likely remained in your wardrobe. I wanted to help and didn't want to disturb you. I thought I'd just fetch it."

Clearly, my laundry was not in the curiosity cabinet. I looked at the pearls in her hand.

"I was only holding them, Miss Sheffield. They were on top of the cabinet—right on top, and . . . I'm sorry. I'd never seen anything so lovely."

It seemed my first test of integrity would not be for Mr. Clarkson after all.

"Would you like me to tell you about the objects in my cabinet?" I asked. I closed the door behind us, locking us both in the room. I knew every item that was in the cabinet and did not want her to leave until I ascertained that all were present. If not, I would restrain her myself whilst Orchie went for a constable.

"Oh yes." She did not seem the least bit anxious, which brought some confidence and relief.

I relieved her of the pearls. "These are not genuine—a rope this long would be beyond my means. They are made of blown glass—my collection includes mostly glass—and then filled with wax to make them heavy." I handed them back to her, and she hefted the weight in one hand.

"They shine so," she said.

I smiled. "They are painted on the outside with a gelatin stripped from fish intestines. Even the most discerning eye has difficulty telling the difference. Many a rich woman has been tricked."

I set the pearls back into my cabinet and saw her eye drawn to the perfume bottle. "That was my mother's."

"Did she pass on?" Alice asked in a quiet voice.

"In a manner of speaking. She left this behind." I unstoppered the bottle and Otto of Roses escaped into the room. "Sometimes, without anything to touch, to hold, to feel . . . to smell, it can seem as though the person had never been with us at all."

Gently, I lifted a fragile glass bottle with its cork still inside. "A tear catcher."

"Ooh, I have heard of them. You catch your tears in them when someone dies."

I nodded. "And then, when the bottle dries out, the time for grief is over, and the living must move on. 'Put thou my tears into thy bottle: are they not in thy book?'"

"The Bible," she said.

"Psalm 56. He keeps track of our sorrows, so we know he pays us mind and carries our burdens, and therefore we need not do so forever."

"The tears are almost dry. If you'd take the cork out, it'd dry up right away."

I looked at her and then at the bottle. She was right. It was my responsibility, after all, to uncork the bottle and let the tears I'd collected—for Mother, for Father, for Harry—to dry rather than adding to them. To allow the Lord to lift my burdens rather than keeping them corked and close at heart.

I took out a pretty hand mirror and gave it to Alice.

"Gold!"

I laughed. "Brass. One of the first lessons I learned as an evaluator. Sometimes brass masquerades as gold, and gold as brass. The trick is to discern the difference. This mirror I paid dearly for—believing it was gold. I've not made that mistake again."

Orchie knocked on the door, and I called out that all was well before returning to my cabinet, looking over the few further pieces.

"What's this one, then?" Alice lifted a little blown-glass daisy with a bumblebee affixed to it. It fit around a small cup inside which one placed a candle.

"A fairy light. After my mother left, I had difficulty falling asleep. Orchie, Mrs. Orchard, brought this light to me each night and lit a small candle inside it. It worked: by the time the candle had burned down, I was asleep."

"My sister Mary would like such a thing," Alice said. "She's not slept well since our da died."

While she was distracted, I opened the tiny, secret drawer to ascertain that the ring was still inside; it was, next to the mustard seed necklace. I did not show them to her but closed the drawer again.

"We should both return to our duties," I said. "I shall remember to bring my laundry down so you need not come to retrieve it."

"Thank you. That was lovely of you to teach me about your things while counting everything to make sure I hadn't stolen or such."

I kept my face impassive but held back a smile. She'd known all along.

"What is that?" She pointed to the green bottle toward the back of my cabinet, shaded from immediate view. "It looks like spirits. Do you drink spirits, Miss Sheffield?"

I stood silent for a moment, battling between pride and honesty, and then took the bottle in hand. "I do not drink spirits, Alice. But my father did. Like your father, he died from an overindulgence of gin."

She held my eye then, not realizing, perhaps, how her own forthright admission some days past had freed me to be honest in return. "I'm sorry," she said.

"I, too."

"Does it do you good to keep the bottle, then?" she asked.

"That's an odd question." She looked frightened for a moment, like she'd overstepped. "Perhaps I keep it to remind me of what I lost him to. It might be better to remember what I've kept of him." To reassure her, I set down the bottle and picked up the fairy light. "Perhaps young Mary would like to borrow this until she can sleep again? Mrs. Orchard has some tallow candles you might take with you."

"Are you sure?" she asked.

"Indeed I am."

"Then we shall treasure it!" She clasped her hand around the wee fairy light.

I smiled. "That's what treasures are for!"

Alice took my laundry and left the room, and I looked once more at my treasures. I had thought she'd been taking from me, but in truth, she'd given. I would dispose of the gin bottle that very day. I needed nothing to remind me of what had happened, and maybe with it gone, I could allow the finer memories of Papa to assert themselves in my mind. I uncorked the tear catcher.

Once I was certain no one could see, I opened the tiny, hidden drawer again and lifted out the ring. I counted four gems present, mourned the missing amethyst which represented the hole in my heart, and slipped it on my finger.

Five questions to be resolved. Four stones and a hole. I counted them in my head as I touched the remaining stones. Had Harry been selling portions of the collection? Had he sold or planned to sell Arthur's items? Had he tarried in Austria of his own free will? Did he care about the things others cared about, or was he simply selfish?

I came to the final setting, the hole where the amethyst

should have been. A week after Harry had left for Italy and Austria, the amethyst had fallen out somewhere, and I could not find it. I wore the ring anyway. When two months had passed from the time he'd said he'd be back—the empty setting was like the hole in my heart—I yanked it off once more and placed it within my cabinet for good.

Why hadn't he proposed? That fifth question, the one closest to my heart, yawned like the empty setting.

Was what we shared brass or gold, Harry?

Treasures are to treasure, I'd told Alice. I closed my eyes, and the tears squeezed out. Mama. Papa. Harry. *I am never kept. Prioritized. Valued above all. In the end, I am no one's treasure.* I took the ring off again, denied it light by placing it in the back of the dark drawer.

I sat for but a moment, collecting myself, and the words came back to me but slightly changed. *Put thou thy tears into my bottle: are they not in my book?*

I closed the door behind me—and then I locked it. Orchie, after all, had a set of keys should she need to enter in.

After telling the stories to Alice, I'd recalled a premise my father had taught me and which I'd often repeated. "*The story is always good. It charms, it enchants, it informs, it entertains. It brings in a higher value. But it's not always true. Believe what you see with your own eyes, Eleanor; observe carefully and without emotion. That will reveal the truth. I wish I had.*"

He'd meant with my mother; I knew without his having to say it.

Regardless of who tried to blindfold me for the games of bluff going on round me, I must remove the blindfold and then trust myself to see.

I went to my father's room, which had been unlocked, and checked to ensure that his treasures were all in place. They were. In one drawer was my mother's jewelry, given to her by Papa. I suppose one could credit Mother for not selling it after leaving my father. I held the heavy garnet necklace in my hand. Maybe *I'd* have to sell it.

Not yet. Perhaps she'd want it someday. Perhaps she'd want *me* someday. I held my breath as I put it back into the drawer and locked the door behind me.

Uncle Lewis's study seemed in good order too. My gaze caught on a shelf about halfway up his bookcase. It was his medieval Book of Hours, the beautifully illustrated prayer guide which had been hand-lettered and painted in centuries past. Had that been there when I'd come to find the bills? I couldn't remember. Something had bothered me at the time, but I'd been too flustered to investigate. Perhaps he'd been using it to guide his prayer? I checked it closely. All was well.

I locked that door behind me too.

I returned to my room and opened the drawer in my cabinet once more. The necklace I lifted out this time was the mustard seed pendant. I'd wear it, but tucked under my dress. "I find that I do still have faith in myself, in the man who purchased this for me, and in you, Lord. But in all cases, I'm sorry to report, that faith is very, very small."

The morning post delivered some packages I'd been waiting for—the silver for Mr. Herberts, purchased from a trusted supplier. Aware that the gas bill was soon due, I was eager to deliver the commission and collect the fee. I took out my magnifying glass and my notes and quickly inspected the face and back of each piece of silver, finding them to be genuine. I was thrilled that this would bring in some much-needed income and fairly skipped through the examination.

"Mr. Clarkson?" I thought it would be kind to ask his assistance, as he had been Mr. Herberts's original contact.

"Yes, Miss Sheffield?"

"I wonder if you might have a look at these coins. They seem fine to me, but a second set of eyes is always helpful."

"Certainly." Clarkson sat down at my desk with his magnifying glass, the musky pine scent of camphor-laced paregoric syrup, which quelled his otherwise-constant cough, surrounding us both. I saw him take it by the teaspoonful, always careful not to overdo. It was costly.

He took care with each coin and, in the end, returned to two that I had thought were fine. "I believe this one to be a forgery."

"What?" I pulled a second chair up next to his and turned up the lamp. "Surely not."

"Surely so." A clear note of triumph trumpeted through his voice. I could not blame him. I might feel the same way.

He put the coin he'd found to be authentic in my left hand and the one that he'd found fraudulent in my right.

I flipped the right-hand coin on its side and held the lamp close. "I can see a faint line where two halves of a mold were put together as opposed to this being poured and struck. Someone has made a mold and replicated the coin." I had neglected to look at the sides, having rushed and reviewed only the front and the back. An error I would not have made had I not been so distracted of late.

I then looked even more closely. "And there are pits from air bubbles as well." That would not be the case in a true coin. "I should not have thought these particular sources would be selling frauds to us."

"It may not have been intentional. Even they may make an innocent or hasty mistake," Clarkson reassured me. "Accept the ten; we shall source one more," he said. "It's rather rewarding to work side by side, is it not?"

"It is," I admitted. "I'm sorry for this error."

"I've not seen you make another."

"I'm grateful you found the error before we sent them to Mr. Herberts."

His face sobered. "I am too."

Look closely at what's in front of you, Eleanor. Take your time, and verify.

At the end of the next workday, Mr. Clarkson presented me with a small, long box. "I wondered if you would consider accepting this from me," he said.

I started to shake my head because it would not be

appropriate, but his gentle smile implored me to at least unwrap the ribbon and open the box.

When I did, I saw a lovely new magnifying glass. The handle was carved to fit a woman's hand and the glass was powerful and perfectly clear.

"I thought perhaps yesterday's mistake may have been due to the glass and not the valuer," he said quietly. It was a considerate offer which allowed me to keep my pride.

"Because the gift can be of use to Sheffield Brothers, I gratefully accept," I said. "Thank you, Mr. Clarkson. This is a lovely gesture."

"I hope to be of service to both you and the firm," he said. "Till tomorrow." He put his hat on and left through the workshop door.

CHAPTER *Ten*

I had no faith at all in the doctor who had been tending to my uncle. He'd said there was nothing wrong and that I should stop fussing about it, wasting his time, and only call him if there was blood or crippling pain, in which case he would suggest laudanum.

I decided to ask Dr. Elizabeth Garrett. She'd just opened the St Mary's dispensary in the Marylebone section of London, not terribly far from my home, and was the first woman doctor qualified under the Society of Apothecaries.

Her dispensary was charmingly calm, with warm-brown woods, lamps that had tiny roses painted upon them, and comfortably upholstered chairs sized especially for the bodies and gowns of her women patients. This time, though, she had agreed to come and visit me at my house.

She was but five or six years older than I, her dark-brown hair softly pulled back from her face. Her father had once managed a pawnshop in Whitechapel, and he had on occasions long past called upon my father for valuations, Uncle Lewis had once told me.

After Orchie showed her in, I met her in the parlor.

"Miss Sheffield," she said, "I'm sorry you are not well."

I folded my hands. "I'm quite well, thank you. It's my uncle about whom I hope to speak with you. He's upstairs, but I thought perhaps I could describe the situation first, and then you could determine if you might see him?"

"I'm happy to listen and advise—as a friend. But I am not allowed to practice medicine on men."

I hadn't realized. "Just advice, then, perhaps?" My voice echoed my strain. "I've no one else trustworthy to enquire of."

She sat across from me as I explained Uncle Lewis's situation.

"Decay of nature," she said softly.

"I'm afraid I don't understand."

"Old age, Miss Sheffield. It pursues all of us. To some it visits inconveniently early, I'm sorry to say."

"What can be done?"

She shook her head. "Little. You can care for him here at home."

I thought about the future: our bills, our waning business commissions, the growing realization that I might have to sell all that we owned to forestall debtor's prison. Our bank account, upon investigation, had not held anything near what I hoped it would, though I saw that we could, by year's end, just cover our debts. "And should I be unable to?"

"Then the only option is to have him declared a lunatic and placed in an asylum. He could stay there until the end unless he became a disruptive presence."

The shock of that forced me to my feet. I sat down again. That would not happen. Uncle Lewis had been a disruptive presence even before his dotage! I could sell all; we could move to smaller quarters. Even better, we could increase our commissions.

"Thank you. I'm so pleased to be able to see a woman doctor. Perhaps there are many more of you to practice soon?"

She laughed, bitter as the willow bark tea she prescribed for headaches. "Alas, no. After I found a loophole, the Society of Apothecaries closed it and has banned admission to women. I'm afraid British women must study medicine abroad if we're to study at all. Then when we return, it's unlikely we'll be licensed to practice. Our world is still not amenable to our fair sex, Miss Sheffield."

As she turned to leave, I gathered the courage to ask a question I'd had for many years. "Dr. Garrett, I have a friend whose brother died of asthma after having been exposed to horses and hay, to which he had sensitivities. My friend's father claimed that had a doctor arrived earlier, the brother's life would have been saved. Is that true?"

She frowned thoughtfully. "It's always possible, but

unlikely. There is but little we can do when the lungs spasm and close. Caffeine, laudanum, alcohol, sometimes smoking tobacco—these are suspected of helping. But if the lungs squeeze closed, there is naught one can do."

"Thank you. I'd suspected as much." I was exultant and could not wait to share this reassuring news with Harry. Even as a friend—if that was indeed what we now were—I would want to bring him comfort and peace. I bid her good day and walked with her to the door, where I offered to pay her, and she generously declined.

Orchie tidied up the parlor while I returned to the workshop. Mr. Clarkson waited for me.

"Miss Sheffield?" His voice seemed stern.

I suddenly felt uncomfortable. "Yes, Mr. Clarkson?"

"There's been an error in my pay remittance. The sum is larger than expected."

I smiled and exhaled with relief. Mr. Clarkson had passed his test of integrity. He could be trusted. "That's no error, Mr. Clarkson. You've been such a help, and especially with the Herberts commission, it seemed fitting."

"That's not necessary," he said. "I will do whatever I must to see the firm succeed. However, if you insist, the extra will be a welcome benefit to my sisters. I shall see them soon."

"How kind," I replied. I had not insisted, but I had placed the amount and offered.

He caught and kept my eye. "I take care of my own."

I tilted my head. Did he mean his sisters? Me and our firm? Had he heard Harry express a similar sentiment as we'd left Watchfield? Where Harry's tone had been reassuring, I heard something flinty in Mr. Clarkson's.

I nodded and began to walk toward my desk.

"Miss Sheffield?" He spoke up once more, but gentler.

"Yes?"

"I'd first asked your uncle about my remittance. He informed me that you had taken over the ledgers and accounts."

He did not look comfortable with this; most men would not be, I supposed. I held only the faintest hope that Uncle would regain his sensibilities, but I sought to reassure. "I hope it will be temporary, Mr. Clarkson."

He nodded and spoke reassuringly too. "Of course; I anticipate it will be."

To my great surprise, not only was I invited to the next meeting of the Burlington Fine Arts Club, but Mr. Clarkson received an invitation as well. He was pleased, and I was pleased for him. It could bring nothing but benefit if offers of membership were extended to each of us.

The meeting was to be held at the London home of Lord Parham, who had an extensive country estate near Bath as well; I had been there with my father. I was delighted that the next event would be held at the home of someone with whom I had a passing acquaintance. In fact, Parham had given me my first piece of glass, one of the small balls he'd had floating in the fountain at Bath. I hadn't kept it, as it was well before I'd started my own collection.

Mr. Schreiber and Lady Charlotte were at Lord Parham's home, of course, and she very kindly made social introductions for Mr. Clarkson and me.

"Gentlemen . . . and ladies," Lord Parham's voice boomed into the crowd. "I shall lead a tour of my display cases soon, but I thought tonight we might provide a bit of entertainment for some of our newer attendees."

Charlotte looked at me sidelong. Had she known this was to happen? Lord Parham distributed small leather notebooks and thin pencils—to me, to three or four other men in the nearby crowd, and to Mr. Clarkson.

"Do you know what this is about?" he whispered. "Did they do this last time?"

I shook my head.

Lord Parham continued, "In each room, I've identified an object of particular value and desirability. Perhaps some of our newer guests would be willing to note the suspected provenance and value of each?"

We smiled, attempting to appear good sports. "A test," I whispered to Clarkson, who nodded his agreement.

The first item was, I knew, an ice cream cooler. It was Sèvres porcelain from, I thought, about the time of the French Revolution. The Nordic blue-and-gold design looked rather Russian to me. I guessed that it had been made for Catherine the Great because she was said to have loved things that glittered and were cold—Russia, diamond sashes, and ice cream. I noted a value and moved on.

Next was a French chest of drawers paneled in Chinese

lacquer. I noted what I thought was the proper date. A flintlock pistol, a piece of field armor, a gilded perfume burner, the latter surely from a court. Perhaps Versailles? I hazarded a guess.

I wrote my thoughts in my notebook, and Lord Parham collected it along with the others. He handed them to a man nearby, and several people, including Lady Charlotte Schreiber, followed that man out of the room.

We trailed Lord Parham, and I greatly enjoyed viewing the other items in his extensive collection, but I kept looking for the group that had disappeared to come back. Soon they did.

Charlotte drew near me. "Your answers were quite right." She squeezed my arm. "As were Mr. Clarkson's."

It had been a test, and we'd passed!

We mingled among the crowds, and Lord Parham approached me—a singular honor. "Come, my dear," he said. "I'd like to show something to you."

He led me to his library, which was peopled with marble statues, and pointed out one which reposed on his desk. "Do you recall this?"

I closed my eyes and reached through the catalog of thousands of pieces I'd seen in my life. Something about the slightly pink coloration of the marble brought the statue to the front of my mind.

"My father," I said. "He sourced this for you."

He smiled, but rather than warm me, it unsettled me.

Perhaps it was that his lips were as thin and red as earthworms. "Yes. He was a fine man."

We talked for another moment, and out of the corner of my eye, I spied an urn, Grecian, presumably. Something about it troubled me. As we walked past it, I stopped and looked it over. Suddenly I knew what was wrong. I thought I might be of even more value to Lord Parham, and thereby other collectors with whom he might speak, if I pointed it out.

"What is it, my dear?"

But would he want to know? Should I speak up? He was my father's friend after all, and I should treat others as I would like to be treated. "You have a home filled with beautiful, authentic treasures," I began. "I don't want to cause alarm, but I believe this Greek urn to be a reproduction."

"Of whatever do you speak? It's beautiful."

I gently touched the urn. "It's beautiful, of course, but it's perhaps too beautiful. If this were, indeed, five hundred years old or more, the surface would have pits and cracks. The inside would be slightly darkened from having held contents of any kind."

His face grew angry. "It is in perfect condition because I paid a premium for an untouched urn."

"There are no untouched urns from that era, sir." I kept my voice respectful. "They were created for use. I'm sorry, Lord Parham. But I thought you might want to know."

He turned on me. "I think you've gone rather beyond yourself, young lady. I'll have you know that Mr. Crespin—whose family sourced antiquities for many years before there were Sheffield brothers wailing in a nursery—personally located this item for me and sold it to me years ago. Your father overindulged you, and your uncle is in his dotage. I feel no need to indulge your arrogance, nor am I in my dotage. If I may say so, I do not think many will do business with those they may learn are indiscreet."

I looked around the room, not sure how to answer. Parham would not meet my eye; only his many marble statues looked at me, blind, deaf, and dumb as they must remain to keep their places. *A mute of statues.*

"I'm sorry. Please forgive me." I had hoped to win his confidence with my honesty; instead, had I alienated him with my pride?

Lord Parham did not answer. As I turned away from him, I saw the dark shadow of a figure move quickly away from the door.

I straightened my dress and walked out of the library; the guests were leaving, and Mr. Clarkson glanced up at me nervously. My legs felt about to buckle, and my face burned with the curse of the fair-skinned. I wished for nothing more than the privacy to have a good cry.

"I shall see you tomorrow," Mr. Clarkson said to me. Had his voice grown cool?

When I returned home, I went quickly to my room; Orchie was already abed. I closed my door and, after undressing, pulled the coverlet over my head and cried until my nose was blocked. I repented. I rolled this way and that and wished I had kept my fairy light to soothe me to sleep.

The next morning, Mr. Clarkson was in the workshop before I was. Uncle Lewis was present too. I was to have a dressing-down.

Mr. Clarkson did not begin with any preliminary niceties. "The worst thing you can do, Miss Sheffield, is to let them know they've made an error and have them publicly shamed."

"I said nothing in public!" I protested, shocked by his presumptuous tone. "There were but the two of us in the room." I dismissed, willfully, the shadow waiting outside the door. How had Mr. Clarkson even learned of the conversation?

He sighed and spoke more softly. "I apologize for my tone, Miss Sheffield. It was uncalled for but came completely out of concern for the firm. Lord Parham came to speak with me and asked that we, your uncle and I, rein you in somehow. Said you'd made a mistake in pointing out something amiss in one of his statuaries. Could you . . . could you have made a mistake? As you did with the coins?"

"What mistake with the coins?" Uncle Lewis blustered back to life, his tone matching Clarkson's earlier one.

"I shall explain later. I do not think this time, the urn, was a mistake. I'm certain it was not."

"Were you certain about the coin for Mr. Herberts?" Clarkson asked, more subdued.

"Please, Mr. Clarkson. You yourself said my error was an anomaly. I was distracted."

Uncle pressed on as if he had not heard us. "They'll never forgive you if they think you've let on they have false pieces in their collection. It brings their eye, their judgment, and their taste into question. Never embarrass a rich man. Once anyone has shown acceptance of an item later found to be a fraud, it calls their entire ensemble into question, something they will never allow. Most are not as wise as they think they are and do not appreciate that being pointed out.

"You've made, perhaps, a fatal mistake, m'dear," Uncle Lewis said sorrowfully. "As Sophocles put it, no one loves the messenger who brings bad news. I should have explained all this more clearly. To my great regret, I did not."

I didn't share with them Lord Parham's warning to me last night. *"I do not think many will do business with those they may learn are indiscreet."*

"No one knows but the three of us and Lord Parham," I said. "Are you saying that if I find something which is counterfeit, I should lie to protect delicate elites?"

"If directly asked, answer honestly," my uncle replied. "Sell honestly, advise honestly, collect honestly. But don't go looking for trouble, offering bad news unsolicited. Unfortunately, the truth is not always a welcome houseguest. Many are willing to ignore a weak or missing provenance to own the notables their peers crave."

I nodded. That was true. Looters, thieves, the rich and covetous—the world was populated with them. There were also those who collected out of love, appreciation, and the desire to tell a story about themselves and others through their things. The difficulty, then, was in determining who was honest and who was not. What and who were true, and which were forgeries.

My confidence was shaken and I called my own judgment into question too. To where had my self-sufficiency fled?

"Donate the Lydney Collection to the South Kensington, claiming your decision was made due to the inspiration of the members of the Burlington," Clarkson implored. "Marry and have sons to carry on the work of the firm. If you have any questions about an object, bring it to me directly. I applaud you for doing so with the coins, and if I find there to be any irregularities, I shall determine what to do."

I looked up in shock. Was Mr. Clarkson now asserting authority over our family firm—and me? And proposing himself, in a roundabout manner, for marriage?

CHAPTER
Eleven

On Sunday, Uncle Lewis made a special effort to ready himself to go to church with me. I should have been glad of his company, but I did not feel like attending that day. I struggled mightily with all that was in front of and behind me, and I did not sense the Lord's guiding hand or encouraging word.

We took a carriage to St George's; Uncle could not, of course, walk the distance. It was a dark day, wet and weary. The city smelled of stewing leaves which had not been swept up and whisked away, and the heavy dusk of coal hung in the air like a funeral veil. As we traveled, I reminded the Lord of his promise, given in the book of Saint James: *"If any of you lack wisdom, let him ask of God, that giveth to all men liberally, and upbraideth not; and it shall be given him."*

I'm asking, dearest Lord. Why won't you answer?

The church was a marvel, majestic gray stone with a roof hefted by Corinthian columns. Inside, the many clear windows captured whatever light nature allowed and funneled it into the sanctuary, where it shone, ethereally, upon those gathered to worship. We sat near the back, as it was not as far for Uncle to walk. Once in our pew, Uncle closed the door behind us as I settled myself.

Preparation of the heart.

Prayer of penitence.

Scripture reading.

Creed.

I recited them all by rote. The words should have been a blessing to my heart, but that heart was so heavy. What I needed most was a personal touch, a reassurance from God himself that I was not alone and that all would be well.

Lord! I'm here, and I need you, my heart cried. *Are you here?*

More silence. Perhaps, like my mother, he'd fled to those with better promise.

I closed my eyes and saw Papa taking my hand in his one luncheon after church, weeks after Mama had left us.

"There's no need to refuse to speak to God on difficult matters," he'd said. *"It's not as if he doesn't know what you're thinking."*

Very well then. *Are you true, God? Brass or gold?* As a girl, I'd learned about *pia fraus*, a pious fraud. In the name of science or faith, a claim would be made that could not be backed up. The claimant believed that passing on the faith was so important to the recipients that it mattered not at all if the claim was entirely accurate. At one time, Uncle Lewis and I had cataloged and cared for famous reliquaries, small but very expensive boxes of gold and gems which were thought to have once stored a bone of a saint or a piece of the true cross. Uncle, who preferred religious antiquities to all others, had joked that if all the pieces of the true cross had been gathered, there would be more wood than could be harvested from every oak grown in England. But people touched them, and they believed, and it helped.

"How could it help if it's not real?" I had asked him. *"And if it's real, why is there no help?"*

"All people want to believe what they wish to believe, but we must all eventually look to believe the truth, whether or not that's what we wished."

Perhaps this was also true of matters of the spirit.

Was God loving and present? Or had I been taught a *pia fraus*? I dared not ask that of anyone, ever. But God, were he to prove true, must know the doubts which shadowed my soul. I touched the collar of my dress, under which rested the mustard seed which was so very, very small.

Marguerite and I were to spend that afternoon together. I arrived and her housekeeper opened the door.

"Eleanor." Marguerite came down the stairs. "Tea first?"

"Yes, please." I closed my umbrella, left it in the hallway, and followed her into a cozy sitting room. I noticed that the paper was peeling, slightly, from the wall and had darkened from damp near the window. The room smelled of wet flour, the paste which held the paper to the walls. Marguerite was meticulous about appearances. She must be in dreadful straits to not repair these.

"I've received an invitation from Lord Lydney," she said. "I assume we're going."

"You're coming to help me finish the inventory?" I teased.

"No, dearest. I wouldn't have the slightest idea what to do nor the interest to learn. He's having a social evening. He knows you would not attend without me. I suppose by winning me first, he believes I'll deliver you on time."

"I've had the invitation, of course, but I've not decided if I'm attending the social events."

"Of course you are," she rebuked me. "For my sake."

I tilted my head, took a sip of my tea, and asked, "How so?"

"One never knows whom one might meet."

This was true. Marguerite did need to marry again, and Watchfield was a good place to see who might be available. As forward-thinking as I tried to be, I was a realist, too.

We drank our tea, and I stood and looked at her wedding portrait, hanging on the wall. "Mr. Clarkson made the strangest comment the other day. He said I should be married posthaste and have children . . . and leave difficult evaluations to him."

She came behind me. "Was he proposing?"

"I do not know."

"Are you interested?"

I sighed and faced her. "I do not think so. Though perhaps I should be. Up until the past week or so he's been a perfect gentleman, and I've enjoyed working with him. We have some common interests, and he could be considered attractive."

"Not every successful marriage has to be a love match." She looked at the portrait of her late husband. Her marriage had been arranged by her parents. He had been much older than her, and while she had not been miserable, she had not been happy, either.

"I agree. But if I am not to have a love match, I must have a trust match."

"Yes," she said. "Do you trust Mr. Clarkson?"

"I do not know." I returned to the settee. "Mostly, I think. And yet there is something, I'm not sure what yet, that puts me off giving him my full faith. When he loses his self-control, he can speak most injuriously. And yet perhaps it is his zeal for the firm which causes those words." I changed the topic. "Now, as for Harry's social event . . . I do not have the necessary clothing. Nor do I have the funds to purchase anything new." I explained to her the sorry situation of our many bills, leaving out the portion about my perhaps being thrown into debtor's prison at the New Year. That unsavory detail would remain with me.

"And then, the other night at the Burlington, I made a terrible mistake." I did not cry in her presence, but I felt pressure behind my nose and eyes, so I stood by the window to cool my face.

"I'm sorry, dearest. Will they refuse you membership?"

"I do not know. I hope that Lady Charlotte will come to my defense."

She took my hand. "Let's do something to bring good cheer. Follow me."

Marguerite led me upstairs to her suite of rooms. Next to her bedroom was a small dressing room with a wardrobe, mirror, dressing table, and a commode for her jewelry.

"Remain here. Remove your dress."

"What?" I could not imagine what she was undertaking.

"I shall serve as lady's maid," she said.

She soon returned with a delightful amber gown, embroidered with sepia flowers, which seemed to lightly rain down the watered silk. The puffed sleeves cinched in above the elbows, and the neckline was just low enough to accommodate a drop necklace. "The bodice is darted to show off your tiny waist . . . ," she teased.

"Oh, Marguerite! Really."

She insisted I slip into it and then that I face the mirror. I gasped as I did. Was that me? The colors beautifully set off my reddish-brown hair and picked up the amber bits in my brown eyes.

"This isn't strictly in keeping with official mourning," Marguerite said. "Though the good Lord Lydney does not seem to be observing strict mourning."

"Can you blame him?" I asked.

"No. I cannot."

She brought out a plum-colored gown which was equally

suited to my coloring and, with just a few tucks and stitches, would fit me perfectly. I liked it even better. "I have not seen you wear these."

"I sold some jewelry," she said matter-of-factly. "I'm not mourning Edwin anymore. I must move on. You may borrow these; no one has seen them yet."

"They are too dear. I would be worried about spilling something on them or causing a tear."

"They are not as dear as you think—they are not new. Hard times fall upon people of all stations. Even the privileged have steep hills to climb on occasion."

I fought myself, looking in the mirror. "You know I abhor this type of thing."

"I had no such idea. I've seen you polish silver much longer than anyone else would just to have it shine for your clients. I have seen you use the finest tweezers to pluck a piece of lint from a ring. I've smelt the oils on you as you buffed the walnut chairs given to your care. Why, then, Eleanor, do you not care for yourself in like manner?"

"In the end, I am no one's treasure," I spoke softly. I do not believe she heard me.

"Let's go to Watchfield, dearest. I shall serve as chaperone and lady's maid, and you shall introduce me to some wealthy old man who needs a friend and wife—a trust match. And along the way, I'd like to see my beautiful friend cared for, cherished, and shown in the best light."

I thought for a moment. Charlotte Schreiber, after all,

dyed her hair. Alice lived in a slum but wore a stiff, white collar.

Why not? Why not!

"Yes, I will." I held up one finger. "On one condition."

"Whatever you like."

I grew somber. "You introduce me to the person to whom you sold your jewelry."

I did not have enough for November's rent, fast upon me. I would begin to sell my mother's jewelry.

CHAPTER *Twelve*

WATCHFIELD HOUSE, OXFORDSHIRE

Marguerite and I walked into the adjoining rooms which had been assigned to us at Watchfield House. Had Harry chosen them himself so I could be near to and comforted by a friend? I wondered when I should see him. I wondered if he was thinking the same.

Uncle, of course, had stayed in London with Orchie to tend to him. Mr. Clarkson would join me early the following morning to finish the inventory.

We dressed for an evening of music and games followed by a dinner; I could not imagine where the funds were coming from to pay for it all. Sir Matthew Landon had made it clear that Harry had been left no income from his father. The string musicians warmed their instruments in the distant background while Marguerite helped me into the beautiful aubergine gown. I clasped my mother's gold-and-opal choker round my neck. It would catch the lamplight and create tiny rainbows.

When I returned to London, I must sell it.

"Here, then." Marguerite pulled my hair back and up, tightening it into curls and then loosening them into waves which cascaded around my shoulders. She rubbed my cheeks for color and instructed me to bite my lips for the same.

"Absolutely not!" I protested. But when she turned her back to get herself dressed, I furtively bit my lips. It could not hurt, after all.

When I entered the reception room downstairs where all had gathered ahead of dinner, all eyes turned to me. This time, they were looking at me afresh. The conservator's daughter? I was dressed as richly as any in the room. I glanced over and smiled politely at the lovely Signorina Viero and her mother. Signorina Viero smiled politely back, but her widowed mother did not. I turned, and as I did, Harry entered the room. Although I'd believed that I was doing this for myself and not for Harry, I soon realized an unasked for but happily received reward. He gasped. Audibly.

I nodded and then turned back to Marguerite, who grinned.

I introduced her to people I knew. One man, a widower of perhaps forty years of age, seemed particularly enchanted with her, so I nodded my departure and went to speak with some others in the room. Dinner was served, and afterward, games.

Charlotte would have been proud. A variety of board games had been set up around the room. As chance would have it, I found myself at the large table where Signorina Viero also sat.

There were Greek figures of love scattered across the porcelain board, and each of us was assigned a piece. The dice were tossed, and we were to move forward or back depending on the instructions given on the square upon which we landed.

"Discretion," I called out. "I shall move three steps forward, which lands me at Hope." Fitting, I thought, for such an evening.

The man to my left landed nearby on the square marked Indiscretion. "I'm quite pleased that my wife is at another table," he teased, and we laughed with him. Each of us made our way on the game board through the stages of Flirting, Courtship, and then toward Engagement.

Signorina Viero took her turn and landed on a square whose romance requirement seemed rather strange.

"Silenzio," she said in her lovely, lilting accent. She looked at me and smiled coyly. "To remain silent." An uncomfortable moment passed, and the game continued.

Her mother bustled about the room, much as a hostess would. At the end of the game, Francesca joined her and seemed to signal the waiters that water and champagne should be served. She then went over to the quartet, and as I was nearby, I could hear her instructing them to play some soft music whilst the games continued but to prepare for dancing afterward.

Even Marguerite, Harry's reluctant champion, stared. "More hostess than guest," she noted almost absentmindedly.

Harry announced that we would divide into teams to play sardines. He handed out cards with letters and numbers on them. The card numbered one would be the "sardine" for that team, lettered A all the way down to E. The sardines would hide somewhere in the house—"private rooms and servants' quarters off-limits," he said—and we would all seek to find where our team's sardine had hidden. As soon as we did, we would pack in with him or her until the team was fully assembled. The last person to crowd into his or her "sardine tin" would lose and be required to sit out the first dance.

Lord Grimsby, the man who had his eye on Marguerite, was the sardine on my team, C, but I saw him trade cards with someone else after spying which team card had been assigned to Marguerite. We gave the sardines time to spread out and find a hiding place; then the room emptied.

I calculated there were perhaps fifteen members on each team, and it would take us all some effort to work out into which space our team would cram. That would give me enough time.

I slipped to the back of the house first. Why had that room, and that room alone, been locked? Without a key made available to me? I must know.

Because Harry had said that servants' quarters were off-limits, I thought it likely that I could make my way up to the third floor via the back staircase unnoticed. I wondered if perhaps the door had been unlocked since my last visit. Perhaps because I'd asked after it . . . or because there was a party being held, if it were a supply room of some sort.

The music swirled in the background, becoming quieter and then finally still as my own heart's pounding grew louder. I had not taken a lamp. I rounded the corner of the first-floor stairs, and the area grew, suddenly, completely dark. A door slammed shut in the distance, and my heart leaped.

Nothing. I let my eyes adjust and then rounded to the next landing. As I stopped to squeeze my gown into the smaller space, I heard a footstep fall just behind me.

Who could be following me? Why?

I waited a moment and then made my way up the narrow staircase to the top, where there was but one door at the end of the long corridor. I tried to twist the handle, but it was firmly locked.

I shook the door lightly. Nothing. I heard footsteps one floor below me. There were no other rooms nearby, only a staircase leading to the lower servants' quarters. Should I continue walking? Did someone tarry in the shadows? I could shout, but I was unsure that anyone would hear me this far back in the house and above the music.

Why would I need to shout?

I took hold of myself and continued walking down the stairs, one at a time, till I was one floor lower. I heard some commotion in a linen closet. I pried the door open and heard breathing and muffled voices.

"Are you Sardine C?" I asked quietly.

"But no," came a woman's answer and a giggle. Was that a foreign accent? Was Signorina Francesca in there on her own? Or was Harry . . . ?

I shook the thought from my head. There were dozens of people in attendance, after all.

I wandered all the way down the hallway and opened the door to the small closet in which Harry's father had stored his cigars. A whiff of sweet, nutty, smoky, and stale greeted me.

"Are you Sardine C?" I asked.

"No," a man said. "Go downstairs, and you'll find them."

Ah. He must have found C while looking for his own team.

I went down to the first floor and heard a small scuffle coming from the large coat closet. I opened the door.

"Are you Sardine C?" I whispered.

"Yes!" came the reply. I snuck into the closet and pulled the door shut behind me, then made my way to the back, where seven or eight sardines, men and women, packed in close quarters.

Another woman soon entered the closet and came to join us. There was a long silence. A muffled cough. A hand rested on my right shoulder.

"Don't forget what I told you, Miss Sheffield," a voice breathed in my ear. "He's not proved faithful to anyone but himself."

My gown was so big and the players so cramped that I could not turn to see who was whispering, but this time, I knew. Lord Audley. Claiming Harry was selfish and disloyal. Would he know? They'd gone to university together, and their families had been great friends.

The closet door opened again, and because the light was behind him like a halo, I could see that it was Harry. He asked if this was where Sardine C was, and Lord Audley answered tersely. Harry made his way to the very back, and as he got close, he spied me and smiled.

He'd placed us on the same team; I knew it. I smiled back, though a degree or two cooler than I might have done a year earlier.

He stood as near to me as acceptable, which was very near given that was the point of the game, and we were, of course, in the company of others. His side pressed against my own, and as the door opened and someone new joined us, it gave him reasonable cause to draw even closer. He leaned over and let his cheek rest against mine before turning his mouth to my ear.

"You are stunning. Beautiful," he whispered.

A pleasurable warmth spread throughout me, prompting a smile. The last person finally opened the closet door, and we all tumbled out, back to the dance floor.

Harry took my hand as we exited the closet and I let him hold it, unwilling to let go.

When we returned to the room, the strings were playing the dance music that, presumably, Signorina Francesca Viero had requested. Within minutes, Lord Audley came to ask me to dance.

Marguerite raised her eyebrow at me across the room, and I smiled. I was in no social position which Lord Audley would consider, we'd had no conversations which would lead me to believe he was interested in me romantically, and I'd learned he was already happily affianced to a wealthy American.

I consented to dance, and he was a most pleasant partner. When I looked up, I caught Harry looking at us with badly hidden jealousy. I admit to it: it pleased me.

Lord Audley escorted me off the floor and brought me water with lemon.

"You continue to warn me," I teased him. "It's not necessary. Why do you persist?"

He laughed. "Despite what you may have observed, Miss Sheffield, chivalry is not dead. There are some among the nobility who still act with noble intentions. You may count me among them."

He bowed and left my presence. I was not left unattended for long. Marguerite's skills as a lady's maid had brought plenty of eyes and attention my way. I hated to admit it, but it bolstered my confidence. Perhaps a woman might be allowed beauty and capability, both.

As Harry danced with Signorina Viero, I kept my eyes on others. Then he came to ask me to dance, and I agreed. "I see Audley seeks to usurp my place," he teased, but there was an edge to his voice.

"What place is that?" I asked sweetly, holding his eye as we passed one another and switched round partners and back.

Because I had not yet decided on the collection, he could not say anything personal or which hinted at an arrangement.

"On the dance floor," he offered weakly. Then he laughed merrily, which made him yet more attractive and recalled to my heart hundreds of memories. His rough and sweet laugh had always undone me.

Lord Audley and his fiancée came to stand nearby; Harry was to my left, and Lord Audley just to my right. The gentlemen greeted one another cordially and discussed horses. I turned to his fiancée, and we discussed the fine musicians. When Lord Audley left, Harry drew near me and said, "Audley at your one side, now and in the sardine closet, and me at the other, puts me in mind of *The Shepherd of Hermas*."

I recalled the book; it was an ancient Christian manuscript. I was delighted that Harry was aware of it, and my surprise must have been reflected on my face because he laughed once more. "Ellie, you are surprised? I don't prefer antiquities, but I am happily well-read."

I blushed, caught out, and I knew he spoke the truth. "Do tell me—how does Lord Audley put the story in mind?"

"All people, the story teaches, have two angels: the shepherd of iniquity and the shepherd of righteousness. Each desires to descend into a person's heart and shape her emotions and choices. A person must be careful, the writer cautioned, to understand and manage both angels, but only allow the angel which leads to righteousness to guide her path."

"I'm delighted you think of Lord Audley as promoting righteousness," I teased. "I shall tell him so, next time we partner at dance."

At that moment, a song struck up. My eyes widened. "You arranged for this song to be played!"

"Indeed, I did." He smiled and took my hand. "May I?"

I looked at Harry now, a man and not a boy. He, too, had recalled our first dance.

My mind returned to us at a house party his father once gave.

It mattered not to me that Papa had not been invited to the party the baron was hosting. Papa was an honored friend in many ways, but not a social equal.

I did not seek to be a social equal either. I went to the library to take a book or two back to my room—the baron had given me full permission to do so. On my way out of the library, I saw Harry.

"Ellie. Come with me. Meet me at the summerhouse."

I shook my head. "I cannot. Papa is expecting me back upstairs."

He sighed. He wore black tie and tails; I was in a teal gown that one of the ladies from church had helped me to purchase. Pretty, but not above my station. Harry pulled me through one of the hidden servants' doors into a linen supply room near the ballroom to try to persuade me.

"They won't notice if you are gone. He's old. He will be asleep soon."

I laughed. "Papa is not old, and he will be up reading long after the music stops."

At that, the musicians magically struck up the next song, a slower song, one with the violin's siren cry to intimacy.

The room was small, but we were alone. Harry held out his hand, so I set my book down on the floor. Then he took both my hands in his. "May I?"

His hands were warm, and then mine were too. I looked up, startled, as he put one arm around my waist. I had not, in my ladies' day school, envisioned that this would be how my first dance would transpire: intimate, two of us, no chaperone, no crowd.

He pulled me closer and against my better judgment, I let him, and imperfectly, then perfectly, to the beat of the music we danced our first dance. At the end of the song he held me from him—reluctantly, it seemed. I disentangled our hands.

He bowed. "For now, my lady," he said. "For now."

When the present dance was over, Harry spoke once more, softly. "Regrettably, I have duties to which I must attend. Do you depart in the morning?"

"I will stay and complete the inventory. And then Mr. Clarkson, Mrs. Newsome, and I will depart for London."

"Ah . . . Mrs. Newsome." His eyes twinkled. "I shall have to invite her to my Twelfth Night festivities so she may bring along her charge. In the meantime, I will call on you in London, if you'll allow."

If I were honest, I did not truly mind his machinations to keep me in his presence. But would he want me here for Twelfth Night if I decided against him with the collection? That decision would have to be made first. It seemed, after my mistake with Lord Parham, that awarding the collection to the South Kensington might be the only way in which I might save my family's firm. I nodded my assent.

Harry kissed the back of my hand and ensured his lips stayed pressed against my thin glove much longer than socially required. Then he pulled away from me and seemed reluctant to depart. Finally he bowed and took his leave.

Out of the corner of my eye, I saw the widow Viero staring at us both. Harry left, and she came to speak with me about pleasantries and the forthcoming holidays and her homesickness. Her English was broken. I switched to Florentine, which surprised her, I think. "My father saw to it that I was well educated," I said.

"Admirably so, *che bella*. And your mama? She is not with you tonight?"

"No." I shook my head quickly and bid her *buonasera*, good evening, then took my leave before she could ask further questions about my mother. Someone would likely tell her soon enough, anyway.

On my way up to my room, I turned my glove so that the back of it, where Harry's lips had been, touched my own lips. It was the closest I would get, perhaps ever again.

I waited an hour, nearly two, until I thought all were asleep. I listened carefully and heard nothing but the arthritic bones of an old house cracking in the cold. I slipped into a heavy dressing gown and slid my feet into furred slippers. Then I took the back stairs down, one at a time. To be true to my duty, I must learn what was in that upper room.

CHAPTER

Thirteen

The kitchen had been quickly cleaned and emptied. The scullery maid slept in her corner. She was too young to be snoring, but likely the poor lass had done more than her share of work that evening, so snore she did. I let my eyes adjust to the dim light and then turned the corner toward the butler's pantry.

I slid my hand up the side of the pantry door and found it locked. I sighed with disappointment. The keys were in the butler's room, most likely.

I dared not break into a room where a man slept. A dim light flickered on in the butler's room; he had a window which looked onto the hallway, and I did not want him to see me. I quickly crept back up the stairs to my room and sat on the bed, thinking. Praying. Nothing came to mind.

I flipped open the Bible and paged through it, passing the time, looking for a word of encouragement.

Ten minutes later, I pushed it aside. As I did, it knocked my bag, in which the chatelaine of keys jingled. I'd told myself that I'd keep them until I no longer needed them for inventories and such. Truly? I wished them to be mine.

In any case, I'd tried all the keys on the upper room. I closed my eyes and thought and prayed. I considered that the baron's room—well, not Harry's room, but his father's—was directly below the room I wished to access from the hallway. Perhaps there was another entrance? I knew Watchfield had other secret passageways and staircases. Harry and I had slipped through them on occasion.

Perhaps there was one in Lord Lydney's suite of rooms? I did have the key for that.

I slid my slippers back on, took the keys from my bag, and slipped out the door again, taking a small candlelit lamp with me.

Down the hallway, quietly, so quietly. Murmurs and laughter swelled from another room.

I found my way to the suite of rooms and inserted key after key into the lock, hoping one would work before I was discovered. I could certainly not claim I was inventorying at this time of night.

Finally I turned a key, holding my breath. The door opened, and I stepped inside.

The furniture in the room was covered with linen preservation sheets, but the cabinets and armoires were not. Something caught my eye on the dressing table. The mantel clock. Harry had not sold it! He'd simply removed it from public view, and who could blame him? It and its constant, silent condemnation were not pleasant to bear whilst his father was alive, and now he was dead, Harry wanted that condemnation banished.

I looked around the room's walls, seeking a door which might hide a hidden passage upstairs, but found none. Then I noticed that one wardrobe was much larger than the others, certainly larger than would be required for the clothing of a man rarely in residence.

Instinct. My papa had always told me when I felt something, trust it. Trust myself, even if it was the tiniest feeling that I was right. A little trust in myself was all I needed. A small amount of faith would work wonders.

As I opened the wardrobe door and stepped inside, I found it empty. I next saw a thin panel of wood toward the back which did not match the rest of the cabinet. I ran my hand over it, pressing in as I did, and it popped up. It was a locking lever. When I pulled down on the lever, the back of the wardrobe opened and a narrow staircase appeared out of nowhere, exactly as a secret door reveals a hidden room. I began to climb the stairs with excitement.

At the top of the stairwell, I pulled down on a second lever, repeatedly, but it stuck; perhaps the wood had swelled from lack of attention or the joint had been poorly made.

Just when I was about to give up, I tugged once more and—reluctantly, it seemed—a door opened into the room.

One small window allowed a faint trickle of moonlight to leak in in addition to the light of my lamp. When my eyes adjusted, I could see exactly what was in the room.

Armor. A golden helmet with a dragon for a crest. A circular shield upon which was pressed the protective image of Mary, mother of our Lord. A cutting spear. Another shield embossed with the face of the evening. Finally, the sword, in the fashion of Excalibur.

Armor styled after that supposed to have been used by King Arthur, for whom Harry's brother, and his father, had been named. Shields inlaid with gold and silver, richly embossed with images depicting war. This was Arthur's portion of the collection—the very pieces his father had accused Harry of selling. And yet they were right here in a tiny, hidden room accessible only through the late Lord Lydney's rooms. He would have known of that secret lever, a lever only someone familiar with the tricks of ancient woodworking—my father had taught his lordship, as he had his daughter—would have been able to puzzle out.

I was overwhelmed with relief. Harry had not, as his father had claimed, sold Arthur's riches! It had been a lie.

I heard a noise. I turned and stared at the suits of armor. It seemed to me that one of them moved. *Eleanor. Be rational. Suits of armor don't move on their own.*

Someone could hide in that suit. I would not see him until it was too late.

I tentatively walked over to one and pushed it; it swayed on its hanging rack. I looked up. The eye slits were empty.

Now that my sight had fully adjusted to the dark, I looked around. There was a costly and rare piece of armor from a Polish hussar. To my knowledge, it had never appeared on any inventory, and I'd not seen it. I saw a piece of rare Chinese armor. That, too, was completely unfamiliar. In the far corner was a bejeweled reliquary for which I'd never seen an account.

There was more than Arthur's collection here. There were items I believed might have been stolen, including a rare piece of medieval barding, armor made to protect horses. Not only were they not documented—which could be damning, because they were hidden for what reason?—they were too valuable for the late Lord Lydney not to have flaunted them openly if he could.

I would document them, and when I'd ascertained that I'd found someone both knowledgeable and trustworthy, I would make enquiries. I remembered what I'd told Harry the night after the funeral, in the summerhouse. *"During the last war, Italy was looted."*

The gateman was Harry's father's man. As was his valet—unquestionably loyal up until his lordship's death. This locked room on the third floor, of course, could have been accessed by the valet, who, according to the gatehouse man, had the only other key. He could have placed the stolen goods safely within. *"He is my father's man,"* Harry had said, *"and his man alone, through and through. There would be the devil to pay if we were caught."*

The devil, known as the accuser, desires someone else to pay for his misdeeds and cloaks himself as an angel of light whilst making others look bad. Likewise, Lord Lydney had blamed Harry for the theft, knowing it would cast a deep shadow of suspicion. Perhaps he'd instructed his valet to place Arthur's items in the secret room during one of his visits back to England, then written to me with his false claim. He'd have assumed, then, that I would see Harry as untrustworthy and donate the collection—including Arthur's items—to the museum. Had his claim that Harry preferred to remain in Austria in the company of Francesca Viero also been a mistruth? Likely.

I thought back to Harry's statement that his father loved the game Questions and Commands. Of course, if the commander was not satisfied with the answer given in response to his query, he would demand a forfeit. Perhaps, in this case, the collection? He could also require the responder's face to be smutted with coal, thereby publicly shamed.

The late Lord Lydney wanted Harry to both forfeit and be shamed. I was growing more certain of this day by day. It was an evil game played from beyond the grave, a way to punish the son he'd not loved for the death of the son he did love, using someone else's hands—mine—like the clock's, to bolster his own baseless claims.

Looking at the size of some of the pieces in the room, it became clear why a second, outside staircase was required; by no means was there enough room for the armor to have been transported through the narrow passage in the wardrobe. Was there?

I went back to look, and within seconds of my peering down the stairs, I watched as the wardrobe door below clicked shut, sealing off the baron's bedchamber.

Had someone followed me—trapped me? I quickly tiptoed down the stairwell and tried to push open the door. It would not open.

I looked for another secret panel with which I might open the lower door, hoping there was a lever trigger on each side. I felt up and down the sides of the inside of the wardrobe, which was now only open to the above chamber in the dark. I felt nothing of interest or value. The air grew thin, and soon I was inhaling my used breath. It was hot and moist, and I grew light-headed.

Movement caught my eye, and I gasped. It appeared that the door which opened to the upper room was also slowly closing. If I did not make it up the stairwell before that exit closed, too, there was no guarantee I could unstick the lever a second time. I would be well and truly trapped!

CHAPTER Fourteen

I clawed my way up the stairs just in time, reached my hand out and pushed the door open, and then stumbled onto the floor of the small room. It seemed this door had an automatic hinge. Did the bottom door, too?

Or had someone tried to trap me in here?

I looked at the door to the hallway, the one which Mr. Clarkson had sought the key for, and felt an immediate sense of relief. It looked of the style of a double lock, which meant it had one key for the outside and one for the inside. I had my keys. *Thank you, God. Please, may one of them work.*

I struggled with each key on the chatelaine, forcing them into the lock one after another with no luck. I tried twice, thrice. My clothes were damp with my efforts, although the room, which was unheated, was frigid. I grew chilled.

Perhaps I could pick the lock. "I'm sorry," I whispered to the memory of Arthur and took his thin rapier to see if I could wriggle the point into the area which seemed like it was a keyhole.

Nothing.

Finally I sank to the floor and in anger used the sword hilt to hit the serpent icon—how apt—on the back of the lock. When I did, the snake popped out and revealed a lever. A simple lever. I pulled it, and as I did, the lock disengaged.

"Thank you," I whispered.

I went back down to the late Lord Lydney's suite of rooms and slipped inside once more, walking to the armoire. I saw the lever now because I knew it was there, but it had been very cleverly disguised. Like recognizing evil, I thought.

I looked once more at the clock.

There was no *tick, tick, tick*; the hands were stilled once more, but unfortunately, the hands of the late Lord Lydney—a shepherd of iniquity—were not. His hands continued to move from beyond the grave. But this time I had caught him out and I would, if I could, still them permanently.

The next morning, Mr. Clarkson was already in the study when I went to meet him to complete our inventory. He greeted me kindly and we set to work, dividing the remaining rooms in the house between us. When I passed through the bright salon where Harry's mother's porcelain had been kept, I noticed that this time, all her figurines were in place. Had any truly been missing before? I ran my finger along the glass upon which they stood. The glass was completely clean. It could be that the housekeeping had been better kept up since Harry was back in residence. Perhaps Signorina Francesca oversaw that, too? Or perhaps the person who had moved them was bright enough to realize that he or she could not leave a telltale trail of dust?

Downstairs, in the Italian room, I ran through the majolica, the fine Italian earthenware that had been famous, and very collectible, since well before Henry the Eighth wooed Anne Boleyn. It seemed to me that a piece or two was missing, but when I checked what was there against the latest inventory, every piece had been accounted for. There were dozens of pieces. This was only one account. It would not be unusual for me to have misremembered. Perhaps the pieces I'd recalled had been a part of another assemblage.

Everything seemed in place. Mr. Clarkson left for a train which would take him to visit his family in Bristol for a few days. Within the week, we would need to prepare for a large dinner hosted by the Burlington Fine Arts Club in support of the South Kensington Museum, which still desired the Lydney Collection. I hoped to make a good enough impression to overcome the mistake I had made with Lord Parham. Surely, if he desired the fraud to remain secret, he would keep that secret himself. Then I could curry bonds of professional camaraderie with the others. I'd learn more about what the museum hoped for its future and if it might be the better home for the Lydney Collection. Regardless of my feelings for Harry, I had to make an objective decision.

I returned to my room, ready to pack for my return to London. When I arrived, I saw Marguerite there, waiting.

"Are you ready to leave?" I asked. "I have some wonderful news to share with you."

I told her about the fact that I'd found Arthur's collection in a hidden chamber, and that the mantel clock, too, had been found. "So you see?" I concluded. "All things thus far point to Harry being the man I thought he was. I am diligent in the ascertainment, though. I have a list."

She smiled weakly.

My heart was troubled; she normally jested about my note-taking habits. "What's wrong? Is it Lord Grimsby, the man who seemed to favor you last night?" I sat down at the table near the window. The clouds shivered flakes of ashen snow over the tawny dead lawn.

"He was a wonderful companion," she said ruefully. "Until he made it clear that he was interested in a . . . dalliance. The kind of arrangement one might propose to a woman of lesser moral qualities. I don't know what gave him the idea that I could be open to such an arrangement."

I reached across the table and took her hand. "I would never, ever have expected that of Grimsby. I'm shocked. It was an idea he brought with him, and most probably brings with him everywhere. Nothing you've done, dearest. We shall look for someone else."

She nodded, but her mood had not lifted. "Perhaps happiness will not be attainable for either of us." She looked wistful, and I wondered if it were only her interactions with Grimsby which had made her doubt the potential for my happiness, too. A picture of the beautiful Francesca Viero came floating through my mind.

"Let's pack your pretty gowns," I said. "The plum one was a decided success yesterday evening. Of course, I shall have to sell some jewelry of my own now." I thought back fondly on the necklace. It had had a swan song, of a sort, the night before. "Did you ask about my selling some jewelry?"

Still uncharacteristically glum, she answered, "Yes. I'm so sorry, but he's not buying anything further for the moment. Apparently there are more sellers than buyers."

Ah. "I shall find a way to carry on," I said. I must find someone discreet—I would not want our clients to know that I was in nearly desperate straits. It was one thing when the rich sold some of their treasures to buy things even more costly. That was not, as would be known, our case. "Still, dearest, that is not the end of the world."

This time she took my hand. "I've heard it said trouble comes in threes."

The disappointment of the potential suitor. One. The fact that there was currently no buyer for my jewelry. Two. "What is the third?"

"Last night I heard . . . well, I heard that Harry and Signorina Viero were married in Venice."

I pulled my hand from hers as though I'd been clutching an ember. "From whom did you hear this?"

"From the *vedova Viero*, the signorina's mother."

I shook my head back and forth, unwilling to believe it was true.

Marguerite continued, "I asked how they'd been able to flee from Venice without passports, without British papers, especially during a period of war. She answered that as her daughter was married to an English nobleman and the son of an ambassador, they were given smooth passage."

"Oh." My eyes looked down at the table.

"I asked the signorina," Marguerite went on.

I looked up again. She'd risked a social breach for me, as only a dear friend would. "And she replied . . . ?"

"That they had not truly married. That they'd claimed it, for protection, but that it was not a true marriage in any way, legally or . . ." Now she let her sentence drop off.

"Which is why none of us has heard of it." The tiniest bit of relief began to seep into my heart.

"Maybe." She hesitated before adding, "She's titled. And wealthy."

"I know. I remember that about Stefano." I recalled the words Harry's father had used in his letter to me: he'd once expected me to be a caretaker and wife, a daughter-in-law, but he had not suggested I would be a welcome addition to his family. I was neither titled nor wealthy.

Perhaps I'd merely been a youthful dalliance to Harry. A passing of the time during school holidays. Now he'd come into his title . . .

I let a minute elapse so I could control my emotions and my voice. "From time to time I've considered that perhaps once Harry learned of his father's intention to have me dispose of the collection, he decided to keep his affections for the signorina quiet until he'd won the collection back. That he tarried in Venice—and Austria—because his heart and mind were set on someone else." I said it so she would not have to.

"Maybe," Marguerite agreed once more. "I'm sorry, Eleanor. I had not anticipated this . . . possibility. Should you speak with the signorina yourself?"

No, I would not speak with the signorina. "I'll speak with Harry."

Had all he spoken to me been from true affections of his heart? Or had they been misleading actions to further selfish goals?

Perhaps *this* Lord Lydney was the shepherd of iniquity.

CHAPTER *Fifteen*

BLOOMSBURY, LONDON

Once I had returned home, Orchie divulged that there had been another visitor to the house wishing to speak to my uncle about an urgent matter, but Mr. Clarkson had spoken with him and he had left, reassured. She did not look happy when she said that.

"Did he not handle it well?" I asked.

"Oh, he did," she said. I ascribed it to her suspicion of anyone outside the family, as she had shown with Alice. Or perhaps she did not like to see my uncle's place being taken, professionally. I did not either. But I believed Uncle's illness had caused some longtime clients to turn away from us, and

Mr. Clarkson would earn their trust and perhaps keep them on good terms. It was imperative that we make a good showing at the South Kensington dinner. And that I sell some of my mother's jewelry.

I did not know where to turn. I was more accustomed to buying than to selling. In the workshop, Mr. Clarkson kept a small drawer in which I'd seen him place professional cards and notes for contacts. Perhaps he would have something in there?

In his drawer, I found those bits of paper with contact information, but nothing that would indicate where I might discreetly sell my jewelry. I could certainly not let it be known, publicly, that we were struggling, so discretion was all important. I was just about to leave his desk when I saw, propped up against the back, a daguerreotype. I picked it up.

It appeared to be a family. A father and some children, anyway. No mother. Some lovely little girls and a lanky young man. I peered closer. Yes. It was a young Mr. Clarkson. He looked innocent and sweet. Behind them appeared to be a shop—the curiosity shop? I took the photo to my desk and magnified it with my glass. On the shop awning was the word *Clerk's*.

I could not be certain, but the street looked somewhat familiar. East End London, maybe?

The door to the workshop opened, and my heart leaped into my throat. My new glass dropped to the floor and the daguerreotype with it. Fortunately neither broke.

"It's just me," Orchie said.

Relief. "Yes?"

"Next time you see the lady doctor, could you ask her for a bit more of that willow bark tea? My aches are getting worse." She put her hand to her back. "And perhaps you might ask her if there's something to quieten him down. At sunset, he's all twitchy and tense."

We did need more tea. But she'd also given me a splendid idea. I would bring the jewelry to the pawnshop once owned by Dr. Garrett's family and ask for discretion.

I went into my father's room and sat down on the bed. *Papa. Is this the correct thing to do?* He would not, of course, answer me directly, but I knew him well enough to know that he would tell me to do what was necessary to save the firm and the family. I opened the drawer and pulled out the soft velvet pouches which held my mother's jewelry. I left but one elaborate set: a gold-and-pearl necklace with matching teardrop earrings. Papa had given the set to her on their wedding day. I'd wear it with Marguerite's amber gown to the charity dinner for the South Kensington and then be done with it.

I took the omnibus past the slaughtering waste ground, where the air still smelt of blood, finally heading into Whitechapel, an amalgam of English slum misery and immigrant stepping-stone hope. I stepped down from the omnibus into the cold mist. The streets teemed with men and boys; a few clutches of women stood near to one another, their large skirts wounded with rips and tears. I turned a corner, and as I did, I saw three tough-looking men fall out from an alleyway and follow me. They kept a distance at first, but as

I sped up, they came closer. They whistled, and I could hear them muttering about how pretty and fresh I was. I clutched my bag closer, regretting the decision to come to this part of town alone with a hoard of expensive gems.

They were nearly behind me. I smelled the dirty sweat wicking from their wet woolen outerwear. I heard them breathe. *A threat of footsteps.*

I finally ducked into the shop at 1 Commercial Road.

"Can I be of some assistance?" The reedy man behind the counter smiled at me. He had but a few more teeth than my prison friend Jeanette.

The ruffians loitered outside the door. When I looked at one, he tapped his capless head as if in greeting and grinned wickedly. How would I be able to leave—with money on my person? My vision blurred as my apprehension grew.

"I'd like to sell some jewelry," I said.

"Do you have ownership papers?" he asked.

Well, no. And I had not expected that question, though I would have asked it myself.

I shook my head. "They were my mother's, and she's gone now. I do know the Garretts. My family has been in the evaluation business for some years, and my father, William Sheffield, worked with Mr. Newson Garrett on occasion."

He looked at me skeptically. I did not blame him. And I did not receive as much for the jewelry as I had hoped. I was mindful of Marguerite's warning that there were more sellers than buyers at the moment. It would, in any case, keep the wolf from the door for a month or two longer.

As he counted the money behind the counter, I asked him, "Have you heard of a shop named Clerk's? A curiosity shop, perhaps?"

He looked toward the ceiling, appearing to think, then back at me. "There was a pawnshop named Clerk's here some years ago. I think they was run out."

He smiled, silent now, and handed the money to me, but I did not move to take it. I glanced at the men waiting for me and my money, eager to mishandle both, I was certain.

"I cannot leave safely," I said to the shopkeeper.

"Did you come alone, then?" His voice indicated his surprise. "They are not accompanying you?"

"No, indeed. Here is my card." I handed it to him, indicating my professional legitimacy, and his face lightened. "I'm certain you understand my need for discretion," I said.

"Yes. And I shall hail a hansom cab." He went to his till and took out some more money, then handed it to me. "I thought you was with them, and they are bad men. If you were, then the goods might have been stolen no matter your story about your mother." He tucked my card in his cash drawer.

And yet you bought them anyway. I dared not say that aloud. He would not then be so accommodating in assisting me.

I had the cab leave me off a few blocks from my home to save a pence. As I walked, I sensed and heard footsteps following me once more. It could surely not be the ruffians from the pawnshop.

Perhaps it was those men who had accosted my uncle. Predators were known to lie in wait for prey, if required.

I raced home and, once inside, fast locked the door behind me.

The dinner was to be held at the museum itself and had a dual purpose: raise funds and encourage the wealthy to part with some of their treasures to make the South Kensington the most expansive and complete museum in all Britain, if not the world.

Lady Charlotte and her husband had kindly agreed to escort me to both the dinner and the event which followed; I would meet Mr. Clarkson there, of course. The Schreibers' carriage was closed tight against the November wind, and Charlotte had brought blankets to spread across our laps. I slipped my hands inside a fur muff which had been a Christmas gift some years earlier, plunging them deeper till my left knuckles knocked my right.

There were better than a hundred of us—perhaps two hundred—eating in a grand dining room within the museum; the dinner was overseen by Mr. and Mrs. Herberts, generous patrons of the museum. I saw Mr. Clarkson, too, from across the room. He smiled at me encouragingly. I suspected his conversations on behalf of the firm were going well.

"Do you know William Morris has agreed to decorate this dining room?" Charlotte's face conveyed her excitement. I knew she was a great fan of Mr. Morris, as was I. "He's planning to call it the Green Dining Room. We shall come back together, I'm certain of it, and see what he'll do." She squeezed my hand. Her friendship had come to mean so much to me in such a short time. She was not a mother, per se, nor an equal friend, like Marguerite. Somewhere, perhaps, in between.

Many of the guests spoke well of the late Lord Lydney. He had been a friend to many of the collectors, and they praised the things he had purchased and which my father had assisted in locating. Did they know him only superficially and therefore had been tricked? Or had I seen the baron in the wrong light? Until the discovery of Arthur's pieces, I might have thought so. Perhaps they had been hoodwinked as well.

Dinner was served on plain white porcelain, which was very daring indeed as most hostesses used highly decorated plates. Mrs. Herberts had no doubt planned the menu to be as artistic and impressive as possible; the food needed nothing but a fine bone foil. The serving table stretched nearly as long as the room. Platters of lobster, pink as winter cheeks, were placed next to ramekins of rich butter as creamy as the clover the yielding cows had dined upon. Fruit long out of season had been tucked into French pastries. Silver spoons rested on pearl platters, each overflowing with black seeds of caviar which popped with satisfyingly briny goodness when placed between the front teeth. Jellies. Sweetmeats. Jowls of beef. It was endless. Above the serving table was an Italian master's fine portrait of Epicurus, the Greek philosopher who believed that pleasure was the absence of suffering.

After dinner, Mr. Herberts proposed a toast to the museum, spoke about the current needs, and explained how individuals could support the common effort. He looked directly at me and smiled. I held my head high and smiled back.

Lord Parham turned toward me and scowled.

As I turned away from him, I felt, more than saw, eyes upon me from across the room. A sense of forewarning caused the fine hairs on the back of my neck to rise.

I looked up.

It was my mother.

As I met her gaze, she quickly turned toward her dining companion. I looked down at my plate; my appetite had fled along with, I could sense, the blood in my face.

I had seen her but once in a dozen years, at a distance, outside the opera. I was not, after all, likely to mingle in the clique in which she circulated. She was still beautiful, more beautiful than I could surely say of myself; she always said I favored my father, which I took to mean I was at a distinct disadvantage.

We were dismissed to wander the galleries nearby, which had been lit by lamplight and especially opened for the event. I stood and walked away from the table quickly, not trusting my voice or emotions to remain steady until I'd had a chance to recover. The warren of open rooms extended in all directions. I wandered down a hallway which looked rather less crowded, hoping for some peace. I suppose there was a part of me which hoped she would follow me, seek me out, strike up a conversation, and express her regrets.

I ambled through the galleries pretending to look at the

various pieces of art but truly trying to manage my thoughts and feelings. If she hadn't left us, perhaps my father would not have married himself to his gin bottle; perhaps I would not be left alone to manage my uncle and his illness and our firm and the troubled currents I must navigate.

At the end of a long vestibule, I saw her in a nearly empty gallery. She spoke animatedly with a man. Her new husband? She'd been but a paramour until my father's death, when she was freed to remarry. I did not know if she had. Her companion did not seem to respond to her with the enthusiasm she directed toward him.

Her sole piece of jewelry was a thin gold chain, and I became uncomfortably aware of the much richer jewel which graced my neck—hers. Her gown, upon focused inspection, looked quite thin and a bit dated. In spite of myself, I began to pity her just a little. Perhaps she was in dire straits? I recalled Marguerite's comment. *"Even the privileged have steep hills to climb."*

As I viewed her through the gallery, it struck me—I was also viewing her through the glass cases. She was an ornament—treasured but perhaps, judging by the man next to her, set aside to be dusted and shown off but on occasion?

I willed her to look at me, and she did. If she had indicated any friendliness, openness, or pleasure at seeing me, I would have approached her in the hope of a reconciliation. Instead, as she faced me and our gazes met once more, she glanced at my neck, scowled, and turned her back toward me definitively.

Had I not been dependent upon Charlotte to return me to my home, I would have fled. *I am no one's treasure.*

Someone cleared his throat behind me, and I turned.

"Oh, Mr. Herberts, Mrs. Herberts." I put on a calm false front. "Thank you for kindly inviting me this evening."

Mr. Herberts properly introduced me to his wife and then asked, "Your Mr. Clarkson has left you alone?"

"Oh, I'm certain he's nearby. Perhaps I should seek him out."

Mrs. Herberts tucked her arm in mine. "We shall escort you."

We wandered through the fine art gallery, and then Mrs. Herberts stopped at the ceramics room with its lovely display of Italian majolica.

"Look, dearest," she said to her husband. "Such that you love."

We passed an open room. "It's sparsely populated, as you can see. Lydney's armor would look very well in here," Mr. Herberts said in a voice best saved for wooing.

I was certain that it had been the armor, and not the porcelain or furniture or even fine art, that drew the museum trustees to Lord Lydney's collection. His pieces were vast and wide. *Lorica hamata* from the Roman legions. Steel-plated armor from the soldiers of medieval kings. Rare Japanese samurai cuirasses. The collection was invaluable, should someone choose to sell it, irreplaceable for display.

"It very well may," I said.

"The room would be named for Lydney," he said, "with a

prominent plaque thanking the highly recommended curation and care of Sheffield Brothers."

At that, my eyes widened. I hadn't expected that. All collectors, donors, and visitors would be made aware of our firm each time the collection was viewed.

"Would all of the pieces be on display?" I asked.

He laughed and shook his head. "Not permanently, of course. Many would be cataloged and stored—but available, should someone ask."

Buried in a storeroom? Where no one might ever view them? I wasn't certain what Lord Lydney, the deceased, might have thought of that.

"The armor would see plenty of light," he reassured.

We soon drew near where Mr. Clarkson spoke with Mr. Denholm, one of Mr. Clarkson's recent patrons, a friend of Harry's father, and the wealthy owner of a chain of chemist shops. Mr. and Mrs. Herberts left to tend to their other guests, hoping, I suspected, that I was sufficiently won over. I did think how wonderful it would be to see the Lydney Collection magnificently displayed among these other pieces and my family's name acknowledged and thanked.

I stood near, but not among, Mr. Clarkson and Mr. Denholm as they continued their discussion. Mr. Clarkson coughed and took a tiny nip from a paregoric bottle and then returned to the conversation. Shockingly, Mr. Denholm was speaking of how he had been sorting through donations to the museum and, on occasion, swapping a piece which had been donated with something from his own hoard.

I held my tongue, but my face must have expressed my utter disbelief. I could not believe that Lord Lydney would have agreed to have his collection donated to men who would rifle through it for their own profit and pleasure. He was a very possessive man.

"What is it, Miss Sheffield?" Mr. Denholm tried to cover his disdain with forced sweetness.

"Do the . . . do the benefactors know that this transpires?" I asked. "Or do they . . . well, have they expected that their donations remain with the museum?"

I had not invited trouble. This time, I'd been asked.

Still, I felt Mr. Clarkson's forewarning look.

"Our generous benefactors expect that we, the experts, will best know what to do with their donations," Mr. Denholm soothed. "And they trust us to do so. Unquestioningly. I exchanged something better for something lesser, which is in the best interests of the museum, is it not?"

Mr. Clarkson's face remained animated.

I nodded lightly—though I doubted either noticed—and began to walk toward the dining room in search of Charlotte and Mr. Schreiber, who would see me home.

If I were to assign the collection to the South Kensington, could some of the best Lydney treasures be diverted into private hands? Smothered in a forgotten attic at the museum itself? And yet, if I gave it all to Harry, there was no guarantee that he would not break up the collection and sell it after it became his. Once ownership was assigned, the new owner was free to do what he wished with it.

I was approached by many during the course of the evening, all of whom made me feel most welcome. Charlotte came up to me. Had she heard about my difficulties with Lord Parham? If she had, she did not say so.

Charlotte looked at those who had been paying court to me. "They are bees to the pollen, Miss Sheffield," she said, gesturing to a pretty ornament of a bee landing on a flower, nearby. "Bees to pollen."

"And yet," I replied, "once the pollen is yielded, there is no guarantee that the bees will pay court. Bees, after all, move on once satiated."

She smiled. "Wisely put."

During the carriage ride home, we talked about her new ambitions to transition from a personal to a professional collector, and how heartening I found that. "I desire a similar arrangement for myself," I said.

Her husband took her hand, and she teased, "In a marriage or a collecting partnership?"

"Both, I hope," I said. "But if not . . . perhaps alone?"

She dropped her husband's hand and laid her hand on my arm. "My dear. That is not yet possible. You do realize that whilst I may acquire and purchase, accept commissions and trades and all manner of other engagements, the payments must all be remitted to Mr. Schreiber. You cannot run Sheffield Brothers on your own. Now, that fine Mr. Clarkson has quite a keen eye, and he's been very busy tending to all the right people."

Indeed, he had been. I'd seen that for myself. He was

very good indeed at valuing and solicitous to my uncle and Orchie and me. He'd tended to our business as if it were his own. But as I closed my eyes and envisioned my future, I saw the rugged face of a man with earned care lines, smiling, as always, at me.

CHAPTER *Sixteen*

The following week, Mr. Clarkson and I were in the workshop when the morning post arrived. I shuffled through the letters, holding my breath lest more creditors arise like ghouls from an autumn swamp. I turned over a thick, official-looking correspondence.

I turned. "Mr. Clarkson, there is a letter for you here." He did not normally receive mail at Sheffield Brothers.

He looked surprised but took the envelope from me and returned to his desk. I turned back to our post and noticed there was a letter from our landlord reminding me that not only was December's rent due very shortly, but a portion of the amount we needed to make up was quickly coming due.

I hadn't forgotten. The coal bill was due too. I would review the accounts shortly and ascertain if we had enough to cover them all; with the sale of the jewelry, I hoped that we did.

"Miss Sheffield!" Clarkson stood and waved the letter in the air like a victory flag. "It's a letter suggesting I apply for membership to the Burlington Fine Arts Club!"

Relief flooded through me. "I'm delighted. I'm delighted!"

He read the letter. "Your name was not mentioned. Could someone have sent you an encouraging note?"

I shuffled through the post again; there was not much there. "No."

"Perhaps tomorrow," he replied, a little more subdued. "I'm certain we'll both be invited. Or . . . you could just apply?"

"Only once I'm certain I'd be accepted," I said.

He nodded, but uncertainly.

Saturday evening at dinner, Mr. Clarkson shared his good news with Uncle Lewis.

"Eleanor?" my uncle asked me.

"Not yet," I said quietly. "Or perhaps not at all."

"That bad business with Parham," he muttered. "I told you it was fatal."

"Thank you for your encouraging words."

"People are afraid to go against the powerful. You need a protector."

I said nothing. No one powerful seemed to be willing to stand up to Lord Parham for me. I did not have a protector.

We finished our meal in silence, and I stood. "If you'll excuse me, gentlemen."

"But wait," Orchie said as I was about to leave the dining room. "Something arrived for you in this afternoon's post."

The invitation to the Burlington? Perhaps some clerical error had delayed its delivery. My heart raced.

Orchie handed a letter to me, and I left to read it in my room. Once there, I turned up the lamp and could see the distinctive seal on the back of the envelope. It was from Harry. A blend of joy and dread, excitement and fear coursed through me.

Dearest Ellie,

I shall be in London soon and will hold you to your promise to allow me to call whilst I am there. I have some matters to attend to, regarding both my father's estate and some matters with the horses, of course. I should enjoy seeing you at your convenience. I've been invited to a dinner and showing at Dante Rossetti's house on Cheyne Walk. I know how you enjoy his art. Would you like to attend? Skating, first, a night or two before? I can send round the exact details, if it all appeals.

I await your acceptance.

I miss you.

Yours,
Harry

On Monday, I would reply in the affirmative. Then I would ask him, face-to-face, about Signorina Viero.

Sunday morning, icy misery sluiced from the sky. I wrapped my cloak tightly round me and indulged in a hansom cab.

My uncle was unwell, so I walked alone into the church as the organ played; friends nodded a greeting, and I nodded back. It seemed to me that though the Lord had promised to be with us, ever, always, his Spirit was perhaps concentrated in church, where so many like-minded were gathered in a small space. The amber candles shone through the morning's darkness, scenting the air with honey from the hives from which the wax had been harvested. *Provenance.*

I entered the pew where we normally sat and closed the door behind me as the order of service began.

The greeting. A prayer of preparation. A prayer of penitence. *I'm sorry that I spend much time allowing myself to be filled with anxiety and wondering what purpose you are working. Your ways are higher than my ways. Please forgive me.*

A Scripture reading. The liturgy of the Word.

"This is the Word of the Lord," the Reverend Hill spoke loudly.

"Thanks be to God," we responded.

Prayers of intercession. *Jeanette and the other women at the prison. Uncle. Orchie. Marguerite. Charlotte. Alice.* More difficult: *Harry. Mr. Clarkson. Mr. and Mrs. Herberts. Lord*

Audley. I held my breath before reluctantly moving forward strictly in obedience. *Mama. Signorina Viero.*

The liturgy of the sacrament. I awaited my turn to stand and move forward to receive Communion. I moved down the aisle and approached the rail. As I knelt beside the others, I held my hands open one over the other in a cruciform to receive the bread.

"The body of Christ, the bread of heaven." He placed the bread in my hands.

"Amen," I whispered and ate of it.

The chalice bearer next approached. "The blood of Christ, the cup of salvation."

I guided the chalice toward my lips and sipped. "Amen."

As I rose to leave, I clearly heard, "I am here."

I turned to see who had spoken. No one looked back at me.

I looked up at the cross hanging above the altar. Once more I heard it, this time quietly, in my heart. *I am here.*

Tears welled. He'd heard my plea and answered me, reassuringly, once more.

Thank you for speaking to me, Lord. Please, do not stop, for I sense my trials are far from over.

That week I indulged in what I felt was a second necessary extravagance, a hired carriage for several hours. First, I took the carriage back to the pawnshop in Whitechapel. Before I alighted from the carriage, I held the beautiful gold-and-pearl set in my hand and tried to imagine my father fastening the heavy necklace around the neck of my mother, who must have loved him on that day, their wedding day, surely? She loved all things that glittered, and he'd loved her.

I squeezed back the tide of melancholy threatening to drag my heart under. I had loved her.

How had it gone wrong?

There was, I now knew, no chance of her wanting it, or me, back. I opened the door and strode in.

The shop's owner evaluated the set with a rather colder eye than I just had and gave me a handsome sum. He looked approvingly at the carriage tarrying for me outside.

"I'll see you soon," he called after me, hopefully.

I did not tell him that I had no more jewelry to sell.

I tucked the money deep within my gown's inner pocket and then instructed the driver to take me to the prison.

"Yer old man in there, eh?"

I didn't answer. Whether he meant my father or my husband, I didn't care for him to know that I had neither. I paid him to wait for me while I made my visit.

My boot heels echoed sharply through the long, stony corridors. There was little joy to be found within, and with a deathwatch of cold blowing through the building, the prisoners burrowed into wherever they could to keep warm. The closer Christmas came, the more likely they were to sink into the slough of despond, as Bunyan had written, missing gifts, family, friends, and even Christmas pudding. Who could blame them?

Jeanette waited for me in the usual area; it was she alone.

"Th' others are not well," she said. "Old Rosie died this week. Cholera."

Old Rosie had not been as old as Mrs. Orchard.

"I'm sorry."

"I am too." She held her hands out. "They're a bit better, as you can see. I've a friend who's been able to trade something for the tallow candle nubs, and she lets me rub it in."

I smiled encouragingly, but the flesh on her hands looked as torn up as ever. The bones were bent in awkward and unexpected configurations from rheumatoid arthritis. "Last month when I was here," I said, "I noticed a young woman, perhaps eighteen years of age, who was newly admitted." I explained which cell I'd seen her placed in.

"Oh yes, that'd be lil' Nancy," she replied. "She never comes out of her cell unless she's ordered to. We've tried, miss; we really have."

"Why doesn't she come out?"

"Sadness. And fear. Fear'll do that to you in here, then. You start thinking people don't like you or they're coming for you."

"Do they?" I whispered. "Come for you?"

She nodded. "Sometimes. We've got old Mistress Hopkins who helps keep them away. When she can. We make a ring around the new ones, try ta help who are most likely to get it."

I dared not ask, *"Get what?"*

"She reads, though."

"Mistress Hopkins?"

Jeanette cackled. "I think not. Lil' Nancy."

"Maybe if I brought a book next time, you could ask her if she'd like to meet with us?"

"Oh yes," Jeanette said. "Maybe that'd break her out of her fright."

We talked about her children, who had been allowed a brief visit and two of whom had come, and she asked about my family and my work. Then we prayed together, about my troubles and hers, and bid our good-byes. As I made my way to the carriage, I asked the Lord for a special financial provision of some kind to buy gloves for the ladies.

On the way home I thought how badly I did not want to be imprisoned. I thought of my overwhelming debt and laughed to near sobs. The carriage driver looked back at me with alarm.

I regained my calm. My strength. I believed the sale of the jewelry would provide enough to clear our debts, and then the New Year would surely bring further commissions. Mr. Clarkson had been currying favor to ensure that happened, as had I.

When I returned home, there was a card from Charlotte. "She came by calling hours," Orchie said, smiling. "I didn't tell her that except for Mrs. Newsome, who's practically family, we don't have callers. When I told her you were at the prison, she said you should feel free to call upon her tomorrow, if you like."

I embraced Orchie, and she shrugged me off as if she were

uncomfortable, but I could see in her face that she loved it. She was almost family too. I must do what I could to help us all. I could not see her in the workhouse, dying of cholera as many had this past year.

Perhaps Charlotte had come by with good news.

The moment Charlotte greeted me in her parlor, I knew she did not have good news to share with me. Her face was kindly, as always, but not filled with the exuberant joy I'd seen in it before.

I wondered if we'd ever dine together in the Green Dining Room that Mr. Morris was going to design.

Her parlor was lovely—frosted lamp shades, and those lamps blazed brightly against the dark assault to the spirit that was deep winter. Her maid brought out tea—Earl Grey—and biscuits.

It had been so long since we'd had the margin for Mrs. Orchard to make biscuits that I rather overindulged myself. Or perhaps I just enjoyed their sweetness to counterbalance the bitterness I suspected my friend was about to deliver.

Surprisingly, Charlotte did not deliver bitter news. "I have a few objects upon which I would enjoy your opinion."

I knew she did not require my opinion on anything. I determined at that moment that I would live in forthright honesty and not fear, as I had promised the Lord in my prayer. "A test?"

She smiled; I did not think she was offended by my direct

statement. "We, as admirers of art, are not afraid to test items, are we, Miss Sheffield?" She picked up a figurine and knocked it, gently, against her teeth. It would, quite likely, have been a most peculiar sight to those who did not understand that teeth will tell the truth even when the mouth lies. If one knocked a piece of porcelain against one's teeth, it was easy to tell if it had been restored or not. Originals would feel firm and bony; those parts which had been restored would be slightly sticky to the tooth touch.

She continued, "We should not, therefore, be afraid of testing others—or of being tested ourselves. It is only by testing, or being tested, that we understand whether the substance or the person is as it appears to be or is merely masquerading."

She took my arm in hers, and we walked to her husband's study. "I agree," I said. "I thought that our time at Lord Parham's, with the notebook and parade of items shown to those being newly considered, was a test of some sort, though it had been presented as an amusement?"

"Ah, yes." She let go of my hand in front of a small writing desk. "Lord Parham. Apparently he had some questions about your evaluations, and if you had perhaps been looking over the shoulder of someone else marking notes."

"He suspects me of cheating?" I was suddenly more sympathetic to Alice.

"He was not so direct, but it was understood that his concerns could jeopardize any request for membership which you may present." She turned to face me. "And, perhaps more ominous, Miss Sheffield, he directed doubt toward your firm's reliability."

I understood. He sought to derail me.

"No one has asked me to do this, but I believe you to be as capable as you appear. So, Eleanor, what do you say about this French writing desk?"

I looked it over carefully, not wanting to rush as I had with Mr. Herberts's coins, but also wondering if she wanted the truth or, like Lord Parham, a honeyed misdirection. "I do not think it is French," I finally said. "We English prefer oak, but the French find it rustic—unless it is bur oak—preferring walnut or rosewood instead." I had looked the piece over. "Sunlight and wear seem to have aged it uniformly. Except here." I pointed to the drawer. "A new wood. Married, badly, to the old."

She smiled. "Yes, that is exactly how I would have put it." She took my arm again in a most friendly way, and we returned to her parlor.

"Just last week, someone brought this piece of Derby ware to me. What do you say about it?"

I gasped. "Lovely!" I turned it over. "Early 1770s. The anchor and the overlinked *D* for Derby tell me everything."

Charlotte smiled again and indicated I should take a seat. Her maid freshened our tea and biscuits. "The maker's mark will tell us everything we need to know about a piece, won't it, Eleanor? If it's genuine."

I agreed with her. When our calling hour was up, she took my hand once more and said, "Do not despair."

Is she the powerful person I need to see my way through?

"The club will not meet over Christmas, of course. But in February, after you've made your decision about the Lydney Collection . . ." She let the sentence dangle. "And it will be held at Mr. Denholm's house in March. I understand he is quite close to your Mr. Clarkson and greatly admires you as well. Perhaps that would be the time to apply for membership."

I tilted my head. Was she in favor of my donating the Lydney Collection to the museum? That would be sensible; after all, she was a great supporter. But she did not seem to be the kind of person whose affections could be bought.

Maybe. I just did not know.

CHAPTER Seventeen

One day shortly after, Mr. Clarkson and I were in the workshop; I repaired broken porcelain which had belonged to a client's mother, and he sent out correspondence to people he had met at the Burlington in hopes of garnering more commissions.

The door to the storefront opened, and he stood up. "I'll see who it is." I remained hunched over my work. Within a minute he returned. "They'd like to speak with you, Miss Sheffield."

Without asking who *they* were, I knew instinctively. Debt collectors.

I went to the storefront, and Mr. Clarkson followed me.

I could hardly dismiss him; this was business property, and they had called here rather than at my house. Perhaps he wished to ensure that I was not left alone with them, and for that, I was grateful.

A constable again. Two men in black overcoats, collars turned up against the muck and wet they had ushered in with them and which had fouled my floor.

"Miss Sheffield?"

"Yes. And you are . . . ?"

"We're here on behalf of Mr. Christopher Dodd. He requests his funds be remitted immediately."

"Mr. Dodd . . ." My mind raced to place the name.

Mr. Clarkson came up behind me and spoke softly. "The Sèvres porcelain platters for Lord Canterwood. We purchased them from Dodd and delivered them to his lordship. Was Mr. Dodd paid? According to these men, no."

What had happened with the money paid for the platters? I shook my head. I did not know. I turned back to the men in front of me. "May I have a few days to investigate this? Please, leave your card, and I'll see to it that your monies are remitted in full."

They agreed, with a quiet, gentlemanly threat to return if the funds were not received within a fortnight.

After they left, Mr. Clarkson turned toward me. "Did you know about this?"

"No. But I shall speak with my uncle about it."

"He probably won't remember," Clarkson said. His voice was cool and casual, and it startled me. Was he unfeeling toward my uncle? Or was there perhaps something else amiss?

"We won't get others to sell to us on behalf of those who would commission us if this becomes common knowledge." He spoke like a man with experience.

"I know." I returned to the house and sought Orchie. "Do you know if my uncle might have squirreled away money?" Because if it was not in the bank, where had it gone?

She shook her head. "Oh no. There's no money stashed."

"I need you to look carefully. In his room. I cannot do it, but you can under the auspices of cleaning."

She agreed, and in the meantime, I unlocked my father's bedroom door and then his curiosity cabinet. I plucked his watch from it and then locked the cabinet again. It was the partner watch to the one which had been stolen from Uncle Lewis. "I'm sorry," I whispered. "But I must do this to save us all."

Orchie came back. "I found no money in his room. I searched everywhere."

I brought the watch to Mr. Clarkson. "Would you know of anyone who may be interested? With the remittance, I could pay Mr. Dodd."

He considered my request and then said, "I would. Leave it to me. And . . . I heard you called on Lady Charlotte Schreiber."

I nodded slowly, questioningly.

"Some members of the Burlington mentioned it to me. They know we are close. . . ."

I caught my breath.

"We do work together," he amended.

"Yes, that is true."

"Was the visit successful?" He put down the pincers with which he had been adjusting the balance wheel of a pocket watch.

"I believe so," I said. "She asked me to identify some Derby ware, and I did. She had me look at a writing desk, which I knew was not French, and I pointed out the mismatched wood which was badly married."

He looked up at me. "It's never good when things—or people—are badly married. Your wood—was one refined and one common?" He held my gaze. "One old, one new?"

One aristocratic, one middle class? I felt he was referencing Harry and his title and me and my middle-class status. I did not look away. "Perhaps. In any case, I had the idea that she found my answers satisfactory, and she reassured me that there may be another opportunity to join the club soon."

He rested his hand on my arm, lightly, but for a moment. "I fervently hope so. But if not, I am ready to be a formidable presence for us . . . for Sheffield Brothers, I mean."

"After all," he'd left unsaid, *"we are both middle class."*

"Thank you, Mr. Clarkson." I hoped my voice reflected my genuine gratitude.

Then he lifted a letter toward me. "Mr. Denholm has asked me to secure ancient Egyptian artifacts for him. He's asked me personally, but I wonder, in light of the situation that the company finds itself in, if you'd prefer that the commission go directly to Sheffield Brothers?"

I sat down for a moment. I'd had no idea that Mr. Clarkson was accepting commissions outside of the firm, but I supposed that must be all right because Clarkson himself had connected with Denholm long ago. He had not been a Sheffield client first. We did need Mr. Clarkson and his abilities as much as he needed us and our name and reputation—both of which seemed to be under review.

"You may do whatever you prefer. It's completely at your discretion."

"I think it would be quite enjoyable for us to locate such a treasure together," he said. "You and I. Would that appeal?"

I heard the implicit arrangement in his suggestion. We would work together. Nothing more. Not yet, anyway. "I would find sourcing the items together quite satisfactory," I agreed.

"Splendid. I shall inform Mr. Denholm that you and I will find him something unquestionably old and rare and deliver it forthwith. Then I'll send a note by messenger to one or two people I think might be able to help us."

"Thank you," I said. "I shall look forward to it." I loved the hunt and the chase and the satisfying feeling of providing to our clients something rare and beyond their expectations. And the story, of course.

Mr. Clarkson was certainly qualified to partner with me, and I with him.

He'd done well caring for our business. And my uncle. And perhaps me.

As I gently packed the china for the next day, I looked up at the shelf with Lady Lydney's pelican. I would complete the repair on it soon.

For my outing with Harry, I would dress with care, as had become my pleasant habit, at Marguerite's urging.

Alice knocked at my bedroom door. "I took a extra hour or two with your white dress. No spots now, and I took one a your uncle's razors to remove any of the little nibs poking out on your cloak. See?" She ran her hand down the cloak like a mother might run her hand down a child's dress, to smooth it.

"It looks beautiful, Alice. Thank you so much."

"'Twas a wise choice. With your reddish-brown hair and all, resting against the white, why, he won't be able to resist you!"

"How did you know I was planning to wear this for an evening out?" I teased. Eager anticipation heated my face, and I knew my eyes must be shining with expectation, too.

"I have someone I'm sweet on," she said. "I understand."

She handed my white fur muff to me. Mrs. Orchard had buffed my ice skates, as it had been a year or more since I'd worn them.

Alice left for the evening, and Orchie served Uncle Lewis a tray in his room. I declined to eat. My stomach was fluttery, not only in anticipation of our evening together but because of the question I knew I must pose. I must ask Harry about the signorina.

I sat in the parlor, the lamps turned just slightly lower but with plenty of coal for once, as my mother's necklace had fetched a bit of relief. I looked up at the clock.

Five minutes late. That was fine. The extra time would allow me to quieten myself a bit, regain my composure.

Five more minutes passed, and he had not arrived. I picked up a lady's magazine and began to page through it. There were ideas for Christmas celebrations and advertisements for sewing notions and the very best advice for keeping help, but I was distracted, of course. I could not remember a line I'd read only moments after I'd read it because, while my eyes might be following the sentences, my mind was elsewhere.

Fifteen minutes overdue. I set my cloak and my muff aside. Perspiration trickled down my arms, and I repented of having put so much coal on the burner, so I turned it down. My enthusiasm snuffed.

Orchie looked into the room. "You all right, then?"

I shrugged, and she left, her mouth set.

I pulled my watch out and compared it to the time on the parlor clock. Yes, it was exact.

When he was thirty minutes late, I turned the lamp down, the coal burner off, and returned to my room.

He'd forgotten me. Again.

Piece by piece, I unwrapped myself and hung the clothing with care in the wardrobe. I did not want to undo Alice's careful work. I weighed my heart: it was real; it was chipped with wear; it was heavy. I opened the tiny drawer in my curiosity cabinet and lifted out the Adore ring. Then I returned it. I did not take off my mustard seed necklace, for it implied fidelity to and from the Lord, who, despite my questioning in pain, I still believed would prove true.

Nearly thirty minutes later, Orchie knocked on my door. "Miss Eleanor?"

"Yes?" I tried to force cheer into my voice, but I feared I failed.

"Lord Lydney has arrived and conveys 'is most sincere apologies; the late hour was out of his hands. He would very much like to speak with you."

Of course he would.

"Please inform the baron that I had been looking forward to accompanying him at the appointed time but am indisposed at present."

Silence. "You are certain? I . . . I quite like him, miss. It's only been an hour, and I believe him."

"I am certain," I replied firmly.

"Very well, then." She wandered down the hallway and the stairs, and I could hear her voice and then Harry's in return before she firmly shut the door.

The door should, perhaps, remain firmly shut.

"Give the collection to the museum," a voice seemed to whisper from my shoulder. But was it the angel of righteousness guiding me or the angel of iniquity offering up a cold dish of revenge?

CHAPTER
Eighteen

The following morning Uncle worked with us—a rare occasion, and it should have brightened my mood to see him happily looking at silver with his inspection glass and making precise evaluations of a difficult piece.

Yet my mood was not brightened. It felt positively funereal.

Orchie knocked on the door about ten o'clock. "Miss Eleanor, if you don't mind, I'd be most obliged of your presence in the house for a moment." She looked awkwardly at Mr. Clarkson, who smiled at her in return.

He waved in a manner of giving permission, which did not settle well with me. I wiped the glaze from my hands and followed Orchie to the house.

Not another debt collector. Please!

In the parlor stood a man holding a large case. "Miss Sheffield?"

"Yes?" My voice wavered.

"I am here at the request of Lord Lydney. If I may?" He first handed a note to me—it was sealed with Harry's wax and seal and begged my forgiveness, then requested the opportunity to explain in person.

I folded the note, and the man opened the case and stood it up on its side. Inside hung twelve silver pocket watches, each on a silver chain. I drew near to them and looked closely. The first was set at one o'clock, the second at two o'clock, the third at three o'clock, and so on all the way till twelve o'clock.

"His lordship requests you select one of these, which I will return to him, as a manner of informing him of the exact time you would be willing to accompany him to ice-skate at Hyde Park today, and he reassures he will be prompt. If you decline to send a watch back, he will understand." The man smiled and winked at me. "But I won't. I'll lose my commission."

Alice had come behind Orchie, and the two of them clapped with delight.

"Do it, Miss Sheffield," Alice said. "Remember all my hard work!"

"And me, polishing the skating shoes," Orchie added.

I walked toward the watch seller. "I could not see an honest man be put out of his commission."

I lifted the watch which indicated seven o'clock and handed it to the man, who tipped his hat and hurriedly began to close his case. "Said there was something extra in it for me if I got back within an hour."

The three of us burst out laughing.

I shouldn't have been as enthusiastic as I was. Maybe it was just because Orchie and Alice were so enthusiastic for me. I needed to ask Harry about the signorina in any case, so I would go.

Later, I dressed with care once more and plucked my white fur cap from my wardrobe. At half past six, I looked out the front window and saw Harry's carriage waiting. I would not rush. At five minutes before seven, I heard the door open and Mrs. Orchard show him in. I could not hear what she said, but her tone was more like a birdsong than a pug's grumble, and my heart followed suit.

I met him in the parlor.

"Ellie." He glanced at Mrs. Orchard. "Er, Miss Sheffield. Please accept my apology, and I'm very thankful for your gracious willingness to visit the skating rink this evening." He kept his language formal in front of Orchie, whom he always treated with as much respect as he'd have treated a mother, which tickled me.

"The pleasure is mine." I hoped I did not let on how pleased I was to be there with him, but Orchie's eyes told me that I looked as happy as I felt.

He took my arm and walked me to the carriage; the walk to the street was slippery with ice and packed snow.

He instructed the driver to take us to Hyde Park and then explained, "I had planned for another couple to accompany us yesterday evening—a friend of mine and his wife. When she took suddenly ill, I was left trying to find someone else to chaperone. I could not, and then I was too late. I tried to reach your friend Mrs. Newsome for this evening but could not. I was most concerned that you would think I had not taken your situation into consideration—that you would prefer to be seen not alone with me, but in the company of a chaperone as you often are, with Mrs. Newsome. Failing to secure anyone—I admit that I do not know many ladies' chaperones, or any, really—I hope that you are comfortable accompanying me alone?"

I did hesitate for a moment, wondering what others should think. I was not, strictly speaking, of the class of ladies who must be chaperoned each moment, but I appreciated now that his tardiness the night before had been due to care for my reputation. "I think as we are old family friends, it will be acceptable," I answered.

He flinched when I called us friends. Yet for the moment, that's what we were.

"I'm glad our friendship can be salvaged from the difficulties of the year," he responded quietly.

Then I flinched. It was not what I wanted either. Perhaps it was all that remained.

We made awkward talk until we reached the park, and I noted that his tone of voice was as gentle as ever but perhaps not as beseeching as it had been in months past.

There were others skating, of course; it was a festive event when the rink was lit up with torches.

Harry took my hand and led me out. "I came earlier. To make sure the ice was thick enough and firm."

I warmed. "What a thoughtful and protective gesture."

"I told you, I take care of . . . ," he began but did not finish saying *my own*.

He held my hand and kept me at arm's length for some time as we skated side by side. Although my ankles wobbled for a moment, they soon remembered what to do.

"Do you remember when we first came here?" he asked me.

"Yes," I laughed. "Awkward as fawns."

He laughed with me. "You were never an awkward fawn. I, on the other hand . . ."

He switched from holding my hand to linking our arms—a bit closer. He did not miss a step as he did so and steered me smoothly up the Serpentine.

"You are not awkward in any way," I said. "Not anymore."

He grinned at me as he had when I first fell in love with him, and I nearly stumbled.

Best say it now, I thought, *before you lose your nerve.*

"Harry, Mrs. Newsome learned something rather disturbing when we were last at Watchfield."

He looked intently at me. "What was that?"

I took a deep breath, and as I blew it out, a whorl of mist curled into the coolness between us. "She'd heard that you and the signorina were married in Italy."

He came to a smooth stop. "Shall we take a seat?"

I agreed, and he led us to one of the benches nearby.

"We were not married," he began, "but in Italy, we told people that we were. It was a chaotic time; war efforts were under way, and people did not know whom to trust and whom not to trust. Viero asked me if I could take his family treasures, his sister, and his mother out of the country till things were settled. He was in a hurry—there were people after him for his efforts too."

I nodded. Harry had told me so before, and I'd believed him.

"There was no time for papers, which were not strictly required but would make it much easier to take the signorina and her mother. Under my father's diplomatic immunity—ambassador to Austria, no less—they would travel with relative ease. So we told people we were married. But we were not."

My face must have reflected my misery. He continued to try to reassure me.

"We have not been introduced in England as husband and wife. She does not travel with me. We have not entertained. We are not . . . close. There was no need to tell you because there is no charade now, in England."

"I'm inclined to believe you," I said but then thought, *All people want to believe what they wish to believe.*

"You must believe me."

I could not bring myself to say, *I do.* "It's just that you were so late." *And your father insisted the reason you were late is because you preferred to stay in Austria with Francesca, till you learned he was dying and would leave stewardship of the collection in my hands. You would, of course, keep up* that *charade, till it was all yours once more.*

He looked down at his hands and then up at me once more. "Last year, this year, last night . . . I know. As much as I try, it always seems I'm never what the people whom I care for need me to be: Father. Brother. You."

A hush of snowflakes sifted over and around us, providing a gentle lace veil which encircled our intimacy.

"I spoke with Dr. Garrett about Arthur," I said. "She affirmed that there is but little one can do when the lungs enter a deadly spasm. Even if you'd returned with the doctor earlier, it is unlikely Arthur would have lived."

He looked at me wonderingly, then spoke, his voice gruff with emotion. "You asked her that, just recently, on my behalf?"

I nodded, and he gently pulled both my hands from the muff and enveloped them in his own. "Thank you, Ellie. I rode as fast as I could. I returned with him at all possible speed." He blinked twice, thrice. Was he blinking away tears? I had never seen him cry.

"Be at peace."

He circled his finger around one of mine, the one on which he had once slipped the Adore ring. "Where . . . ?"

"Put away. The amethyst fell out, and I could not find it." I offered a weak excuse. "I didn't want the other stones to fall out and be lost too." He knew me well enough that he could guess I spoke a half truth.

He tightened his finger around mine once more, and my hand clasped reflexively over his. He held my gaze for a moment, and I was quite light-headed. When he bent toward me, I thought he was going to kiss me, but he didn't. "Will you attend the dinner at Rossetti's with me tomorrow evening?" he asked. "You will not be looked down upon for not bringing a chaperone."

I would imagine not. Mr. Rossetti's crowd was quite progressive.

"I'd be delighted. I'm curious what Mr. Rossetti's collection might contain. He's quite notorious . . . and purchases often."

"I know." He lifted me to my feet and set my muff on the bench, which surprised me. "That's why I thought you might like to attend. You and your collections." He lightly touched my nose. "I would like my family's collection to remain at Watchfield—for me and especially my family. But no matter what you determine to be the fate of my family treasures, Ellie, it will not change my affections for you. Nothing ever has, and nothing ever will."

"Thank you," I said softly. "I needed to hear that."

"But I've decided I must be done striving. I cannot spend my life trying to prove myself to my father, to your father . . . to you. That striving led me to make decisions which, although helpful to others, did not lead to good turns of circumstance and robbed me of my peace. I must be true to who I am and hope that is enough."

I nodded. This, then, was the cause of his more confident

tone. He led me back to the rink, which had become more open as others had fled the snow and cold. The torches were still lit, though, casting an amber glow over the ice.

Harry drew me near him as though we were dancing, and in some ways, it was more intimate than dancing. He could take me in his arms for an extended period and was not expected to hand me off to another partner.

There was no music but that which played in my head. The wind picked up, and instinctively I nestled closer to him. In response, he pulled me in. Perhaps ten minutes later, I started to shiver.

"Although I am reluctant to do so, I must return you home. It's grown too cold."

His driver was ready for us and had kept a small coal brazier going so our feet would be warm.

We said little on the way to my house, but this time, it was not due to awkwardness. Neither of us wanted to break the circle of intimacy.

CHAPTER
Nineteen

Harry's driver pulled up in front of Queen's House, 16 Cheyne Walk, the home Mr. Rossetti had lived in for some years. Harry stepped out first and then helped me from the carriage. I wore the amber gown Marguerite had lent me and that I'd worn to the South Kensington benefit dinner. I hoped none of the others should remember it, had they been in attendance.

As we approached the door, the distant church bells quieted but were replaced by a strange noise: a trilling caw followed by staccato cries. I looked at Harry.

"Rossetti keeps peacocks." He smiled wryly.

"In his home?" I asked in wonderment.

"During the colder months, yes."

I nodded. I'd heard that artists were peculiar. I'd not had a chance to meet many of them.

Once through the door, the peculiarity continued. The foyer was a hodgepodge of cultures—Chinese lanterns set atop what appeared to be an expensive Italian leather cello case. Delicate Persian rugs overlaid with worn bearskin. Some walls were crammed with random knickknacks, others bare but for costly paintings, some of which were Rossetti's own. Two hedgehogs in a cage looked up at me with as much astonishment as I felt looking down at them.

I glanced at Harry, and he winked.

Daringly, I winked back, and he blushed just a little.

The colors Rossetti painted with were rich but always dappled with light. His subjects reclined in languor among what seemed to be easy riches—always women, always otherworldly. Harry led me to the main reception room, where Mr. Rossetti stood with one of those otherworldly-looking women.

"Miss Eleanor Sheffield, Mr. Gabriel Dante Rossetti."

"Miss Sheffield." Rossetti took my hand.

Harry asked if he might leave my side for a moment to speak with another friend, or would I like to come with him. I preferred to speak with Mr. Rossetti, so he left me to the polite felicitations of our host.

"How did you and Lord Lydney meet?" I opened the conversation.

"My father and mother, as you may know, were born in

Italy," he said. "They were forced to flee because of their support for Italian national unification. Naturally, that cause remained close to my heart, and Lord Lydney and I often socialize in the same circles. We both know Garibaldi and the Vieros, of course."

"Stefano."

"And the beautiful Francesca," Rossetti added. "Whom I've just met for the first time. Would that she'd let me paint her."

My ears tingled. "Recently? You met her recently?"

"Yes. At Watchfield House," he said. "It was a pleasant gathering—many British and many Italians. Good fortune for our lovely Francesca that Lydney was there to protect her. Some rather threatening men, opposed to the unification in defense of the pope, attended too. They have a long reach, even in England." He shrugged. "Enough of Italy." After caressing the cheek of the dark brunette by his side, he took my hand in his own. "I would like you to see some of my collection. Perhaps, then, when you understand the kind of eccentricities I most appreciate, you might keep an eye out for anything I'd enjoy?"

Oh yes. I would love for Sheffield Brothers to undertake him as a client. But I could not shake from my mind the vision of Harry protecting Francesca.

We walked into the room where a string quartet played and a somber young man sat at a dilapidated pianoforte. On top of it was a lamp with a Venetian glass shade of unimaginable worth. My instinct was to run to it and secure it somehow so the young man pounding on the keys didn't cause it to tumble to the floor. Alas, I suspected that gesture would be misunderstood.

I heard a scuffling noise at my feet and looked in amazement as a squirrel ran by.

"Did you . . . ?" I asked Mr. Rossetti.

"A member of the family," he said.

Room after room held beautifully painted panels, Russian Orthodox icons, and especially, given the Italian birthplace of Rossetti's parents, Roman and Venetian works in porcelain, paint, and pottery.

"This is all truly beautiful. If I find an appropriately named madness of marmots, I shall immediately know with whom they should be settled," I teased. "But where are your paintings, Mr. Rossetti? I am most eager to see them close up, having admired your talent from afar."

He laughed. "Come, Miss Sheffield. I will show you something not many in the house have seen." We went up a dark stairwell, guided by his small lamp, and as we ascended, I heard peacocks screaming on the lower level while music entirely too somber for a gentle evening with friends played on the first floor. Rossetti led the way, pulling me behind him. Was it quite safe to follow him, alone?

At the top of the stairway, Rossetti unlocked a door. The room was dark; the roof had been partially replaced with window glass, so on a bright day the sun could stream in from all angles. This night, though, the glass was smothered with drifts of snow, and the only light came from the dim lamps which sputtered even as Rossetti tried to raise the light level.

The room was filled with paintings on easels, some nearly complete, some skeletal sketches. In the corner, an unfinished painting reposed, and Rossetti led me to it.

The painting was of a woman at her dressing table, long tresses of hair like endless ocean ripples spilling in front of her, caught in a comb whilst she stared into the distance. Her dressing gown slipped from shoulders as milky white as the roses behind her. He'd labeled it *Lilith* with a piece of paper propped against it. I looked once more at her dressing table. The pink-and-gold perfume bottle looked familiar to me. Where had I seen it before?

"The painting glows with a life of its own. I could almost enter the woman's reverie."

"Do you think this painting will be worth its commission?" Rossetti pressed, a tint of urgency in his voice.

"I do not doubt that this will be highly sought after. The talent is undeniable."

On the way out of the room, I noticed a second painting which was nearly complete. "May I?" I asked.

He nodded his approval. "*A Christmas Carol*," he said. "I've named my artistic interpretation after the sung custom, as Dickens himself did."

"The model is not someone I recognize from your other work."

His face flushed with pleasure. "I'm delighted that you

know of my work. Her name is Miss Ellen Smith. She's a laundress."

I smiled and thought of my own dear Alice. In the painting, Miss Ellen Smith played a costly golden instrument.

"Thank you, Mr. Rossetti. Seeing your art is an early Christmas gift."

He took my hand in his own and kissed the back of it. "Should you find yourself in need of a situation, I should love to paint you. That beautiful auburn hair . . ." He reached a hand up as if he were about to take one of my locks in it, and I stepped away. Still, a compliment, honestly given and graciously received, is one of life's small, unrestricted pleasures. I was happy to have been both offerer and recipient with Mr. Rossetti.

Of a sudden, I remembered what had bothered me and returned to the painting of the lady at her dressing table. "This pink perfume bottle. It looks familiar. I do believe I have seen it before." I knew I had. It had originally rested on her gilt dressing table and then later been stored near Lady Lydney's porcelain pieces with a few other pieces of exquisite glass. It being a perfume bottle—like my own mother's—and glass meant it had made an impression on me which I now recalled.

His smile cooled to wary. "It belonged to Lady Lydney."

"Has it . . . ?" I must ask. "Has it been sold to you?"

"No, no, of course not. It was loaned to me by my friend Lord Lydney. I have already returned the item in question."

I exhaled relief. Harry was not selling off items from the collection—at least as far as I could see.

We turned toward the doorway. Harry stood there; he'd come looking for me. By the look on his face, it was clear he'd overheard our conversation. "I believe my mother would have enjoyed seeing her items in the portrait," he said rather pointedly. "And her perfume bottle was not a part of the collection."

I blushed. He knew I'd been questioning him. And yet—was that not my charge? "It was kept with a few other glassworks in the pink room," I said with assurance. "And marked on the inventory, so I was not aware that it was a personal item. But I am glad I have asked because now there is no doubt."

Harry graciously acquiesced. His irritation melted away, and my defensiveness softened as we made our way downstairs. Dinner was served, and I did find the conversation enlightening; I was seated next to Mr. Murray Marks, who had a firm which competed, in a friendly manner, with Sheffield Brothers. He and his wife were delightful, and I thought strengthening that collegial connection could not hurt.

He was a member of the Burlington Fine Arts Club.

As we made pleasant conversation throughout the meal, my mind was teased back to the *Christmas Carol* painting Rossetti had shown me. After the meal, the ladies rose to make their way to the parlor for tea and the gentlemen to the smoking room. As we stood, I was delighted to find one other person in attendance whom I knew.

"Lord Audley." How strange it was that I should be comforted by his presence—only in this unusual atmosphere.

"Miss Sheffield. I'm amused that Lord Lydney has brought you to this rather raucous gathering."

"There are many treasures herein." I felt the need to defend Harry whilst he spoke with someone across the room.

As soon as Audley moved away, I slipped back toward the dark stairway. This time, I did not have a lamp for light.

In a nearby corner stood the most magnificent stringed instrument. I thought I had seen it, too, in Watchfield House. Was it that very same one? If it had belonged to Harry's family, was it a personal object, like the perfume bottle, and therefore able to be freely given? Or was it a documented part of Watchfield's art and therefore something Harry could not give away? I was nearly certain that very piece had appeared in the *Christmas Carol* painting that Rossetti had shown me. I tiptoed up the staircase, turning the corner once, twice, thrice till I reached the top floor again. Unsurprisingly, the distractible Mr. Rossetti had forgotten to engage the lock when we'd left it an hour or more earlier; I opened the door.

Inside, I tried to turn the lamps on again. One sputtered on; one did not go on at all. Sometimes the gas had trouble reaching all the way to the topmost floors of houses, especially if it was in demand, as it was during the winter months.

Even in the dim light, I could make out the golden

stringed instrument on the *Christmas Carol* portrait. It was Italian.

But so was Mr. Rossetti's family.

I was tired, distressed, and most likely seeing familiarities among the unfamiliar; I had viewed so many treasures in the immediate weeks past that they ran together in my mind. I looked at the instrument closely. It was nothing I truly recognized; it was not from the Lydney Collection, I was certain. I nearly cried with relief. Between this truth now affirmed and locating Arthur's treasures, I believed Harry had not been selling off pieces of his father's art against the injunction in the will. Nothing else had been found missing! I was pleased with myself for checking, though, as I'd determined to be thorough no matter what I might find.

Suddenly I sensed someone else in the room. Had Harry followed me again? I heard a noise, a soft noise, but very definitely one which had not been present moments before.

I stood still and heard it again. I sensed it was from a far corner of the room. Should I flee? Or walk rather casually out of the room?

As I reached the door, knowing I could now flee down the stairs, I turned to stare at the corner whence the noise came.

I looked up. And up. Craned my head and looked higher. Then I laughed aloud when I saw it: an owl on its perch.

CHAPTER *Twenty*

It was the middle of December, and I had about two weeks in which to make my decision. The tense feeling at the workshop and home was a direct foil to the merriment of the season. I prayed constantly about the decision I was to make, but the answer was never clear to me.

Perhaps God was not going to tell me what to do. That thought heartened me, just a little. One does not need to give detailed instructions to adults. And yet, I desperately did not want to make a mistake. The gravity of the situation was not lost on me, as I had little money to spend on Christmas festivities, gifts, or decor in anticipation of the rent and other bills due on January 1.

If I were to give the collection to Harry, once he owned it, he would be free to propose marriage and thereby provide some financial stability for myself and my family, if not my firm.

If I were to give the collection to the South Kensington, it had been implied that many commissions and a heightened awareness for the firm would follow—though there had been, of course, no guarantees. Those commissions would be of financial benefit, but—honesty allowed me to admit—I should be quite proud to be the first Sheffield *daughter* to rescue and helm our firm, though I understood I would need a man beside me to do that.

I did not want to be responsible for its downfall, humiliation, and closure. Apparently I could do that as a woman on my own.

One day, Mr. Clarkson told me the sum he'd received for my father's watch; it was not as much as I'd hoped for, but it would be enough to pay our debts by the end of the year, including Mr. Dodd's invoice, which had precipitated this sale, plus a little more. In my enthusiasm, I embraced Mr. Clarkson as I would any friend. He smiled, which warmed his face and made him positively handsome, though he was always rather pale due to his coughing illness.

Mr. Clarkson and I had also sent out several enquiries regarding an Egyptian treasure for Mr. Denholm and had settled on a limestone block from a tomb, dated thousands of years earlier. Mr. Clarkson carefully wrapped the block in linen, and we then set out to deliver it.

The Denholm home in London was grand; he had purchased it from an aristocrat whose family had seen better days. Our hired carriage pulled up in front of the square and let us off. Mr. Clarkson carried the bag which, to my eyes, looked rather larger than required for the limestone. Perhaps he had wrapped it thoroughly and carefully and in many more layers of padding than would typically be required. That would be understandable. It was most valuable.

The butler led us into the parlor. Mr. Denholm was there and, surprisingly, so was his wife. Her gray hair was pulled back with sapphire hairpins which twinkled authentically, as did her necklace.

She reached out her hand toward me, and as she did, I noticed a sapphire bracelet over her white gloves; the stones were beautifully faceted and picked up the light.

"Please," she said, "let's have tea."

We four sat around a beautiful table of the finest French walnut while her day maid, in white and black, served tea from a silver urn that I suspected was Russian. The room was decorated with holly and ivy, cheerfully anticipating the Christmas season.

"I like old things," Denholm said loudly. "When your money is new, it's important that you surround yourself with things that are ancient. Gives you credibility and gravitas." He laughed at himself, and Mrs. Denholm smiled gently and looked at me. She understood how indelicate it was to mention money but was certainly not going to correct her husband.

"Well, don't tarry; let's see it." Mr. Denholm stabbed toward the bag in which we'd brought his treasure.

"I would like Miss Sheffield to do the honors," Mr. Clarkson said. "She was instrumental in fulfilling this commission. She both sourced and authenticated."

How kind of him to give me credit! Perhaps it was an intent to restore confidence in my abilities with the members of the Burlington; Charlotte was working on my behalf in that area too.

I stood to speak while Mr. Clarkson unwrapped Denholm's piece some feet away. "You'll see that although this is limestone, it is nearly white, and not the greenish-gray we've come to expect. That means it was from the tomb of a more highly ranked individual. We've verified that the stone is correct for the time, and the inscription is written in the hieroglyphics for the era. See here?" I pointed to the sides. "It's properly chipped. If it's old, it's going to be chipped. Think of the people who have touched this, Mr. Denholm. The man who quarried the stone—likely a slave who had nothing for himself, but whose efforts are held here in our hands, thousands of years later. The artisan who carved it—he does not remain, but his work does. Perhaps the widow and children touched the stone as it was laid, thinking affectionately of the man who was gone but fearing what lay ahead for them."

Mr. Denholm touched the stone in appreciation.

I continued, "Then the hands of the discoverer. The hands of those who transported it—tempted, perhaps, to steal such a valuable object but knowing that the probability of death awaited them if they were caught."

"Quite right." Denholm was still caressing the stone.

"Then the hands of the man who owned it before you, and finally . . . your own hands."

At that, he grasped the stone in both hands. "Yes. Mine now."

He set it down, and his wife had the maid pour more tea. "My bracelet is always in the way," Mrs. Denholm said as she lifted her teacup.

"Your jewelry is lovely," I commented, now she introduced the topic.

"It's medieval." She smiled proudly and touched the bracelet. "Edwin procured it for me."

I peered into my teacup and steadied myself. "How generous of him."

I looked at Denholm, who beamed.

I looked at Clarkson, who blinked a warning to me.

The bracelet could not possibly be medieval. Stones from that era remained more typically rounded; they only began to be faceted in the style of her stones within the previous hundred or so years. It was possible that the bracelet was real but more contemporary. It was also possible that it was a fraud.

Clarkson stared intently at me. I remembered the words my uncle had spoken to me. *"Truth is not always a welcome houseguest. Many are willing to ignore a weak or missing provenance to own the notables their peers crave."*

Perhaps Mr. and Mrs. Denholm knew that the bracelet was not real and would not appreciate my making them aware that I knew too. I did not know.

Mr. Clarkson and Mr. Denholm took a short parade around the room to review a recent acquisition; I spoke with Mrs. Denholm, as women will, about charitable causes, as she led me through her home.

"I do so enjoy my time visiting with the women in the prison," I said.

She looked surprised. "Enjoy?"

I smiled. "Some are not so very different from you and me, except, perhaps, they have started out planted in soil which was rockier and then made decisions which are difficult for the poor, but not always the well-to-do, to overcome."

"I would like to feel more useful," she said. "I shall make enquiries with the committee."

Soon, we stood and said our good-byes. I overheard Mr. Denholm saying something to Mr. Clarkson about a second Egyptian piece. Apparently Mr. Clarkson had split the commission for two pieces between himself and the firm. I could not blame him, but if that continued, and I was not invited to become a member of the club, it would not be for the betterment of Sheffield Brothers.

"About the bracelet," I said to Mr. Clarkson on the way home, "should we have told her that the era was not correct? Are the stones even real?"

"They did not ask for it to be assessed."

I shifted uncomfortably. Still, I thought she'd prefer to know.

"The commission from Denholm for the Egyptian art will cover many, if not all, of our expenses in January," he said, trying to reassure me. He laid a hand on my arm, and I smiled but then politely moved away. *Our* expenses? What expenses did *we* have?

A counterfeit of conservators. A collusion of collectors. My father had not allowed Sheffield Brothers to operate in such a manner. I knew he would have kindly pointed out the truth.

The whole matter made me feel unclean.

The kitchen smelled of wheaten baking breads and sweet plum puddings being prepared and set aside to ripen. I'd spent a small amount of the Denholm commission on Christmas preparations, and it was well worth it. We had given Alice a little extra to stay and help Orchie in the kitchen, and it was a merry time, the three of us in our aprons. Now the expenses were caught up, I'd quietly instructed Orchie to send a food packet or two home with Alice in the weeks before Christmas.

"Here." Alice handed back the fairy light to me. "My sister is sleeping much better now—thank you, Miss Eleanor—though she was reluctant to see this go. I'd like to see if I can buy something else pretty for her at the market. Would you like to come? To see the Christmas wares and such?"

I thought of Jeanette. "I'm looking for gloves. Perhaps they'll have some there?" I certainly did not have the funds to purchase anything on the high street.

"They will, Miss Sheffield. They will."

I'd found some silver paint from the workshop, and we were applying it to the walnuts which would be hung from the tree on Christmas Eve when we heard a knock on the door upstairs. Not everyone had Christmas trees, of course, but as my father had always tried to make things cheerful after the disappearance of my mother—and we all loved beautiful things—our family always had a small one.

"I'll see to it," Orchie said, and moments later she re-entered the kitchen followed by a large wrap of ivy. Large as a man. Then the man behind it popped out!

"I've come to deliver Christmas greenery." His eyes were bright with the winter chill.

I stood motionless, but my heart raced forward. *Harry.*

Uncle Lewis had heard the commotion—and no doubt had smelled the baking—and soon bungled down into the kitchen.

"Well, if it's not Father Christmas," he greeted Harry warmly.

Harry responded with a man-to-man smile. "Not quite Father Christmas. But if you'll allow me to stay, I'll be happy to help you hang the greenery around the staircases, windows, and such."

A dubious look crossed my uncle's face. It was unlikely that Lord Lydney, first or second, had ever participated in anything like household chores, but we did not have a manservant. "Have you hung greenery?" my uncle asked.

"No. But I'm game to try."

"Good sport. Let's have at it." My uncle smiled, and I mouthed, *"Thank you!"* to Harry. It was the first thing Uncle had looked forward to doing in a while. I heard them laughing and dropping things and resisted the temptation to go upstairs and look.

"Perhaps he's just needed a man around," Orchie said quietly.

Perhaps she was right, I thought. It seemed to do him good, and it was true that Uncle was sprightlier when in the workshop with Mr. Clarkson, too.

We women joined them in the parlor—Orchie bringing tea—to admire their handiwork. I gestured toward one piece of bough which had slipped from the window casing and, instead, hung like an escaped lock of hair. Harry tucked it into place while looking at me, and I caught his meaning. I nearly felt his touch on my scalp, recalling the moment outside the stables when he had tucked a strand of my hair into place.

The room sang with Christmas cheer now it was suddenly transformed into holiday merriment. The fresh greenery coolly scented the air, and the frosted lamps twinkled in the softening afternoon light. Harry returned to his carriage for a moment and came back carrying holly. "I remembered you love it," he said.

"I do," I responded with a smile. "Thank you."

"Because she's prickly," my uncle muttered fondly, and Alice and Orchie laughed.

Uncle spoke up once more. "I haven't visited Glastonbury for such a long while. 'Tis a shame."

Each of us turned to look at him; though the comment seemed to come from nowhere, I knew what had caused his mind to travel along that path—the prickly holly had recalled the legend of Glastonbury's holy thornbush.

"I should like to visit at least once more," he said, chin quivering.

Was he aware that he was growing more and more ill?

Alice spoke up, though she had never addressed my uncle before. "Is there a story there, sir?"

Uncle Lewis nodded. "There certainly is, Miss Carolina."

Alice's face deepened nearly as red as the holly berries.

I stepped in. "Her name is Alice."

She turned toward me and whispered, "He often calls me Miss Carolina, but I don't mind."

Uncle smiled and corrected himself. "Delightful, delightful Alice. Thank you for indulging an old man his interests, and if you've no place to go, I shall tell you the story of the holy thorn of Glastonbury. Dreadful state of affairs when young English girls do not know our history. I shall set that to rights."

I brimmed with deepening affection for everyone in that coal-warmed room. "Please, have a seat," I said to Alice and Orchie. "I shall serve this time."

Orchie looked ready to protest, but for this one moment, I wanted her to enjoy the story and not worry about serving.

Alice sat next to me on the settee and held her cup with her small finger extended. This time, I pursed my lips to quell a smile.

"You'll remember from your Sunday school lessons," Uncle addressed Alice, "that our Lord had the Last Supper with his disciples the night he was betrayed. He drank from a cup—now known as the holy grail. After the Lord's death, Joseph of Arimathea, a rich man who was a disciple of Jesus, made sure his body was respectably buried, giving up one of his valuable properties to see it done."

Alice bit into a biscuit and nodded. "I do remember that."

"Legend says that, after that time, our Joseph was so disheartened by what had transpired that he sailed from the Holy Land to England—quite a long journey—for time to mourn and think."

"Long journey indeed, I should say so!" Orchie exclaimed.

I watched Harry as he watched my uncle, deep regard on his face and in his eyes. My uncle had ridden with Harry once or twice when Harry was a boy; my father and Harry's father never had.

"When he landed in Glastonbury, he used a walking staff made of hawthorn wood from the Holy Land to right his sea legs into land legs once more. When he made it to the top of the hill, named Wearyall for his tiring journey, he thrust that staff into the ground."

I watched my uncle return to life, his voice and blue eyes clear, his memory sharp, completely engaged in the stories and objects which had defined his life.

Alice leaned over toward me. "It's clear where you get your love of telling the stories," she whispered, and I nodded my agreement.

"Then what?" Orchie asked.

I knew she'd heard the story from him, perhaps many times. I sensed she was excited to see him so animated again.

"Then the staff blew, which is to say, flowered. Right there, after it took root. Each year from then on, it bloomed at Christmastime to commemorate the birth of our Lord, and then in May, as English hawthorns do. It, and plants grown from its cuttings, are the only ones who bloom twice."

I poured more tea for each of us.

"Is the story true?" Alice asked.

I knew Uncle's faith and his profession were both valuable to him, and he would not offer a mistruth in defense of either. No *pia fraus*.

"I do not know. I suppose no one does. A staff blooming has happened once before, for certain." Uncle reached for the copy of Scripture which rested on a side table and paged through the beginning. "'And it came to pass, that on the morrow Moses went into the tabernacle of witness; and, behold, the rod of Aaron for the house of Levi was budded, and brought forth buds, and bloomed blossoms, and yielded almonds.'"

He closed the book. "In any case, it does represent and remind us of all that *is* true about our faith, does it not? It comes with a cost. Even with faith, life is sometimes wearying, but we persist in walking forward. And there are miracles to be had if we look for them. This bush was not an English hawthorn, but one from the Holy Land. How else did it arrive? That is a mystery and enough to give one pause for thought, is it not, Miss Carolina?"

"It is," Alice said, not bothering to correct him regarding her name.

Orchie stood up to clear the tea and biscuits; I did not assist. To do so once more would be to encroach on her territory.

Alice followed her back downstairs, and Uncle bid good-bye to Harry, then tottered off.

Harry and I faced one another in the parlor, silent. I did not want to ask him to leave, and he did not seem to want to go. As the room grew dim, he finally spoke up. "I'd best leave. I have one more visit to pay before nightfall."

"By all means," I said. I did not ask whom he was going to visit. I did not have that right and did not want to overstep. He offered anyway.

"I'm calling upon your Mrs. Newsome," he said.

"Marguerite?" Now I was intrigued.

He nodded. "I've heard she's fallen upon somewhat-difficult times and collected some greenery for her when I collected yours."

I wondered if he'd heard about my difficult times; he did not say. "Oh, Harry," I spoke quietly. "That is most considerate. Her parents will visit from Dorset over Christmas. I know this will make all the difference to her."

"Perhaps it will win her affections toward me."

"She's always championed your cause," I said.

"Then your affections," he said. "I would like to be your champion."

I reached up and touched his jawbone, tempted to draw my finger across it to his lips, but I refrained and let my hand fall by my side. We must have nothing personal between us until I decided.

"I'll be spending Christmas at Watchfield, of course," he said. "But would it be possible to escort you—and your uncle—to Glastonbury before I take my leave?"

I looked up wonderingly. "That would be utterly delightful! However, this season is somewhat slow as far as commissions are concerned." I could not bring myself to tell him the complete truth. I did not want to be shamed in front of him, and anyway, I had the solution well in hand.

Strong and self-sufficient.

"My pleasure. It will be a Christmas gift for your uncle." He kissed my forehead lightly and bid me good eve.

CHAPTER

Twenty-One

I met Alice on a corner very near the thoroughfare where she had once guided me to safety. Her clothing was a bit better cared for, and it appeared that she had a nearly new cloak on. I commented on it.

"Oh yes," she said. "I'm bartering. You started that, after all, trading your washing for my services. Now I've traded a month's worth of laundry for this cast-off cloak of a rich lady my sister met."

"The cloak's so pretty, and the red sets off your dark hair so well."

She laughed, as my sentiment was reminiscent of her comment regarding my white dress and auburn hair. This day, we were not employer and laundress; we were simply friends.

The cobbles on the street had become uneven over the course of time, and I had to take care to make sure I did not trip and fall. The winter air hung with moisture of a thickness somewhere between exhaled breath and mist, while the chill of it prickled my nose. Alice led me down a few alleys; as we grew closer and closer to our destination, we were wooed by the lovely melody of brass instruments from street musicians afar.

The market street had shops in proper brick buildings with proper doors, of course, but there were also tented purveyors of all kinds of food, clothing, trinkets, and treats.

"We'll shop here," Alice said. "Pretty things for fewer pence."

We walked up and down the road, and I soon became aware that even in the street market I would probably not have enough to purchase all the things I'd like to. Alice must have come to the same conclusion because she bought very little.

Toward the end of the street market, we came upon a large tent, flapping in the wind like a ship's sail but much dirtier. Water dripped off each corner, but underneath nestled a curiosity shop of sorts with many different items on offer. We stepped inside.

"I'd like to buy a jewel for my ma. I know they're not real and such, but she'd still think they were pretty."

We stood next to the worn glass case protecting the

jewelry from darting hands. I scanned the case, up and down, and then my eyes stopped on a garnet brooch.

"You like that'n, eh?" the salesman asked. "And right you should."

He took it out of the case so the gem and I could become better acquainted, but I think he was more than a little surprised when I withdrew a magnifying glass from my reticule. I inspected the jewels. They were real. Very valuable.

"How much are you asking for this piece?"

He named an impossibly small sum. The piece was worth fifty times or more what he was asking for it. Unlike the elites I knew, I suspected he would be gladdened to know the true value of the pieces in his collection.

"I'm going to be forthright," I told him. I withdrew one of my cards from my handbag. "This is not paste—it is composed of real garnets and is worth many, many times what you're asking for it." When I told him what I thought it was worth, he gripped the counter.

"Are ya certain?" he asked.

"Her father and her uncle have been doing this kinda thing for a long time," Alice spoke up. He had met her before and seemed to trust her.

"What should I do with it?" he asked.

"Sell it," I said. "I can give you a name."

He nodded. "How'll I know they won't cheat me?"

"Give them the card I just handed to you and tell them what I told you it was worth." I'd send him to the pawnshop where I'd sold my mother's jewelry.

Alice's barter for her cloak reminded me of that fine idea. "You might have other things mismarked. Perhaps we could strike a bargain. I'll look at your jewelry and figurines and tell you if you have anything else you might bring to the pawnshop for more than you're asking. In return, you allow my friend here—" I nodded toward Alice—"and me to select a few items for our friends and family well under the value of your gain. You will come out far ahead; I can promise you that."

He nodded, and the bargain was struck.

I spent perhaps an hour looking over his cases and found three or four items that would fetch him much more in Whitechapel than he would gain here. For the following thirty minutes, Alice and I wandered through his shop and found soft gloves for the prison ladies.

"Alice!" I called out to her. "Look!"

In a far corner was a fairy light, twilight blue with tiny pinpricks throughout, which would seem like starlight when a candle was within. She picked it up and then hugged me. "This is just perfect for Mary!"

Then we found a beautiful paste bracelet for her mother. "It's not real, is it?" she asked me, worried, I guessed, that it might be too dear.

I shook my head and then breathed on it. Alice looked at me oddly, and I laughed. "Real diamonds are cold. If you breathe on them, the fog will evaporate right away, if it even sticks at all. But false diamonds are much warmer, so . . ." I puffed on the bracelet again and counted. "One, two, three, you see? It takes much longer for my breath to disappear."

She clapped her hands. "Shall I ask for it?"

"Yes, certainly. We have done him a favor worth many times what he is giving us in return."

We packed up our purchases. "Being at the market with you puts me in mind of Saint Nicholas Day. Our purchase of gifts for others reminds me of him."

Alice raised an eyebrow. "Another story, Miss Eleanor?"

I smiled. "Of course! I always loved Saint Nicholas Day as a girl, though we haven't celebrated it much since my father died. You know my uncle is fond of religious relics and tales. His mother—my grandmother—was Dutch, and celebrating Saint Nicholas was one of their especial customs for my father and my uncle. Papa would tell me the story of how Saint Nicholas would deposit a treat or some coins in the shoes of anyone who left them out for him. Each year I would dutifully leave out a pair of shoes, and in the morning, I would find some sweets or a coin or some small treasure." I winked at Alice. "Saint Nicholas is the patron saint of unmarried girls. Perhaps we should speak of him kindly and see if he might assist us somehow, though his feast day has passed."

Alice laughed.

I stopped walking.

"What is it?" she asked. "I didn't mean to make fun . . ."

"Oh no," I said. "It's just that, well, I didn't buy anything for my uncle."

We turned back to the market, and as I had not needed to spend all of my money for the other gifts, I had some remaining. In one of the market stalls, I found an old book, a tiny volume of pocket proverbs which might have been printed a hundred years earlier. I bargained for it.

Alice grinned. "I don't know that I believe in patron saints of unmarried girls. Girls like me 'ave to be a bit more practical." She steered us to a stall selling Christmas greens.

"We already have holiday greens," I began.

"Not the right ones," she insisted. She led me to a small booth which sold the few flowers tough enough to prosper in such a season, as well as row upon row of hanging mistletoe balls.

"How much?" She pointed to the balls of entwined holly, ivy, and ribbon. From the bottom of each ball hung a piece of mistletoe—under which one could kiss one's desired.

The greensman named a price, and Alice scoffed. "No. Just for two of them, tha's all, not the lot. Just two."

They agreed on a price for two very small ones, and she handed one of them to me. "Merry Christmas. Let's see if your Saint Nicholas or my mistletoe balls are better at bringin' round the men."

I laughed, and she saw me to the thoroughfare, where we parted ways.

That night, I waited till I heard my uncle snoring and then quietly opened the door to his room. Despite Orchie's best efforts, things were askew, as he had become disorganized and was fearful of sleeping with the wardrobe doors closed. Sometimes he emptied the wardrobe completely. Orchie had told me he would not allow her in the room to tidy up any longer.

I found his shoes and set them far enough out from his bed that he would be certain to see them upon awakening. Then I slipped the small, antique book of proverbs into one of the shoes and a boiled sweet into the second. It was some days past Saint Nicholas Day, but I did not think Uncle Lewis would mind.

I crept back out, beaming, and could hardly wait to hear his whoop of joy come morning. I'd make sure we'd celebrate it on the proper day in the years to come. Papa would have liked that.

A few days later, on the morning of my prison visit, I was up before Orchie. I went into the kitchen and set the kettle on the burner. Then I ambled into the parlor and turned the lights up against the soporific winter darkness which slowed morning ambitions. With the room brightened, I saw the twist of Christmas green with which Harry had swagged the windows.

I closed my eyes and relished the memory of him doing it. For me, it had ever, always, and only been him. But I could not let that guide my decision.

I emptied the large reticule I normally carried when tending to an evaluation, filling it, instead, with the gloves and other gifts. I took the omnibus and then walked the remaining distance. Though it was about a fortnight ahead of the Christmas celebration, I was eager to bring my gifts to my friends.

When I arrived at the prison, I was surprised to find a

familiar face waiting for the warder to allow her through. "Mrs. Denholm!" I exclaimed. "I am delighted to see you here."

"I contacted the committee shortly after your visit, and although they told me I might wait until the New Year, I thought, what better time to spread some cheer than Christmas?" She held out a basket with some religious tracts. Next to the booklets snuggled tiny linen pouches.

"What is in these?" I asked.

"Spices mixed with salt." Her voice was hesitant. "I thought they might appreciate that with their meals."

"An inspired gift. I've never heard of it being offered, and yet it's perfect. They'll be so very happy to have you visit."

I walked down the halls, silent as a tomb in the merriest of seasons. Instead of the smell of bread and puddings, I discerned cold stone and dripping iron. When I made my way into the room in which we were allowed to meet, Jeanette and my other prison friends waited for me. Jeanette pushed a younger woman out to the center. Little Nancy.

I came close and forced myself not to recoil at the scent of their dirtied clothing, wishing I could help in some further manner.

Jeanette caught me out. "Only the rich prisoners gets the laundry," she said. Ah, yes . . . the rich prisoners. There might have been equality in sentencing, but in prison, the equality of treatment stopped. Prisoners with the funds to afford better treatment were allowed services, special meals, suites of rooms, and even servant help, if they could pay for it.

Those who could not—which was most—did without the most menial of help. And spiced salt.

I sat down and asked if they'd like us to take turns recounting the Christmas story.

"You tell it, Miss Sheffield," one of the ladies said. "We hear our own voices often enough."

So I did, and as I did, it struck me that most of the people in that story were as poor as the families these ladies had come from. "I have something for you. Gifts!"

"Father Christmas," one of the women said.

"I don't thin' she looks like no one's father." Little Nancy smiled for the first time since I arrived.

"For coming to my defense, you get the first gift," I jested. I pulled out three back issues of one of my ladies' magazines.

She nodded warily. "Improving literature?"

I rubbed my neck. I had worried that the women might grow discontent or sad by looking at issues women outside the prison faced. Perhaps I'd been right. "No, I'm sorry. But perhaps something entertaining? Would you have preferred something more improving?"

"No, indeed, miss. This agrees with me just fine." Nancy read aloud some of the article titles. "'Society is now one polished horde.'" She looked up and laughed. "Ain't that the truth!" She paged through one more. "I do like these dresses, I do. When I get out, I'm going to learn to sew. Or maybe do up hair for some fancy ladies. I'll enjoy reading these; thank you, miss." Little Nancy clasped the periodicals to her chest.

"Much better than those who always want to improve us in one way or t'other."

"When you're done, you can tear the papers out one by one to roll up your hair into curls."

They all clapped. "Ooh, what a lovely idea," Nancy said.

I handed out the pairs of soft gloves and tiny jars of ointment which I had scooped from my own. Each woman came in turn to thank me; one curtsied, which touched me deeply.

"I'm like you," I said. "There is no need for that."

Jeanette came to speak with me last, just before I took my leave. "Thank you for the gloves and the trinkets for the young ones. But the best gift is that you come here and sit with us and don't forget us. That's what matters the most."

I could not speak for a moment; then I told her how I looked forward to our hours together and said that I should see her in the New Year. "We are friends."

I heard a voice call my name as I walked the road to the thoroughfare. "Miss Sheffield!" A fine carriage pulled alongside me and stopped. "I just now see you are walking. Please, allow me to escort you to your home."

It was Mrs. Denholm. For a moment, I was ashamed that she'd seen me walking, hem dragging in the mud once more, boots all spattered underneath. I wanted her to see me as strong and capable and worthy of her company.

I looked at her friendly face. Would I, then, turn down the very charity offered me by someone with better circumstances when my friends in prison had no such pretensions?

"Thank you, Mrs. Denholm." Her driver helped me inside. "The offer is very kind and much appreciated."

We talked companionably all the way to my Bloomsbury home and workshop, and she bid me good-bye. "I shall hope to see you after Christmas!" I said as I stepped from the carriage, and she responded in kind.

I opened the door and shook the snow from my shoulders. Orchie stood there, smiling, holding out a telegram. "Your Lord Lydney will be round first thing tomorrow to take you and your uncle to Glastonbury. The journey is long, so he's made arrangements at a coaching inn for accommodations that evening. He and your uncle will stay in one room, and you in another."

"How kind." I kept my voice and, I hoped, my spirits calm. But inside, my heart sang. *My* Lord Lydney!

CHAPTER Twenty-Two

Orchie helped me to pack a bag, and when she left the room to prepare one for Uncle Lewis, I slipped a few additional items into that bag and then closed it tight. I was not certain if Uncle completely understood that he was going to Glastonbury before Christmas, his fondest desire.

Harry's driver arrived very early in the morning to take us to the London Waterloo station. We soon settled into the first-class compartment, and within an hour of departure, the train's gentle rocking motion lulled Uncle Lewis fully asleep, head resting against the window. His mouth hung open a little, and a bit of drool eased from its corner; he looked rather like a young boy.

I wondered what his hopes and dreams had been. Had he wished for a wife? For children? He'd had neither, and now it was up to me to care for him.

Harry talked about his time in Italy and the few affairs he was completing for his father, but he did not bring up the collection. We talked about our past and the state of my business.

"We have fallen upon some rather difficult months," I admitted.

"Can I be of assistance?" he offered.

"I'm afraid not," I said. He could not help me in any material manner while the decision was still outstanding. Year's end, when Sheffield Brothers' commission with the Lydney Collection would end, and by when my decision must be made, fast approached. I had little more than a fortnight. "I believe things to be well in hand and getting better," I added.

"You will let me know, at any time . . . if you need anything or if things become urgent."

I smiled. "Thank you. I will."

Conversation and laughter knit us together during the travel, and some hours passed before the call for Westbury, three-quarters of the way through our journey.

"You know, there is a chalk horse etched upon the high hills on the Salisbury Plain outside of Westbury."

"I did not," I said. There were many horses carved upon the white chalk hills throughout England, some going back many hundreds of years, each with a legend of its own.

He nodded. "Knowing how I loved them, Mother always

arranged for us to see it when Father insisted upon a family visit to Glastonbury—he and Mother, Arthur and me."

"Do you miss him?"

"Father?" Shock pitched his voice and Uncle stirred.

I shook my head. "No. Arthur."

He squeezed my hand once before releasing it. "Yes. I do. He and I were quite close as boys, at least during school holidays. My father poisoned the well from which we were both required to drink, so that changed things." He looked up and smiled. "He once had a white horse, too, you know. Before we were certain he was sensitive to their hair. Named Excalibur, of course."

"I found Arthur's armor," I said.

He looked past me, through the window, though addressing my statement. "Had it been missing?"

"I thought perhaps it had been." I could not discern from his voice whether he was surprised or had known. He had not sold it, in any case, as his father had secretly accused.

We changed trains once, then arrived at Glastonbury and took a hired carriage first to deliver our luggage to the coaching inn, which used to be the inn the old abbey used for pilgrims. I thought of Mr. Herberts and his pilgrim's coin and wondered if he treasured it as my father had. The George, as the inn was now called, was three stories high with a castle crenellation on top; Harry had arranged for us to have an entire floor, for privacy, and dinner that evening as well.

We left our bags and then departed for the sights.

"I'm surprised at how well he is walking," Harry said as we made our way across the dormant green lawns. My uncle had brought along a walking stick—whether to steady himself or to recall the legend of Joseph of Arimathea, I did not know. If I were to hazard a guess, 'twould be the latter.

To the unprepared eye, there was not much to view. There were no amusements or cafés or shops to draw visitors. There was a trinket seller peddling false thorns, in the damp; they had been poorly encased in glass. Uncle Lewis waved them away impatiently.

We picked our way into the stones of the ruined abbey. The walls were uneven in height, open to the elements, skeletal. All sort of opportunistic plants availed themselves of the cracks and crevices which damage had left, in which to generate a new life. The silence resonated in a manner that voices never could, and if I believed in ghosts, I would have said they tarried here, warning, hoping, seeking, hiding. I settled my uncle on a derelict bench and then sat down myself. Closing my eyes, I felt the weight of a place where Christians had worshiped for more than one thousand years. I sensed that holy presence; we were in a church, after all, only one that had been destroyed during the Reformation and was now open to the air, its pitted stones heaving and black moss hiding in its cleaves. I opened my hands and lifted my palms; my breath curled upward toward heaven, echoing Psalm 141. *"Let my prayer be set forth before thee as incense; and the lifting up of my hands as the evening sacrifice."*

"It's like a reliquary," my uncle said. I opened my eyes at his mention of those little jeweled boxes we had appraised so many years ago when he was teaching me. "The whole place is. Except instead of holding fragments of questionable bone and wood, the abbey ruins hold the hopes and dreams and prayers and worship of twelve hundred years' worth of pilgrims and believers."

"That's beautiful." I took his arm and felt him shiver. "Shall we return for dinner?" I asked.

He nodded, and as he turned to Harry, I saw tears in Uncle's eyes. "Thank you, young man."

Harry clapped him on the back and then we returned to the George. We were all to refresh ourselves before meeting in the dining room. An hour later, a knock came at my door. I opened it to see Harry alone.

"Your uncle is very tired. I do not think we should wake him. I will ask my driver to stand guard near the room, if you like, and are willing to dine with me alone? There will be others in the dining room," he hastened to add.

I smiled. "I should say no on principle, but I'm hungry now and do not want to wait."

He held my gaze, the lines on his face sketching in the weathered angles. "Nor do I." Unlike our evening of games at Lady Charlotte's home, the waves of intimacy rushed in and did not recede.

I smiled to myself. Perhaps I should consider putting Alice's gift to good use this night.

The fire was lit in the dining room, and though it was not truly late, the room was cleared of everyone except for Harry, myself, and the serving girl.

"I thought there would be others here. The offer holds. Would you like to have a tray sent up rather than eating together downstairs?"

"Can you be trusted?" I teased.

"No," he teased back and held out the chair for me to sit. We stared at each other in the flickering light. "You have ruined me for other women," he finally said.

I held my breath, surprised both by the admission and the rise of emotions it brought forth. A carriage rolled by in the street outside; the horse hooves clopped rhythmically as they disappeared into the night mist. I looked at the wooden plank table at which we sat. For perhaps five hundred years or so people had sat round this very table, eating, drinking, laughing, talking, arguing. What had they been thinking? Hoping? Fearing? The inn's walls were a good three feet thick, but I could still hear muffled voices and laughter on the floors above us. I told all this to Harry, and he took my hand in his own.

"I do find that interesting, my lovely Ellie. But I am most interested in the two of us who are here, now—so very thankful that we are here. But as you have kindly shared your stories with me so faithfully, perhaps it's time I share one dear to me. This afternoon, I meant to tell you the story of the Westbury horse."

"Please, tell me!"

The serving girl placed a platter of roughly cut bread and cheese on the table between us, then a pitcher of water and two glasses of soft cider.

"Well, when we were younger men and Father dragged us out here, Arthur and I would threaten that when he and Mother were asleep, we would ride off into the night toward the Westbury horse."

"Why?"

"Legend says that when the church chimes exactly midnight, the chalk horse comes to life on the hill and walks to Bridewell Springs to drink. We wanted to see that!"

I raised my eyebrows. "Did you?"

He shook his head rather somberly and waited for the serving girl to set our plates of meat in front of us and then leave. "No . . . Arthur, you remember, was sensitive to horses. So we'd have to take the carriage, and then Father would know."

I reached across the table and took his hand. "Arthur was a good young man."

He nodded, and we began to eat. After a few minutes, he said, "You'll remember the Uffington chalk horse."

"Of course! The most famous in England."

"Because it's on the road to Watchfield House, whenever we returned for the school holidays or were back in Oxfordshire after one of Father's diplomatic journeys, I always knew I was home when I saw the white horse on the hill. It comforted me as nothing else could."

I wished I could have comforted him.

"Do you know the stories about the Uffington horse?" he asked with eagerness.

Some of them, for certain. But I did not let on. "I should love to hear you tell it." I had dined sufficiently and pushed my plate away.

"The Uffington horse is said to be a wish fulfiller. If one wants to have a wish granted, he should stand on the hill, on the eye of the horse, and turn three times to the right, then whisper his wish—or for me, a prayer."

"Have you done that, then?" I asked.

"Yes," he said. "Recently. But just nearby. I'm not about to stand on the eye of a horse, even one made of chalk."

I laughed and waited for him to tell me what his wish—his prayer—had been, but he did not.

"I love those stories and am delighted that you have shared them with me, for by doing so, you've shared your heart. I should have known your favorite stories were about horses," I jested.

"And yours about collectibles," he quipped right back.

I nodded. "You have me. I think treasures mean so much to me because they remind me of people, even when time has passed and I may no longer believe what I once did. Perhaps it's much like the relic collectors. They want a fragment of bone or of the true cross because when things seem dark, and it appears God is elusive and does not seem to be responding, they want something to hold on to. Something to prove that the one in whom they trust, at the deepest level, is who they believe him to be."

"That is true." He picked my hand up and kissed it. "I should return you to your room, though I'd prefer to stay and talk through the night."

"That would not do at all," I agreed. "I should like to go upstairs first, and then perhaps you could join me outside my room two or three minutes later?"

He nodded a puzzled agreement, and I took my leave.

Once in my room, I removed the mistletoe ball—Alice's gift—and the hook with the small bit of thread that I'd packed in my bag.

I cradled it in my hand. *Should I hang it?*

Properly, I was not to engage in an overly personal manner with him until I had made a decision about the future of the Lydney Collection.

However, I could honestly say that my decision would be based upon the facts, as presented to and interpreted by me, no matter how I felt about Harry.

I then went outside the door to my room and hung the ball with care on the lintel above. When Harry rounded the corner a minute later, he laughed, though softly, as not to wake the others. I smiled in return.

He came close and reached up to brush my hair back from my face. My face was flushed, I could tell, both from his nearness and from the fire by which we had been sitting for an hour or more.

Harry cupped my face in his hands, and I closed my eyes and savored the moment. Then he bent toward me and kissed my lips, gently at first and then more insistently.

I remembered the first time he'd kissed me—awkwardly, hesitantly, worriedly.

Now he was confident and sure. The first time, I hadn't kissed him back properly. Now, I did.

When he pulled away from me, we both stood reorienting ourselves to time and place, and it took me an unwelcome moment to catch my breath and focus my mind.

"I'd best say good night and leave," he whispered. "This time."

CHAPTER Twenty-Three

BLOOMSBURY, LONDON

The bells rang out joyously on Christmas Day—it was a clear, sunny day, but I hung on to my uncle's arm so we didn't slip on our way into or out of church. Orchie had attended a service much earlier in the morning; though she worked for us, officially, she had no family but ours, so we three would spend our days together. Mr. Clarkson had undertaken to spend some time in Bristol with his family.

"I smell Cornish pasties!" Uncle called out as we stepped into the house.

"You do, indeed." Orchie greeted us at the door. She whispered behind her hand, "And goose and pudding and a mince pie and all such as you and I want to eat, too." She handed a box to me. "This just arrived."

I opened the box, and in it was a small card that said only, *Merry Christmas! Yours, Harry.*

There were three Christmas crackers. One marked *Mrs. Orchard*, one marked *Mr. Sheffield*, and one marked *Miss Sheffield.*

Carolers knocked at the door, and Orchie ran to greet them with a fresh tray of biscuits—where she'd procured the ingredients for them, I did not know. But I was glad to offer the joy-filled singers a treat, and as I held the door open, listening to their songs of faith, cheer, and hope, I wondered if, perhaps, 1867 would be the year in which all three might be restored. *Oh, tidings of comfort and joy. May it be so.*

After a hearty dinner, we repaired to the salon to read and rest. Uncle fell asleep by the fire, and when he awoke, he asked Orchie, "When will dinner be served?"

She looked at me nervously. "You're hungry again, then?"

"Again? You haven't fed me yet!" he roared.

I stood. "Let's fetch the Christmas crackers, shall we?"

Uncle nodded pleasantly, and I brought them from the foyer table, where I'd left them.

I handed Orchie's to her first. She tugged the ends, and the cracker popped open, revealing a token good for a tin of ground drinking chocolate at a shop nearby. "Oh, what a delightful treat this is!" she said and truly did seem delighted.

My uncle tugged the ends of his cracker next, and after a little difficulty, he maneuvered it to snap open. Out fell one of the tawdry thorns in glass baubles from Glastonbury. "He can't have thought those were true relics, antiquities . . ."

"No, I do not think so," I said. "I believe he jests with you."

My uncle laughed. "It's great fun. It's been so long since someone played a prank on me, and I quite enjoy it." I was glad that his thoughts seemed lucid for the moment and that he could see the fun in a man-to-man jest. It honored and respected Uncle Lewis as a man, rather than offering feminine pity.

"Go on then," Orchie said. "Crack yours open!"

I tugged the ends of mine, and as I did, a festive spray of confetti, a note, and a tiny pouch flew out. I read the note. *I am who you believe me to be.* I blinked back tears as I returned to our conversation over dinner at the inn.

Then I opened the pouch. In it was a beautiful amethyst, the perfect size to replace the lost one in my Adore ring.

I did not believe Uncle understood the meaning of the replacement gem, but Orchie did. With it, the ring, and perhaps my heart, would be made whole.

We said our fond good nights and I brought my jewelry repair kit from the workshop to my room, then closed and locked the door. Opening the drawer, I withdrew the Adore ring. I ran my finger over the rough hole whence the first gem had fallen and been lost. I settled the new amethyst into its spot, folded the tiny prongs down around it, and slipped the ring onto my finger for a moment before taking it off once more.

I would wear it again, but only if Harry placed it on my finger.

At my desk, I sorted through the papers that Sir Matthew, the late Lord Lydney's solicitor, had given me. He'd charged me with learning if Harry was now trustworthy—indeed, worthy at all.

If Harry lost the collection, he would lose all his beloved Arthur's treasures.

If he keeps the collection, he might sell all of Arthur's treasures—and the rest.

If he lost the collection, the pelican in her piety might be stored out of eyesight forever.

He's not even asked for it back.

Stories are powerful, but they are not all true. Which was the true story? The story that Harry's father told everyone, including Harry himself: that he was selfish and not to be trusted? Had I believed that story? Should I have?

But his father had lied about Arthur's collection. That much was clear.

I turned the lamp down and changed into my dressing gown.

Signorina Viero had spoken of Harry's valor. That was true, wasn't it?

Some valuers claimed that something of little value was quite costly. Others claimed that something of great value was worth nothing. Both deceived for their own gains. Was Lord Lydney like one of them? In the end, as Papa had taught me, I must not believe the stories people told me but rely on what I saw with my own eyes and judged with my own instincts.

Yes, Harry had been late in returning from Austria. But otherwise, and even in that, I had never seen the man prove untrue.

Yet, whispered the specter of my misgivings. *Or have you?*

Lord Audley, who had proved most friendly to me and who knew Harry and his circle well, had warned me, *"My help comes as advice: he'll exploit your goodwill, you know. As he always has, as his father condescended to your father. Their benevolence has never been selfless, has it, Miss Sheffield? Nor have either proved faithful, at the end."*

I'd set about to find the answers to five questions to prove Harry true. Did he care about others' interests? His risking much for his friend Viero, and his gentle gift of Glastonbury to my uncle, would say yes.

Did he tarry in Austria longer than was required? His earnest desire to earn his father's affections, which I had oft witnessed, and Francesca's affirmation would say he did only what he'd felt was required.

Had he sold pieces of Arthur's collection? Most certainly not.

Had he sold treasures to pay for his own interests? I could find no evidence of that.

The fifth question, dearest to my heart, remained unaddressed but hinted toward. Why had he not proposed marriage?

If I awarded the wealth to the South Kensington, I would

curry favor with those who would help me keep my firm, and a home for myself, my uncle, and Orchie. But they would hide some of the treasures—and perhaps allow their powerful benefactors to rifle through and "trade" them.

No promise has been made by the South Kensington collectors. Nor could one have been.

It would put you on equal footing with Lady Charlotte. Perhaps I could achieve that on my own.

The plaque with the Sheffield Brothers name outside the donation will bring constant attention. This was true.

In the end, I had been charged with determining where the valuable art belonged, and I believed the pieces belonged together, on display, in the home for which they had been collected.

I believed the story about Harry that I saw with my own eyes, not the one his father had promulgated.

I quickly wrote two letters—one to Sir Matthew Landon, the solicitor, informing him of my final decision. One to Harry, thanking him for his lovely Christmas gift and apprising him that I was returning the collection to him, and had informed Sir Matthew as much.

Should I post the letters?

In the end, I could only trust myself. I could not award Harry the collection because I loved him, though indeed I did. I must give him the collection only if it was the right thing to do.

I sat and prayed and thought. Then I decided.

I dressed once more and crept out of my room into the

dark household. Stood, letters clutched in my hand, and looked at the grate. The coal had dwindled to embers, hissing protest on their slow journey to death. I put on my cloak and hat and pulled up my boots. I walked down the dark, slippery way and placed the letters deep inside the green postbox before I lost my nerve.

It was irrevocable. It could not be undone.

Christmas passed, as did Boxing Day, and the following week Mr. Clarkson would be back in the workshop. Harry had written how pleased he was that I had chosen to keep the art and artifacts at Watchfield. He assured me that he would take good care of them and that he looked forward to seeing me very soon. His letter seemed enthusiastic, but had I perhaps hoped for more?

Maybe he would speak of more in person, at Twelfth Night.

There was but little to do as the season was quiet. Most of our clientele would be at their country homes or celebrating in London with family until after Twelfth Night. When Mr. Clarkson did not return to work as expected, I decided to pay him a visit, to ensure that he was well.

Marguerite accompanied me; it would be most improper for me to visit alone, something Mr. Clarkson would certainly point out.

She had first to see her parents off on the train, so by the time she arrived at my home, it was late afternoon and the sun, such that could be seen through the veil of coal mist, had already begun to wane in strength.

"Thank you for coming."

She nodded. Her face was more drawn than I'd seen it for some time.

"Are you quite well?" I asked.

"Yes." She took my hand. "My father introduced me to someone."

"Well, then!" I exclaimed. I caught the look on her face. "It did not go well?"

"No potential for either love or trust, I'm afraid. Father said beggars cannot be choosers and that until I choose more wisely, perhaps he and Mother would forestall their visits. I'm not quite a beggar . . . not yet."

I laid my hand over hers. "It's difficult to make such choices."

She nodded. "And you? You are certain about your choice?"

I shook my head. "I am not certain. But the choice has been made." A drift of doubts wafted against my previously confident resolve.

The driver rounded the corner into a neighborhood which was on the edge of disrepute. "Have you been here before?" Marguerite asked.

"No cause to. Perhaps I should turn back?"

"No, dearest, once begun . . ."

I agreed with her, and soon we pulled up in front of a tall

house whose door was as untended as the unruly child who opened it. "Whatcha want?" he asked.

"We're here to see Mr. Clarkson," I said politely. "Can you tell him Miss Sheffield has come to call?"

The lad sneered. "Tell him yourself. He lives upstairs."

Marguerite and I made our way up the stairs. An older man, perhaps the lad's father, followed us, calling out unseemly remarks.

I turned around, but the man had blocked our way down. "Perhaps Mr. Clarkson will be so good as to escort us to the waiting carriage," I said. Marguerite nodded her agreement.

Once we reached the door at the top of the stairs, I knocked once, twice. Finally the door opened.

"Miss Sheffield! Mrs. Newsome." Mr. Clarkson appeared flustered, and his eyes were slightly glassy. "I would not have known to expect you."

"I had some concern for you," I said, "when you did not appear at the workshop as expected."

"Do come in," he said. "I've been a little unwell." The threatening man still blocked the stairway down, so we had little choice. Clarkson glared at him, and he disappeared into his own rooms on the lower floor.

Mr. Clarkson's front room was threadbare and empty of nearly all expected furniture. Wherever he was spending his income, it was not upon creature comforts. The light was wan, and the entire room smelt of spoilt meat that had still been cooked, the camphor scent of his paregoric syrup, and the pinching musk of the chemicals which warded off moth infestations.

Mr. Clarkson coughed and could not seem to recover himself. "The damp. The coal . . ." He shrugged. "I hope you had a merry Christmas!"

"Indeed so," I said. Marguerite hung back by the doorway, but I scanned the room. In a corner cabinet, I noticed a fine figurine. A shepherdess and a shepherd, dancing in a field with two tiny sheep between them.

Where had I seen that before?

I kept my face steady and did not allow myself to glance at it again lest he notice what I had suddenly realized. It was one of Harry's mother's figurines from Watchfield. A very expensive piece, indeed.

Stolen?

"Have you notified the South Kensington committee of your decision to donate?" he asked cheerfully.

I backed a bit toward Marguerite. "No. In fact—it's just as well you know now. I have returned the collection to Lord Lydney, whom I believe to be the rightful owner."

In an instant, Clarkson's face transformed into a twist of red rage. "You've done what? You foolish, foolish woman. You have utterly ruined yourself and your firm."

It was no longer *our* firm. It was *my* firm.

"I don't believe . . . ," I began, shocked by his sudden lack of decorum, especially in front of Marguerite. I'd hoped to tell him that we could continue to build upon the clients we'd always had and that he had procured, but he did not let me finish my sentence.

And yet, I should not have been shocked. He had spoken to me out of turn, surprisingly so, once or twice before. I had, perhaps, not wanted to see the seriousness behind those incidents, knowing the firm needed him still.

"Just as good a time as any to let you know, then, that I shall not be returning to Sheffield Brothers. I don't need you anymore—I've plenty of clients eager to work with me now."

"You've been cultivating clients outside of your work with Sheffield Brothers, using our materials, workshop, and reputation?"

"One has to look out for oneself, Miss Sheffield. It seems I was correct. Rather than the help and entrée I'd always hoped it might be, your firm's name would now be a shackle to me. By alienating Lord Parham and giving the collection to Lydney, you've no chance—none—of being accepted as a member of the Burlington."

"But Lady Charlotte Schreiber—"

"You are naive, Miss Sheffield. You shall see. You followed your misguided heart and gave those riches to a man who cares not for you because you were blinded by unwise affections. Lady Charlotte follows her husband's lead—as she should."

"I gave the collection to the person whom I thought deserved it, to keep it *in situ* where I believe it belongs. You'll recall, Mr. Clarkson, that my father played a significant role in acquiring and caring for those pieces. I had his best interests in mind as well."

"Your father," he sneered. "In his cups mostly."

I turned away to temper my retort, and as I did, I noticed a medieval chalice lightly rimmed with what appeared to be precious gems. I stared at it up and down. It looked old. Was it real? I felt I'd seen it before.

"Come, Eleanor." Marguerite took my hand. I glanced once more at the shepherdess figurine, and this time, Clarkson saw me. He seemed emboldened, somehow. Unafraid of my recognition.

"Good day, Miss Sheffield. I'll be watching your downfall with sad resignation." He snatched some papers from a desktop and then threw them toward me. I bent to pick them up and saw they were invoices.

"That's right," he continued. "Monies owed by Sheffield Brothers to clients—just like Mr. Dodd. I had been holding them off on your behalf until the collection was donated to the South Kensington and I could negotiate on behalf of Sheffield Brothers. Now that will never happen, and you're on your own."

I looked down. Three invoices.

"They are outstanding debts, Miss Sheffield. Due now. Past due, actually. Who shall want to sell to you without immediate payment, which you shan't be able to offer without a steady clientele? These people—" he pointed to the papers in my hand—"already know the situation. And others shall too. Word travels quickly."

"You had no right to speak on behalf of the firm. Or me. Or to take our mail or receipts."

"Could you have paid them a month ago? Last week?"

No.

"Lord Lydney will assist me."

"Lydney?" He barked a laugh. "He is shameless and undeserving of either the collection or your affections. A thief like his father."

His father had been a thief; that much was true. The stolen antiquities in the room above his bedchambers—I had checked the inventories, and many had never been noted—proved that. Had Clarkson seen them when he'd done the Lydney inventory without me?

"Good day, Miss Sheffield. Good luck. And good riddance."

He closed the door behind us.

CHAPTER
Twenty-Four

TWELFTH NIGHT, JANUARY 1867
WATCHFIELD HOUSE, OXFORDSHIRE

By sheer force of will, I held the disturbing knowledge that I would have to contact new creditors very soon. The beastly threat of debtor's prison had been quickened and fed, but I must put that aside during our time at Watchfield. If I were to be affianced, I would, perhaps, be able to hold the creditors off longer because they'd know my solid standing and that I'd have connections to highborn clientele.

"Harry's kept the tradition," Marguerite said as we approached the front door. Indeed, he had. Or his new housekeeper had—he'd mentioned in the telegram he'd sent with specifics to the weekend that he'd hired new household staff. None remained, now, from his father's era. Erased, excised, and dismissed.

I read but did not trace the writing on the wide, dark oak double doors—18 † C † M † B † 67—not wanting to remove the chalk with which it had been drawn. "Eighteen sixty-seven," I said. "*Christus mansionem benedicat*; may Christ bless this house."

Yes, please, may God bless this house in 1867 and beyond in a measure in which it has not ever been blessed.

Harry's new man must have seen our carriage arrive because he soon opened the door without our needing to knock.

"Miss Eleanor Sheffield," I said and then indicated Marguerite. "And Mrs. Marguerite Newsome."

He showed us into the house, assigning a footman to direct us to our rooms.

"Harry has engaged rather more staff than his father had," Marguerite said to me quietly as we followed the footman up the wide staircase. I had been thinking the very same; the house had been cleaned and polished throughout, which was no simple task given the miles of woodwork.

Marguerite's room was next to mine. "I shall take a brief rest and then help you ready yourself for dinner later?" she asked. She had circles under her eyes; perhaps it was simply that she'd grown thin. Also, I did not think she had fully recovered from the punitive silence her father held toward her when she did not agree to his whims. I squeezed her hand and agreed.

I changed out of my traveling dress and then took the

keys to the house—which I had not yet returned to Harry—with me.

I made my way along a corridor to the study. Next to it was the large room, at the back of the property, in which Lady Lydney's porcelains had been stored and displayed.

I walked to the case where I expected the shepherdess figurine would be missing. But it was not! Mr. Clarkson had already returned it. How? When?

I turned away from the case and looked out across the lawn toward the stables. Harry was riding Abalone, but it appeared to me that the guests he was with were riding new, sleek thoroughbreds. Horses I did not recognize. Had the guests brought them? Truly unlikely. More likely, of course, was that Harry had bought new horses. Even my untrained eye could see that they were very expensive animals. Among the riders, I spied Lord Audley, curiously cheerful and unusually friendly with Harry.

Why? It did not feel right.

As I turned to leave the room, Signorina Francesca appeared in the doorway and seemed surprised to see me. She wore a simple dress of red and white. "Miss Sheffield. I am so pleased to see you again."

"And I, you," I said.

After a moment, she spoke once more. "If you will please excuse me, there are Italian guests soon to arrive."

"Your brother?" I was certain my voice reflected my hope.

She shook her head sadly. "I wish it were to be, but it is not. They are . . . known to our family. Mama invited them."

"I'm so sorry about your brother," I said softly. And I was. "I will pray for his safe return." I walked back to my room and found Marguerite waiting for me.

"Where were you?" she asked.

"Looking at the art."

"Aren't you done with that, now you've made your decision?"

"Yes. I still enjoy seeing it, though." I also remained concerned about a shepherdess disappearing whilst under my firm's care.

Marguerite had brought a lovely gown of rose for herself and for me a beautiful teal creation, cinched in the back. The color set off my hair. "Surely you must be coming to the end of your new gowns," I teased.

"I surely am." Her tone was not quite so teasing. "Let's make the most of them."

We joined the others who were mingling in the large reception room ahead of dinner. I saw Harry, and he caught and held my gaze. *"Later,"* he mouthed to me, and I understood. He had one hundred guests to tend to this evening, but he would find me. I knew he would.

My dining companions were pleasant and personable, friendlier, dare I say it, than the typical aristocrats who had surrounded Harry's father. As friendly, at least, as those who had thus far blocked me from the Burlington Fine Arts Club, aristocratic and middle class alike. There was one table toward the end of the room which seemed to be a bit louder than the others. I turned my ear toward them; they were speaking

Italian and seemed to be angry with Signorina Francesca's mother. Harry looked firmly in their direction and things quieted down.

The meal was, of course, made up of spiced foods, as Twelfth Night celebrated the arrival of the three kings, and their spices, to worship Jesus. There was spiced meat and spiced ale and soft cider—I wondered if Harry had ensured there would be beverages without any spirits in them on my behalf. Oranges studded with cloves and gold ribbons decorated the tables, and for our final course, beautiful Epiphany tarts: six-sided, star-shaped tarts to hearken back to the star of Bethlehem, filled in with many light-colored fruit jellies so they would resemble the finest stained-glass windows.

Afterward, the men retired to the smoking room and the ladies to converse among themselves until the musical entertainment would begin. As Marguerite was engaged in happy conversation, I decided to use the opportunity to sneak up the back staircase to the third floor for just a moment. Over the course of the meal, I had remembered where I thought I'd seen the chalice at Mr. Clarkson's rooms. In the third-floor room—perhaps. Had he had the key all along? Or found a way in? Though the figurine seemed to have reappeared, I needed to check that. I'd promised myself, for my own sake and my firm's, to be thorough.

I slid away from the others and then through a false door which I knew led to the servants' area. No one paid any attention to me as they rushed to clear the dinner things.

I quickly made my way up the back staircase, in the dark. When I reached the top, my heart sank with realized dismay.

The door had been completely removed and replaced. Not that I'd had the key to the former lock—only Harry's father and his valet had, apparently. But what did this mean?

Harry had seemed so nonchalant when I had mentioned finding Arthur's treasures. He had remained casually inattentive when I'd mentioned that I did not have the key to this room. But since then, he had made it an apparent priority to have the door and lock replaced. Or had he discovered Mr. Clarkson's theft? If he had, did he blame me or wonder if I had been involved, somehow?

I tugged my dress down and returned to the ballroom, where the musicians were just striking up, but I could not shake my interest. Perhaps I should see if the room could still be accessed by the hidden door inside the wardrobe. The idea pecked at me until I acquiesced out of a code of honor. I was no fool, though. I was not going to be trapped there again.

I rested my hand on Marguerite's arm, and she concluded her conversation and followed me back to my room. "What are we doing, dearest? Did things not go well with Harry?"

I shook my head. "No. I want to investigate something, and I need you to help me."

I took the keys, and we made our way to the late Lord Lydney's chambers once more. We slipped into the room, and I gently closed the door behind us. The room appeared to be the only one in the house which had not been refreshed. The shrouds remained, as did the dust.

"Why are we in here?" Marguerite whispered. "Investigating in secret? You've already given the collection to Harry."

"Can I trust him? I just need to know. For myself." I glanced at the mantel clock, staring at me from the dressing table.

She nodded. "I understand."

I opened the wardrobe door—it had not been tampered with. Harry most probably did not know it existed. "There is a trick door here." I unlatched the door, and Marguerite gasped as the staircase appeared.

"Do not let the door close," I instructed her. I did not know if, previously, the wardrobe door had been pushed shut or had snapped shut of its own accord, but I was not going to risk either. "Hold it open the entire time I am gone. I'll return soon."

I climbed the staircase. There was a new moon, and therefore no light came in through the tiny window in the upper room, but I let my eyes adjust, and soon I could see, squinting like Uncle Lewis. I had expected to find the items removed, but to my relief, the suits of armor remained in place, bloodless beings. The eye slits in the helmets followed me. I imagined I heard breathing and hoped it was Marguerite.

"Eleanor. I hear voices. Come now."

I saw the small chalice, matte metal beckoning from across the room. I approached it and sighed with relief. It was not the same one—this one had tiny jewels arranged in the shape of the cross on its side in addition to those on the rim. The one at Clarkson's certainly had not.

The room seemed intact. Except . . . The costly piece of barding, the medieval armor which protected horses and which I'd suspected was stolen, was now missing. Had it been placed somewhere else?

But where? Outside of these items, there was no official armory, though there were other pieces here and there throughout the house.

Had it been sold? Fear swept across me. Had this entire room been used as a staging area? To contain Arthur's goods—which Harry might have had placed here out of his sight—and other items which could be sold once he was free to do so? Had his father collected stolen barding, as I suspected? He'd had no use for or love of horses and their accoutrements; that was certain.

Harry did.

I pulled myself together. Even if he did sell it, he now had the right to do so . . . the legally purchased pieces, in any case. I had had to sell my family treasures, after all. But I'd decided to return the collection to him based, in part, on his not selling the treasures and believing his father to have lied about Arthur's collection. I could ask him . . . perhaps.

"Eleanor? Are you quite all right?"

I stepped down the narrow stairwell and out through the wardrobe. "I'm not certain." We returned the keys to my room and then walked to the ballroom, where the music was under way, and so was the dancing.

Lord Audley made his way over to me. "Is your dance card full, Miss Sheffield?"

I shook my head. "Not at all, Lord Audley."

"As Lord Lydney has detained my fiancée with a dance, perhaps you might partner with me for the next?"

"Of course." I looked once more at the beautiful woman partnering Harry. "I'm surprised you trust him with your intended," I teased.

Audley laughed aloud. "I wouldn't go that far, Miss Sheffield. But I am content."

I looked him in the eye. How had his feelings toward Harry so quickly turned?

The tune changed, and we danced; there was little time for conversation as the dance required us to switch partners back and forth quite often. On one occasion, I partnered with Mr. Rossetti, who smiled indulgently at me, and I affectionately smiled back.

Mr. Rossetti sought me out after another dance or two, and we stood drinking lemonade. We were very near a group of Italian guests, and Mr. Rossetti could barely contain his irritation. I overheard quite a bit of the conversation before they turned their backs to me, and a sudden crescendo from the orchestra interrupted.

"They speak quite often of honor," I said.

"The more they speak of their honor, the faster we count the spoons," Rossetti replied. "If I may paraphrase Mr. Emerson."

"You know them, then?"

"Oh yes. The Italians in England are familiar with one another and our Italian visitors. My father was both Italian and a collector, so . . ." He shrugged. "They are here to visit. They are happy the war is over—as am I. I am happy because I, like my father before me, wanted Italy unified. They are happy because they can make a profit."

"Why have they been invited?" I set down my nearly empty glass.

"They are friends with the Vieros," he said. "Or perhaps *acquaintances* would be a better term. They are not good people, Miss Sheffield. They are powerful, but in England, they are reluctant to tangle with the aristocracy. But they will."

Harry was dancing again. This time, not with Lord Audley's intended, but with Francesca. I watched them together. They seemed comfortable with one another. They smiled and talked and laughed, and she was perhaps even more beautiful in the winter than she had been in the autumn; her newly pale skin was set off by her dark hair, a set of white-and-gold wedding cake beads glittering at her throat. The beads were a Venetian specialty, often created by women because they were so small that the great strength required to blow larger glass objects was not needed. A delicate hand was, though, and the beads were infused with emotion. Because they were pretty, ornate, and decorated with hearts and flowers, they were often referred to as wedding cake beads, and sometimes, but not always, used to celebrate said occasion.

What wedding was she planning to celebrate? Or had she already celebrated one?

Rossetti must have been watching me watch them. "They

have known one another a long time because of her brother," he said. "Friends from an early age due to family connections. That is all."

I realized sorrowfully that Rossetti might equally have been describing Harry and me.

Rossetti partnered me at the next dance, and afterward, Harry sought me out.

"Ellie," he said. "My turn?"

He took my hand in his and led me out to dance; our hands melded together as perfectly as if they had been carved from one piece out of marble. Perhaps, should I ever come into a wealth of my own, I would commission such a piece to be carved.

"Of course, Your Lordship." I tried to keep a light tone to my voice. "You have outdone yourself. I have never been at Watchfield when it has seemed so vibrant."

He laughed. "I'm filled with relief and gratitude that all that belongs to her may remain within her," he said. "Thanks to you."

I looked down for a moment before meeting his gaze once more. "They belong here."

He answered me firmly. "Indeed, they do."

I waited for a moment, half expecting him to say something like, *"As do you."* But he did not. Of course, we were in a public environment, and he continued to look over his shoulders at the Italian guests. When he did, he appeared disturbed.

Someone motioned to him, and he bowed graciously to

me and said in the sweetest whisper, "I will seek you out tomorrow so we might have a more private conversation, dearest Ellie."

The night drew to a close, and I stopped in front of the late Lord Lydney's chambers on my way back to my room, thinking about the barding missing from the upper room, anger welling. "You planted a seed of mistrust," I whispered at the door, "to kill my seed of faith. And it's thriving despite my efforts at every turn to uproot it."

There was no voice in return, of course. But in my mind's ear, I could hear the old man's death-rattled laughter.

CHAPTER Twenty-Five

The next morning, at breakfast, I was delighted to see my friends Charlotte and Mr. Schreiber.

"We've come up for the day," Charlotte said. "We had family obligations last night, but Lord Lydney graciously extended the invitation to today as well. We are most eager to see some of his friend's Venetian pieces and hope to view them this afternoon."

It was too cold for a stroll outside, but the fires were lit and some of the guests who had not returned to their own homes the night before sat around reading or doing jigsaw puzzles.

Within an hour, Harry came into the room in which I was conversing with Charlotte.

"May I speak with you for a moment?" he asked. His voice was unusually urgent. I excused myself from Charlotte and followed Harry to a quiet storage room off the library.

"Do you know anything about Roman-era treasures? Glass and such?"

"Some," I admitted. "I have studied them, of course, and we have valued or placed quite a few pieces."

He seemed impatient. "No, Eleanor, not in general. Pieces connected with Watchfield House."

He rarely called me Eleanor. In private, Ellie. In public, Miss Sheffield. It alarmed me.

"No. I do not understand. Whatever do you mean?"

"Will you please come with me?"

"Of course." I followed him to the gatehouse. We did not make pleasant conversation; we did not make conversation at all. He seemed as agitated as I'd seen him since Arthur's death.

When we reached the gatehouse, he proceeded directly to the area in which crates were received and stored. In the room stood Francesca—who appeared to have been crying—her mother, and a group of the Italian men I had seen arguing the night before. In front of them were several crates—the crates with the Viero family treasures—and one that was open and empty.

"I'd like to introduce Miss Eleanor Sheffield," Harry said in English and then asked me, "Florentine?" I nodded my agreement, and he switched languages.

"Miss Sheffield is with Sheffield Brothers, the firm which

my father has used for many years to care for, and accumulate, our collection."

"A girl?" one of the Italians asked.

"My uncle and my father trained me; my uncle is still quite an expert," I explained. "However, the late Lord Lydney, his lordship's father, did trust me with the disposal of his collection. I inventoried these very crates some few months ago when they were returned from Austria."

The Italians nodded and spoke to me politely. "Then you will be able to tell us where our treasures are. *Molto bene.*"

"Although it was right next to the crates where the Venetian treasures were stored, this smaller crate was empty when I saw it," I explained. "There was nothing in there but straw. Were the contents yours?" I asked Francesca.

"No, they were ours," one of the men insisted.

Harry turned toward Francesca. "Can you explain?"

She nodded. "When we were about to leave Venice—you, me, and Mama—these men, who knew of Stefano and his plan to remove our family treasures from harm's way, approached me."

One of the men smiled, but there was a bit of menace behind it.

"They said that surely Roman treasures were as important as Venetian treasures, and as we would be traveling under cover of your father's diplomatic immunity, as husband and wife, the Roman treasures would make it to Britain unharmed too."

"Why did you not tell me this?" Harry seemed as

bewildered as angry. But had he known the Roman treasures had made their way out with the Venetian ones? Was this yet one more elaborate charade to protect Francesca? Or himself?

"They implied that to keep Stefano safe in the war, from their roving gangs of thugs—" she fairly spat out the words at the men—"I would have to keep their goods safe until they came to collect them after the war." She turned back toward Harry. "Please forgive me. I did not think it would be a problem—simply that they would remain quietly in England with my crates until Stefano came back. Only Stefano has not come back."

"This seemed like a fair deal, *non è vero*?" one man said. "You keep our treasures safe; we keep your treasure safe."

"No, it does not seem right at all!" Stefano's mother cried out. "Where is my son?"

"And where are my valuable artifacts?" another man asked. "Perhaps they will both be found at the same time."

I, and likely everyone else, heard the unspoken threat.

I drew Harry aside. "Did they know that crates were received in the gatehouse before this morning? Did they know this is where the Venetian treasures have been stored, out of sight?"

Harry shook his head. "No. They had no idea where they had been stored—nor did Francesca or her mother—on purpose. I did not know until this morning that there had been any Roman treasures." He ran his hands through his hair.

"Who inventoried the Venetian goods?" Francesca's

mother asked. She looked at me. She knew I had done it, or at least Francesca did. Was she implying . . . ?

"When I completed my inventory, that crate was empty," I said once more.

"So you were in control of them, then!" The man who spoke moved threateningly toward me, and Harry stepped between us.

I moved closer to him, grateful. "Perhaps they had been emptied in Italy," I said. "Before I even saw them."

"No," one of the Italians said. "Further, I had someone check on them in Austria."

"You opened crates on my father's diplomatic property?" Harry nearly shouted.

The man shrugged. "I paid dearly for the Roman glass—they are old and very costly. I demand their return. You are clever, Miss Sheffield. You have connections, Lord Lydney. I am a patient man, and my buyers are not expecting their goods immediately, as Italy is being put back together. I suggest you find my *tesori* before I return to England mid-March. If not, then I will take the Venetian treasures as payment instead. Or—" he looked longingly at Francesca—"perhaps I shall simply take the Venetian *tesoro* herself."

Harry moved to stand next to Francesca protectively. It was a gallant thing to do under the circumstances. And yet. My heart, which had been racing with intimidation, now dipped into multiple miseries.

The Italians left the room. Francesca apologized once more to Harry, who waved her off with a combination of chivalry and irritation, and she exited with her mother. That left the two of us in the gatehouse.

Harry went to speak with the gatehouse keeper, but of course, he had not been here when the crates had arrived, as the staff had been completely replaced.

"I will check with the former gatehouse keeper," he said. "I believe he lives nearby. But he would not have had interest or knowledge or the courage to steal. I know him sufficiently well." He turned toward me. "You have never seen these pieces? You are certain?" His voice was not accusatory, but it was not the intimate or playful tone in which we normally conversed.

"No, Harry. They were not here. I am not lying, and I did not take them."

I began to shake. He came close to me and put his arm tightly around me. "I know, Ellie. I know. I am staggered. We must find them somehow."

"Where?" I asked.

"Could Mr. Clarkson . . . ?" he suggested.

I shook my head. "I do not think so. But if he did, they would be at his home. I will enquire immediately upon arrival in London." *Unless he'd already taken them to Bristol and shipped them overseas.* I did not raise that concern yet. One step forward before jumping three more.

In truth, I thought that stealing Roman treasures was beyond even Mr. Clarkson's folly. And even if he had, it would have taken him longer than two short months to find buyers who had the means to purchase such treasures—unless those buyers were already in place, in London, and Clarkson knew he could depend upon their greed and discretion.

"Could the Vieros have done something with them?" I asked. "They withheld this information from you."

"It's possible," Harry said. "I am not happy about that. But they would not have known where to sell them. There is no benefit to them in a threat to Stefano. I only wish she had told me about them, but most probably I would have refused to transport them, and I understand her fears for Stefano. There are criminals in every country, and they particularly flourish during times of war."

I nodded. "I guess these treasures are looted, then? Stolen?"

"That would not be a bad assumption," Harry replied. "I just cannot say. I knew nothing about them until now. I will telegraph some people I know and see if they can apply this new information to finding Stefano. He has hidden before in underground networks, and as Rome is not yet free, he may still be gathering information. Or he may be injured. I assume we would have heard if he were dead, but it's a chaotic time."

I agreed, and we returned to the house together. Until Stefano returned, and especially with this new threat, Harry would have to guard Francesca even more closely.

If the treasures had been stolen and delivered into private hands, it was entirely possible that we would never see them again. What would that mean for the Viero ladies if Stefano did not return?

A short while after we arrived back at the house, Charlotte

pulled me aside. "We were going to view the Venetian treasures," she said. "But I understand from Signorina Viero that plans have changed somewhat. What has happened?"

Perhaps it was because I had no mother to guide and comfort me, perhaps it was because I knew she would understand the value of the Roman pieces, or perhaps it was because I needed a friend. I told her what had transpired. She spoke the words I feared, but which were true.

"They disappeared, then, under the watch of Sheffield Brothers?"

I deflected that. "Not exactly. It seems they were here on the property."

"But whilst you were the trustee." Her voice was not accusatory but was flecked with the gravity for which my situation called.

"That appears to be the case."

"If I can be of assistance, dearest . . . This must be a tremendously discomfiting situation."

"If you stumble upon someone quietly wanting to sell ancient Roman glassware, do let me know." I laughed, though it unwound in a rather less restrained manner than I intended. She rested her arm around me until I steadied myself.

I would not cry while others watched.

I returned to my room, and as Marguerite and I were packing to leave, there came a knock on the door. "Ellie?" It was Harry.

I opened the door, and he came in, but out of decorum stood just inside the door.

"I must unravel some of this if I can," he said quietly. "Where have they gone? Were they there at all? And then I shall be in touch. I wanted you to know right away."

I nodded. "Thank you for telling me."

"Are you certain you did not see them? You could tell me, you know. . . ." He let the sentence dangle. "I could help."

I thought of my comment to his father's memory the night before. *"You planted a seed of mistrust . . . and it's thriving despite my efforts at every turn to uproot it."* Now such a seed was thriving in Harry's heart, toward me. "I have not seen them, Harry. Ever."

"Of course." But his tone wasn't as certain as his words. "Do let me know if you learn anything from Clarkson."

"I shall." I had not told him yet that Clarkson had resigned. I could never tell him now that I'd seen the barding was missing, that I'd been rummaging in his father's chambers, in secret, because I'd feared one of my employees had stolen from him.

Perhaps he already suspected as much.

"One more thing," Harry said. "It's a simple thing, but I wonder if you still have the chatelaine of keys? I've had so many locks changed and will be changing more that I'm afraid you would find it quite useless in a very short period."

"Certainly." I had, of course, kept the keys, hoping I might be reengaged to care for the art, if not engaged for marriage. I returned to the bureau and removed the chatelaine, then reluctantly handed it to him. *An unfastening of keys.* When we were ice-skating, he'd said nothing could change his affections for me. But had they changed?

He had not asked to engage Sheffield Brothers to continue caring for the collection this year after our term had expired.

Marguerite, who had been in my room when Harry knocked, came up behind me and put her hand on my back.

"Good day, Lord Lydney," she said, her voice cold, his champion no longer.

Harry, startled at her sudden appearance, grew more formal. "Good day, Mrs. Newsome. Miss Sheffield."

But he held my gaze for a moment before he left.

As soon as I returned home, I wrote to the three creditors—the invoices Mr. Clarkson had flung at me—and told them I was making arrangements to pay them immediately. Then I sent both letter and telegram to Mr. Clarkson, asking if he and I might meet for a few minutes to discuss a professional matter. If he had stolen and sold the Roman-era treasures, I did not know how I could repay them. The Vieros could have us all thrown into debtor's prison.

I did not receive a response from Mr. Clarkson. Shortly after, I quickly wrote to Charlotte.

Dearest friend,

I hope this note finds you well. I should enjoy having you come to call at any time, or perhaps we might take in one of the exhibits at the British Museum together.

I'm enquiring after Mr. Clarkson, who is no longer with our firm. Was he in attendance at the last meeting of the Burlington Fine Arts Club?

Secondly, at Watchfield over Epiphany, you'd mentioned your willingness to assist me in these difficult times. I would be so obliged if you would be willing to make enquiries on my behalf with the club? If I—and Uncle Lewis—are to build up our reputation and clientele once more, perhaps that might be a place to begin.

Yours very truly,
Eleanor

Her reply came quickly, by the next day's post.

Dearest Eleanor,

Mr. Clarkson was not in attendance at the meeting a few days earlier, though Mr. Schreiber did see him in attendance at a South Kensington event just a few days prior.

I shall do my best on your behalf, dearest. But as Signorina Viero has divulged the news of the disappearing Roman treasure among confidants, it is making a quiet, but certain, circulation. That may make for a difficult situation.

I shall come to call soon.

Affectionately your friend,
Charlotte

My father was dead; my uncle was not; therefore my father's items would have to go first. I took all but one of the few remaining treasures from Papa's curiosity cabinet, arranged to sell them, and then arranged to sell the costly cabinet itself. That very afternoon I was to deliver the final item, a snuffbox made of gold with scalloped leaves that grew from the top, enameled in white to look like the feathers of a swan. Papa had shown it to me when I was a girl.

"I admire swans, my girl, for many reasons. They are graceful, they are beautiful, they are rich in English history, and the ones on the Thames all belong to the queen. When two of them put their heads together and crane their necks, they form a heart."

I took his box in hand and opened it. It was beautiful on the outside, but inside, it was empty; Papa did not take snuff.

He finished telling me his story. "The swan, you know, mates for life; once it's chosen a mate, it will not choose another unless its mate dies."

He'd shared the story before my mother had left, of course, and she had outlived him. I think he'd always hoped she would come back.

I sighed. Now the most valuable items that remained were Papa's medieval pilgrim's flask, which I had long hoped would be reunited with its companion piece at Watchfield, and Uncle's Book of Hours.

Alice knocked on my door. "Laundry?"

"Oh yes," I said. "I'd quite forgotten." I reviewed the

number of dresses in my wardrobe—certainly not an affluence, but by no means pecuniary, either. "That clothes seller you know . . . ," I began.

She dropped her basket. "Has it come to that, then?"

I sighed. "Not yet. Not yet."

Later that afternoon, Orchie came into the workshop. "Is Mr. Clarkson not back from Bristol? He's been gone quite some time."

I drew myself up. "Mr. Clarkson will not be returning. When I decided that the valuables should remain *in situ* at Watchfield House, he decided he could do better without us."

"Oh." She looked startled, and I knew she must have been wondering how we would make ends meet.

"Uncle is still quite good at valuations," I said. "And I'm hoping to meet with some of the collectors who have enjoyed working with Sheffield Brothers over the years."

"Lord Lydney?" she asked, hoping, I thought, that he was going to ride in and save the day.

"We shall have to see" was my only response. There was nothing yet to say. Truthfully, I'd hoped that we might have become affianced in January. But perhaps that was not to be, then or ever. I simply did not know.

"At least he won't be rummaging about in Mr. Lewis's study anymore," Orchie said with a sniff.

"Lord Lydney?"

She shook her head. "No, of course not. He's a gentleman. That Mr. Clarkson."

"He was rummaging?"

"Yes. I hate to bring it up . . . Well, at the time, I thought it was because he was doing something proper to help. Now, well . . . I can't say, can I?"

I set the snuffbox down and went up to my uncle's study. He was in there, reading. I scanned the room.

"What is it, dear girl?" His eyes looked clear this day.

"Is anything missing?" I asked.

"Besides Mr. Clarkson, you mean?" he asked, bitterness seeping into his voice. He stood and looked around. "I do not think so." His voice took on a tinge of knowing shame. "But I cannot be certain."

My eyes landed on the medieval Book of Hours. Once, I had noticed that something had seemed off about it. I plucked it from the shelf and turned the pages, one by one. Near the middle, one of the pages seemed a little loose.

I opened the book as wide as I could without harming the binding and then used a glass nearby on Uncle's desk to look at it. It did appear to be the correct page. But it also appeared as though the page might once have been removed and replaced. If so, it had been done very carefully. The book was hundreds of years old. There was no knowing when such a repair might have been made if it had been done at all.

"What about your miniature portrait?" I asked. It was one of Uncle's favorites.

"Oh, dear. Is that missing?" He knew exactly where to look for it, on the wall in a case, and indeed, it was gone.

CHAPTER

Twenty-Six

Some days after I delivered the snuffbox to its new owner, I tried once more to reach Mr. Clarkson by mail. When that failed, I went to the local police station and explained my situation.

"He was a former employee," I told the constable. "Since he left our employ, we've noticed that several costly pieces of art are either damaged or missing. I've written to no avail. His home is in a somewhat . . . downtrodden neighborhood. My father is dead, and my uncle ill disposed."

The constable nodded knowingly. "I can accompany you. I will not be able to search without a warrant, though."

"I understand. Perhaps we can simply speak with him."

We began walking down the street, a film of wet coal sticking to us as we did. There was no sense making conversation; this was not a companionable visit. I did appreciate the protection offered, though.

The city was in a depression brought on by severe weather conditions, a cholera epidemic, and financial hardships. There were no children out playing; windows were closed except for the occasional one opened to dump wastewater onto the street. For that reason, we walked nearer to the center of the road but, of course, were in danger of stepping into half-frozen horse muck there. We soon came to the street where Mr. Clarkson lived—or had lived, I suddenly thought. Perhaps he had returned to Bristol for good.

I rather doubted it. The money was in London, and he wanted to make a name for himself in the bigger city. Or rather, once upon a time, to add his name to Sheffield's.

The officer knocked on the door and the lewd man who had followed me and Marguerite the last time was shocked into polite complacency.

"We're looking for a Mr. Robert Clarkson," the officer said. "Is he present?"

The man shrugged. "He lives upstairs. Haven't seen him for a few days. Nor heard him cough," he added in what appeared to be a surprising afterthought.

The officer walked upstairs, and I followed him.

He knocked. "Mr. Clarkson. Metropolitan Police. Please open the door."

There was no sound at all.

"Mr. Clarkson. Please open the door."

Nothing. Then, sadly, a cat mewing. The officer turned toward me. "Do you think something might be wrong?"

I nodded. "I have never heard him go for days without coughing, as his neighbor has mentioned."

The officer looked at me and then leaned back before rushing forward and pushing his shoulder into the door. The door, flimsy to begin with, splintered off the hinges and fell inward.

The cat leaped backward but did not flee.

"Stay here," the officer instructed me.

While he went from the main room to the kitchen area and then to the back, I looked around nervously. The stench of rubbish which had not been removed stained the air. There were no lights on. Mr. Clarkson's coat and hat remained on the rack inside the door.

A few minutes later the officer returned to the main room. "I'm afraid he's dead, miss."

"Dead?" I nearly fell backward out the door. "Are you certain?"

"There is a dead man in the bedroom. I cannot be sure it is the Mr. Clarkson for whom you're searching. Does he have any relatives?"

I tried to quell my beating heart and keep the contents of my stomach quiet. "His father and sisters are in Bristol. I know of no one else."

"He'll have to be buried soon," the policeman said. "There is no time to wait for someone to arrive from Bristol." He took his hat off. "Let me go downstairs and get the neighbor. Better he identifies the body."

I nodded. If there had been no other choice, I would have offered. But there was.

The policeman soon arrived with the wide-eyed man from downstairs who followed him into the bedroom and then, somberly, out again.

"It's Clarkson," the officer said. "I'm going to bring in another man to review this with me, and then we will contact you. I know you were concerned about stolen items. Is there anything you can see that belongs to you?"

I looked around the room, which was peculiarly empty of nearly anything personal. No *objets d'art* remained. Even Mr. Clarkson's post basket was empty. It was as if someone had been here before us. Perhaps that was merely a flight of fancy.

"Not in immediate sight," I said.

"We will save his belongings, and I can show them to you after there is a cause of death assigned," the officer said.

I agreed and with a shaking hand wrote down my name and address so he could be in touch with me.

The cat rubbed against the bedroom door.

"I'll take her." She tried to flee, but I threw my cloak over her and then wrapped her in it to keep her from scratching me. I waited while the officer propped the broken door and instructed the neighbors not to enter, that he would soon return.

He saw me to the carriage, and when I walked into the house with the cat, Orchie looked at me questioningly.

"Mr. Clarkson is dead." My voice cracked a little with incredulity and sorrow over his difficult beginning and lonely end. "This was his cat, and we'll care for it henceforth."

The mid-February sky churned with winter's continued demands, and my stomach churned, still, with the news of Clarkson's death. Mrs. Denholm had noted the weather and kindly offered to pick me up for our prison visits and return me to my home afterward. I gathered that she understood the firm was in somewhat-uncomfortable straits, though it was not a topic she would ever raise. Perhaps she simply wanted companionship on the journey. I did too, and it was a pleasant time together for both of us.

The February day opened with unexpected sunshine, and that brightened both our moods as we began the short journey to the prison.

"How is your uncle feeling?" she asked. I did not know who might have told her that he was doing poorly, but I could not lose the opportunity to bring up professional concerns with someone who might be of help.

"He's coming along well. He's retained an extensive memory of all the items he has valued over the course of decades, which is of great value to Sheffield Brothers."

She smiled politely, but the topic did not seem to interest her. I asked after her husband and children, and she told me of their happy times at Christmas.

"Did that nice Mr. Clarkson join your family for Christmas

dinner?" she asked. "I know he has told Mr. Denholm that he dined *en famille* with you on Saturday evenings."

She did not know.

I leaned across the carriage aisle, close enough to be friendly but not overly personal. "I'm sorry to have to inform you that Mr. Clarkson has recently passed away."

"Oh, dear me, no! Whatever happened to him? Consumption, I'll suppose. That dreadful cough of his . . . ? Mr. Denholm had arranged for our apothecary to continue to provide paregoric for the poor man, to help calm what could be calmed. In the end, perhaps it was not enough."

I nodded slowly. I had known, of course, that Mr. Denholm owned one or more chemist shops in addition to his other business endeavors, and I had also known that Mr. Clarkson had been sourcing art for him of late. I had not understood that they had grown to be friends to the degree that health concerns would have been discussed.

"Will your firm continue?" she asked.

"I believe so. Perhaps, if Mr. Denholm desires to add to his collection, you might suggest—" I was about to say *me* but changed my mind—"my uncle."

She smiled and took my hand in her own. "I don't know that Mr. Denholm listens much to me, my dear, nor anyone. But I can certainly raise your uncle's name."

We pulled up in front of the prison. Jeanette and Little Nancy waited for me in the area in which we gathered; the others had caught a dreadful chill in the dank prison, and one had died.

"The meat was rotted," Jeanette said. "I had terrible flux afterward but made it anyways. She di' not."

"I'm very sorry," I said. The woman in question was perhaps thirty years old and had two children for whom I had purchased Christmas gifts. Her smiling face and constant prayers for me flashed through my mind, and I bit my lip so that I would not cry at her loss.

"I, too," Jeanette said.

Despite the somber news, I did want to bring some cheer into their day.

"Your hair looks beautiful," I said to Nancy. "Bouncy."

Her eyes shone. "It's them magazine pages, miss. They work real good when I get them a little wet-like."

"Her young man from the outside has been by to visit," Jeanette said.

"I'm only in here for a year for stealin' a bit o' bacon," Nancy said. "He told me he'd wait. Then, perhaps I will train to be a lady's maid or some sort with my new hair skills."

We all laughed. "I think you would do very well indeed. Then you can earn your bacon rather than stealing it."

I shared with them about my time in the countryside, and the dances and the foods and that I had a new cat, though I did not share the difficult means by which the kitty had come to live with us. At the end of our hour, Jeanette asked, "Will we see you again next month? March?"

"Undoubtedly."

❧

"They're 'ere." Orchie's voice squeezed with panic as she ran into the workshop clutching her apron in two fat, red fists. I glared at her so she would not disturb my uncle, who was rearranging a few pieces of art which had been brought in for repair. His table and shelves were jumbled, but he held everything with delicate care. It would not do to upset him.

Perhaps I should limit him to silver, portraits, and jewelry. No marble, glass, or porcelain which might be easily broken.

"Who's here?" He looked up.

I set my writing paper aside; I was in the midst of sending out letters of enquiry to the many well-to-do clients Sheffield Brothers had served over the years.

"Possibly Lady Charlotte Schreiber," I said with a calmness that I did not feel inside. "I've invited her to call."

"Oh." He turned back to his work, and I smoothed my dress on both sides and followed Orchie to the parlor.

Debt collectors? But I had one month yet, and I'd paid a few of our creditors with funds gained selling our remaining treasures. I summoned courage as I went to face them.

Instead of debt collectors, I found two police officers, one of whom was the constable who had escorted me to Mr. Clarkson's rooms.

"Miss Sheffield?"

I nodded. "Yes, of course."

"I wanted to come by and speak with you about your employee, Mr. Clarkson."

"Please, have a seat."

Orchie ran for tea, more for a reason to eavesdrop than to be polite. The two men sat awkwardly on the gently curved rose-fabric sofa.

"First, miss, I want you to know that he was decently buried, though in a pauper's mass grave. It was consecrated ground, however, as we had no indication at all that the man took his own life."

"Had that even been a consideration?" I asked with alarm.

"All things are a consideration, miss," the other officer answered.

"We had the body examined, and it appeared that he died of natural causes. Most likely consumption."

"He had looked so well just before the time. Yes, he coughed, but not unduly so. His skin seemed to have been pinkening not a few weeks before he died, and he was able to keep up with energetic work. He was young . . ."

"I understand this is upsetting," the officer said.

"Indeed. Were there . . . were there any marks on him at all?"

"Not that we were told of, miss. Do you have any reason to believe someone would want to do him harm?"

I shook my head. "Not really."

"Then perhaps that is best left alone."

Was that a warning? Was there a reason for the warning? Or was this simply the typical protocol when a relatively poor man died?

The first officer held out a large box to me. "All his

belongings in here, miss. Not much—seemed to me as if his rooms had been cleaned out ahead of our arrival. I asked the neighbor, and he denied it, but who knows? Perhaps he'd been the thief. Can't have been much, by the looks of his rooms, and if any of it were stolen from you, well, you'll keep that, then. Would you care for the clothing, too? I can see it delivered."

"No, no, that's quite all right," I said. "You can donate it to some charitable cause."

"You did say you might know where to find his family? We will send notification if you can provide an address."

Orchie returned with the tea, but the men were just standing to leave.

"I shall see that anything valuable is returned to his family."

"Very well then," the constable said. "Good day, miss."

Orchie closed the door behind them. "I thought it was them debt people coming for us," she said.

"Fortunately, not yet. And not ever, I believe. I have worked out a strategy. But in the meantime, I need to return to my letters in the workshop and send them out to perhaps convince some of our former associates that they would like to return to us."

I brought Mr. Clarkson's box into my bedroom and left it there. Later that evening, after dinner, I sat at the small table in my room and looked through his things. Many empty bottles of paregoric syrup, though just a few of them came from Jackson's Chemists, the chain that Mr. Denholm owned. Perhaps Clarkson had only begun to use his syrup of late?

I looked at the Jackson's bottles. They looked to be the same as the bottles from the other chemists. The lingering pine scent reminded me of Mr. Clarkson; although he had not been kind to me in the end, he had been a great help to our little firm.

What had turned him into the man who'd spoken to me so viciously? Or had he been the same man, the same character, all along, just hiding it well? His own little charade, perhaps.

His kitty rubbed up against the box, and I petted her; she hadn't let me till now.

"I'm sorry, small cat," I said.

There were a few trinkets in the box and some photographs of his family. A watch and a personal pen and ink set; I would see them returned to his father. Perhaps they would have some sentimental value.

Oddly, there were bits of broken pottery. They did not appear to be valuable, but they were in various sizes. A linen bag was wrapped around one of them. I opened the bag and inside found damp, slightly molded tea leaves. I closed the fabric bag, and as I looked at the shard it had enfolded, I saw that it was stained.

My heart sank. An old trick of the fraudster. Using tea to appear to age new porcelain.

Oh, Mr. Clarkson. What else have you done?

I didn't need to wait long for that question to be answered.

At the bottom of the box was one more slip of paper. An invoice, with a personal note scribbled upon it by Mr. Clarkson. The invoice was due to Lord Tenteden, a relatively new client to the firm, for an extraordinary sum. We had, apparently, purchased a silver set for him and then sold it to someone else; we needed to return his monies. Rather than remitting the funds due to Lord Tenteden, they had somehow gone to pay earlier invoices.

How could I pay this one and keep the firm's respectable name and my father and uncle's treasures? I had sold nearly everything, but we were finally safe for the moment. Or so I had thought.

I must secure another commission. And make arrangements with Lord Tenteden. But at least I could be assured this was the final invoice—nothing remained in Mr. Clarkson's possession.

I sent Lord Tenteden a well-worded, respectful telegram asking for perhaps two more months to pay this invoice, due to my just having discovered it upon the death of Mr. Clarkson.

He responded tersely, saying he would give me less than a month, till March 15.

I responded in the positive. I had written Clarkson's father shortly after his son's death to offer my sympathies. Now, I wrote a second quick letter to Clerk's Curiosity Shoppe, Bristol, the same shop that appeared in the photographs. I reminded him that I was an acquaintance of Mr. Clarkson's and said I would like to visit, if that were possible, and to send permission by return mail.

I hoped I would hear back shortly. I hoped it would be properly delivered. But even if I did not receive word, I would undertake the journey. Perhaps the missing Roman pieces would be found in Bristol.

They must be. March pressed in.

CHAPTER
Twenty-Seven

A week or so on, I had not received word from Mr. Clarkson's father. I did not know, in truth, if that was the correct shop for Mr. Clarkson's family, or even if they were who he'd said they were. I withdrew funds for Mr. Clarkson's last pay packet and tucked it into the box with his other things. It was the end of the month. I needed to conclude this matter so I could, hopefully, return any Roman objects I might find before Signorina Francesca was in real danger of losing her goods—or her well-being—and pay my firm's debts before I was in danger of losing my freedom.

"Thank you for accompanying me." I squeezed

Marguerite's hand as we waited at Paddington Station. It was perhaps three or four hours to Bristol. We could take the train out, conclude matters as required, and return the same day. Although I required little for the journey, I took a large bag with me to transport Mr. Clarkson's goods, such as they were, to his father, and have space to return with any stolen goods I might find.

The train exhaled a grimy puff and several hot belches before jostling to a stop; we boarded one of the second-class cars. First class was entirely out of our reach, of course, and perhaps I should not have splurged on second class. But I did not want to ride with the ruffians certain to harass us on the cheaper carriages.

Some three hours later, we disembarked from the train and asked a carriage to drive us to Clerk's Curiosity Shoppe. I gave the address to the carriage driver. He shrugged, then the horses did, and we took off.

He finally deposited us at a broken-down building at the end of a lonely spoke of a road near some rough taverns on the canal side. The shop itself seemed dilapidated, its brightly painted exterior dimmed and weathered with the years.

We entered the building and the door chimes swung wearily. A young lady came to greet us. "May I be of some help to you, ladies?"

Before speaking, I took her in. She was perhaps fifteen years old and had long, well-cared-for hair. She looked like Mr. Clarkson, but her skin was pink, and I did not hear the cough that punctuated his life up to the full stop end.

"I'm looking for the father of a Mr. Robert . . . Clerk." I took a guess that was Clarkson's real name.

"One moment." Her smile dimmed, and she returned with an old man who looked to be bent sidewise a bit, like a table with one leg shorter than the others.

"May I be of some assistance?" he asked.

Marguerite stood closer to me for support.

"I'm Miss Eleanor Sheffield, of Sheffield Brothers," I said. "This is Mrs. Marguerite Newsome."

The old man's eyes bulged. I stood patiently; Marguerite was young and beautiful and certainly not the chaperone many expected.

"I was the employer of a Mr. Robert Clerk, or Clarkson. Would that be your son?"

The man nodded. "Was my son. Why? I ain't got any money to pay for anything he might have done wrong, and we're all responsible for our own sins; ain't that right, miss?"

I thought it interesting that would be the father's first suspicion.

"I have brought his effects to you," I said. "Maybe you'd like to view them in private?" He might become emotional when he saw his late son's belongings.

He led me to the back of the shop, which was much larger than expected. It was four or five times as deep as it was wide, and there was row upon row of shelves holding every kind of art, some of it very valuable indeed. As we made our way to the back, we passed a kiln which might be used for casting plaster. Nearby, on a shelf, were rows of shepherdess figurines—the exact statuette as the object which had belonged to Lady Lydney.

Although I was aware of the gravity of the task at hand, I wanted to examine these and did not know if he would be willing to accommodate me after I delivered Mr. Clarkson's goods. "May I?"

Mr. Clerk nodded nervously. I picked one up. It was truly well made—clear glazing and a fine, steady hand had painted it. The colors were just a bit too bright for something which would have been older, and the blue was slightly off. Blues were difficult to reproduce. Each of the figures, I could see, was a little smaller than the original, with which I was familiar. It would necessarily be so. A cast must have been made of the original, and whatever figures yielded from the shell would have lost a bit of space. The tiny printing on slips of paper in front of each one indicated prices much too high for reproductions. There were addresses, too. Most of them overseas. Bristol, as a port, was a convenient place from which to send art to far-flung locations whose collectors would never meet with one another and thereby understand each had a copy, none the original.

Mr. Clarkson. It needn't have come to this. He must have removed the original from Watchfield, made a mold, and then returned the original, selling the copies overseas. Now I knew he had a kiln at his disposal, I could clearly see his deceitful story.

"Most of our business is in foreign parts," Mr. Clerk said proudly.

"Surely you know these are copies?" I asked quietly but firmly. My hand quivered a little at the realization that we were at this man's mercy in a strange city.

His eyes darted down for a moment, and he called out to another young woman behind him. He likely hadn't expected to have knowledgeable guests in the back rooms. "Change these prices, then." He mentioned a more reasonable figure. I did not know if he meant to keep that price after I left, but after my silence at the Denholms' home, I could not go along with false reserve.

The day was dark, and gas was dear, so the aisles between the shelving were dim. Of a sudden, I wondered if it was wise for us to follow him down them. I had rather thought we'd be having a conversation closer to the front of the store.

Might the man have a weapon? Would he be angry when I delivered my news?

I stood still in front of another shelf which had a small table nearby. "If you don't mind, I think we've gone quite far enough," I said. "I simply wanted to hand over Mr. Clarkson's things to you. Some look to be tenderly cared for, perhaps family bequests. I thought you might want them. I know I would."

"All right, then," he said gruffly. "What is it?"

I lifted the items, one by one, from my bag, and set them on the table before him. His eyes widened, and his mouth did too. He put his fist into his mouth to stop a cry of grief as he sorted through his son's possessions. "To think of him being killed in the end."

"But your son was not proved to be killed, sir. The police conducted a brief investigation and said he perished from consumption. He was taking quite a lot of medicine for it," I offered—helpfully, I hoped.

"Bah." He waved his hand through the air. "I saw him at Christmas, and whilst he wasn't pink as a piglet, he was nowheres near death. I've seen those that die of consumption—his mother died of it when he was but a lad. He did not look sick unto death. No one needs to prove that to me."

I could not argue that. I did not think he'd looked sick unto death either. I felt another pang of sympathy for Mr. Clarkson. I, too, had finished coming of age without a mother.

"He was a knowledgeable man." I did not want to speak ill of the dead. "I know he cared very much for your family."

"We could not have kept this shop running, paid our rent and bills, or put food on the table without the money he sent us," his father said bluntly. "I know that rested hard on him. His ma's family owned the property where our London shop was, and after she died, we had to leave."

I hadn't known that. It did not excuse his cheating, but it did, perhaps, explain it.

There had been a better way, but that was all over now.

"You should be careful, miss." Mr. Clerk wiped his rheumy eyes with a dirty rag. "Them that got him might come for you."

The Romans? Had Mr. Clarkson taken the Roman goods after all, attempted to sell them, and been found out? I now knew he was a thief.

Marguerite leaned toward me. "Let's leave."

I could not leave, not just yet. "Mr. Clerk, may I beg a favor? There are things missing from my shop. . . ."

"Are you accusing Robert of thievery?" he asked, drawing so close I could feel his fast exhales upon my cheek; his breath was dank and smelled of rotting teeth.

I leaped back. How to answer? "I'm wondering if he might have brought them here to repair or repaint and then, due to his untimely passing, was not able to return them to London."

"Ah," he said and eased. "That's different, then. Have a look around."

He handed a lit lantern to me, and Marguerite followed me down the aisles.

"Must we?" she asked.

"We must," I said. The shelves mostly held inconsequential bits and pieces of people's lives. It put me in mind of Mr. Dickens's story *A Christmas Carol*, wherein Mr. Scrooge's drapes and clothing were sold off after his untimely death. There was art to be had, though: beautiful portraits and jewelry and music boxes and cuff links and, in one corner, a basket of coins purported to be from the Roman era. There were many of them, too many to be all from an unknown Roman hoard. They weren't priced, so I said nothing.

"Trinkets," his father offered. He began to cry again, and I felt pity for him. But I must continue looking for the Roman items which had been taken from Watchfield House.

I wandered all throughout the place, and never did I get

the sense that the man was hiding anything from me. As I opened the last door in the back, a nest of rats was disturbed, and one flew out toward Marguerite, who screamed, "Eleanor! Let's leave."

She did not have to prod me twice; I had a horror of rats.

I followed her to the front of the shop, profoundly disappointed that I had not found the Roman treasures. Perhaps they had never been in the crates, and the Vieros were in on some hoax which would, in the end, entrap Harry.

Perhaps Mr. Clarkson had already liquidated the items, having stolen them whilst I completed the inventory on our first visit after the funeral. They were small items, I'd think, having been in a small crate. There would have been enough time. If he had done that, though, it was far too late for me to recapture them. I had no proof, and it was unlikely that Mr. Clerk would show me his bills of lading, if indeed he kept such records.

On the way out, I glanced over the glass cases in the front. There were no items of Roman glass, but I did spy two things that were dear to me. My father's watch . . . and Uncle Lewis's.

Mr. Clarkson had arranged for my uncle to be accosted when I was at the baron's funeral. Why? For the money and the watch, of course. And to make it seem like he was helpful, like family, and that we required his protection and assistance? Certainly.

But he had not only stolen from us. He had allowed my uncle to be beaten in the process.

My anger rose; I could feel myself flush and had a pain in my chest.

Mr. Clerk saw me looking at the watches. "They's sold already; the man just hasn't come by to pick them up. I have a few other things I can show you, though." He looked thin. He sounded desperate. His eyes still watered.

"No thank you," I said quietly. One, I had given to Mr. Clarkson to sell and had not balked at the fee returned. There was no way now to prove that he'd had a hand in stealing the second. Perhaps this small family could use the money to make it through the next months. There would be no further support coming from Mr. Clarkson and I had, still, the pilgrim's flask and the Book of Hours.

I gathered up my empty bag and, as I did, glanced at a small print hanging on the wall. It was the one which had been stolen when the panes had been broken in the workshop. Mr. Clarkson had been behind that, too. Perhaps to, as he'd said, show me how much we needed a younger man to protect us. But what protection could a man who had allowed my uncle to be beaten have offered?

His father saw my gaze. "Is that yours?"

I nodded, and he took it off the wall, handed it to me, and bid me good-bye.

CHAPTER
Twenty-Eight

Once on the train, I explained about Mr. Clarkson's wicked doings.

"I know he's dead, Eleanor, and cannot harm you any longer," Marguerite said. "You were right to not fully trust him. But this matter with the Romans and their treasures—I'm frightened. I don't like this at all. I admire your courage in following through, seeking them in Bristol, but I think courage has tipped into folly. Promise me—no more misadventures. Lord Lydney can locate the items which have been removed from his property."

I promised her. "I'm sorry I brought you."

She smiled wanly. "In future, I shall charge more for my chaperoning services, dearest. And . . . Mr. Clerk seemed to think his son did not die of natural causes," she said.

I nodded. "I had wondered about that myself. I'd even asked the police officer. He'd assured me it was a natural death. Of sorts." I recalled the uncomfortable conversation.

"Do you have any reason to believe someone would want to do him harm?"

"Not really."

"Then perhaps that is best left alone," he said.

"I shall have to tell Harry I have not found the Roman treasures."

She smiled. "That brings to mind: a mutual friend has mentioned in recent conversation that Harry is breeding horses now and has been for some time. His father never arranged an income for him, of course. The breeding provides an income to buy more stud horses, which provide more income . . . and while he's not rich, things are growing in the right direction."

My eyes rose, and so did my spirits. "Truly?"

"Truly," she said. "That does not put the man solidly in the clear as to where his finances have come from, but it is something."

A few days after my return home I received a telegram from Harry.

> Nothing turned up here. Have you found anything? Will be in London a week hence, 8 March. May I call? I hope all is well. My best, H.

It wasn't exactly a personal letter, but it wasn't impersonal, either. Therein lay the difficulty. I telegraphed back to Watchfield that I looked forward to his visit but had found nothing. I did not yet tell him that Clarkson had died. I would tell him that in person.

I would also then tell him that there was no sight of the Roman treasures and, therefore, all was not well. Would he feel obliged to protect Francesca until Stefano returned to England? What if that did not happen? Would she relinquish her Venetian treasures in lieu of those which had been stolen? Would Harry feel he had utterly failed his friend if the family treasures were liquidated?

I felt a certain kinship with Francesca. I, too, had been releasing my family's treasures to preserve the lives of those I loved.

It was time to tend to my work, and I was happy to do so.

"Another commission!" I said as I entered the workshop. It would not be enough to pay our remaining invoice, but it would pay the rent and gas. Uncle sat in his chair in the workshop. We'd brought in the most comfortable parlor chair for him, as he often fell asleep whilst working, but when he did work, he was very sharp indeed. Dr. Garrett had told me that the older memories persisted, but the more recent ones, like if he had eaten dinner or not, slipped away most quickly.

His desk and table were covered by all manner of items. It was quite crowded, and I did not know how he kept track of it all, but in truth, my father had been the organized one and Uncle Lewis the one who'd tended toward untidy.

"He's been emptying the wardrobes and closets again," Orchie whispered. "Afraid someone is hiding inside them. Won't let me go in even to fetch the laundry, though he'll hand it off to 'Miss Carolina,' otherwise known as Alice."

I turned back to the note at hand. I'd been invited to meet with Lord Grimsby, the man who had made an indiscreet suggestion to Marguerite but who was, perhaps, as powerful as Lord Parham. Grimsby had indicated that he was interested in commissioning a purchase of some majolica; among my remaining treasures was my father's sixteenth-century majolica pilgrim's flask. Perhaps he would be interested? I hated to sell it but needed to pay that final invoice by the fifteenth. Grimsby had indicated that, furthermore, he would like to speak with me about the Burlington Fine Arts Club. His mention reminded me that Charlotte had not yet called, despite her promise to do so.

I was an outcast.

I hesitantly agreed to meet Grimsby at the South Kensington, in a public place. I could not afford to turn down what might be an enriching commission.

I met Lord Grimsby in the forecourt of one of the galleries.

"My dear Miss Sheffield." He presented his arm to me. I took it, but with a certain stiffness that allowed a distance to remain between us.

"As a widower, I am always thankful for female companionship, especially when looking at art," he said. "Beauty for beauty."

A certain heaviness settled in my stomach. "You were

going to show me some of the objects you most admire and would be interested in . . . my uncle's procuring majolica for you?" I knew better than to suggest I'd do it on my own.

"Yes, yes, my dear. But let's not rush."

Let's rush.

We walked through the section which included some fine majolica, in which he appeared interested. I was glad I had been deeply educated in the Italian pottery because it gave me a solid foundation upon which to make conversation.

He stopped for a moment and patted my hand. "I would like for us to be friends, Miss Sheffield."

I inhaled, sorry that Marguerite had heard this same sort of offer during the Epiphany celebrations at Watchfield, but glad that her encounter had given me a warning.

"I would be most pleased to work with you as a representative of Sheffield Brothers," I said.

At that, he looked up sharply. "I had rather thought of a more personal friendship. Along the lines of a companionship. It would be mutually beneficial. I have great sway at the Burlington, of course, and among others who collect. Lord Parham is an old friend, for example. Mr. Denholm, who will be hosting the Burlington at his home on the fourteenth of this month, has been seeking my friendship. Couldn't we be . . . friends . . . too?"

"An irregular friendship with you, or anyone, is not something I would find of interest, Lord Grimsby. I'm sorry."

He sighed deeply. "I had rather expected you would say

that. It's too bad I am not an antique, Miss Sheffield, that I might invite your undivided attention."

I pursed my lips to keep from laughing. *But you are an antique, Lord Grimsby. And despite your title, wealth, lineage, and a family provenance, there is nothing of remarkable character to note.* "Alas . . ." was all I allowed myself to say. "A woman's reputation is a dear thing."

He nodded. "Yes, quite right."

"The majolica?" I asked as we returned to the forecourt of the gallery.

"I shall contact you as soon as I am ready to proceed," he said, his smile distant and practiced, insincere.

"Of course," I said. "Until then."

He bowed. "Until then."

There would be no commission.

I would sell my uncle's Book of Hours, although how I could explain its loss to him in his fragile state of mind, I did not know. I would also sell my father's majolica pilgrim's flask. They were all that remained of value in our house, but they would cover the expenses that we owed for now and for several months that followed, and keep me out of debtor's prison.

Selling them publicly would certainly call attention to our dire straits, something I was loath to do following hard upon Mr. Clarkson's death, which had already caused some loose and speculative talk among the collecting community. Perhaps Lord Tenteden would agree for a discreet swap—one or the other of my remaining treasures to cancel his outstanding invoice?

When I returned home, there was a note for me.

Will call on you tomorrow, at the workshop, and will have our friend with me. Please advise if this is not suitable.

Harry

CHAPTER
Twenty-Nine

I sat in the parlor nearly weeping with relief. Lord Tenteden had agreed to my suggestion. He offered a meeting in five days, on the thirteenth—in advance of his deadline, and the soonest moment he would be back in London—to trade both my father's flask and my uncle's Book of Hours for the debt we owed him. He'd told me, in his note, that he was most amenable to the arrangement, so I moved forward with confident relief.

I hadn't wanted to give them both up, but I had little choice.

Harry arrived in the afternoon, and the friend was, of course, Francesca. "Please, come in," I said as Orchie took

Francesca's cloak and Harry put his hat and coat on the stand inside the foyer.

Francesca held a rather large box in her hands.

"We are in London for a short time as her mother is visiting friends. We thought this might be a good occasion . . . Well, given the current circumstances . . . she—we—are wondering if you would be willing to value one or two of the Venetian items," Harry said. His voice was as laden with sorrow as the iron clouds burdening the horizon this stormy spring day.

"Certainly," I said. "Let's go through to the workshop." I turned on the lamps in the workshop, lighting up the entire room. Francesca unwrapped the first item, which was the beautiful water pitcher I had seen when I had first done the inventory.

"Oh, this treasure." I was captivated by it once more and reviewed it carefully, looking for cracks and fissures, examining the paint and the smoothness of the glass. "It's perfect."

When I named a figure, Francesca inhaled sharply. "Are you sure?"

"Per certo," I said. "I am certain. But why are we valuing these? They will go back to Venice, surely, to your family palazzo?"

"Unless I need to sell them, signorina," she said. "To replace the Roman treasures. It is not Harry's responsibility to repair this situation. It is mine alone."

Instinctively I reached out and touched the back of her hand in sympathy. I had agreed, this very day, to trade my father's and uncle's remaining treasures to help my own family. I wondered if Harry would be able to purchase the Venetian treasures. Despite what Marguerite had insinuated about his growing income with the horses, I did not think he had the required funds readily available. Not without selling his own family treasures.

"Would your brother agree?" I asked.

"We don't know where he is," she replied. "Perhaps replacing the treasures will bring him back."

She looked on the verge of tears, so I moved swiftly to the next item to give her time to regain self-control, something Marguerite often did for me. "This next piece?"

She handed it over. It was a most beautiful Venetian loving cup, a larger cup with two handles made for a couple to drink out of at a marriage celebration. The French called it a *coupe de mariage*, and once a couple drank out of it at the same time, they could not be separated. This beauty was created from Cristallo glass with jewels shot throughout. It was likely to be sixteenth century.

"I did not see this in the inventory."

"There are two," Francesca replied. "I kept one in my room, and Mama has the other one."

Had she hidden other treasures, too?

I was just about to offer a value when someone knocked at the shop door. I went to it and opened it, about to ask whoever was there if they might come back in a few hours, when the men standing outside pushed their way in. I anxiously sorted them into a collective. *A mob of Italians.*

"Miss Sheffield," one man said, his English heavily accented. "How good to see you again. This time, we visit your shop."

"Signor Pazzo," Harry said. "How convenient to find you here at the same time as we have come for a visit."

"We followed you," Pazzo replied brazenly. "Perhaps we may have a look around. We might be prepared to make a purchase or two."

"I'm certain there is nothing here of interest to you," I said, but it did not stop the three men from looking at the items in the display room. When I moved forward, they followed. When I stopped, they stopped, but ever closer to me.

Francesca's lovely pieces were still on the evaluation table in the workshop. *"Bella, molto bella."* Pazzo caressed the loving cup and glanced covetously at the pitcher. He began to make his way toward the back of the workshop, where we kept our private items and notebooks.

"Harry?" I said quietly.

"See here," Harry said, but for the moment, they paid him no mind.

A shout came from the back and Pazzo's compatriot ran toward us with a tiny but beautiful bottle, perhaps one that had held oil at an ancient dinner table. A bottle which appeared to be early Roman, and one which I had never seen.

"That is mine!" Pazzo turned accusingly toward me. "You have said, Miss Sheffield, that you have not seen my Roman treasures when clearly there is one here in your shop."

Harry turned toward me. "Miss Sheffield? Is that yours?"

I shook my head. "I have never seen it." I turned to the man who had fished it from the back, near where Mr. Clarkson had once hidden our art from the purported ruffians. "Perhaps you placed it there only to 'find' it moments later!" Had Harry been involved in that setup, too? It was unthinkable. And yet . . .

The Italian man ran at me, and Harry stepped between us. "See here! You'll recall I have been in Italy, have many friends here and there, and am capable of protecting what and whom I want to be protected—here or there. Including Miss Sheffield. There are, after all, only three of you, and there are many, many I can call upon."

The man shrugged, moved back a little, but did not respond with any humility or acknowledgment. I had the feeling their confrontation had ended in a temporary draw. "I don't need more than three," I heard Pazzo say quietly.

Harry turned toward me wonderingly and with a newly added look of suspicion. "You have never seen that?" He pointed toward the Roman bottle.

"No." I shook my head. Pazzo walked to the back, where his friend had found the Roman bottle, and examined a few other items. All of them were mine or belonged to clients.

Harry picked up his mother's pelican. "Mama's . . ."

"I was repairing it, you remember." I was shamed by the desperation in my voice.

"Months ago? Before you'd returned everything to Watchfield . . . and to me." He tucked the pelican into his pocket and held my gaze.

"Yes, I simply . . . simply forgot," I said. "With so much going on."

Francesca glanced at me with skepticism. "Did you simply, simply forget about taking the Roman items, too?"

"No." My feelings of kinship with her dissolved. "I have never seen them before, did not know of their existence." *Unlike you, for example, who knew about them all along.*

"We will then search this entire building," Pazzo said.

"No," Harry responded firmly. He stood in their way, and they did not push past him.

"That would require a search warrant from the police," I replied. "You will then be required to have proof of ownership for the items. Do you have proof of ownership?"

Pazzo sneered. "I do not require the police to do my work." He wrapped the precious bottle in one of my linen cloths from a stack next to the delicate figurines. "I suggest you find where the rest of these items are, Miss Sheffield. If one is here, the others are too. I have some other pressing meetings already arranged. They will allow me to return in, say, ten days. That should give you enough time to find them. If you can't find them, be sure that I will find you, wherever you are."

"They aren't here!" I insisted.

"Ten days." He tipped his hat and left through the door whence he'd come in.

Francesca cried softly in a corner. "Where is my brother? Where are the pieces of art? Will I have to sell my family's heritage because this woman stole their goods?"

"Francesca," Harry began, "I hardly think . . ."

And yet, when he looked at me, there was a shadow of doubt in his eyes.

I pulled him aside, tears threatening to spill from my own eyes. "They planted it, Harry—planted it here to blame me. That's why they followed you here."

He waited just a moment. "Do you need the money?" He spoke softly. "You referred to it at Glastonbury."

I shook my head vigorously. I could hardly blame him—it all seemed so unusual. I'd spent the last months questioning him, wondering if he was trustworthy, without a moment's thought to how he must have felt about my doing so. Wondering if he would sell his family's goods because he needed the income. Now it was his turn to decide.

"I am who you believe me to be," I said quietly.

A moment ticked by. "I believe that the bottle was planted moments ago, too," he finally said. "They planted it to send a message to me: they can reach out and harm whomever they choose to harm. You. Francesca. Stefano. They want their treasures, or they want their money."

"Perhaps." I still wondered, silently, if Francesca was somehow involved with them—and perhaps the planting of the bottle.

Harry continued, "I trust you unreservedly. We must trust one another."

And he did—against all the odds. I was grateful I had not questioned him about the missing barding and risked further eroding his belief in my trust of him, too.

A love match. A trust match.

"Let Mr. Clarkson take care of your clients until I sort this," Harry said.

"He's dead," I whispered. "Mr. Clarkson is dead."

Harry's face drained. "Ellie, do not leave the house until I return. Have Orchie or Alice leave to get what you need. They won't send the police after you because it's most likely some of their goods don't rightfully belong to them either. They are dangerous but believe themselves to have honor. If they've said ten days, they will wait ten days. But they will not wait longer. Do not let anyone in, and keep the doors locked. Do you understand? I must try to resolve this, and it may take a little time. But I will resolve it within ten days. Do not leave! Promise me."

"I promise," I said.

He embraced me quickly and then escorted Francesca and her Venetian treasures into his waiting carriage.

CHAPTER *Thirty*

MID-MARCH 1867

On Sunday, I told my uncle that I was unwell and we would not be attending church that morning. I did not tell him I'd promised not to leave the house.

"You look well enough to me," he replied with a tremble.

"I'm certain I'll be in fine sorts within a week or two," I told him. Our roles, too, had changed. He now looked to me for reassurance and provision where once I'd looked to him for those ingredients which made up a confident life.

On Monday the eleventh, Alice arrived. I pulled her aside

and, after explaining the situation, asked if she might be willing to help me for a week.

"Lord Lydney thinks it better if I do not leave the house until he's resolved our concerns, and I tend to agree. However, it's most important that I communicate with a client I am supposed to meet on Wednesday. Would you be willing to take telegrams for me?"

"Of course I would," she said.

I telegraphed Lord Tenteden and asked if we might meet at my workshop. I did not hear back.

On Tuesday, I had Alice send another telegram. Still no response. No matter what I had promised to Harry, I had to venture out of the house.

Because the treasures were so valuable, I wrapped them carefully—sneaking the Book of Hours when my uncle was napping—and took a hired carriage. I arrived at Lord Tenteden's lofty London town house and asked the carriage driver to wait for me—an extravagance, indeed, but it seemed safer, given the current circumstances.

I walked up to the door and rapped the knocker. After a moment, a butler appeared.

"I'm Miss Eleanor Sheffield," I said. "Here for an appointment with Lord Tenteden."

He looked me up and down and then handed a note to me. "Good day, Miss Sheffield," he said and closed the door.

Bewildered, I stood paralyzed for a moment before picking up my bags and walking back to the carriage. Once in the carriage, I opened the note.

Miss Sheffield,

It has come to my attention that there is some doubt placed upon your valuations and the authenticity of the objects represented by your firm. I have heard this from my friend Lord Parham only of late.

I shall be at the Burlington Club meeting tomorrow night, and shall make further enquiries. Until my confidence is restored, I am afraid an exchange of your antiquities for the debt owed is not possible. I shall send someone to collect the funds on the morning of the fifteenth, as previously arranged.

I slid the note back into the envelope, dread encasing me. I would, of course, not have the required funds two days thence.

At home, I asked the driver to tarry once more whilst I delivered the antiquities; I hid them under my bed and instructed Orchie to answer the door to no one.

Then I went to the telegraph office myself. The first telegram was sent to Lord Tenteden, assuring him that my valuations were proper, but that I could have his funds, in any case, in a matter of a week, if he'd be so gracious as to wait.

Next, I sent telegrams to Harry, both at London and at Watchfield, as I knew not where he was. I told him the amount of money I needed to have by Friday morning for a most urgent debt, and could he respond posthaste. I remembered my confident promise to myself that I would not rely upon his money to pay my debts. I had truly tried every other means.

Perhaps I should have availed myself of his offered generosity earlier on. I comforted myself with the thought that I would give him the flask in return, and it would be at Watchfield as it was meant to be. And that Uncle could keep his Book of Hours.

For the present.

None of us slept well on Thursday night. I stayed in the parlor and prayed, and Orchie made batches of Cornish pasties till the wee hours. The more agitated we became, the more agitated my uncle grew. No word from Harry, nor any money.

On Friday morning, the fifteenth of March, I dressed serviceably and began my work, hoping that Harry would appear with some funds. At ten o'clock a knock came on the door and I opened it to see a man whose cherubic face belied the sharpness of his voice.

"Do you have the funds for Lord Tenteden?" he asked. "It's the fifteenth, and my client has been quite patient, after all."

"The funds are en route," I said. "Lord Lydney will deliver them very shortly. A few more hours—perhaps Monday at the latest."

He did not smile and bid me a good day.

I closed the workshop. I shut the lights off behind me though it was but midmorning. I returned to the house and calmly gave Orchie instructions on how she should proceed should what I expected transpire.

Why hadn't Harry responded in any way? Had he well and truly left me to my fate? More worrisome—and likely—he himself had met with harm, perhaps in the matter of the missing Roman antiquities.

Orchie cried quietly.

"I shan't be too long, I hope." I tried to sound more confident than I felt. "Lord Lydney will surely appear and bring a cheque. Please have him proceed to the house of detention with a receipt after paying my debt in full." I gave her the name and address of the man to whom the funds would need to be delivered.

"And if he doesn't come?" Orchie asked.

"Then please send a note to Lady Charlotte Schreiber and ask her if she might locate a buyer for the pilgrim's flask." I did not know if that would be enough once the expenses for the court were added to my debt. My heart hurt, but I must suggest the last possible item which we might sell to keep ourselves afloat. "And perhaps the Book of Hours," I added softly, "if need be." That should cover their complete expenses for some months, should it take longer for me to be freed. "You might call upon Mrs. Newsome to see if she can help further. But I instruct you to pay the household expenses for you and for Uncle first. Do not use the money to release me until all household matters are arranged and Lord Tenteden is paid." I would not have them in the workhouse or the asylum, even if it meant I might remain in debtor's prison.

Orchie nodded. I did not give her further instructions because I did not know what else to do or say. I remonstrated with myself that I should have arranged this with Harry sooner, or have sold the pilgrim's flask sooner along with the snuffbox and curiosity cabinet. In truth, though, I hadn't because I thought I'd had until the last moment to save what remained of my papa, with the promise of Harry's assistance at any time.

Truly, I had to admit and confess, it was pride which had done me in. I hadn't wanted Harry's help. I wanted to remain strong and self-sufficient in his eyes and in my own.

This time, it was not Harry who had waited too late. It was I.

Promptly at two o'clock, the debt collector walked to my front door. A constable was at his side.

I opened the door. "Yes?"

"Are you Miss Eleanor Sheffield?" the constable asked. I was grateful that it was not the same policeman who had escorted me from Mr. Clarkson's home.

"Yes," I said.

"Come with me, please."

He put me in the police cart, which was dry but uncomfortable. Neighbors looked out from their windows, and I was glad that he'd let me walk on my own. Soon the gossip would spread like a kitchen fire among the neighbors. Who at the South Kensington would be the first to hear?

The streets were rough, and I heard the cries of London—watercress, flowers, pies, cheese, chair repair. For the first time, I understood what it was like to have no say at all over my own life. I must do only as the law permitted me to do.

I was at the mercy of those who did not necessarily value mercy.

We pulled up in front of the prison, a place I had arrived at many times in better circumstances. Once inside, I appeared before the warder, who recognized me.

"Are you able to pay this debt in full?" he asked.

"Not presently."

"That would be a no, then." He wrote something on a piece of paper. "You will be held here, in detention, until you appear before a magistrate to plead your case. At that time, he will assign a prison term. You will remain in prison until your debt is paid or your time of incarceration, as he warrants it, is completed. Is that clear, miss?"

"Yes," I said. "When . . . when will I appear before him?"

"As soon as convenient," he reiterated. "For him."

"Perhaps a week or two," the constable whispered to me as he took his leave. "Good luck, miss."

I was whisked away to the next room, where a female warder checked me for contraband.

We walked in silence down a long, narrow corridor. Should I have wanted to, I could have reached my arms out and dragged my fingers along each wall. If I had, I knew the blackened filth that had hardened upon them through the years would stain my gloves like the shame staining my soul. It seemed to me that the hallways grew narrower as we walked, and I found myself heaving for breath.

As she led me down the hall, I felt as though I were suffocating with the foul stench of filthy air which, like those women trapped within these walls, rarely circulated. I'd overheard the warders talking once about how they nearly lost the contents of their stomachs when they first entered those deeper hallways, and I swallowed hard to avoid a similar reaction. Faintly, I could also smell the pinch of chloride of lime, which was used from time to time to "freshen" the air. Jeanette had told me that it burned her lungs. Now she struggled to breathe deeply at all.

The woman warder opened a door and nearly pushed me in. "Enjoy your first night under Her Majesty's roof," she said with a cackle. She stood outside while showing me the contents of my room.

She indicated a slit on the wall. "Push that—" she pointed to a red flag on a rough hook—"through the slit if you are sick or in need of the closets in a hurry. Yer food'll be delivered and you'll get exercise in the morning and chapel on Sunday."

"Thank you," I said politely.

She laughed. "There's no need for high manners, missy. You answer to me now."

She clanged the door shut and left me to look around the room.

The moment I heard the lock engage, I felt unable to breathe, as though I were facedown in a bath and someone held my head so I could not raise it to air. My lungs hungered. I sat on the small bed, and the room itself seemed to close in around me. I was acutely aware that there were imprisoned people on top of me, and likely below me, and in every room all around. I wasn't underground, but I felt as though I were.

There was a small window, but it was high and dim. *You shan't be here long,* I comforted myself. *Harry will certainly arrive with the funds within hours. You won't be here for even a day.*

I stood in the center of my cell, which was perhaps six feet by ten feet and whitewashed. There was a small shelf upon which rested a wooden bowl and a wooden spoon. The lower shelf held a Bible, a book of prayers, and a hymnal, though I knew most of the prisoners could not read at all.

There was no desk, nor anything with which I might write. How could I reach out for help?

Help would have to come to me.

The plank which served as a bed had splinters sticking up, which I tried to smooth down, to little avail. At the head was a pillow of sorts. It was a rough feed sack which had been stuffed with coconut fibers. The end remained untied, which made me wonder what kind of vermin had squirmed their way in and were already sleeping.

Surely they would wake the moment I laid my head upon them.

At the foot of the plank was a folded woolen blanket. I opened it, gently, and dust motes escaped into the air. Once open, I could see that it was stained—with what, I did not know—and greasy. I let it fall to the floor.

I sat on the plank, grateful that I had been allowed to keep my own clothes for now. I suspected that if I were convicted for the debts, I would be issued the ill-fitting prison clothing my prisoner friends wore and the boots that "talked"—that is, their soles flapped openly from the boot bottom.

Several hours later, a bowl of food was pushed through a narrow opening on the floor, as well as two pewter mugs. As soon as the warder walked away, two small rats came up and sniffed the bowl.

Rats!

Their shoulders were hunched over and their heads were down in what I assumed was an attack position. The pair of them stared at me, whiskers twitching, eyes unblinking—the phrase "beady little eyes" had never seemed so apt—and so deeply black no pupil could be distinguished. I made a move toward the bowl, and as I did, the vermin advanced toward me boldly.

My stomach churned and roiled again. I closed my eyes and waited till the feeling passed. By the time I'd opened them again, the rats had eaten of my dinner. They'd stayed away from the pewter mugs, though; they remained filled nearly to the brim, so I pulled them into my cell. I sniffed. One held beer—which I would not drink—and the other, water.

I was so very, very thirsty. I drank the water.

An hour later I pushed the red flag out and prayed that someone would see it. She did, and I rushed to the closets before I was sick.

I slept not at all that first night under Her Majesty's roof. I suspected a leering eyeball through the peephole in my door. I shivered, fully clothed, and tried not to cry, though the others around me had no hesitancy to sob as loudly as they might.

CHAPTER Thirty-One

I woke in despair and distress, feeling forsaken, despite my familiarity with Saint Paul's words to the Corinthians: "*We are troubled on every side, yet not distressed; we are perplexed, but not in despair; persecuted, but not forsaken; cast down, but not destroyed.*" I washed my face with the cold, slightly brown water that had been brought to me. I spent the early hours of the morning tending to my hair, with my fingers, and trying to be hopeful, thinking of what I would do, once out, to support my uncle, Orchie, and myself.

Orchie was surely too old to be hired on elsewhere. Uncle continued to grow ever more confused. I had thought of living with Marguerite, but she had no income of her own, and when I viewed the situation as clearly as I must, she needed to marry to tend to her own future.

Sheffield Brothers would be lost once it was understood that we did not pay our suppliers. We needed a powerful protector, and we did not have one.

Midmorning, I went with the others to the area where we were to take some exercise. I sat on a rotting wood bench in the middle of the small yard; the day was blissfully dry if cold. Then I realized why the bench was empty of all but I: it was infested with woodworm beetles chewing through the damp wood. I jumped up, looking around for the regulars who did not like fancy misses, and a few approached me. One came close enough to look in my face and then I heard a voice ring out.

"Hey! She's one of us. She's mine!"

I broke out in a rash of relief as Jeanette made her way over to me.

"Miss Sheffield?" Her voice was suffused with wonder. "Is it really you? Why are you here?"

"It is I," I said. "I have been remanded until I can see the magistrate for some debts that my uncle owed and for which I signed."

She gathered some of the other women around her. "You all put the word out to everyone. She is not to be touched or harmed."

The others nodded in agreement, and suddenly I felt enveloped in a circle of friends and affection. My heart filled with gratitude and I closed my eyes for a moment.

"Or when saw we thee sick, or in prison, and came unto thee? And the King shall answer and say unto them, Verily I say unto you, Inasmuch as ye have done it unto one of the least of these my brethren, ye have done it unto me."

"Thank you," I said to Jeanette, to all of them.

"Of course," she responded. "We are friends."

I walked with them for the permitted hour; I did not know if I would be allowed to see them at chapel the following day. Perhaps the prisoners in the private quarters went at a different time. But knowing they were here and nearby and companionable and protecting me helped buoy my spirits.

"Are there—are there always rats?" I asked.

"Some says they make good pets."

My face must have reflected my horror because she laughed gently at me. "Dear, kindly Miss Sheffield. Did ya not know this was our life? After all these visits?"

"I did not." But I vowed to do more than kindly social visits should I ever find a way out of here.

She looked at my face. "Ya didn't sleep, did ya?"

"Does it show?"

She nodded. "Dark circles. Plus, none of us sleep. It's the planks. And the noise."

"Sobbing," I agreed.

"And raving," she said. She looked surprised when I tilted my head. "You have no ravers?"

"No," I said.

"Oh, you will," she said. "They always starts in on Saturday nights afore church on Sunday."

I drew in a deep breath.

"I'll pray for ya," she said, as she always said she would.

"And I for you," I replied.

I returned to my cell and pondered my situation. I was cold, my clothes and thin gloves offering little protection. I was thirsty. I had spilt some water on the floor the night before, but because it was so cold, it had not yet dried. When at home, I never gave a second thought to desiring water, but now that I could not have fresh, it was all I could think of. I wanted some greens. I wished for Cornish pasty, when it had not been long since I'd thought myself ill-used for having to partake of it so often. I wondered if my uncle was well and how Orchie was coping and hoped and prayed that I would be able to tend to their needs quickly. I understood freshly the hopelessness my friends in prison felt when they had no say over their own lives and little or no hope of ever being released.

I found them, now, to be more courageous than ever. That gave me courage.

But when night came on, I found myself struggling to breathe again. The walls tilted closer, and I could hear crying down the hallway. The person in the cell to my left retched loudly, and I had to press my jaws together from underneath, with both hands, to overcome the reflex to retch myself.

Then the raving began, with first one woman, then another, talking, pleading loudly with unseen people, and crying out remembrances of past crimes committed against them. One screamed of the horrors of fire.

I closed my eyes and prayed for them and for myself and for Jeanette, and for Harry to hurry, all the while clutching my Bible.

If there is a fire, no one will come for me, I thought. *I will be left—we all will be left—to perish.*

No one is coming for you anyway, Fear taunted.

Where is Harry? Why hasn't he paid my debt? Perhaps he never intended to see me out of prison. Perhaps this is as good a way as any of disposing his responsibility to me.

I did not believe that, even as I rubbed my empty finger. My heart believed that I knew the man, even as it clenched in worry.

Hours ticked by and a familiar dread bolted me up in bed.

Perhaps Harry really had wanted me out of the way—and had assisted that Italian man in planting the Roman bottle in my workshop.

Perhaps the person who had killed Clarkson had also gone after Harry, and then I would likely have no way out. If he were to die with no heirs, could the collection be given to the South Kensington after all? That would be the likely default.

What if the Italians had apprehended Harry? Perhaps he had found something out that upset him, and they had arranged to detain him beyond the tenth day?

"If they've said ten days, they will wait ten days. But they will not wait longer," Harry had said.

It would be ten days on Monday.

I eased my back against the wall and felt a settled presence gather around me.

I'm thankful for a reassurance of your presence, dearest Lord, in moments of trial.

I prayed the majolica alone would bring enough money to pay back Lord Tenteden. I prayed my uncle would be far enough along in his wanderings that he would not know if I had to sell his Book of Hours for us to live. I prayed Charlotte would help with that sale—she might want nothing further to do with me, and that would be understandable. Then who would sell the items to free me? Could she even sell them, without my uncle's permission? He might not, after all, have the legal competency to make such a decision.

I prayed Harry was well.

I love him.

Early the next morning I had a visitor. I did not think I would be allowed visitors whilst awaiting my sentence—only once I was under correction.

When the door opened, I saw the chaplain there. "Reverend Bradly Clay," he introduced himself. "I've come to invite you to chapel this morning."

"I had planned to worship alone in my cell."

He smiled at me. "I suspected as much. It is quite usual when someone is newly introduced to the prison, they are so filled with shame that they do not like to be seen by the others. That denies them a powerful opportunity for joint sympathetic worship and does not allow us to tend to your needs. Eucharist may be served in quarters, but that is frowned upon. You may find it strengthening to attend."

I nodded, tempted but not convinced.

"I understand you have been a part of the women's committee which has regularly visited the prison," he continued.

"I have."

"Perhaps it would bring a strong message to them that you expected to find comfort and joy in the church within the prison as much as without," he said. "I shall leave the decision to you, Miss Sheffield. There is darkness here, as you well know. But remember, 'He discovereth deep things out of darkness, and bringeth out to light the shadow of death.' The book of Job."

I smiled. "I am overly familiar with the book of Job, Reverend. Thank you. I shall attend."

After he left, I smoothed down the sides of my dress and shook from it what dust and wrinkles I could.

I used a corner of the greasy blanket to wipe the dust from my boots, then put on my gloves, thankful once more that I had been able to retain my own clothing. I repented taking my small graces for granted.

The bells were rung to call us to chapel—I recognized them from my former visits—and I left my room and made my way toward the chapel. Although I had visited my ladies in a room nearby, I had never been in the chapel itself.

Reverend Clay was right; I did appreciate his message and

knew the words to the songs sung, so I was able to join in. Soon, it was time for Eucharist.

One after another, the women transformed from somber to peaceful. Old women, young women, women with no teeth and whose lips had sucked in toward their jaws and gums to compensate.

I took the Eucharist myself and, thus strengthened, prepared to return to my cell. However, a new warder came and took me firmly by the hand.

"Come with me," she said.

CHAPTER Thirty-Two

The warder led me to another part of the prison.

"This is your new room," she said, opening the door.

"Why?" I asked. "What of my old cell?"

She shrugged. "Just be happy tha' someone paid for you to be moved. I'll be delivering your food, and you can have visitors, if you like. Should any think to find you here." She smirked.

I nodded, and she left. I looked around the room. It was larger; the window wasn't clean, but not completely blocked, either. The bed had a mattress and was not merely a plank. The pillow was sewn shut, though it did not look to have down or feathers. This was still prison.

There was a small desk and a chair and no grate by which rats might enter.

I nearly cried. Who would pay for better quarters for me but not pay for me to be released?

I sat on the chair for a moment and soon heard a fall of footsteps on the stone hallway. They stopped outside my door. I stood, tense. Then came a knock.

"Ellie?"

I flew off the chair as the door opened. "Harry!"

He held me tightly for a minute, for two, before whispering in my ear, "I am here now, and all will be well. I shall see to it; I promise."

I blinked back tears and took him by the hand. "I have no second chair to offer you," I said as I led him into my cell.

He stroked my hair. "The least of our concerns, but quite like you. We shall sit side by side—properly—on your bed as if it were a sofa."

I nodded. "Why . . . ? How . . . ?" Although the day was dim and the window remained dingy, suddenly my room and my spirits became bathed in golden light.

"I had no idea," he said, "that you were being threatened with debtor's prison if your invoice was not paid by the fifteenth of March. Why did you not tell me?"

I spoke softly. "Pride. You'd always admired my strength and self-sufficiency. I did not want to lose that. I suppose, too, that I wanted to prove I could manage Sheffield Brothers on my own. I came very close. When the Roman piece was found in my shop, I couldn't ask you for money, as it would seem as if I took the bottle to pay my debts. Like you, my striving to earn others' approval has not led to amiable circumstances or peace. By waiting too long to ask for help, to have a plan in place should all fail to go as I assumed it would, I have risked myself and, worse, others."

He reached across and took the cell Bible from its shelf. Turning to the book of Isaiah, he read, "'Since thou wast precious in my sight, thou hast been honourable, and I have loved thee: therefore will I give men for thee, and people for thy life.' You are precious, your actions were honorable, and I am here to help you."

I blinked back tears and whispered, "Thank you." Then I leaned into him before speaking. "Can you free me?"

He nodded, and I nearly collapsed with relief. "But you must remain here for another day or so until I have the Roman treasures arranged for. I was in the countryside arranging a sale of my own so that I could cover your debts and the debts incurred by the theft of the Roman treasures. I did not return until early this morning. When I did, I found your telegram and came with all speed. I've paid for you to have better quarters—and protection—until I can pay those debts and free you, and protect you from the Italians, as well."

"Yes, thank you. How shall I ever repay you?"

He ran his finger along my jawline. "You need not, lovely Ellie."

"Will you sell the Venetian treasures?"

He shook his head. "By no means. Viero entrusted them to me, and I shall see them safely back in his hands."

I'd never loved the man more than I did at that moment. I recalled what Audley had told me. *"Despite what you may have observed, Miss Sheffield, chivalry is not dead. There are some among the nobility who still act with noble intentions."*

"Pazzo and his men won't breach the prison. It's very likely those goods are stolen, and they won't want to draw an authoritative eye. In any case, it will be moot very soon." He took my hand in his own. I was acutely aware that my hands were not as clean as they might have been had I been able to wash them with clean water, at home, and use a nailbrush.

"The water . . ." I shrugged, pulling my hand away before he could remove the glove to hold my hand, skin to flesh.

He looked at me questioningly. "What is it?"

This was not the moment to be concerned about such matters, but . . . "I . . . I had taken such care with my gowns, my hair, my hands and such since Marguerite prompted me. And I must say, it affected you. And now?" I looked down at my serviceable gown and what I knew to be, under the gloves, slightly careworn hands. My hair was still fresh but hung a bit awkwardly for lack of pins and a good brush.

He cupped my face in his hands. "Dearest Ellie. You are beautiful to me in every manifestation. You are clothed in strength and dignity." He looked as though he were going to kiss me, but he did not. "May I?"

I nodded and closed my eyes in reverie as he removed my gloves, slowly, finger by finger, gently easing the fabric from my hands until they were bare. He then took my hands in his own, drew my fingertips to his lips, and kissed them.

It sent heat throughout me, down to my toes, a welcome warmth and reassurance in this most hostile environment.

A moment elapsed, and I took his hand and kissed the back of it. "You have ruined me for other men."

Harry laughed. "Good!" He glanced at his watch. "I must leave soon and conclude the matter at hand. You shall see, Ellie, a surprise I have for you. A most unexpected friend has come to our rescue, and all will soon be revealed."

He stood. "I must leave to make final arrangements." This was not the time or place for a passionate kiss, but for a kiss of reassurance which he offered tenderly, caringly, sweetly, and which I received in kind.

He left, and I closed the door behind him and then beamed. It was just as Uncle Lewis had said. There were miracles to be had if we looked for them!

The next morning, Monday, I was fully prepared to leave the prison. Harry would certainly have had time to make his final arrangements. I could not wait to get back to my home and reassure my uncle and Orchie that not only was I no longer in prison, but our problems would shortly be solved. I tidied up my bed. I did not eat lunch. I would prefer to save my appetite for food at home—even Cornish pasties!

The afternoon began to grow old, and I grew anxious. Near dinnertime, I became worried. Where was Harry? It was the end of the tenth day, after all. My heart began to squeeze each beat out a little more firmly.

Had something happened?

Just after dinnertime, when the spring sun had already set and the dingy window in my room turned from gray to black, a knock came on my door.

"Miss Sheffield?"

"Yes?"

"Someone is here to collect you. Your debt has been paid."

I sighed with relief. He had not forgotten after all!

I followed the warder down the narrow staircase and hallway, and she indicated there was a carriage waiting for me outside.

I bid her good-bye and walked through the door to the circular area where carriages waited during visiting days, pulling my cloak tightly around me. Today I saw but one carriage, though it was very fine indeed. When I drew near, I saw a hand waving me toward him. It was not Harry but Mr. Denholm waiting.

"Hello," he said.

"Mr. Denholm," I greeted him. "I did not expect to see you here." When Harry had mentioned an unexpected friend, he must have meant Mr. Denholm, who had, after all, no lost love for the late Lord Lydney, especially as he would have preferred the collection to go to the South Kensington. Harry, not willing to sell Stefano's treasures, must have promised to sell some of his own treasures to Mr. Denholm to pay back the Romans—and pay my way out of jail, too.

"I imagine not," he said. "But I've paid your debt in full and have delivered the receipt from Tenteden to the warder."

He opened the door, and I looked inside before entering. My friend Mrs. Denholm rested within, which assured me that I could enter.

Once inside, I saw the tears filling her eyes.

"I'm sorry," she said. "I . . ." She looked so forlorn, and suddenly I felt afraid.

She. I. *A casualty of women.*

"Clarice!" Mr. Denholm barked. "That is enough." I turned and looked at Mr. Denholm, who firmly closed the carriage door behind him. "I now have a favor to ask of you, in return for my paying your debt."

A whip cracked and the horses startled, and we were off into the dark, wet night.

CHAPTER
Thirty-Three

"I don't understand." I turned first to Mrs. Denholm, who sat on the bench beside me, and then across the aisle to her husband. "Didn't Lord Lydney sell art to you to free me?"

Denholm laughed. "No, no, Miss Sheffield. There has been no word of any sort from Lord Lydney. I'm afraid, as I'm certain Mr. Clarkson conveyed to you, that choosing to return the Lydney Collection to Watchfield House proved most unwise. Your only help has come from one you have spurned—and cheated. Me."

"Spurned? Cheated?" I asked. My hands, inside my thin gloves, felt as though ice sheathed them instead.

"We'll return to that momentarily," he replied.

We raced over the cobbled streets much more quickly than I would have thought safe, the carriage jostling Mrs. Denholm and me together. The gas lamps sent streaks of light through the hazy mist but did little to lift the gloom either within the carriage or without.

"How did you know I had been remanded, then?" I asked.

"There was talk of your debt at the Burlington last Thursday," Denholm said. "Lady Charlotte Schreiber took up your defense despite discussion of the shame of it all, and speculation about how you were going to remit what you owed to Tenteden. And then chance smiled upon me."

Mrs. Denholm took my hand and spoke quietly. "You've me to blame, I'm afraid. When I visited at the prison today, your friends told me that you had been remanded for a debt which had remained unpaid and asked me to pray for you. I'd hoped to do more than that. I'd hoped that Mr. Denholm would undertake your cause in the same charitable spirit with which you have undertaken the Visiting Committee." She dabbed her eyes. "Alas."

"But why me? And now?" I addressed Mr. Denholm. "What have I done to harm you?"

He did not answer. We pulled up in front of his home, and he let his wife out of the carriage first, then helped me down, a gallant measure I found most ironic. We walked up to the front door, and I was surprised when Mr. Denholm let us in himself. No man opened the door. A thought crossed my mind: the only people who had seen me with Denholm were the man himself and his wife. The carriage driver would not recognize me for my tightly fitted cloak. The prison warder had only the receipt from Lord Tenteden stating that my debt had been paid in full. Mrs. Denholm could not testify against her husband . . . should it come to that.

Denholm held the door open for his wife. She turned to me and whispered, "I shall be nearby even if you cannot see me. No harm shall come to you." Then she walked into the house, and I followed her. I took both of my gloves off and dropped them to either side of the door, just outside.

The lamps were all turned off. There were no maids to be seen, no menservants. The house smelt faintly of roast beef drippings and beeswax. The clouds must have cleared somewhat because by the light of an almost-full moon I could make out the display cases in the parlor. They appeared to be half-empty.

"Follow me," Denholm commanded. "Your imprisonment provided an unexpected opportunity, one I intend to capitalize upon."

I turned to dash, and he caught my arm.

Mr. Denholm led me down a set of stairs and then another, until we reached a lower floor, completely underground. The walls were somewhat damp, and there was a locked room behind iron bars. In nearly every way it reminded me of the prison whence I had just been freed.

Once below stairs he lit some lamps and unlocked the iron gates before ushering me into a large room. To one side, there appeared row after row of bottles of wine. To the other side, where he lit even more lamps, I saw row after row of shelves which held dozens of treasures, if not one hundred. Many of them I recognized from our earlier visit.

I turned toward him, bewildered. "You've moved some of your collection from the display cases and walls?"

"Just this afternoon," he said. "After Mrs. Denholm returned home. You see, Miss Sheffield, I came by some most disturbing information last week at the Burlington meeting. I don't mind telling you I was a little discomfited by it all. Would you like to sit down?"

"No thank you." I eyed the door. Could I dash for it? He saw my glance and closed the gates tightly.

"Please, come over here," he said. "I am not the kind of man who mistreats a woman—and my wife is just upstairs."

I had little choice but to hope he spoke the truth. I prayed that Harry would arrive at the prison and find me gone and then seek me out. But how would he know where to look for me?

Mr. Denholm stood in front of a large statue of Psyche. "Beautiful, is she not?" he asked. "Look closely, Miss Sheffield."

I took the lamp he held out to me and looked the statue over very closely. From far away, she looked perfect. Up close, though, one could see that the marble used for her face was slightly different from the marble used for her body. Because statues were ungainly and heavy, they were often made in pieces and reassembled. This made it easy for someone to steal a portion and replace it with an inferior piece of marble—or even porcelain.

"Her face is not original."

He nodded. "Yes . . . I learned that not too many weeks ago. Mr. Clarkson sold this piece to me, unfortunately. I lost significant funds on it and have no means by which to recover them, as the transaction was done under his name. It caused me quite a bit of shame when a fellow collector commented on my being duped. I brought it up to Mr. Clarkson during a visit in which, out of the depths of my kindness, I gave him some of our chemist shop's paregoric. He then treated me disrespectfully by lying to me about it. That, I would not brook. I vowed to see him undone."

I recalled what Denholm had said when I'd shared a possible story of the Egyptian stone upon its sale.

"Then the hands of the discoverer. The hands of those who transported it—tempted, perhaps, to steal such a valuable object but knowing that the probability of death awaited them if they were caught."

"Quite right," Denholm said, still caressing the stone.

Undone? Or dead? I looked at Denholm sharply, but he said no more. He had provided paregoric to Clarkson. Had it been tampered with? Bottled in a strength to which Mr. Clarkson was not accustomed? I could not know—nor could anyone at this point. The bottles were long gone and Mr. Clarkson pitched into a pauper's mass grave.

I recalled what Uncle Lewis had said to me upon learning that I had spoken with Lord Parham. *"They'll never forgive you if they think you've let on they have false pieces in their collection. It brings their eye, their judgment, and their taste into question. Never embarrass a rich man. Once anyone has shown acceptance of an item later found to be a fraud, it calls their entire collection into question, something they will never allow. Most are not as wise as they think they are and do not appreciate that being pointed out."*

Uncle believed I'd made a fatal mistake, but perhaps it was you who did, Mr. Clarkson. I'm so sorry. It's never good to think you're cleverer than your clients.

"How can I assist?" I asked Mr. Denholm, warier than ever now that I understood the danger he might present. "I'd like to return to my home and see that my uncle is well."

"I understand he is not well," he said. "Poor man. He's been taken to hospital, having found out that his niece was remanded to debtor's prison after signing for debts he owed. Perhaps he's been returned home by now. Or perhaps . . ." He left the sentence to dangle.

"Who told him?" I nearly shrieked, no longer worried about myself.

"I did, of course. After I went to your home over the weekend to see about receiving the monies owed me for falsely sold goods."

"You've just said Mr. Clarkson sold Psyche to you on his own account," I replied. "Independent of our firm."

"Yes. But I have many more pieces, Miss Sheffield, including one or two sold to me by Clarkson as a duly recognized representative of Sheffield Brothers."

That part was true. If my firm had been involved in

some misdoing, and it seemed it had, I wanted it set right. I nodded.

"Good. Here is a bargain I'd like to make with you. I have paid your debt and freed you from prison. I want you to tell me, confidentially and completely, which pieces are true and which are frauds. I do not want to openly display any which might bring me further shame."

Now I understood. "And what confidence do you have that I can, or will, do so?"

"I have complete confidence in you," he replied. "You're young, I know, but your father and uncle have trained you since you were a girl. And it takes some courage for a chit of a woman to speak up to Parham and tell him that his prized Grecian urn is a reproduction."

"He told you?" I asked.

He shook his head. "I heard you tell him. I'd been standing outside the library."

Ah. The shadow. "Very well," I agreed. "I am only one woman with my opinion and experience, but I shall do my best. And then I am free to leave?"

"Yes. Upon my word."

What that was worth, I did not know. I believed if I needed help, I could scream and his wife would help me. I hoped she would. In any case, the prison could, eventually, follow the trail of the paid debt to the person who had paid it. If harm were to befall me, I believed he knew the authorities would learn where to look. He wouldn't risk that.

It wouldn't be easily explained away . . . as Mr. Clarkson's death had been.

I walked around the shelves, lamp held high, looking from both twelve feet and twelve inches.

Everything seemed legitimate on the first shelf. On the second shelf, I saw a Palissy platter which seemed to be very old but gently restored. It was beautifully painted, a moving image of God pulling Eve from Adam's rib. The damp of the room had caused the linens which bound the crack to lift slightly, and I lifted them even a bit further. When I did, I could see the distinctive letters *PULL*. This was not a Palissy. It was a Pullman, perhaps ten years old, if that. I said as much to Mr. Denholm.

"Thank you, Miss Sheffield. This was not even one I had suspected, as it had been a donation to the South Kensington."

So—he admitted he had sampled and acquired treasures for himself out of those which had been donated? I was gladder than ever that I had returned Harry's family collection to him.

Harry. A thought: If he went to fetch me from the prison and I was not there, he would certainly visit Tenteden, who would tell him that Denholm had paid my fine. He would then know where to find me.

I smiled. Perhaps in this one instance, I might be permitted to believe that Harry and I were cleverer than my client.

"You're smiling?" His voice was not polite.

"I'm glad to have found the truth out," I said honestly, though I did not clarify which truth I referred to.

The explanation seemed to satisfy him, as he relaxed.

I looked at the next shelf, filled with porcelain. Prominently displayed, just up in the front, was a shepherdess figurine exactly matching the one from Harry's collection.

Was it one of Mr. Clarkson's frauds? I picked it up and examined it as closely as the dim light allowed me. I tapped it against my teeth. I looked at the maker's mark and the glazing and the fine cracks. It was the original, which I believed had last been seen in Mr. Clarkson's rooms. That would mean, along with the ones in Bristol, the one at Watchfield was a reproduction.

Had his room been emptied of anything of value, or perhaps anything which might be condemning, by Mr. Denholm, or more likely one of his men?

It was a most damning piece of evidence. Chills ran up my spine like ice cracking. Mr. Denholm had arranged for Mr. Clarkson to be killed, but likely it would never be proved.

Careful not to show my recognition of the shepherdess lest he seize upon the moment to harm me, I moved on. Upon the next shelf sat an Egyptian bowl. I knew immediately it was all wrong.

"The bowl appears to be very old—but it's quite possible that the pottery was aged and cracked to make it look much older than it is." I ran my finger over the picture. "The bow and arrow being used to confront an enemy—and that is correct. However—" I tipped the bowl toward him—"the horses are not attached to the racing chariot. They are free-floating. That is not a mistake that a practiced artisan would have made. And this bowl would not have been preserved for so many years if it had not been crafted by a practiced artisan." I faced him squarely, more confident now that I was in my area of expertise. "I'm sorry, but this is not right."

"Yes . . . someone called that into question last Thursday night," he said. "Parham, I believe. It was the second error, the second incidence of fraud at the hand of your firm."

"I have never seen this piece."

He took out a bill of lading. On it was written the Egyptian stone that Mr. Clarkson and I had purchased on his behalf. The chariot bowl was listed just under. The tally had been adjusted, and just beyond that, I had signed off on the pieces.

"I signed this before the bowl was added," I insisted.

"There is no indication of that," he said. "In fact, the handwriting is consistent throughout."

"Of course it is," I replied. "Because we both know Mr. Clarkson was a forger—and a very good one at that." I thought of the many pieces he had painted.

"I think you knew about the bowl. You accepted the praise when Mr. Clarkson complimented you on sourcing the Egyptian treasure. In any case, it matters not, as he legally represented your firm at that time."

That was true. I saw the difficulty of my situation. Mr. Clarkson had used my good name to cover his misdeeds.

Harry, please come. I looked over the remaining shelves and found nothing of interest until I spied a page from an illuminated manuscript, neatly framed. I lifted it down.

It matched my uncle's Book of Hours. I had examined that book and found the pages intact, but at least one of them had been loose.

I read the page. It was, of course, painted in Latin. To the person able to read Latin, the errors would be immediately noticeable. If not, it would merely look like beautiful serif painting. I had to be honest.

"This is a painted copy of an illustrated page, not the page itself," I said. "The Latin is not right."

He looked shocked. "I had not expected this."

Because you do not read Latin, I thought.

"I thought Mr. Clarkson had torn apart a true book and was selling the pages," he said. "Yet another fraud." His face grew red. "I believe your uncle's signature was on that receipt."

Perhaps it was the real signature. Perhaps it was Mr. Clarkson's forgery. But if it were from even six months earlier, we would have difficulty proving that Uncle was not sensible enough to sign, especially as he had been signing for other commissions which had had no problem. I did not want them all called into question.

I believed that Mr. Denholm—and perhaps Mr. Herberts—were the only clients that Clarkson could have cultivated in his time with us who were wealthy enough to have purchased these expensive frauds. When—if—I was allowed back to my workshop, I should make a careful review of the books to ensure that.

"How shall you rectify this?" Denholm asked. "I want it

fixed but done quietly. As I've said, I do not want my peers to know of my folly."

Of course you do not, although they probably already do. What would my father have done? My uncle? Despite it all, they would have been honor bound to see the situation mended, and I felt that same compelling duty. I thought to strike the bargain I'd offered Tenteden. "Perhaps I might offer you the complete Book of Hours," I replied. "In exchange for the false page, the false chariot bowl, and the monies you paid Lord Tenteden on my behalf."

Denholm considered for a moment. "Yes. I will agree to that."

"And if any other pieces are found to be fraudulent but connected with Sheffield Brothers, you will agree that this exchange makes them all paid in full. Forever."

He smiled. "I have not purchased anything else from your firm, Miss Sheffield. Nor shall I in future. But you keep discreet about my follies, and I shall keep quiet about yours."

"No need to keep quiet on my behalf," I said. "I have done nothing wrong, and the wrongs committed by Mr. Clarkson I have made right."

He opened a bureau drawer in a small office off the wine cellar and withdrew a piece of paper which listed some vintage bottles. On the back of it, he drew up the agreement, and we both signed it. I held out my hand. "I'll keep that."

He put the document behind his back, and at that moment, we heard a clattering of footsteps come down the stairs. "Eleanor! Miss Sheffield."

Round the corner came Harry, an Italian-looking man, and Mrs. Denholm.

"What is the meaning of this?" Harry demanded. He was taller than Denholm, younger, stronger, and titled. Even Denholm shied back.

"I could ask the same thing," he said. "What do you mean by storming my house?"

"He did not storm in," Mrs. Denholm said quietly. "I invited him in."

Harry came through the iron gates and took me in his arms. "When I saw your gloves outside the door . . . ," he said, emotion filling his voice. "Was he holding you against your will?"

"I left the gloves to let you know I was inside, should someone deny it," I whispered. I looked up at him and then at Denholm, whose face had a determined look of surprise. He had not expected Harry to remain faithful and committed to me. Perhaps because he himself was untrue. "Not truly against my will. Not yet."

"What is the meaning of this?" Harry asked Denholm once more.

"I'm sure Lord Tenteden told you when you went to collect the funds," I answered as Denholm seemed to have gone dumb.

"I was arranging for those funds when Antelini—whom I'd stationed outside the prison—came to get me, telling me that you had been whisked away from the house of detention by someone you'd greeted as Denholm."

Ah! Bless Mr. Antelini. "Mr. Denholm paid the amount due to Tenteden, and he and his most kind wife collected me from the prison," I said. "In return, I notified Mr. Denholm which of his art might have raised some . . . concern. Mr. Denholm? Could you please show your wife, Lord Lydney, and Mr. Antelini the document we just signed? I'm sure we can count on both the honesty and the discretion of all involved."

Denholm reluctantly showed the document to those present, thereby ensuring that our arrangement would stand.

"The Book of Hours," Harry said. "I shall pay—"

Denholm stood firm. "I am not interested in your money, Lydney. I am interested in the Book of Hours. If Miss Sheffield does not agree to abide by her part in this arrangement, we shall have it seen in court."

My uncle, my family firm, my name—these were worth more than the Book of Hours, as it was unlikely that my uncle would soon even remember he owned such a treasure.

"I abide by my word, Mr. Denholm. Do you?"

He nodded.

I was in a hurry to return to my home, to see if my uncle—and Orchie—were well and if he had returned from hospital. I wondered, too, if Harry had already paid for the Roman treasures. If not—were Pazzo and his men at my home?

As we turned to walk up the stairs, I took Mrs. Denholm's hand in my own. "You are a most dear lady and a friend. In friendship, I must advise you that the medieval bracelet which was a gift from your husband is not medieval, as the gems do not have the appropriate cut for that era. I'm so sorry."

She blinked. "Thank you, my dear. Better to know when one has been dealing with a crook."

She glanced firmly at her husband and then led the way up the stairs. Her husband did not follow us.

Halfway up I turned to Harry. "Wait. Your shepherdess is down there."

I retraced my steps, but by the time I reached the bottom of the stairs, I could see that it had been removed from the shelf and tucked away somewhere in the bowels of the dank wine cellar, along with Mr. Denholm.

I did not have time to tarry—I needed to get to my uncle.

CHAPTER

Thirty-Four

Harry helped me into his carriage—Mr. Antelini joining us—and we drove as quickly as possible to my home. Harry held my hand, but we did not speak, both because we were not alone and because there was little to say until we understood what had happened to my uncle.

The carriage stopped in front of my house, and the driver tied the horses and then opened the carriage door. He helped me out, and I raced up the steps.

I pounded on the door, as I had not taken a key with me to prison, and hoped that someone would be there.

I sensed a presence behind the door, but it did not open. "Orchie! Orchie, it is me, Eleanor," I called loudly, caring not if the neighbors eavesdropped.

The door was quickly unlatched, and then Orchie gathered me into her arms. She looked to have aged a year or two though only four days had passed since I'd left.

"You're back!" she sobbed.

I nodded. "Harry is behind me. Uncle Lewis?"

I stepped into the house and looked into the parlor, which was dark and cold. Surely he wasn't already laid out there on the long table?

Orchie came up next to me. "He's in 'ospital."

"Oh!" I was overcome and about to say more when she held up a hand.

"He can return home tomorrow. He's much improved. Your Dr. Garrett saw that he was cared for."

Tears flowed for a moment, and then I wiped them away with my handkerchief.

I sank into the sofa. Harry entered the house, and Orchie took his hat and coat and placed them on the stand just inside the foyer. Mr. Antelini was stoking the coal fire when Orchie joined us in the room, bringing tea service.

"Mr. Sheffield was unwell, as you know," she said. "I told him you'd gone visiting, and that seemed to bring him peace until that horrible man showed up demanding money or Mr. Sheffield would end up in prison just like you had."

My chest heaved with anger toward Denholm, but in a clear moment, I also had sympathy for his wife, who was a very kind person indeed.

"Well, then he seemed in pain and was clutching his chest like this—" she pressed against her breastbone—"and so I did what you told me to do and sent Alice for that nice lady doctor. She took him to hospital and found a man doctor to care for him, though I don't know as to how we're going to pay for that. . . ."

"Do not worry about that," Harry spoke up.

She smiled at him. "And then they said he could come back home on the morrow. It will do him a world of good, Miss Eleanor, to see you home."

"I shall fetch him from hospital myself," I said.

"We shall," Harry amended, taking my hand in his own. "Together."

Orchie looked at our joined hands. "Well, I'd best be preparing a bag: clean clothes—if they can be found—for him to wear home."

I shook my head. "No. You go to bed now. It's been a difficult time for you, and you look as if you need a good rest. I can pack the bag."

She yawned. "I don't mind saying I could use a bit of sleep—" she came over to me and kissed my forehead—"now you're safe."

Harry asked Mr. Antelini to wait outside. Antelini nodded to me.

"*Buonasera*, Signore Antelini," I said. "*Grazie mille.*"

"*Prego*, Signorina Sheffield," he replied. "You are most welcome."

Orchie, ever tending to my reputation, had not actually gone off to bed but was tottering about in the hallway and then the sitting room nearby, loudly enough for us to know she was still there but distant enough that we could speak in private.

"You are safe now," Harry said. "I can leave Antelini stationed outside for the night, but unless you fear Denholm, there is no further threat."

"Denholm will do nothing openly," I said. "He's a coward. And he knows you are protecting me now. The Roman goods? I'm so sorry, but I have concluded that Mr. Clarkson stole them whilst we were doing the inventory and then sold them overseas, from Bristol. They are paid for? For the moment? Because I shall find a way to repay you."

"Yes. I paid for them earlier today. The Italians are satisfied. They will not trouble you, or Viero's sister, anymore."

I smiled at the manner in which he referred to Francesca, more formally—it was to please and reassure me, I knew. "I am sorry you had to sell some of the collection," I said. "That must have been difficult, having just had it returned to you."

He ran his hand through his hair, which looked even more deeply auburn in the glow of the coals. "I did not sell any of the collection, Ellie."

"How, then, did you pay for the Roman goods?"

He sat on the sofa next to me; it had not been made for a man as broad as he was from years of riding, and so we were rather close. I did not mind. I suspected he did not either.

"There were a few reasons I wanted that collection returned to me," he began. "First, I wanted to keep my mother's things."

"The pelican," I offered shyly, remembering the question of whether I had intentionally kept it.

He leaned over and kissed my cheek. "The pelican and other things. I wanted my brother's items. I wanted my ancestral treasures. But mostly, Ellie, I wanted to keep that collection because, in the end, that collection will be yours."

A flush of warmth spread through me. Was he implying . . . ? Was he next going to propose marriage to me?

He drank some of his tea and then set the cup down. "It became apparent to me some years ago that my father had no intention of providing an income of any sort to me, though he was well able to."

I sighed. "That was, unfortunately, clear to all of us."

He looked sad for a moment, then pressed on. "Although he could have claimed them, the horses were left to me by my mother when she died. He did not demand them, having, one hopes, some respect in seeing her final wishes through. Despite his acrimony toward me, he truly loved my mother."

As did Harry, I knew. When his mother died, he'd been left without a defender.

He continued, "I decided that I could breed the horses, and I began to do well at it; the studs are high quality, and word began to spread. Little by little I've built quite an enterprise. Even whilst traveling back and forth from Italy. It's grown more quickly in the last year or so."

"Marguerite had mentioned something along those lines," I admitted.

He turned fully toward me. "Until I had sufficient income in place, Ellie, I was in no position to take a wife."

He held my hand but said nothing more. Should

I prompt him? What woman wanted a proposal to come from a prompting?

Well, I did, perhaps. "I understand and am gladdened to know that is remedied." I would say no more.

"I had to offer Signorina Viero the cover of my name to transport her safely from Italy and then again for a few days whilst I arranged for the payment for the stolen Roman goods. For her safety and for her brother's." He smiled. "Viero is well. He will return for his sister and mother within a month or two."

"I am so glad to hear of that," I said, and I was. "So there is no longer need to give Francesca the cover of your name?" I hinted.

"No." His face grew somber. "Because to pay for the goods which have gone missing, I sold Abalone."

I set my teacup down so hard it nearly clattered. I thought I heard Orchie scurrying in the background, but she did not appear. "Harry. No. Not Abalone. Not only is he your favorite, but he must be the foundation of your stud—so well-known, such good lineage."

"It was necessary. He was the only asset I had which could bring in enough resources to cover both the Roman goods and your debt." He met my gaze. "I do not regret it. My honor means more—and I have done for Viero what I said I would do. My love for you means more—and you are safe now."

"Perhaps you might buy him back someday?" I offered.

He shook his head. "No. Our understanding is that this would be an irrevocable arrangement." He looked sad and boyish for a moment. "As it turns out, Abalone was more generous to me in the end than was my own father."

He looked down at his hands. I thought of taking him into my arms but sensed that this was not a moment for clucking and feminine pity, as Uncle would say. Instead, I drank the remainder of my tea and then flipped the cup over.

I pointed to the maker's mark on the bottom. "In order to claim his own work, a maker stamps or paints his unique mark on the cup and then glazes over it, making it permanent.

"Now I—" I turned the cup back over—"could tell without looking at the mark who had made this. I am very used to seeing them, of course, so they are easy to recognize. The distinctive design that the maker used. The colors he preferred. How he was able to make something both beautiful and useful." I smiled a little, recalling my discussion some months past with Marguerite. "But if there is a question, the mark will always tell."

I set the cup back down. "You, my love, have been proved to be authentic." I gently touched his face, those weary lines, and continued, softly. "You have your Maker's design all over you. His mark is stamped in your loyalty. Your kindness. The way you put others before yourself."

I touched his hands, each in turn. "The friendship you offer to all and your fidelity toward them, in your vow to Stefano and others. Your courage in taking his mother and sister to safety. Your beauty as I see it and have always seen it."

He took my hands in his own and raised them to kiss the backs. "Thank you, Ellie."

"You will collect me in the morning to fetch my uncle from hospital?"

"Undoubtedly," he said, his voice slightly roughened. I saw him to the door. He put his coat on, and I took his hat from the stand and put it on his head in as wifely a manner as I could muster.

He smiled before leaving. He knew.

But still, he had not proposed.

I closed and locked the door behind him. Orchie, hearing that all was now quiet, toddled off to bed. The fire was dying out, but although I should have been spent, I was not. The events of the night and, indeed, the days which had come before it, had added nervous energy, and I feared I would simply lie awake for hours till I saw Harry returned for me and my uncle safely home.

I'd pack Uncle's bag.

I went down the hallway and pushed open the door to his room. It smelled foul. It was a muddle. I did not care what his preferences were; I was going to tidy it up. I was a firm believer—perhaps passed along to me by my Dutch grandmother—that a tidy environment would lead to an organized mind.

First, I picked up all the clothing that had been strewn on the floor. I tidied the personal items on his dressing table and put his shoes neatly next to a chest of drawers, for now.

Once close to the chest of drawers, I could smell the most dreadful odor. I nearly turned away from it. Could it be a dead animal? I could not ignore it. It was unsanitary, at best.

I opened the lowest drawer and within it found perhaps two dozen Cornish pasties in various states of mold and decay. I held back a gag and went to fetch an old sheet in which to wrap them for permanent disposal.

I used a rag to ensure I had cleared the drawer out from front to back, and then I wiped up the side of the drawer. As I did, the rag caught on something. I wiped again. It caught again. I knelt as low as I could, peered inside the drawer, and found what seemed to be a hidden lever.

Yes! As I looked it over carefully, I saw that it was crafted by the same firm which had made Lord Lydney's wardrobe. Perhaps my uncle—or father—had sourced them both. This tall chest of drawers had hidden door latches. I tugged on one lever, and the drawer above it, which had been locked, opened.

I took out the first thing my hand touched. It was the miniature portrait from his study—the one I'd suspected Clarkson of stealing. Perhaps Uncle had just wanted it near him? Or he'd suspected Clarkson of stealing things too, and didn't especially want this one to be taken?

I turned it over in my hand, and as I did, the top portrait fell off. Underneath was a portrait of a young woman who looked, just a little, like Alice. It was clear that the portrait had been painted many years ago, but it was very finely crafted. At the bottom of the portrait was painted, in the tiniest script, *Carolina*.

That must have been why Uncle had referred to Alice as Miss Carolina from time to time, as his mind slipped further back. I could not know, nor would I ask him, but I suspected Miss Carolina had been a sweetheart, perhaps one forbidden to him and thus hidden in the portrait locket. I tried to open the larger two drawers, which were above the two I'd just opened, from the front. They, too, were locked.

I felt around for another secret latch, found it, and tugged. When I did, the drawer above popped open just a little, and I heard a sound like glass rattling.

"Oooohhh." A moan escaped my lips. *Could these be? No. How could they be?*

Oh, Harry. I'm so sorry. Abalone, irrevocably sold.

I looked in dismay at the items hidden in this drawer, and then very gently eased open the drawer just above it. Nestled in old clothing, things I had not seen my uncle wear for some months, were treasures. Roman treasures. All ancient, and all made of glass.

CHAPTER *Thirty-Five*

I looked the Roman treasures over carefully and then brought them to the workshop, where I looked them over once more with my eyeglass. Precious—some of them. Irregular, others.

I sat there for a moment, and then a thought bolted me from my chair. Might there also be a hidden drawer in Uncle's study?

I ran up the stairs and sat in his large chair, opening all the drawers. Nothing was new, except I now saw a false-fronted drawer, manufactured, of course, by the same craftsman who had made the others. I reached inside and triggered the lever; the drawer popped out just a little. I pulled it open and looked inside.

"Oh, my goodness!" I reached my hand in to pull out stack after stack of invoices with banknotes pinned to them. Uncle Lewis had apparently withdrawn the money to pay some of our larger invoices—perhaps ones he normally delivered in person? He had then placed them here for safe-keeping, forgetting that they remained unpaid.

Of course, I could not sleep. I lay awake nearly till morning's light thinking about the treasures, mulling over some irregularities I'd noticed in a few of them, and praying about what to do. I finally got up and readied myself for the day. The water in which I washed was unbelievably warm and clean, and I was grateful for it in a new way. I put on one of my best dresses, cared for by the skillful hands of Alice.

Soon, Orchie was up. She knew something was awry as soon as she saw my face. "What is it?" she asked.

"I found some items in Uncle Lewis's room," I said. "As I was tidying it up last night and preparing a bag for his return home. Some pasties. Old and rotted. And money. Lots of banknotes."

She flinched. "Oh. Dear me. I looked, that once, and found no money. Hadn't smelled any rotted food, but then he wouldn't let me in too often."

"Everything was hidden in clothing drawers locked by unusual levers. I did not know he had such bureaus. Some other drawers had false fronts, so you couldn't have known last time you'd looked for me. Papa had a bureau like that too. I think they must've had twinned sets as young men."

"I'm glad to know I hadn't overlooked anything." Her face pinked.

I nodded. "The banknotes I found were pinned to invoices which had not been remitted. Invoices I have since paid, of course, with money from items I have sold. Nothing new—not since you'd directed the post to me."

Orchie sat down. "Oh, I'm sorry. But 'appy is this day!" Her smile filled her face. "You can certainly use the additional funds."

"We can," I agreed, sighing once more with relief that our house was now on a firm foundation. "But . . ."

Her face moved from joy-filled to tentative.

I continued, "The worst part of all is that I found some Roman antiques. They appear to be ones that were entrusted to Lord Lydney and then stolen. We had thought Mr. Clarkson . . ."

"That cannot be!" she said. "Why would your uncle have stolen them, and when?"

"I think they are what they appear to be," I said. "I shall ask him when he is home and settled if I feel he is up to it. Whilst we wait for Lord Lydney, I shall place them in crates, softly cradled and well wrapped, in the workshop."

Harry appeared shortly after breakfast. "Are we ready, then?" he asked.

I nodded. "I have something to share with you in the carriage."

As we made our way to the hospital, I told him what had transpired. "I cannot be certain, of course, because I have not seen the exact treasures that Signorina Viero agreed to transport. But I believe them to be old and Roman, and they look to be the kind of thing that would have been sold along with the bottle that Pazzo has already reclaimed."

"How could this be?" Harry asked.

"I do not know," I answered. "We shall endeavor to find out. But, Harry . . . some of them appear to be fraudulent, and I can't be certain, but a few might have been stolen, as you suspected."

"Would it be criminal to have them in England?" Harry asked.

"Most certainly, if they are stolen. The sentiment might even be stronger in Italy, where they belong."

We pulled up in front of the hospital, and the driver waited whilst we went in to retrieve my uncle. When he saw me, his face lit up, and he nearly leaped out of the chair where he'd been waiting to depart. "Eleanor! You are back. You are not in prison." Tears rolled down his cheeks.

I hugged him to me. "I am not in prison. Lord Lydney and I are here to take you home, where you belong, and where you will remain."

Uncle grinned and waved his walking stick in the air, almost losing his balance until Harry steadied him from the side. We drove back to Bloomsbury, and once home, the three of us helped him to his room.

As soon as he walked through the doorway, he turned to Orchie. "I told you not to clean this up!" His voice held as much fear as anger.

"Nor did I," she said firmly, confident at dealing with his antics.

He saw the drawer which had been opened by the lever pulled out, and a sudden light of realization and remembrance flashed across his face. He then turned toward me, his voice more boy than man. "You found them."

I responded in a voice both steadfast and quiet. "Indeed, I did."

He looked at Harry. "I don't suppose you would like to help an old man out of a pinch?"

"I already did." Harry kept his sense of humor, despite what this pinch had cost him. "I've paid for them."

"Oh. Oh." Uncle sat down on his bed, and Orchie propped him up with some pillows and took off his boots. "And here I thought I'd been assisting you, young man."

I pointed toward the drawers, still open. "Do you feel up to telling us what has transpired?"

He sighed and held his head for a moment as if to clear the cobwebs. "As I recall, I journeyed with you and Mr. Clarkson to do the last inventory at Watchfield. I grew tired, and that Mr. Clarkson left me to rest whilst he went to the porcelain room—in which he seemed overly interested." He fell silent.

"You were going to get the key for me," I gently prompted him. "For the room on the third floor at Watchfield House."

"Yes, yes, that's it," he said, his memory invigorated. "I went to ask the gatekeeper for it, he refused me, but then I felt tired, and I sat down for a bit and closed my eyes. When I awoke, I was alone and went to look for the man. Instead, I found the crates. Those Venetian beauties . . ." His rheumy eyes filled with joy. "Then I saw the smallish crate with the Roman art inside. I went to look at it, and I knew your father was up to his old tricks again." He looked at Harry. "Is he here, presently?"

Harry looked at me.

"No," I answered. "He is not. What do you mean his old tricks?"

"Well, whenever he stored things out of sight, and they were stolen, he would keep them in crates with a blue mark across them—" he drew a line in the air—"like that. Then the gatehouse man, or his valet, would keep the goods out of sight until he could place them . . . somewhere. I caught him once, with a relic. Told him he'd have to return it and he refused. Dressed me down and worked only with your papa from then on. Your father wouldn't have let him get away with that either. But I suspect *your* father—" he looked at Harry—"just got better at keeping things hidden."

"So you saw these Roman goods," I said. "And then . . ."

"I knew just by looking at them that some were frauds and some were stolen. He hadn't returned the relic; I had no faith he would return these, either." He turned toward Harry. "I thought if he were caught out, he would blame you, just like he always does. I wrapped them in my clothing and brought them home and put them with the clothing in the drawer and then . . ."

I looked at Harry, who nodded. We both understood that my uncle was blending present and past and had little sense that he was doing it.

"Would you like to show us?" I asked. "I have put the pieces in the workshop."

Uncle swung his legs around the bed. Orchie went for his boots, but he waved her away. We helped him down the stairs and then the hallway, stocking-footed.

We settled my uncle once more in the best parlor chair. I lifted the treasures one at a time—they were all small, certainly able to have been nestled among Uncle's clothing in his travel bag that first visit back to Watchfield. First, a tiny mosaic glass bowl, perhaps one hundred years old, possibly one which held olives. "Was this one of them?" I asked.

"A beauty. Yes, yes. I believe that to be genuine, and if not terribly expensive, dear enough for the likes of us."

I, too, believed it to be genuine. Next, I lifted an early Roman ribbed bowl from the small casket in which I had set it for safekeeping. The glass was a light-green tint and had a beautiful pearlescent oxidation on it.

I held it close to him, and he squinted. "I'm not certain."

"Nor am I," I responded. "But something about it troubles me."

He nodded. "One of the ancient glass bottles troubled me too." He stood, and Harry held him by the elbow. "I left it just over here, on a shelf, so that I could examine it in a better light."

As he started to walk toward the shelf, I raised my eyebrows at Harry, who nodded to me in return. The glass bottle had not been planted by Pazzo. My uncle had placed it there for careful examination and then forgotten it.

"I'm just checking that now," I said. "I'll ask you more about it later." I did not want to tell him that it had been snatched back.

I held up a small Roman plaque. He agreed that it was valid. Then we came to the gold-and-porcelain chalice and platter for celebrating Eucharist. To my eyes, they looked real and perhaps five hundred years old—pre-Reformation. Very valuable indeed.

"Thief!" my uncle cried out. "This is the one I first noticed. These could not be lawfully sold. Indeed—" he turned toward Harry—"once more your father has taken advantage of an unstable political situation to 'acquire' goods from Italy. These were designed, commissioned, and purchased solely for religious purposes and were stored at the Palazzo del Quirinale, where the pope resides."

"Stolen from the church?" Harry asked. "I do not think Viero or his sister would have approved of that, had they known."

"Viero?" Uncle asked. "Who is that? Nonetheless, they must be returned to Italy. I had been planning to do that, to return them to their owners, to set things right for all involved. I meant to find out where I must send them, and then, somehow, I forgot. I'm sorry." He hung his head. "I do not want you to be blamed for this, young man. To be hanged, as it were, for your father's sins."

I came behind him and put my arm round him. "Do not concern yourself. You must rest now. I shall pick up the threads from here. You have done quite enough. Without you," I said in all sincerity, "none of us would have recognized where these belonged. I certainly would not have. You have done well."

He nodded, and Orchie helped him back to his room.

"They must all be returned to Italy," Harry said. "Their proper owners found."

"Your money. Abalone," I answered quietly. "Due to Uncle Lewis. I'm so sorry."

He touched my cheek. "It's for the best. We do not want to be responsible for stolen goods. Once we know they have been acquired illegally, it is our responsibility to see them restored, as your uncle so rightly insisted, though his methods were somewhat—" he smiled—"questionable. I shall ask Viero to take them when he returns to Italy. He'll be here next week." He caressed my face for a moment and then took his leave.

I sat down in the chair my uncle had just vacated; it was still warm, and I was well aware of the symbolism of his leaving the chair and my taking his place. Sheffield Brothers was in my hands now. Had Mr. Clarkson's deceit, coupled with my uncle's well-intentioned theft, brought us to the place whence the firm could not be recovered?

I let my mind relax for a moment and my gaze drift back to the items on the tables in front of me. In an instant, I realized that the ancient ribbed-glass bowl was certainly fraudulent and guessed that the small oil bottle my uncle had taken for examination, and which Pazzo had pocketed, was as well.

I immediately put on my hat and coat and went to call on Lady Charlotte.

CHAPTER Thirty-Six

Charlotte returned to the workshop with me within the hour, as I knew she would.

"Thank you for coming," I said.

She took my hand in her own. "Of course. We are friends."

"I had worried that might not be the case any longer once it became known what Mr. Clarkson had done and that our firm owed debts." I explained to her about my uncle.

"You have done quite well, my dear, with the circumstances you were given. I said as much at the Burlington only last week."

I squeezed her hand. "Mr. Denholm mentioned that. Your support means a great deal to me."

I showed her the treasures, one by one, and we agreed on their value and on which were authentic. Though we could not be certain that all of them had not been stolen, they would have to be returned for that reason alone. I shared my thoughts on the ribbed bowl and the missing oil bottle, and then the insight my uncle had passed along about the sacred items from the Palazzo del Quirinale.

Her eyes misted over. "It will be a sad day when we lose his wealth of knowledge. But yes, I suspect he is right."

I nodded, a bit saddened myself. "I shall endeavor to learn all I can before my uncle is unable to continue teaching me."

She looked up from the table. "Do you think Lord Lydney would be willing to have these exhibited before he has them sent back to Italy? I am sure many of our friends would enjoy seeing them before they are rightfully returned. Perhaps the Venetian treasures might be exhibited too? We were not able to see them when we were last at Watchfield."

Oh yes, I'd forgotten that. It was because the Roman goods had just been discovered stolen. I sensed something behind her request, but as she was not forthcoming with it, I could hardly ask if she had some other rationale. It would be presumptuous. *There may be nothing there but what is on the surface,* I thought. *Her friends would surely enjoy seeing these, and as they are to be returned and Harry has paid for them, there is no harm in it.*

"If Lord Lydney agrees, of course," I said. "I shall telegraph him, and Signorina Viero, and ask if that might be possible. You'd like to host them at your home?"

Charlotte nodded. "Yes, that would be wonderful. Make your enquiries and we shall agree upon a date as soon as you hear back."

Lady Charlotte had asked me to arrive at her home ahead of the others. Her dinner preparations were complete, and she wanted to speak with me privately.

"There will be many in attendance from the Burlington. Although it is not an official club meeting."

My stomach clenched though I knew I was safe. "Mr. Denholm?" I asked.

Charlotte shook her head. "No, dear. His questioning of you at the last meeting made it clear that he was no friend. I would not subject you to another onslaught!"

I nodded, grateful. "It is appropriate that many from the Burlington are here. They would be the most likely to appreciate the Venetian treasures as well as the Roman ones."

"I'd like them to appreciate *you*." She put it bluntly.

"Me?"

"Yes. There was some . . . discussion . . . after all, with the understanding that Mr. Clarkson had not been, shall we say, completely aboveboard. May he rest in peace. I would like you to explain about the Roman treasures to the others present tonight. Perhaps the Venetian, too. I shall introduce you. It may go a long way to setting things right where people's thoughts about you and your firm are concerned."

She offered a chance to stand before those who might

have rejected me and explain myself. I wished it were not necessary, but it was. It also offered me the opportunity to set things right regarding Harry.

"I agree—with inestimable gratitude." I embraced her. "But I believe Signorina Viero should be allowed to speak of her own Venetian treasures."

"A wonderful idea!" Charlotte said.

Her friends—many of whom, if not most, were collectors and valuers—soon arrived, and as they filtered into the rooms and circulated, they watched me with wary interest.

Well before dinner was to be served, Harry arrived with Signorina Viero and two other men, one of whom I gladly recognized as Stefano Viero; the other I did not know.

Charlotte welcomed them, and Mr. Schreiber directed Harry's man, bearing a large crate which I assumed held some of the Venetian treasures, to the library, where he'd set out the Roman treasures for display.

"Miss Sheffield." Stefano took both my hands in his own and kissed each cheek. He looked tired and thin but as handsome as ever, and I told him so.

"Perhaps you are Italian, Miss Sheffield? Such a delightful compliment."

I laughed. "No. But I wish I were, after having viewed many of the beautiful works of glass your countrymen have produced. Thank you for allowing my friend Lady Charlotte Schreiber to share them this evening."

"It is our pleasure," he said. "May I introduce Barone de Bennetto? My friend and a friend of Lydney, too."

Signorina Viero turned her eyes to the handsome de Bennetto, a man with deep-blue eyes and a stubbled black beard. By the look on her face, I imagined they were more than mere friends.

They departed, and I stood there alone with Harry. I could hardly keep my eyes off him, and it seemed he felt the same way, as his gaze did not waver.

Mr. Herberts approached us and spoke up. "I am glad the two of you are here together. I was sold—wrongfully, one now understands—a piece of majolica. I gather it was from your family." He turned to Harry. "I should like to return it to you."

I looked toward the ground. Mr. Clarkson. Again.

"I will be happy to pay for it," I said, "if you remitted funds to my firm or someone representing it."

Mr. Herberts gave me a fatherly smile. "Consider it a gift for the forthcoming occasion."

I looked at him oddly. What forthcoming occasion?

"And I would be happy to patronize Sheffield Brothers if it will continue to offer its services," he said. He looked at Harry as he said it. Harry squeezed my arm and nodded his agreement to Mr. Herberts.

Charlotte had tables set in her large dining room, with lacquered screens separating each table to allow for more intimate conversation, and had thoughtfully seated me with Harry and his Italian friends. The conversation around the table was lively, and my heart filled with happiness and pleasure in a way I could not have imagined possible only a fortnight earlier.

Signorina Viero, seated next to me, leaned over as we ate sorbet. "I must apologize, Miss Sheffield, for accusing you of stealing the Roman treasures, or any of mine. If the truth were known, I was the one who was duplicitous, not telling his lordship that I had allowed the Roman goods to come with our own goods. He was so kind to pay for them, and we will seek, in Italy, to see him reimbursed. I was quite wrong. I hope you will accept my apology."

I took her hand. I had, after all, questioned her motives as well. "War and difficulty and evil people encourage doubts in all of us, signorina. Please do not concern yourself any further. And please, do call me Eleanor."

"Yes," she said. "And please call me Francesca."

I asked her if she would be willing to speak about her family's treasures that evening and she happily agreed.

After dinner, Mr. Schreiber led us into the library. There were not quite enough chairs for all present to sit; the ladies sat and some of the older gentlemen, while the remainder of the men stood. Mr. Schreiber introduced me. "Miss Sheffield has a fine eye for discerning the genuine from the fraud, and a wealth of knowledge upon which to draw. I'm delighted she will now share with us some of her expertise."

"Thank you." My voice warbled. *Why weak?* I thought to myself. *Charlotte has gathered her friends here out of love for you. You are doing what you do best.* I had to decide: Was I going to sit in the chair my uncle must soon vacate? Was I taking the helm of Sheffield Brothers?

I was done striving and trying to earn the approval of

others. I, too, must be on the outside who I was on the inside. My voice grew strong. "I know many of you have heard of the wonderful Venetian treasures that our friend Lord Lydney escorted out of Venice during the months of war which, happily, saw Venice united with Italy. His friends, the Viero family, have graciously allowed us to appreciate these treasures before they return to their home. Perhaps Signorina Viero would be so kind as to come up and tell us about them?"

The lovely Francesca came to the front and spoke of the goblets, in waves of sea-blues and -greens, fitting for Venice, delicately etched with remarkable skill and openmouthed, ready to receive the riches of Italian water and wine.

She next touched the chandelier, which glistened and twinkled, even in the relative dark of the room.

She spoke of the twisted cornucopias, purest glass with threads of gold woven throughout, as intricate as any embroidery I'd seen, and then the delicate blown-glass water jug. When she held up the yellow perfume bottle, swirled like sunrise gauze, my heart felt no pain. *Mama, I wish you well. But we are well and truly parted now.* I had learned that every circumstance in life doesn't have to end happily for the Lord to provide a happy ending.

When Francesca held up the Venetian wedding cake beads, rolled black but with hearts and flowers shot throughout, to celebrate a woman's best day, de Bennetto grinned at her, and she blushed in return. I then knew which bride's neck they would next grace.

She introduced me. "Please, my friend Miss Eleanor Sheffield is going to tell you about the Roman treasures, which had been stolen. They will only be in England for another month or two. When my family returns to Italy, we will take them—openly—with us, to return them to their rightful owners." She turned to Harry but spoke to those gathered. "It is because Lord Lydney paid for these, and then is graciously donating everything back to be repatriated to Italy, that they will find their way into the refounding of the Italian nation."

Stefano led the applause then; Harry looked down in humility, but I scanned the crowd and saw that they viewed him differently now. I did have a fine eye for discerning truth from falsehood, and with Harry I had confirmed that he was all I'd ever known, and hoped, him to be.

I began lightly but confidently, discussing each of the small Roman items, and invited people to come forward and view them when I was finished. I spoke of the goods that had been designed, commissioned, and purchased solely for religious purposes and were to be stored at the Palazzo del Quirinale, fully crediting my uncle. "He is brusque—but well-meaning. He has a good heart and a wealth of knowledge. From him, and from my father, I have learned nearly everything I now know. I honor them."

Lady Charlotte spoke up. "I would like Miss Sheffield to explain how she concluded that the ribbed-glass bowl was not authentic."

A final test! I recalled how she'd encouraged me some

months before. *"We should not, therefore, be afraid of testing others—or of being tested ourselves. It is only by testing, or being tested, that we understand whether the substance or the person is as it appears to be or is merely masquerading."*

I took the glass bowl in hand and held my lamp very near to it. As I did, those near enough could see the tiniest bit of the oxidation melt and smiled or gasped, depending on if they had suspected the fraud. I pointed to the place on the bowl where the pearlescent glaze had softened—something that would never happen so quickly, if at all, with oxidation accumulated naturally through centuries of resting buried underground. "False oxidation. But how?"

I then set down the bowl and held up my rope of pearls, the ones I had caught in Alice's hands when she first came to do laundry in our home.

I remembered our conversation and shared it with those present.

"These are not genuine pearls; they are made of blown glass and then filled with wax to make them heavy." I handed them to the person standing next to me, and she hefted the weight in one hand. "They are painted on the outside with the gelatin stripped from fish intestines. Even the most discerning eye has difficulty telling the difference. Likewise, our Roman thieves had difficulty discerning that the olive bowl, too, had been painted with fish gelatin to falsely age it."

I knew many, if not all, in the room had seen, valued, or even owned false pearls such as my own. I held them to the lamp, and the pearlescence melted just as it had on the counterfeit Roman bowl. It was not worth a small fortune. It was worth nearly nothing.

I smiled at the room, and they smiled back at me; Lady Charlotte came forward to thank me and invited the others to view the Roman and Venetian treasures while they may.

Those gathered came forward to view the tables, many of them stopping to speak with me, our friendly camaraderie and collegiality restored, perhaps even beyond what it had ever been.

Charlotte squeezed my hand before she was to slip away to tend to her guests.

"Thank you, my friend. I can never repay you."

"You need not. That is what friends are for."

Harry came up and put his hand under my elbow. "Well done, Miss Sheffield," he whispered in my ear.

I turned to him. "It would not have been possible without you."

He shrugged. "I'm happy to see you happy."

"I would see you happy as well," I said.

"I'm delighted to hear that. Then there is something you can do for me. I have already asked Mrs. Newsome if she would be so kind as to accompany you to a gathering I'm hosting at Watchfield next weekend. I hope you are free?"

"To my regret, I remain so," I teased.

He laughed and ran a finger along my jawline as was his intimate, most welcome habit. I had the feeling that if we had not been in a room filled with people, he would have kissed me as he had that night outside my room at the George Inn.

CHAPTER
Thirty-Seven

WATCHFIELD HOUSE, OXFORDSHIRE

We traveled to Watchfield on a Friday afternoon. As our train pulled into the station, Marguerite was nearly as excited as I was.

"There is another secret that lies ahead," she said.

"Why is it that each time I come to Watchfield, everyone knows the mystery which remains unspoken, except me?"

She laughed and took my bag for a moment as we stepped up into the carriage that Harry had sent to bring us to Watchfield. "It shan't remain a secret long, dearest."

When the carriage arrived, the driver pulled up for us to alight at the front door. Harry's new man had been waiting for us. He came down the front steps to take our bags and treated me most deferentially. My heart could do nothing but sing.

When we went into the house, the new housekeeper greeted me warmly. "Let me show you to your room, please, Miss Sheffield," she said. "I hope you will find it to your liking."

Marguerite grumbled teasingly as she shadowed me down the hall. "I guess I shall follow along and hope that his lordship has had some accommodations prepared for me as well."

I laughed aloud.

Our rooms were one floor up and were perhaps the finest quarters in the house. Directly above mine would be Lady Lydney's, and both rooms looked out over the extensive grounds. The dogwood trees had come into flower; their pink-and-white blossoms reminded me of the little girl's tea set my granny had given me as a child. The grass was thriving in emerald, and darling little English bluebells nodded their heads like fairies along the cobbled walkway to the summerhouse.

Then I knew. Besides the lovely view, Harry had wanted me to have this room because it overlooked our summerhouse. The wisteria, which had looked so mournful in September, burst with violet bliss.

"Dinner this evening, miss. And then we're to close your draperies until eleven tomorrow morning, and his lordship has asked that you remain in your room." The housekeeper's eyes twinkled. "I shall bring breakfast to your room."

I tilted my head. Could I winkle the mystery out of Harry tonight at dinner?

Dinner was supposed to be a quiet affair, but with the Italians in the house, it was delightfully noisy and emotionally expressive.

The widow Viero sat next to me. "Where are your mother and father? Could they not come?"

Francesca batted her mother. "Mama!"

"My mother and father are no longer with us," I said, honest if not precise.

"What? You have no mother?" She scooted her chair closer to me. "I shall be your mama then." She sniffed loudly as if to dare anyone to contradict her.

"Thank you," I replied as she patted my hand.

I looked toward the end of the table and saw Marguerite involved in a deep conversation with Stefano. Both laughed, and each time I looked, their chairs were closer to one another. By the end of the meal, she'd even let her sorbet melt, completely uneaten.

Mama Viero sniffed again. "I thought we would be leaving England behind soon. If this progresses, I may have to remain or take an 'English souvenir' back to the palazzo in Venice."

I laughed. *I hope so, Mama Viero. I certainly hope so.*

After dinner, a quartet of musicians readied themselves to play in the background whilst we enjoyed cards and conversation. Harry took my hands in his own and held my gaze. "What can I do for you, Miss Sheffield?"

I teased him back. "Any manner of things, Lord Lydney.

But what I most want to know is, why keep my draperies closed in the morning? Why must I remain in my room until eleven o'clock?"

He laughed. "Oh no. You shan't get me to reveal that secret. Nor anyone else. I have sworn them to secrecy."

"Could you be convinced?" I asked.

"No. At least not tonight." He smiled. "Later, perhaps . . ."

This night, I was not wearing a secondhand gown, but a beautiful emerald dress purchased with a little of the banknote bounty found in my uncle's desk. Harry had not asked Uncle to repay the money for the Roman goods; they would be his gift to the Italian people.

The music struck up—the same tune we had first danced to so many years before—and Harry pulled me closer than he had dared as a young man, though we had both desired it, then and now.

His movements were slow and deliberate. I followed. We nearly melded into one another, and at the end of the dance, he led me into the small linen supply room where we had once had our first dance. He drew me near him and kissed me. I answered with a kiss of my own, and emboldened, he kissed me even more deeply. He put his hand on the back of my head and drew me closer so that I could not pull away, even if I had wanted to.

I did not.

His light beard scraped me, and it was a welcome, masculine roughness. After a moment, he pulled away. "We must part," he said. "For now, my lady. For now."

I did not respond. I could not. I had no breath with which to speak.

The next morning, Marguerite remained in my room with me.

"You are not quarantined," I teased. "You should be out with the others instead of remanded to this dark, close room."

She looked around at the fresh opulence of new linens and old, treasured furniture. "What a prison, Miss Sheffield. What a prison. As a matter of fact, I shall serve as your lady's maid this morning. Maybe for the last time?"

"Do you have plans to flee so soon?" I asked. "Perhaps to Italy? I thought, after watching you with Stefano Viero, that perhaps it is you in need of a chaperone and not I."

She laughed. "You are not qualified to be a chaperone, Miss Sheffield. Not yet, in any case."

"My fondest desire is to see you happy again. And I suspect I shall."

She laughed again, and the sound of it gladdened my heart and brightened the room.

She then helped me into a beautiful gown the color of the wisteria which was blooming near our summerhouse and brushed my hair so that the auburn tresses fell around my shoulders.

"Are you not going to pin it up?" I asked. "I look rather heathen with my hair about my shoulders like this."

"You look beautiful," she said. "Free and young and ever

so pretty. Does it matter to you what others say you look like today? You are no heathen, and all know it."

I smiled. "It only matters to me what one person thinks."

"I believe I can vouch that he will find you mesmerizing."

At precisely eleven o'clock—Harry had assured me he would be on time—Marguerite opened the door to my room and led me down the long hallway. I could hear people gathered in the large drawing room, but it had been screened off and in any case, Marguerite marched me right past.

We stepped out onto the dew-kissed grass, our boots barely touching the ground. Whither was she leading me? Soon, I saw. The summerhouse.

As we got closer, I could see that Harry waited for me outside. Marguerite handed me over to him and then kissed my cheek before disappearing back into Watchfield.

I expected Harry to take me into the summerhouse, but he did not. Instead, we stood outside. I was poised to jest with him about what we were to do next or did he not know, but then a horse came from the stables, not too far away.

It was a white horse, ridden by a man in a fine riding suit. As it approached us, I saw another horse leave the stable, this one also white. Soon, a third rider appeared on yet another white horse and then a fourth. The fifth white horse was ridden—though quite slowly—by the ungainly Mr. Herberts, who tipped his hat at me as he passed.

"What . . . ?" I began. I understood why I'd been confined to quarters. I would certainly have seen all these horses and riders being readied.

Harry placed his finger over my lips but for a moment, shushing me. "All in good time, Ellie. All in good time."

The parade of silent white horses continued, and as I counted, the twentieth horse approached.

"Abalone," I whispered. Being ridden by Lord Audley! "What has happened?"

"Audley purchased him," Harry said simply. "But that is not what this day is about."

As he spoke, the first rider circled back on his white horse.

"May I tell you a story?" Harry took my hand in his own.

"Certainly!"

"I've told you how I love the Uffington chalk horse. How when I saw it on the hill on the way to Watchfield, I knew I was soon to be home. There are many stories about the horse, but one of my favorites is the ancient belief that because of the Uffington horse, real white horses could predict the future husband of an unmarried girl. You see—" he turned toward me—"the girl would count the number of white horses she saw until she reached one hundred. Then the first man she shook hands with after that would one day become her husband."

The horses paraded by once more. "I could not find one hundred white horses," Harry said. "For as many horsemen as I know. But I could find twenty. I am hoping that if twenty horses come by five times, that will be good enough for me to claim the one hundred horse myth. Or rather, for you to do so."

He dropped my hand, and we stood, side by side, watching the horses walk. The birds chirped in the air around us, and the breeze rustled the new leaves budding from the trees, fresh leaves which spoke of new seasons of life and hope. I glanced at the summerhouse behind us and in my mind's eye saw us as a young man and woman, and then as a grown man and woman, now. All had come to fruition in the right time.

As Abalone came by for the fifth time, Lord Audley tipped his riding hat toward me, and I watched Harry as he smiled at Audley, struggled a bit with him being on Abalone, and then faced me. Seeing Audley on his horse, and the fact that he'd done all this for a story, which he knew would mean more to me than a simple proposal, confirmed why I had only, and ever, loved this man.

"That is the one hundredth white horse, Miss Sheffield," Harry said.

It was up to me, I knew, to shake his hand. I held out my gloved hand and took his.

"Yes." I nodded. "Yes. Always yes. Yes today. Yes tomorrow. Yes until the chalk hills pass away, which they never will."

Lord Audley smiled and rode away, leaving the two of us alone in front of the summerhouse. Harry kissed me in agreement, in tenderness, in protection and affection and commitment. He kissed me in passion. I answered in kind.

I held out my hand, where my Adore ring belonged, and envisioned it there, amethyst intact. Fifth question—would he propose marriage?—answered now. But it had required faith to trust him, the faith of a mustard seed, and to return the collection to him before I had that last answer.

As we walked back to the house, the crowd which had been gathered in the room, waiting, spilled out onto the lawn and, with cheers and whistles and applause, celebrated with us.

"Marry me in May?" Harry asked as we walked.

"May?" I asked. I wondered why he wanted to wait more than a month.

"Oh yes," he said. "I have not finished with surprises, Ellie. It must be none other than May."

Then I thought, *Yes, May. Because, Lord Lydney, I may have a surprise of my own.*

CHAPTER *Thirty-Eight*

MAY 1867

I did not have a chance to speak with Lord Audley whilst we were at Watchfield, and it was perhaps just as well. I wanted to speak with him privately, away from the eyes of anyone else, but most especially, away from Harry.

I'd sent a note asking if I might call on him at his London house, and he sent a gracious reply, though it was some weeks before he had an available date. The night before we were to meet, I went over the account books once more. I had reconciled all the monies that were due to Sheffield Brothers but then had repaid myself for the funds I had used to pay company matters by selling my and my father's treasures. I knew exactly what was available. It was more than I had expected, and while we were not exactly rich, Mr. Herberts had promised his patronage and I had been invited to the April meeting of the Burlington, where my membership was expected to be confirmed.

Harry had been planning for my uncle to move in with us at his homes in London and Oxfordshire if Uncle liked, or he would arrange for him to remain at our home in Bloomsbury, if that was less disruptive.

So I could afford to make a generous offer, one that I could add to as the years went on, if required.

I arrived midafternoon at the large town house. The butler saw me in and then showed me to a private sitting room, one I had not been in during my earlier visit for the club meeting. "Lord Audley will arrive shortly," he said. "Please make yourself comfortable."

I sat in a very comfortable chair and looked around the room. There were paintings and treasures and such, and pieces of a very nice collection, portions of which I had seen during my earlier visit. But then . . .

I stood and walked over to a portrait of a man on a horse. The man looked like Audley, but not completely. His father? No. Older. A forebear. It was not the man who had drawn my eye, though. It was the horse. More precisely, it was the barding that the horse wore. It was the exact piece of barding which I had first seen—and then noticed missing—in the third-floor room at Watchfield.

"Miss Sheffield." Lord Audley entered the room and noticed where I stood. He joined me in front of the painting.

"It's quite well done, is it not?" he asked.

I nodded, not knowing what to say. I thought I'd offer a leading sentence and see if he picked it up. "Stunning horse. And barding, too. Unusual."

He smiled. "It has my family crest on it." He nodded to the portrait and then pointed at a crest appearing in the stonework above the fireplace. "That is, of course, how Lydney knew it belonged to me."

"May I sit down?"

He helped me round to a chair and sat across from me whilst tea was brought into the room.

Once the maid left, I asked, "Did he . . . did Harry return it to you, then?"

"He did. Apparently he had not been in that room and for some reason became aware that there was a lock with no known key. He had it changed and, when he did, saw this. Among some other items which, I understood, he has seen back to their rightful homes."

"His father?" I asked.

"Yes. Stole it, I suspect, from my father. My father had always said as much, and it cooled all friendship between our two families. It could never be proven. But now it has, and it has been rightfully returned to our country home, thanks to Lydney."

I drank my tea for a moment and thanked God for the most auspicious opening that he, and Lord Audley, had provided. "It's always so rewarding to see something precious returned to its owner," I said pleasantly. "Do you not find that to be true? For example, a beloved horse!"

Audley laughed. "Oh, dear Miss Sheffield. I hope Lydney understands what a gift to him you are."

I laughed back. "I've come to ask you to sell Abalone to me. You knew I would."

"I hoped you might," he answered with a grin.

❧

We sat in my rooms at Watchfield, preparing for the wedding which would take place in a little under an hour at the nearby village church. Marguerite and Francesca were in the room to help me get ready, and we had brought Alice along too. She said she'd come to ensure that my wedding dress was presented exactly so, but the truth of it was she had become a friend, and I wanted her there on my wedding day.

Orchie fussed with a large vase which held many long branches, each with dozens of lovely buds, the same creamy white as my dress, centered with pink tendrils and a button-yellow middle. "They are all over the house," Alice said. "In every room. In the room for the wedding luncheon. By the door. In here. What are they?"

I remained seated in my chair whilst Marguerite finished my hair. "There is a story, of course, my dear Alice. Would you like to hear it?"

She laughed. "There's no escapin' it, I'm sure."

I smiled back. "You'll remember when my uncle spoke of

the holy thorn of Glastonbury—how that particular hawthorn tree was said to have sprung from Joseph of Arimathea's wooden staff when thrust into the ground at Wearyall Hill."

She nodded.

"The trees themselves last but one hundred years or so, but because they were so important, many cuttings had been taken from them. Pilgrims and those committed to seeing the tree blossom grafted pieces of the original tree onto common English hawthorns so that no matter what happened to the original, the tree, and their faith, would be spread, year after year, generation after generation, from old to new. You see? When the original was hacked, it was a pity, but it was not the end. The trees have been spread all over England, and you'll know them by this distinctive: they bloom both at Christmas, to celebrate the birth of our Lord, and in May, as do all hawthorns."

"So Lord Lydney wanted you to wait till these were in bloom, then," Marguerite added. "Your most distinctive wedding flowers."

"Yes," I said softly. "He was worth your championing all along. Our love has bloomed twice, too."

"My fondest desire, to see you happy again, has been met."

Alice sighed. "That story was worth it, Miss Eleanor. That one was worth it."

The ladies led me downstairs to the carriage which awaited me, and we drove off to the church. The guests were already present, as were the men, including Harry.

After all were seated, my uncle walked me to the altar and delivered me to my beloved. "She is yours now," he said. "You must treasure her."

Harry nodded solemnly, and we turned while the vicar helped us to speak our commitment and our vows. As he pronounced us man and wife, I heard a most welcome, most distinctive voice again, deep in my spirit.

I am here.

I looked up at the cross above the altar and whispered back, also deep within my spirit, *I know you are. You always were.*

Harry and I rode alone in the carriage back to Watchfield.

"Did you bring it?" he asked me.

I nodded and handed the ring to him.

"May I remove your gloves?"

"If you are certain that is appropriate," I teased.

"We are married now, Lady Lydney. It is most appropriate, as I shall show you later this evening after our guests have left."

I blushed, and he laughed. "It has been a long time since I have been able to make you blush."

He eased my gloves off, and when my hands were bare, he slipped the completed Adore ring back onto my finger. "This is where it shall stay. This is where it belongs." He pulled me close to him. "This is where you belong."

I closed my eyes in purest pleasure.

We returned to Watchfield, where a wedding breakfast had been prepared for us. Unusually, the table had been set for Harry and me to sit side by side, and when we entered the room, I saw why.

The delicate, most valuable Venetian loving cup had been placed between our two place settings.

"What a lovely thought, for us to use this today," I said.

Francesca smiled. "Today and as many days as you would like," she said. "It is our wedding gift to you and Harry."

I nearly gasped. "Oh, but it is so dear. So precious."

Stefano chucked Harry on the back and then kissed my cheek. "And so are you."

We ate in delight and merry conversation, and then Stefano gave a small speech wishing us well in our married life. As he did, I signaled to Lord Audley, who was seated at the end of the room, and he slipped away.

Harry stood up to speak next. "Many of you will be aware that my beautiful bride was faced with an unusual task some months ago. She was to determine whether the extensive collection housed at Watchfield would remain here or be donated elsewhere. I made no secret of the fact that I wished it to remain, though I said little to Ellie—" he looked at me—"so I would not interfere in her fiduciary duty. I was most delighted when she allowed it to remain. And the reason? Because I knew I would ask her to be my wife and had hopes that she would agree. She did, and now the collection is in the hands of the person to whom it truly belongs. Ellie is now the lady of a thousand treasures. I am a man who needs only one: Lady Eleanor Lydney."

He brushed away my tear, and I smiled at my friends and

my husband as they looked on and chatted fondly. Finally, Audley appeared at the doorway to the room and nodded at me before quickly leaving once more.

"Follow me?" I asked Harry.

He looked at me, curious, but agreed. I nodded to Marguerite, who shepherded the others to follow us out the door.

"Stay here," I said to Harry, and then I began the five-minute walk to the stable where Audley had arranged to wait for me.

"Ready?" he asked.

He handed Abalone's reins to me and walked nearby, as the horse was powerful and unused to my lead. We crossed the green, past the summerhouse, and to the front of the lawn where the wedding party and our guests waited.

Harry came forward. I could see a question, and hope not yet risked, in his eyes.

I handed the reins to him and then leaned up to kiss him in front of all. "My wedding gift to you."

Harry looked at me, then at Audley, and then at Abalone. "But Audley and I made an irrevocable arrangement," he said.

"I made no such arrangement with your lady." Audley laughed, and all present clapped.

Harry held out his hand to him. "You're an honorable man, Audley, and I'm proud to call you my friend." Audley voiced his like sentiment, and then my husband turned back to me.

Harry leaned over and kissed me like he meant it for all to see; then he took my hand and lifted me, in my wedding dress, sidesaddle on the horse. He swung himself up behind me, and to the applause and whistles and laughter of all who loved us and whom we loved, we stole off, alone, into the distant fields and wooded greens where we'd first fallen in love.

EPILOGUE

1873

I watched them from a shy distance. Harry had our five-year-old twins, Hawthorn and Arthur, in the yard outside the stable, learning to patiently and quietly approach the horses. The horses looked to Harry for their cues, and when he reassured them, they stood still while the boys took turns being placed on a horse, a groomsman holding them steady while Harry led them, gently, around the yard.

When the horses were put away, he played boisterously with the boys in a manner his father would never have stooped to. Each boy was given his affection in turn, and when the boys spied and ran toward me, they held hands. Best of friends. Something denied to Harry and his brother which he was determined to see done for his sons.

You intended for Harry to lose all, I whispered inwardly to his long-dead father, whose hands had been permanently stilled. *But he's gained all instead. What you meant for evil has been turned to good. All that was meant to be then, is now, and ever shall be.*

The boys ran up and grabbed me, almost toppling me as they did.

"Carry on," I corrected them. "Into the house and back to studies."

Harry came up and kissed me, his face smudged with dust, marking me as he did. "Your sons," I said. "Chasing horses."

He smiled. "Come to ride with me?"

"No. A package has arrived."

I used my chatelaine keys to open the bureau in his study, in which we kept the delivered post, and he prized the lid off the small crate which had been delivered.

"A Book of Hours," he said. "And a porcelain shepherdess?" We set the Book of Hours on the desk, and he took the shepherdess to the window to look at it in the light. "I recognize this, somehow."

I nodded. "It was your mother's. Mr. Clarkson had stolen it to copy, if you'll remember. But the original was left in his rooms and then, after his death, disappeared. I saw it at Denholm's house once."

"Now I recall."

I held a letter aloft. "Mr. Denholm died a sudden and rather painful death some weeks ago. I sent a letter of condolence to his kind wife and she, in return, has now sent these to me. She couldn't have whilst he was alive."

We discussed it for a moment and then talked about

the day and the week ahead. When I turned to face the room again, I touched Harry gently on the arm. "Look," I whispered.

My uncle, who was normally very far gone into his mind, was standing in front of the desk with the Book of Hours, my boys at his side.

"May we touch it?" Hawthorn asked, his fascination plain on his face.

"Indeed, you may," Uncle replied, and my jaw dropped. I would never have been allowed to touch that as a child.

"Will you read a page to us?" Arthur asked as he touched the page, completely captivated.

"Certainly, my boys," Uncle Lewis answered, and the two boys leaned in as he began to read.

Harry put his arm around me. "Your sons," he said. "Chasing treasures."

I patted my abdomen, where our new baby nestled. "Ours, my love. A cherish of children in a circle of love."

AUTHOR'S NOTE

COLLECTING

It all started with a cow creamer! I first became aware of the mania for collecting, especially among the Victorian and Edwardian British, while watching an episode of *Jeeves and Wooster*: "Jeeves Saves the Cow Creamer." In it, a certain set of men were trying to outdo and outmaneuver one another to acquire and keep a silver cow creamer. Wodehouse played the scenes for absurdity, of course, but in that poking of fun was a truth we all recognize—collecting can become a competitive sport.

Today's culture reflects the continuing interest in collections, and understanding and appreciating what those who came before us collected. How many of us enjoy watching *Antiques Roadshow*, for example? We gasp along with the owners when a rugged, torn blanket is valued at tens of thousands of dollars, or a treasure long believed to be a rare work of art is discovered to be a fake.

Collecting was and is both personal and public. Before there were museums, viewing other people's collections was a way to see what they had gathered from their travels, purchased on their own, or inherited from their family. There's pressure, then and now, for wealthy art owners to donate for the good of all. The largest museum, at least by the sheer number of pieces, is the Victoria and Albert. It has nearly 150 galleries with items from over 5,000 years. The museum had its beginnings in the Great Exhibition of 1851, the brainchild of Prince Albert; in 1854 it became the South Kensington Museum, and finally ended up with its most fitting name, the V&A, in 1899.

REAL PEOPLE

One of my great pleasures as an author is weaving real people in among my fictional characters. In this book, the person who brought me—and I hope you, dear readers—considerable delight is Lady Charlotte Schreiber.

Although I found Lady Charlotte Schreiber in several sources, the richest trove was found in the book *Magpies, Squirrels and Thieves: How the Victorians Collected the World*, by Jacqueline Yallop.

In the book, I learned, "In a departure from the usual model of the gentleman's club, women, too, were invited and by 1867 there were eight female members (of the Burlington Fine Arts Club)." Also, "Charlotte's journals are littered with references to helping out her sister collectors. In November 1869, for example, she spent 'two very pleasant hours' with Mrs. Haliburton, a widowed china collector who became a regular visitor and correspondent, and in June 1884 she called on Lady Camden, in Eaton Square, to discuss china. By the 1870s, Charlotte was already being recognized as an expert, and she was able to use her unusual level of access to the male worlds of curating and dealing to act on behalf of her female friends both at home and abroad."

Lady Charlotte had a most unusual life, marrying a much-younger man (fourteen years her junior) for love, after her first husband's death. You can view part of her collection of fans and parlor games, which she donated to the British Museum, here: http://www.britishmuseum.org/research/collection_online/search.aspx?searchText=schreiber+collection

Dante Rossetti was another real person who appears on the pages of the novel; he was a poet (as was his sister, Christina), an artist, an eccentric, and a collector. There is much to be read about him, too, in *Magpies* and elsewhere. His painting *Lady Lilith*, which appears in my book as the painting he showed Ellie in which Harry's mother's perfume bottle was a piece of staging, was sold by Sotheby's as I was writing this novel. It sold for £680,000, or nearly one million US dollars. The promotional material the auction house put forward tells that the painting was shown at the Burlington Fine Arts Club in 1883, though it was painted, signed, and dated in 1867. Rossetti lived on Cheyne Walk, very near to where Miss Gillian Young, the heroine in my book *A Lady in Disguise*, lived just a few years later.

One interesting—and creepy—fact about Rossetti's life is that he was so distraught when his wife died of a laudanum overdose that he had a manuscript of unpublished works buried with her. Many years later, short of cash and addicted himself, he had the grave dug up to try to reclaim the work and sell it. Too bad he didn't make that £680,000 in his lifetime!

By all accounts, Elizabeth Garrett, later Elizabeth Garrett Anderson, was the first woman physician in England. She began her career as a nurse, then applied to Oxford, Cambridge, Glasgow, Edinburgh, St Andrews, and the Royal College of Surgeons. Each of them promptly rejected her, so she applied to the Worshipful Society of Apothecaries and was licensed through a loophole allowing her to practice medicine. The unexpected loophole was promptly sewn shut after her admittance, but that did not stop her, and other women's, forward progression in the field.

ITALIAN WARS OF UNIFICATION

History classes, for most of us, did not cover much Italian history. Readers may be surprised, as I was, to learn that there were three wars in the nineteenth century which, in the end, allowed the city-states of the Italian peninsula to become one unified Kingdom of Italy by 1871. To keep things from becoming too complex, I've often used the word *Italian* to describe the language and area as we know it today. As in all wars, there was looting, and much of the looting went into private collections.

I drew the desire for Harry's friend Stefano Viero to save his family's treasures from the truth of what went on in his beloved Venice in the years leading up to the 1866 return of Venice from Austria to Italy. In *A Brief History of Venice* by Elizabeth Horodowich, I read, "Most dreadful, however, was the degree to which the French vandalized and pillaged the city. Napoleon ordered all the public statues and sculptures depicting the Lion of St Mark, both in the city and on the mainland, to be removed since they were symbols of a despotic regime. They were added to his imperial wealth. He also shipped the four bronze horses above the doorway of the basilica of San Marco to Paris on 7 December 1797, placing them first before the Palace of the Tuileries and then on the Arc de Triomphe. He put the lion on top of the column in the piazzetta on the Place des Invalides. Newspaper cartoons around Europe depicted the lion of St Mark caught in a net or crushed beneath the feet of a crowing Gallic cock as Napoleon's troops systematically pillaged every corner of the city, including the mint, fleet, and archives. They hired women to pick precious stones out of their ancient settings that they melted down. They took the diamonds from the Treasury of San Marco to be set in Empress Josephine's crown. In particular, in the weeks just before handing Venice over to the Austrians in January 1798, the French desperately tried to remove anything and everything from the city that might benefit their Austrian enemies."

And then, from 1806 to 1810, "In a perhaps ironic reversal of much of Venetian history, the French methodically removed every last item of beauty or value from the city, literally down to the nails on which the city's paintings hung. . . . While figures vary dramatically, approximately 80–90 churches and around 100 palaces were razed during the French occupation.

They carted off the valuable furnishings and artworks from both private homes and religious and charitable institutions to enrich French coffers and museums. Gold, silver, crosses, candlesticks, goblets, and crowns were melted down and disappeared forever. Marble, altars, paintings, relics, parquet floors, mosaics, frescoed ceilings, stuccoed walls, antique reliefs and inscriptions, furniture, porcelains, textiles, carpets, glass, and entire libraries were dismantled, destroyed, or sequestered by the crown. Through later auctions and resales these objects were eventually dispersed around the world."

There were many frauds exposed in this book, as well as the authentication and valuation of precious works of art. Almost all the objects described are real pieces of art, drawn from various sources but described by my own observation and language. All the frauds, and the methods by which they were learned to be fraudulent, were also all drawn from authentic cases.

Because the Continent was often in an uproar and subject to art thefts, almost everyone was deceived at some time. Many of these frauds were not found out until the twentieth century when X-ray, carbon dating, and chemical testing came about. So, in the years when my book takes place, it really was a business built on experience and integrity.

And yet, isn't that what our lives are tested upon, even now? Integrity? That is not a bad thing. As Lady Charlotte says in the book, "It is only by testing or being tested that we understand whether the substance or the person is as it appears to be or is merely masquerading."

ACKNOWLEDGMENTS

I am always so grateful for the wonderful people who graciously contribute their thoughts, insight, talents, comments, and prayers to my books.

Danielle Egan-Miller and Clancey D'Isa of Browne and Miller Literary Agency did an excellent reading of the manuscript and offered many wonderful suggestions for its improvement, as always, coming alongside with excellent advice and encouragement. Thanks, too, to the entire hard-working team at Tyndale House Publishers, especially fiction publisher Karen Watson, for her enthusiasm and confidence in the series, and editors Jan Stob and Sarah Mason Rische, whose keen editorial eyes helped me to shape the characters and circumstances on the page as I saw them in my heart and mind. Jenny Q of Historical Editorial once more brought her thoughtful insight to both the planning and the rough draft and is an editor, an encourager, and a wonderful friend.

Friends and fellow authors Serena Chase and Melanie Dobson deserve a shout-out for their focused, valuable comments and willingness to brainstorm with me through several drafts—thank you, ladies! Mary Sudar, of Sudar Estate Sales, was a generous wealth of information, as was Stephanie Lile of the Harbor History Museum. I am very grateful to several wonderful people at the Wallace Collection in London for their willingness to share insights and resource recommendations, as well as to the kind and helpful Morgy at the Glaston Centre.

My wonderful husband, Michael, not only brings excellent research skills but is the world's best traveling companion. He is also my first—and last—manuscript reader. My children all love on and cheer me at each step of what can be a daunting journey, and I appreciate them more and more each day.

I am deeply indebted to Dr. Alex Naylor and Finni Golden, historical advisers and residents of Hampshire, England. I always say they help me keep my history straight and my English, English, and not American. They have become the dearest of friends—also excellent traveling companions—and we enjoyed a wonderful dinner and night together at the fourteenth-century George Inn. Sadly, Alex was recently diagnosed with inoperable cancer and passed into the arms of Jesus as I finished the edits on this book. In one of his correspondences he wrote, "I have absolutely no fear about the dying nor death, for it is all destined and comes to us all. It is how we bear it that matters. If Christ can bear death as He did in the Mystery of Golgotha, then who are we to baulk at the suffering on our microcosmic level?"

This book, then, is for you, Alex, with all honor, love, and respect.

DISCUSSION QUESTIONS

1. Do you collect anything? What pieces in your collection hold the most emotional resonance? If you're not a collector but had to choose one thing to collect, what would it be?
2. Have you ever felt as though you were not treasured by anyone, as Eleanor does? How did you process those thoughts and feelings?
3. Bad circumstances befall us all. How does what you believe about God affect how you handle difficult times? How much agency do you believe we have, as individuals, to deal with those circumstances?
4. Can you think of a situation in your life that was not resolved as you wished it would be, like Eleanor's relationship with her mother? Do you believe there can be a happily ever after in your life anyway? Why, and how?
5. Are there traditions or stories, Christian or not, that are meaningful in your life in the way that the history of Glastonbury or the stories of the white horses are to the characters in *Lady of a Thousand Treasures*?

6. Do you have someone in your life, as Eleanor has Marguerite, who loves you completely and will speak up and tell you the truth you might not want to hear? Do you play the same role for someone?

7. Have you ever misjudged someone out of your own insecurities? How did you come to recognize that, and how did you move forward?

8. Has your family been impacted by dementia or Alzheimer's disease? How has it affected the roles you each play?

9. If you could own any treasure in this book, what would it be? And do you plan to test your pearls and porcelain now that you've learned Eleanor's tricks?

10. Eleanor tells Harry that he bears his Maker's mark in his loyalty, his kindness, his selflessness. What is the Maker's mark you recognize on yourself? On your closest friends or people in your family? Would you consider telling them what you see?

ABOUT THE AUTHOR

After earning her first rejection at the age of thirteen, bestselling author Sandra Byrd has now published fifty books.

Sandra's delighted to kick off her new historical romance series with Tyndale House Publishers, Victorian Ladies, with *Lady of a Thousand Treasures*. The three-book Victorian Ladies series follows her historically sound Gothic romances, Daughters of Hampshire, launched with the bestselling *Mist of Midnight*, which earned a coveted Editor's Choice award from the Historical Novel Society. The second book, *Bride of a Distant Isle*, has been selected by *Romantic Times* as a Top Pick. The third in the series, *A Lady in Disguise*, was published in 2017. Check out her contemporary adult fiction debut, *Let Them Eat Cake*, which was a Christy Award finalist, as was her first historical novel, *To Die For: A Novel of Anne Boleyn*. *To Die For* was also named a *Library Journal* Best Books Pick for 2011, and *The Secret Keeper: A Novel of Kateryn Parr* was named a *Library Journal* Best Books Pick for 2012.

Sandra has published dozens of books for kids, tweens, and teens, including the bestselling *The One Year Be-Tween You and*

God Devotions for Girls. She continued her work as a devotionalist, this time for women, with *The One Year Home and Garden Devotions*. Her latest book, *The One Year Experiencing God's Love Devotional*, was published in October 2017.

Sandra is passionate about helping new writers develop their talents and their work for traditional publishing or self-publication. She has mentored and coached hundreds of new writers and continues to guide developing authors toward success each year via novelcoaching.com.

Please visit www.sandrabyrd.com to learn more or to invite Sandra to your book club via Skype.

crazy4
fiction
.com